DAUGHTER OF LÎR

DAUGHTER OF LÎR

Diana Norman

HEADLINE

**To Tony and Margaret,
Roger and Ann.
With Love.**

Acknowledgements

Dermot of Leinster is, of course, notorious in Ireland for precipitating the Norman invasion and
beginning the seven and a half centuries of English rule, although the fact that he was responsible for the rape of the Abbess of Kildare is less well known. That crime actually took place in
1134 – we don't know why or what happened to her afterwards, since there is only the briefest
mention of it in the Annals of Loch Cé – but I've set it twenty years later in order to combine
her rape with the rape of her country.

Although I've taken liberties, I don't think that any of the historical personages in the book,
Henry II, Eleanor, Ruairi O'Conor, Asgall, Dermot himself, and others, act out of character,
but I must apologise to the shade of Cardinal Papato who is made into a symbolically dirty old
churchman, though there is no evidence at all that he was.

The only other liberty has been to set the marriage of Aoife to Strongbow in Dublin when it
actually took place in Waterford.

Thank you to the London Library, the National Library of Ireland, my hospitable and
helpful friends in Ireland, and my editor, Sarah Molloy, without whom . . . well, she knows.

British Library Cataloguing in Publication Data
Norman, Diana
    Daughter of Lîr.
    I. Title
    823'.914[F]
    ISBN 0-7472-0075-0

Printed and bound in Great Britain by
Richard Clay Ltd, Bungay, Suffolk

HEADLINE BOOK PUBLISHING PLC
Headline House, 79 Great Titchfield Street, London W1P 7FN

PART ONE

Chapter One

The Archbishop of Cashel was a good man and did not as a general rule approve of women being killed; nevertheless when the message came he went up the stairs to his private room at a rate which made him gasp in the hope of hearing that at least one member of the breed was dead.

The monk who was waiting for him had the remoteness engendered by fatigue, and a satchel.

'Is that it?'

The monk undid the satchel and handed over a roll of parchment. Panting from anxiety and the climb, the Archbishop stretched the roll out on his table and sat down to read it. The membranes of which it consisted differed in size and shape. While they had been neatly stitched to connect one to another, they were inexpertly treated so that their surfaces were rougher than a professional scribe would have permitted and the ink was home-made brown. The writing was childish and, for economy's sake, covered both the flesh and hair sides, but it was hideously readable.

'It's in Latin.' Somehow he had expected it to be in Irish. Who in hell had taught her Latin?

'Yes, my lord.'

'You've read it?'

'It was I who first alerted the Church of its danger.'

Even so, thought the Archbishop, the monk would have to be transferred to where it wouldn't matter if he talked; somewhere remote, some wave-lashed fastness.

Up the stairs came the voice of Gerald of Wales below in the chapter house expounding his view of the Irish people to the gathering of Irish clergy. The stressed words were audible. 'Barbarous . . . primitive . . . wild . . . debauched . . . incestuous . . . you slack . . . correction.'

The Archbishop got up and shut the door to cut off the sound. He was tired of Gerald of Wales; his opinions and his voice. Anyway, if this document contained what he feared it contained, Gerald of Wales was the last person he wanted to see it.

3

He sat down again to continue reading, emitting moans at each new horror.

'Listen to this. She says the Princess of Breffni wasn't responsible for the invasion of Ireland. That's a lie for a start. Of course she was responsible.' Just as Helen had brought down Troy, just as Cleopatra had destroyed Mark Anthony, just as Eve had poisoned the whole world by bringing sin into it in the first place. So Dervorgilla of Breffni was responsible for bringing the Normans to Ireland. He might forgive her for the Normans, but he'd never forgive her for Gerald of Wales . . .

He reached another subject. 'Yes, well, of course the rape was a scandal and perhaps we should have acted at that point. But other women have been raped without making such a fuss about it. And the Lord knows she got her revenge.' He looked up. 'She's safely dead now, I trust?'

'Yes, my lord. She died in the fire at the tower along with . . .'

'I know who,' snapped the Archbishop. 'They must have been mad.'

The monk stood at the west window facing out over the drop from the Rock of Cashel to the plain below. Still on the retina of his memory another view transposed itself continually – perhaps it always would – on anything he looked at; a river with a hill curving down to it and jutting out in a promontory on which stood, like a candle at the end of a bier, a tower which, like a candle, was burning.

'Oh my God,' said the voice behind him. The Archbishop had reached the heresy. He'd dropped the parchment and was clutching at his armpits as if to contain sudden pain.

The monk decided it would be kinder to deliver all the bad news at once. 'My lord, it is feared that there is yet another . . .'

'Another woman?'

'Yes, my lord, that too, but . . .'

'Not another copy?' pleaded the Archbishop, begging to be wrong. 'There isn't another copy of this?'

'Well, my lord, it is feared there might be. It may have gone up in the fire, but there was another woman, and she got away, and it cannot be overlooked that she may have taken a copy with her.'

'Is she being pursued?'

'With tracker dogs, my lord, but without success so far.'

'She must be found. You do realise that? She must be brought down and incarcerated, and the copy must be destroyed. We can't have this heresy even whispered.'

'I do realise, my lord.'

Dear Jesus, sweet Jesus, thought the Archbishop. Let her be caught. Let her fall off a cliff, sink into a bog and God have mercy on

4

her soul. Because the manuscript had been brought to him they would call it the Cashel heresy. His name would be known in history only for this ultimate insult to God. Where in hell had the woman gone?

He pulled himself together. They would find her. The trawl of the Church was inescapable and this shrimp would be caught. She'd be making for somewhere she considered safe. If he didn't panic, if he were calm and used all the cunning that had made him archbishop in the first place he would discover where that was.

'You must be tired,' he said to the monk. 'Have some wine.' He poured it out with his own hand. 'Do you know this heretic's story?'

'Some of it, my lord.'

The monk held the clue then, to the woman's hiding place. 'Tell me all about it,' said the Archbishop, 'Go back before the invasion. What possessed them to appoint the woman in the first place?'

The monk perched on a chair and then slumped. He hadn't sat down in twenty-four hours. 'She was intelligent,' he said quietly, 'and forceful, all the qualities that caused trouble later. And, of course, she was Irish . . .'

Looking out into the winter night sky through the squint which she had slid back because of insistent knocking on the gates, the porteress of Fontevrault Abbey could see only a dim figure and hear a male, retreating voice. 'She's Irish. She's been abandoned. Pray for me, sister, for I have sinned.'

'God forgives the sins of all who turn to Him,' said Sister Teresa, the porteress, automatically, 'What's Eye-rish?' She had never heard the word.

But there was no reply and the figure had gone. Grumbling, because her fingers were becoming arthritic, Sister Teresa pulled back the bolts on the wicket in the gates, lifted her lantern and found herself staring down at a skinny child about six years old who stared back out of brilliant, dark-blue eyes with a mixture of such misery, terror and ferocity that the old porteress put down her lantern at once and lifted the child into the warmth of the convent.

'What's Eye-rish, Mother?' she asked the Abbess, having requested her presence urgently to the porteress' lodge.

'It's a nationality,' said Mother Matilda, 'A strange, barbarous people. Celts, I believe. The question is, how did this one get here and what shall we do with it?'

'Keep it?' suggested Sister Teresa, hopefully, 'It is female. And sent to us by God.' The Abbey did accept novices as young as this child. Generally the intake was restricted to the nobly-born, but there was something so vulnerable about this foundling that the porteress' elderly heart had been stirred to protection.

5

'Or the Devil,' said Mother Matilda. She leaned down towards the child, wrinkling her nose at the nits which clung to strands of the fine, black, wavy hair: 'Can you talk, my little one?'

The child could talk all right. She jabbered angrily away at them, wiping tears from her eyes as if they were shameful and adding swathes of dirt to an already filthy face, but not a word could they understand.

'I suppose that's Irish,' said Mother Matilda, straightening up. 'Well, whatever else she is, she's brave.' She approved of courage. 'Hand her over to the Mistress of Novices for now. Later, we'll see.'

Transferred into a world as ordered as a black and white chess board, where sound broke out with the ringing of a bell and stopped as abruptly, the Irish child lost some of her terror, though misery remained, and so did ferocity. As she absorbed its language she learned much of its beauty, but she also discovered that some of her fellow novices, especially those of her age group, could use it to hurt.

'Eye-rish, eye-rish,' Sister Petronilla, aged seven, would chant at her, 'pagan Eye-rish,' and the others would join in until the Irish foundling threw herself on them, howling and scratching, not to defend her Irishness – for how could she defend a nation that had abandoned her? – but to stop them saying it.

'In my view it was the Prince of Darkness who left his own daughter on our doorstep,' said the Mistress of Novices to the Mother Superior as they walked together down to the river behind a gaggle of little, wimpled girls who were let out for an hour after Tierce, like hounds, to play in the abbey pasture. 'The child is untameable. Only this morning she bloodied Petronilla's nose and pulled Clotilde's hair. I cannot recommend her acceptance into our sisterhood.'

Mother Matilda grunted. At the moment she was more concerned about the coper from Perche who was leading a roan into the paddock for her inspection. Mother Matilda was a hunting abbess and didn't care who knew it; in her view the only ways to God were on your knees and on horseback. The coper was asking a shocking price for the horse, but warfare between King Stephen of England and the Empress Matilda had devastated Normandy and taken most of its horses into their armies.

'How old?' she asked the coper suspiciously; she liked her horses young enough to learn her ways.

'Four, blessed Mother.'

The right age, if the man was telling the truth. She peered short-sightedly into its mouth, ran her hand over its withers and back, and then caught sight of the Irish child who had climbed onto the paddock fence to watch, and who was shaking its head.

6

'No?' mouthed the Abbess at her. The Mistress of Novices might be right, but there was something about the child Mother Matilda liked. Since learning Norman French she had informed them that her name was Finola and had recited a list of kings from whom she was descended. Uncouth kings, the Abbess had no doubt, but royal in their way perhaps. There had been a mother and a father, a fight in which they had both disappeared, and a ship full of nasty men and a long journey. So much and no more had she been able to tell them and even that much had caused her distress, as if her mind wanted to veer away from it. If she cried for her mother, and the Abbess suspected that she did, she did so unheard and unseen in the blackness of the novitiates' dorter.

The child clambered over the fence and approached the horse. With practised, skinny hands she thumbed the roan's lip up to display its teeth. 'Feel,' she demanded.

The Abbess ran her forefinger along the bite of the teeth – and felt the tell-tale roughness of the filing which had shortened them in an attempt to make the horse appear younger than it was. She turned furiously on the coper, who backed away. 'This horse has been bishopped, you son of Satan.'

With a large-sized flea in his ear, the coper and his roan were sent packing and Mother Matilda looked down at the Irish foundling. 'They taught you horse-sense, whoever your ancestors were,' she said.

Suddenly, and for the first time since her arrival, the child smiled and the Abbess made up her mind. 'We keep her,' she said to the Mistress of Novices. 'I have taken an interest in her.' She looked down again into the child's astonishing blue eyes. 'And since Finola is an outlandish and unchristian name, she will be known as Sister Boniface.'

In the spring of 1154 flocks of whooper swans were seen in unusual numbers over Central Europe as they flew back north to their breeding grounds. They flew over what was essentially one great forest in which the villages, towns and cities were just different sizes of clearings connected to each other by trackways and, occasionally, a Roman road, or a river. The assault on the forest was well under way and there were assarted fields in it that had not been there when the swans had flown south, but it still remained a threat which could grow back and overwhelm the tiny labouring figures on the ground if they paused in their efforts to cut it down.

The sound of air displaced by huge wings made the figures look up. Some saw flying food and ran to get weapons with which to shoot it down, others took the swans to be tokens of hope from the Virgin Mary that the coming year would be a good one. But whenever the

7

swans passed over the head of one of the Irishmen or women living or travelling on the Continent, he or she would wave and wish good luck to the Children of Lîr of Ireland who were going home.

In one of those enchantments which were an everyday hazard of mythical times, the one daughter and three sons of King Lîr of Ireland had been changed into swans for nine hundred years. But so potent was their legend that by the time the nine hundred years were up and they had crumbled in human death, they had gained immortality in Irish imagination; the Children of Lîr becoming all swans and all swans becoming the Children of Lîr.

From a swan's eye view there hadn't been a lot of change in the world since the Children had undergone their transformation. The birth of Christ had brought great hope to it, but the termite gatherings which were armies still advanced and retracted, building empires and toppling empires in a swirling but consistent pattern. The Daughter of Lîr would have had reason to honk out her misery at the condition of her human sisters and their continued bondage to their fathers, brothers, husbands and sons, most of them in bondage themselves, but her black, grieving eye might have brightened at the escape which Christianity offered in its celibate sanctuaries of convents where her sisters could lead unnatural, but longer and freer, lives.

It is a coincidental fact that on a day in April 1154 it was a pen from a flock of swans flying up the Loire Valley that broke away from the others and circled over the elegant rooftops of the Abbey of Fontevrault as if intrigued by the sight of a convent which provided not just sanctuary for women, but was unique in Europe in giving them power.

In Fontevrault an abbess ruled not only 230 nuns but over the adjoining monastery of one hundred monks, owing allegiance to no male figure except the Pope and God.

The roofs covered refectories, dormitories, lavatories, hostels, cloisters, a springlike church, hospitals, walkways, fountains, all carved and gilded, contributed by the nobility of Christendom eager to save their souls and provide fit accommodation for their daughters. When kings and queens visited Fontevrault – as they frequently did – they stayed in the luxury of the nuns' guest house and ate at the nuns' lavish table, and the monks were only invited if they behaved themselves.

As if time lay heavy on her wings, the swan circled the Abbey. Below her webbed feet was the pepperpot shape of Fontevrault's kitchens, the finest in Europe, where in a doorway stood a young nun.

The swan trumpeted out a call as the Daughter of Lîr might have done to a fellow countrywoman, for the nun was Irish; with her white, freckled skin, sapphire-blue eyes and the dark eyelashes and eyebrows

8

which indicated that the wimple covered a head of soft, black hair, she was unmistakably Irish to those who recognised the physical types of that faraway country.

One expected a woman of such colouring to be gentle, a vulnerable dreamer. Men meeting Sister Boniface for the first time sweetened their voices, traders with whom she had preliminary dealings inwardly decided that she should not have to pay top prices, and then found themselves bargaining hard to get any price at all.

Sister Boniface looked up at the swan overhead, crossed herself out of respect for the Virgin Mary and briskly shook her fist at it, in case it dropped a mess in her clean courtyard. Then she turned back to concentrate on the scene in the kitchen. She had never heard of the Children of Lîr, or, if she had, she had forgotten, just as she had forced herself and everyone else in the Abbey to forget that she was Irish. If that nation had abandoned her, then Sister Boniface had taken her revenge in abandoning Ireland. What little was known of its people took the form of base words, 'barbarous', 'pagan', 'wild', 'unculti-vated' and if ever the subject came up Sister Boniface used them as freely as anyone else and with more vehemence.

The swan returned anonymously to her flock and continued her slow flight north.

Sister Boniface no more thought of herself as Irish than she thought of herself as a woman. Both were inconveniences of birth which she had struggled to overcome. God had not found her worthy to be born a man, but He had relented when He had created the strange circum-stances whereby she had been delivered to the Abbey of Fontevrault as if she were a parcel, perhaps the only place on earth where a woman could rise to high position without dependence on a man. Sister Boni-face's ambition was no less than to become Cellaress of Fontevrault, then its Treasuress and then its Abbess and then to take her place in Heaven alongside the other souls who had been good and great on earth. Having known powerlessness as a child, Sister Boniface wanted power with a greed from which no penances could absolve her.

Patriotism and gender were for lay people. Sister Boniface was a would-be sexless citizen of Christendom, breathing its purified air with the million of other monks and nuns who knew no boundaries but God's and who, whether they were Irish or Spanish, Angevin, Norman, Flemish or English, obeyed only God's law and spoke God's common tongue – Latin. It was true that her feminine state obtruded itself on her notice with disgusting, monthly regularity, but God might take that away as she bounded briskly up the spiritual ladder.

When the summons came she thought it was in order to put her on the next step up that ladder and make her Cellaress.

*   *   *

9

It came in silence from the hub of the abbey, along the Great Cloister, through the refectory, down long, light corridors to the kitchens, the only place in the convent where there was noise between Sext and None as the chaos created by the midday meal was eliminated. Even there the only sounds were sibilants; pans were scoured, tables scrubbed, tiles swept, slippered feet turned and scurried, platters were scraped and the scullion hissed when she scalded her finger on a turnspit insufficiently cooled down.

The summoner, Sister Jeanne, gave her message in the gestures which were the Fontevristes' communication during The Silence. 'From the Mother Superior, greetings. Would the Lady Kitcheness attend on her in her room,' said Sister Jeanne's hands.

Sister Boniface nodded. She would indeed – she'd been waiting to do so for a month. But even for that, even for the Mother Superior, she would not offend God by leaving the kitchen in a mess. She stayed at her post until the job was done as God would want it done. The meal had been unusually large and elaborate in honour of their guest that day, the Papal Legate; and although it had achieved the standard and quality which Sister Boniface and God required, the disorder in the kitchens caused by its preparation had been considerable.

She remained in the doorway, the bunch of keys at her belt as motionless as her folded hands under her scapula. As if she were the Chantress and they were choir nuns, the kitchen staff glanced at her for direction as they went about their chores. Instead of a baton, Sister Boniface used her eyes. A blink popped a pot off the wrong hook onto the right one, another swept the ashes of the fireplaces in the north and west walls into neater piles, and yet another pointed out the discordant cabbage leaf lurking under the water vat.

At last harmony was achieved. God, who was order, beamed His approval through its shine. Sister Boniface's hands emerged to shape a 'Well done' in the air. The kitchen staff shambled off to have forty winks before Vespers (being excused None) and Sister Boniface was released to pursue her destiny.

She did so at speed, asking God's permission to allow her proper gliding gait to degenerate into a lope. He did. He was good about things like that. He spoke to her in the silent corridors through the whisper of her slippers on the tiles. 'I promised you greatness, daughter. Hurry to receive it.'

'I'll sack the bailiff of Home Farm, Father,' promised Sister Boniface to her God. 'I'll grow a better strain of barley and improve pig production. Your glory shall shine before all men.'

In its valley under the sun of Anjou in the centre of the civilised world, the abbey of Fontevrault had grown in the warmth of God's goodwill and men's during the fifty or so years of its existence. It was

10

the Queen of Abbeys, the home of Mary the Virgin to whom it was dedicated, spawning priories all over the known world so that altogether the Order of Fontevrault now numbered some five thousand souls. To be Kitcheness of such an Abbey carried great responsibility, but to be its Cellaress was to occupy one of the highest roles in female monasticism. For a month now, ever since the final stage of Cellaress Priscilla's illness, Sister Boniface had shouldered her work as her deputy.

Although she was only eighteen years old she had discharged her many functions like a veteran, trading with merchants, ordering the immense amounts of food the convent consumed, overseeing the domestic staff and the management of the home farm where much of the convent's produce was grown, planning menus, laying out money, laying in stores, attending the great fairs and markets, seeing to the repair of the kitchen and its utensils, fitting it all in with her duties as Kitcheness and the relentless hours of worship. She had become thin and not minded it. What she minded was in not having the power that went with the post proper. As a mere deputy she couldn't take seisin of Home Farm and reorganise it to be the efficient unit it should be, which meant sacking its indolent bailiff. She couldn't institute the radical changes she had planned in her head to make Fontevrault's – and her own – status even greater than it was. She couldn't sit at the Cellaress' place at table, nor receive the prestige due to that eminence. She didn't have power.

'Give me that, Father. Give me power and You'll be amazed by what I shall do for You.' Most of the Fontevrault nuns prayed to the Virgin Mother, their patron, when they were in need. But although Sister Boniface loved St. Mary and consulted her on domestic matters, on important things she believed in going to the top. Wanting power, she recognised where it lay.

She entered the Great Cloister and checked her pace as she passed along the stripes of its holy shadows, 'I was wondering,' she prayed casually, 'whether we shouldn't buy a horse, just a little one, a trifle, to win the Saumur races in Your name.' The 'trifle' she had her eye on was sixteen hands and had some form behind it. She waited outside the door of the Mother Superior's room to hear God's view on the subject; she wasn't sure where He stood on her love of racing. Apparently he had none. The only sound came from a cuckoo in the Abbey orchards.

Sister Boniface crossed herself, knocked on the door and went in.

To her surprise, the Mother Superior was still entertaining Cardinal Papato. She had expected that by now the Papal Legate would have returned to Chinon, where he was staying during his sojourn in Anjou. After she'd kissed his ring and the Mother Superior's hand she

11

was even more surprised to find that the Cardinal, apparently, was going to conduct their interview. She wondered why the Pope's emissary should have an interest in the appointment of an Abbey Cellaress, usually an internal business.

She relaxed as he prepared to confer the honour upon her: 'Sister Boniface, you have been chosen for a task important to God and His Church . . .'

His next words diverged so sharply from the route she had expected them to take that, for a moment, he might have been lapsing into an unknown language. She didn't understand. He repeated what he had said.

She wasn't going to be Cellaress of Fontevrault, but something greater and, to Sister Boniface, more terrifying. They were going to make her Abbess of Kildare in Ireland.

'Where is Ireland, anyway?' asked the Fratress of Fontevrault that night after the Kitcheness had delivered her news.

'God knows,' said Sister Boniface, miserably.

When they weren't away on business, the officers of the Abbey of Fontevrault slept in a partitioned-off section of the dorter which demarcated their higher status from the other, run-of-the-mill princesses and noble ladies who were the non-commissioned body of the convent. The size of their beds was strictly in accordance with their rank. The Treasuress, for example, the most important woman in the Abbey next to the Abbess herself, had a bed that was enormous, which was lucky since the incumbent Treasuress was gigantically fat. The shape she and her bed made in the moonlit room was frightening. The empty one reserved for whoever succeeded the late Cellaress Priscilla was the next in size and the Kitcheness, who had the smallest and hardest bed in the room, had looked forward to occupying it, but now she never would.

The importance of the women in this dorter gave them special dispensation. They were allowed, for instance, to miss night office sometimes – all except the Mistress of Novices who was obliged to lead her yawning young flock to that inconvenient interruption in the night's repose – and occasionally, as now, to break the Grand Silence on matters which affected them.

'I think,' said the Almoness, who was a Norman, 'I think it's somewhere off England. On the left hand side, I believe.'

'Wherever it is,' said the Chantress, 'it is a barbarous and backward nation. I suppose you, Boniface, are to be the spearhead of reform.'

'And I wish the lot of you would go with her and let me sleep,' interrupted the poor Mistress of Novices, waspishly. They ignored her.

'Weren't you born Irish, Boniface?' asked the Chantress. 'Is that why they've chosen you?'

There was no reply.

'Dear God,' said the Fratress, 'Perhaps Boniface will be martyred.'

There was a frightened yet envious hush. Even though the world had grown so old, there were still sainthoods to be picked up and martyrdom was a sure way of doing it.

'As a matter of fact,' said the Infirmaress, who possessed considerable learning, 'Ireland was once renowned for its saints and scholars. Whatever's happened to it now, it's still producing the odd one. That Malachy whom Bernard of Clairvaux was so fond of, he was Irish. Bernard had himself buried beside him at the high altar of Clairvaux.'

'I wonder who'll be Cellaress now?' asked the Fratress and immediately caught everyone's interest except that of the Kitcheness, who had curled into the foetal position in the darkness and put her thumb in her mouth. Abandonment was her terror and now they were abandoning her, just as she had been abandoned as a child.

God had come to her aid then, with Mother Matilda. Wrapping her round in His love, He had promised never to leave her. He'd gone further; guaranteeing her power in and over her own life so that she could never be abandoned again. It was why she had become so brisk, some even said 'bossy'. Efficiency was part of her bargain with the Lord. He had broken His promise. She had worked herself into a skeleton to make herself indispensable to this convent, worming her way into its very fabric in her need to be needed by it and by God. Now both had cast her off.

How could they send her back to that place which was associated with such horror that her memory still refused to recall the circumstances of it? Ireland was loss. It floated in her mind like some dismal Atlantis in a cold pagan sea, deserted by God's light, off the map of Christianity, off-stage, off-shore, off-putting. Insecurity infected her so that twelve years of familiarity were obliterated and the structures around her, the women, the sounds of their voices, became as monstrous as they had been to the six-year-old, grief-stricken, hiccuping child she had once been.

There was a creak of stressed wood and a smell of body odour, an earth-moving disturbance, as the Treasuress sat up in bed, clearing her throat for utterance. All the voices stopped at the sound which penetrated even Sister Boniface's misery. This was the voice she had been waiting to hear ever since she'd told the nuns about Ireland. The Treasuress had distressing physical characteristics, one of them being a tendency to fart whenever she bent down, which made her genuflections at mass a noisy procedure and caused the novices to go into hysterical giggles, but she possessed the shrewdest mind in the convent.

13

Her words came deep and musical from her great chest. 'I tell you what, Boniface. You'll go far. Once an abbess always an abbess. Make a success of your abbey out in the sticks and you'll be in line for taking this one over before you're thirty.'

Jealousy that they could not help had prevented the other nuns voicing this fact which had been obvious to everyone but young Boniface herself; now their fairmindedness made them grunt their agreement and call out God's blessing on her.

There was a virulent 'God bless you' from the Mistress of Novices' bed. 'And may your novices have a better example in keeping the Silence than these she-devils here.'

'Oh, shut up,' said everybody.

The thin body of the Kitcheness gradually uncurled. A courage she did not know she possessed – she had little self-awareness – was suddenly enlarged by the challenge to her. Of course, that was it. God had not deserted her at all. He had promised her power, but He hadn't said where. He was a tricky old God sometimes but He loved her for obeying His rules and she loved Him. His light would shine over Ireland, wherever it was, once she got there and instituted His rules in it. And she would, she would. They would not know in Ireland that she was Irish and they had cast her out. 'I'll give them abandonment,' she promised.

And now she came to think of it she would have free rein over this abbey of Kildare; she could make it grow good and prosper, order its nuns, arbitrate their fate, make them happy and obedient to God, punish their transgressions.

And what if she was martyred? She tried to imagine it. She saw herself, her arms protectingly outstretched in front of her abbey door, guarding it from the painted heathen hordes, as a spear went neatly – and painlessly (there was no point in overdoing it) – through her heart, and her soul streamed upwards in its new manifestation as St. Mary Boniface to join St. Stephen and St. Peter and St. Catherine and all the other canonised martyrs in the jewelled palaces and lush pastures – on which grazed unnumbered and excellent racehorses – in the highest heaven of eternity.

He had His plans for her, did God. She should not have doubted Him. When the bell rang for night office she would join the Mistress of Novices and go down and thank Him.

'Remember you're Irish,' shouted Abbess Matilda of Fontevrault as they trotted along the road to Chinon with their escort the next day. The Abbess' normal speaking voice was a bellow, partly because she was getting deaf and partly because it signified her nobility. She never modified it whether she was talking to her nuns, addressing kings and queens and popes, or praying to the saints. The Abbess' blood was as

14

blue as any royalty and certainly bluer than most of the saints'.

'I'm not,' said Sister Boniface. She was tired, but she had recovered her spirits which, as always, had been lifted even further by being on horseback.

'Well you are. It's only because you're Irish that you're to get the abbacy. The Pope was going to send someone else, not a Fontevriste at all, would you believe. But I told him. I said it would be better to have somebody who knew the native language.'

Sister Boniface snorted.

'I didn't exactly say you knew it now,' went on the Abbess, 'I wouldn't lie to the Holy Father. But you used to know it. When you first landed on our doorstep, snivelling little thing that you were, you jabbered away in your outlandish tongue like a heathen.'

The road began to run parallel to the Vienne, loveliest of rivers, and the onslaught of the Abbess' sentences startled a heron out of the reeds. It flew off across the river with slow, offended wingbeats. Sister Boniface shifted uneasily in her saddle. As sure as eggs were eggs the Abbess' next sentence would begin: 'You were a funny little thing . . .' To Abbess Matilda Sister Boniface's presence always evinced a reference to the time that Sister Boniface herself most hated to remember.

The old and the young nun rode through a countryside in which the wildlife was beginning its annual cycle to perdition in its usual springtime way. In the dust of the roadway puffed-out male sparrows fluttered on the backs of crouching consorts, the woodlands piped with courtship and tree buds cast off their blossom which spiralled down in the slight breeze and stuck to the veils of the two women. The superb mares on which they both rode as if born in the saddle lifted their tails to a stallion in a paddock who came galloping down to the fence to whinny at them. Old as she was, the Abbess was part of the cycle, she had become head of Fontevrault only after the death of her husband – grandson to William the Conqueror – to whom she had borne children. It was the girl who would stay aloof from the meaning of the beautiful day by her vow of celibacy. And thanked God for it. It was such an inefficient, messy business.

'You were a funny little thing,' bawled the Abbess, musingly. 'Thin as a lathe; well, you still are. And not a penny piece as a dowry to God and us for taking you in.'

'But you were brave,' mouthed Sister Boniface.

'But you were brave,' said Mother Matilda, 'and you knew about horseflesh.'

The sound of their hoofbeats dropped an octave as they crossed the Bridge of Nuns and then went up again as the horses regained the road and turned along it.

'You insisted that you were descended from some Irish king or

15

other, but Ireland is pickled with kings and, anyway, we couldn't pronounce the name, so it didn't mean much.'

It certainly had not. In those desolate months she had spent her nights crying and her days in verbal, and sometimes actual, fisticuffs with her well-born, snobbish sisters in Christ. Well, she had outdone them all. God had taken her into His hand. God and the Abbess.

'And I realised your potential when you showed me that horse had been bishopped,' shouted the Abbess, 'I knew then you were destined by God for great things. And so you are.' She stopped remembering, and turned to look at her nun with the shrewdness that had extended Fontevrault's influence to all the countries of Christendom – except Ireland. 'You must carry Fontevrault's banner into Ireland before the other orders get there. This is important, Boniface.'

'I know it is.' The debt she owed this woman was only outweighed by her debt to God. She put out her hand to touch the Abbess' glove. 'I'll make it a second Fontevrault or, before God, I won't come back.'

She had been shouting so that Abbess Matilda would hear her and heard her oath bounce off the surface of the river in reverberation.

The Abbess nodded. 'That's right, "With your shield or on it" as the Spartan mothers used to say. And do remember some Irish; it would interest my nephew to hear it. That is, if the boy's in. Can you see?'

They had reached the outskirts of Chinon and on the other side of their road from the river was a high cliff. On the top of it, as high again, rose a castle of blonde towers and walls assuming the shape of the spur on which it had been built. It seemed to lean over and dwarf the town below. From the roof of the highest tower flew a standard. Sister Boniface cricked her neck and managed to make out three red shapes on the flapping material – the red Plantagenet leopards. Only the Abbess Matilda, his aunt, could describe the King of England, Duke of Normandy and Aquitaine, Count of Maine, Touraine and Brittany, ruler of an empire, terror of non-conforming barons, arbiter of a new system of government and law, as 'the boy'.

'He's in.'

They rode up the cobbled, zig-zagging road which led to the eastern fort of the castle, its one vulnerable point, passing through gates, by flanking towers, under barbicans, receiving few challenges from the sentries to whom the Abbess was a familiar visitor. At last they reached the final portcullis. 'Tell my lord Henry,' said Matilda of Anjou in a voice which effortlessly reached the gatekeeper in his upper guardroom, 'that the Abbess of Fontevrault is here with the Irish nun.'

At that moment, in a high room of the castle overlooking the Vienne, two men, a king and a cardinal, were disputing the ownership of Ireland. They sat on opposite sides of a table and both were getting cross, though the Cardinal was concealing the fact better than the King. Ireland was represented by a piece of parchment to which was attached a great leaden seal, and they pushed it back and forth between them as they argued.

'I tell you I don't want it,' said Henry II of England, 'He'll have to take it back.'

'I'm afraid that's impossible,' said the Papal Legate, gently. The parchment, a papal bull, was on his side at the moment and now he eased it across the table to the King.

'I don't bloody want it.' Again Ireland skidded back to the Cardinal's side.

'It appears, my son, that you have it. Want it or not.'

'Look,' said Henry Fitzempress, 'I've just won England after a war that lasted seventeen sodding years. I'm ruling an empire that stretches from Hadrian's Wall to the sodding Pyrenees. I've got barons disputing every sodding step I take. What I don't want is a floating bog full of warring, sodding tribesmen whose only agreement would be in telling me to fuck off out of it.' Ireland, which had been pushed once again to his side, skidded back to the Cardinal and the King got up from the table to prowl the room, as if looking for an escape.

'As well he might,' thought the Cardinal, 'I wouldn't stay here myself if I didn't have to.' One had to be a very powerful king indeed to afford to receive distinguished guests like himself in a room as plain as this. It held the one table, two stools, an astrolabe, about six hundred scrolls, a stuffed owl, two live Norwegian falcons, two muddy dogs, a lot of straw, droppings and dust. The Cardinal had seen better-kept kennels. For that matter, his own huntsmen were better dressed than this king. In his worn leathers, the young man looked like a huntsman himself. But this one commanded a pack of nations and was in the process of bringing most of them to heel. He was stocky, round-headed and had a bluff, open face with honest grey eyes and the Cardinal didn't trust him as far as he could throw him.

'Besides,' added Fitzempress, 'my Mummy advises me not to touch Ireland yet, and I always do what my Mummy tells me. Have you met my mother?'

Impassively the Cardinal said he'd had the honour of Empress Matilda's acquaintance.

'Strong-minded lady,' said Fitzempress.

The Cardinal agreed that she was. During the long and terrible war between Matilda and Stephen of Blois for the throne of England, the Empress had managed to alienate practically everybody, including her own side and the English themselves. Luckily she had ceded her right to the country to her son whose exploits had won the English over

17

because, peculiar people that they were, he had made them laugh. Nobody had ever, ever, been made to laugh by the Empress.

'But the old witch's no fool,' said Fitzempress, 'and if she says Ireland's a pitcher of eels, then that's what it is. Whose bright idea was it to give it to me anyhow?'

The Cardinal shifted his scarlet velvet robe away from a dog who was about to cock its leg on it. 'I believe John of Salisbury engaged the Holy Father's attention in the matter of Ireland.'

Fitzempress showed his teeth in what the Cardinal hoped was a smile. 'Couldn't he think what else to get me for my birthday?'

'He is your servant, my lord, and had your interest at heart. Ireland is too close to England for comfort, were it to be invaded by an outside power . . .'

'I know where it is. And I still don't want it. You tell that John of Salisbury to keep his nose out of my court for a while or I'll cut it off. He'll be lucky if that's all I cut off. Sodding English clerics.' Without appearing to do so, he watched the Cardinal's fingers drum on the table. How much insult the old boy was prepared to accept was an indication of how important this matter was to the Pope. 'Who said the Pope could give Ireland away to people anyway?'

'God,' said the Cardinal, glad to be on firm ground. 'The ownership of all the world's islands is vested in the See of St. Peter.'

'England too?' asked Fitzempress, with interest, 'I thought I owned England. There was this war, you see, lasting seventeen years and afterwards they gave it to me. I didn't realise it was the Pope's. I thought I'd won it.'

'God and His Holiness are most happy that you reign there,' said the Cardinal, beginning to sweat.

'That's nice. Now then. About Ireland.' Fitzempress sat down again. 'The Pope thinks it's an unguarded postern to England, does he? Well, he's right. Adrian is a good Englishman himself. But what's keeping him awake at nights? The thought of Ireland suddenly biting me in the arse? Or the fact that the Irish Church doesn't follow the rule of Rome?'

'My lord, they are a barbarous people,' burst out the Cardinal. 'Shameful in their morals, wild in their rites. Their very lives are unclean; Christian in name, but pagan in fact. When worthy Irishmen like Malachy reproached them with their filth, they were reviled. They marry whom they please, even among the forbidden degrees, so that incest is rife. The sin of divorce is frequent among them . . .'

'Shocking,' interrupted Fitzempress, quietly.

And then, too late, the Cardinal remembered that Eleanor of Aquitaine had been divorced from King Louis of France before she had married Henry Fitzempress. He began to sweat once more. He

18

had been manipulated and he knew it, because against less clever opponents he was a considerable manipulator himself. Fitzempress beamed at him: 'Want to begin again?'

The Cardinal mopped his face.

'So what we've got here,' said Fitzempress, amiably, 'is not a case of "Let's-give-Ireland-to-poor-old-Henry-of-England-because-he-needs-it." What we've got here is "Let's-get-poor-old-Henry-of-England-to-beat-Ireland-into-submission-for-us-and-establish-the-Roman-Church-there." Do I sum up correctly?'

'My lord, I . . .'

'Do I sum up correctly?'

'Regard it as a crusade,' said the Cardinal in desperation, 'from which both the Church and yourself may benefit.'

'I don't like Crusades,' said the King of England, 'all you get from Crusades is dead soldiers and the pox. And while you're out of your own country, some bugger pinches your throne.'

The enormity was ignored. Instead the Cardinal produced from his robe a beautifully carved, small, ivory box. He opened it to reveal a gold ring on which was mounted a giant emerald. Fitzempress took it over to the window and let the sunlight play on it so that a beam glanced around the room like a green spirit. 'Not bad,' he said, 'nice little bauble.'

'I have been remiss, my lord,' said the Cardinal, 'Forgive an old man's memory. I should have given this to you before now. It is an earnest of His Holiness' love for his favourite son in Christ.'

'That's nice,' said Fitzempress, 'because it would be a cheap price for Ireland.' He threw the ring up in the air over his head and caught it behind his back, like a juggler.

'Henry,' said Cardinal Papato, 'take the advice of a weary old man and don't discount the Church. One of these days – not now, while you're riding high – but one day, you are going to need her.'

Fitzempress looked at him carefully. 'Do you think so?'

'I think so.'

A young king grinned with affection and triumph at an old cardinal. 'All right, I'll tell you what I'll do. When that day comes I'll invade Ireland for you.'

'Not before?'

'Not before. And I keep the emerald.'

'My son,' said the Papal Legate, getting up, 'remind me the next time I come to talk business with you to bring a longer spoon.'

There was a shout of laughter from the King and the two men walked out of the room, arm-in-arm.

But Henry Fitzempress didn't win all the points. As they approached the Great Hall his chamberlain came up to him to announce: 'My lord, the Abbess of Fontevrault is here with the Irish nun.'

'My, my,' said the Cardinal, silkily, 'There's a coincidence.'

The King looked carefully unconcerned. 'No doubt the Queen has asked for her presence in order to give her a farewell gift or something. Eleanor is a patroness of Fontevrault after all. And no doubt you, my lord, will want to give the woman some final instructions.'

'No doubt,' said the Cardinal.

'Escort his Eminence to the Queen,' Fitzempress told his chamberlain. 'My lord, excuse me for a short while. I have some petitioners to see.'

'You are excused.' But the Cardinal hung on his heel to watch the King return to the dreary room they had just left, and remained long enough to see two young men come marching across the courtyard and follow the King up the stairs. He didn't know who they were, but they didn't look like petitioners.

Nor were they. The taller, Fulke de Saumur, was an Angevin aristocrat, a relative of the Plantagenets. The ancestry of the other, Sir John of Sawbridge, was as nondescript as his mousey-coloured hair, consisting only of an English innkeeper father who had sweated blood to equip his son with a horse when he sent him off to the civil war to fight on Henry's side. All the two men had in common was intelligence, a commodity the king valued and exploited, whatever class it cropped up in. He'd spotted it in the young English soldier, had knighted him and attached him to a unit of his own devising whose duty was only to himself. Officially the men of this unit were a detachment of his household knights; to the few who knew of their existence they were 'Fitzempress' Ferrets.' They were the king's spies.

Out of habit the two Ferrets glanced up and down the corridor to see it was empty before they entered the king's room and, once in, they locked the door behind them. 'My lord?'

'Lads,' said Henry Plantagenet, smiling with a benificence that made them nervous, 'confess I'm an indulgent employer. Here you are just back from the Holy Land with its harems and date palms, redolent with the perfumes of the east . . .'

'And its dysentery,' said Fulke.

'We've only just got over the shits,' complained Sir John of Sawbridge.

'. . . and here am I preparing to send you off again to an even more mysterious corner of the world at my expense. Do I note a certain reluctance?'

'No, my lord,' said Fulke.

'It is our honour to serve you, my lord,' said John. You could joke with Henry up to a point, but no further. Anyway, he thought, it was indeed an honour to serve this genius of strategy and cunning, not to mention it being a heaven-sent way for a low-born Englishman like himself to achieve preferment and riches. Even while sweating it out in Outremer, with its heat and flies and its even hotter and annoying politics, he had blessed his luck in being plucked from obscurity by this king. As long as Fitzempress was in a position to do him good, John would serve him with all his soul.

'That's right. Your report from Syria was excellent. I want one just as percipient from this next assignment.'

'And where's that, my lord?'

'Ireland.'

Fulke de Saumur hadn't even heard of it. John at least knew of its existence, having once met an Irishman, but he placed it mentally in a remote part of a mist from which the other Celtic countries, Wales, Scotland and Brittany occasionally emerged to cause everybody trouble but in which Ireland itself was lost. He was disappointed; wherever Ireland was it wasn't in the political mainstream and therefore there would be little kudos from going there.

In the dust of the deep windowsill Henry Plantagenet's forefinger drew a wavy line, the coast of Normandy. Above it he drew an old woman sitting on a pig. 'That's England.' With the palm of his hand he made an indeterminate smudge to the left of the pig's snout. 'And that's Ireland. At least, I think it is.'

'That close to England?' asked John interestedly, 'I never knew.'

'That close,' said Fitzempress, 'which is why it's important. And not many people *do* know, not how big it is, not its potential, not anything. It's a mystery you two are going to penetrate.'

'Who rules it, my lord?'

Fitzempress clapped Sir John on the shoulder. 'Now that's an interesting question. At the moment I don't think anybody does. One of these days I shall. The Pope's just given it to me, hoping I'll conquer it for him in the name of the Holy Roman Church, bless him. I've told him to sod off – I'm too busy and anyway I'm not expending my money and men to get him a cheap new parish. But the place is a vacuum, and the only bugger who's going to fill it is me; I can't afford to have some ambitious bastard flexing his muscles that close to my shore. So, unbeknownst to anybody, you two are going to find out about Ireland. Fulke, you'll do a quick reconnaisance just to reassure me there's no immediate danger. John, you're to stay there until you can give me a detailed report for when I do invade – every petty lord, every weakness, every strength, ports, minerals, every wave of Irish bloody grass. Understand?'

'Understood, my lord.'

The Plantagenet looked at his spy. 'Come on, John. You're going

21

into mystery, ancient beauty, holiness. It's supposed to be a wonderful country. You'll love it.'

'I'll love it, my lord.'

'Good. Now then, the only Irish princeling I have any contact with is called Dermot of Leinster. Leinster's on the eastern side of Ireland, somewhere to the south, nearest to England. This Dermot seems to have more modern ideas than the rest of them and has sent me messages and presents of friendship. Wants to get in with me. My reading of the situation is that he thinks one day he might need my army to help him conquer the rest of his country.'

For a moment the joviality, the youth and the genius slipped out of Fitzempress' face like washed soil to reveal the bare bones of the true nature beneath. They saw a conqueror, 'Poor, dear Dermot,' said the man who intended to rule Ireland.

Then he was back to normal. 'So do a good job, young John, and I'll have a nice, rich heiress waiting for you to marry when you come back.'

Affection for his king and a rush of warmth for this unknown, unsuspecting Ireland gushed enthusiasm through the veins of John of Sawbridge, son of an English innkeeper. 'Pick a pretty one while you're about it, my lord.'

'Greed. That's what's wrong with the world,' said the King of England sadly, as he sent off his spies to prepare for the annexation of another part of it to himself. He didn't tell them that he was arranging to get information about it from yet another source. Henry Plantagenet believed in counter-checking everybody.

Eleanor of Aquitaine had brought something new to the Plantagenet court, thought the Abbess of Fontevrault, as she hauled Sister Boniface through the crowd in the Great Hall of Chinon. In the days of the Empress Matilda it had been stern, filled with warlike barons and depressed by the chilly presence of the Empress herself. Under her son it had lost its chill but retained a purely functional quality, though the function had widened to include every possible expert who could fill Fitzempress' greedy brain with knowledge; philosophers, travellers, historians, astronomers, tacticians, physicians, inventors and mathematicians; many of these being Arabs. Left to the King, the court would have been exciting but comfortless, since the King rarely sat down, which meant that nobody else could either. He took his meals on the hoof – not that they were worth taking, since Fitzempress didn't care what he ate and was consequently exploited by his cooks.

The first thing Eleanor had done was to sack his cooks and institute her own from Aquitaine, men who could not only tempt appetite but seduce it with the genius of their craft. 'We'll stay to dinner,' the Abbess told Sister Boniface.

Eleanor had provided chairs and divans on which her court could relax and gossip, she had hired painters from the East to decorate the walls of the many castles she and Henry owned and in which they stayed on their long, unending progress, not with improving religious illustrations, but with strange, exotic gardens and birds, which, she said – and Eleanor had been on Crusade, one of the few women who had done so – were reminiscent of eastern seraglios. She had put glass in the windows of the cold, northern castles, and fountains into the courtyards of the south; she had installed garde-robes in her solars in order that she and her ladies should not have to use chamber pots which she regarded as a backward and insanitary custom. Music had come into the court with Eleanor, so that the Abbess always associated her with the sound of a lute, and with it had come poetry, most of it in praise of Eleanor herself, and usually from some young man who was dying for love of her.

Her courtiers were easily distinguishable from those of her husband, being generally younger and, both men and women, better-looking and better-dressed. What they wore set the fashion. Her male courtiers appalled some of Henry's die-hard barons by being as perfumed as the female, the die-hards believing the proper scent for a man to be sweat.

'One shouldn't really approve of Eleanor,' thought the Abbess, 'but there's no doubt she's got style.'

Her nun, however, approved neither of Eleanor nor her style. Sister Boniface carried into that swirling, multi-coloured, multi-scented Great Hall an odour of sanctity, lye-soap and disapproval. The stories of Eleanor's various sins during her marriage to Louis of France, her behaviour on Crusade when she was supposed to have had an affair with, among others, her own uncle, had lost nothing in the telling in the Fontevrault dorters where they had been recounted with appalled breathiness. Sister Boniface had never actually met the Queen, having been absent on the few occasions when Eleanor had visited the convent, but she knew that the woman had broken God's rules and was therefore nowhere near as beloved in God's eyes as she was herself.

As she approached the dais to be introduced to the Queen, the young nun's face, had she known it, wore a look of rigid superiority as befitted one who was destined for a higher Heaven than erring royalty.

'She's Irish,' shrieked the Abbess of Fontevrault, pushing forward her protegée, 'An Irish mind trained in the Roman discipline with Angevin logic. Ideal for this holy cause, a treasure.'

Eleanor of Aquitaine looked into the treasure's sharp blue eyes and sighed. Here was another one who thought of her as a scarlet woman. Eleanor had long ago decided that the worst of having a reputation for naughtiness was that half her social inferiors looked down on her, and the other half treated her with a nudging over-familiarity. She didn't know which attitude she most disliked. However, she'd had her orders about this nun . . . she smiled her most brilliant smile at her and said: 'My dear, this venture is so fascinating and I'm dying to hear all about it. Let's go where we can talk privately.'

Trailing silk and a scent of jasmine, she took the nun's hand and began leading her towards a side door. The Abbess would have followed them but was deflected by one of Eleanor's courtiers who, at a glance from Eleanor, went up to her and began talking horseflesh.

Sister Boniface found herself alone with the Queen of England in a walled garden where, Eleanor told her, 'nobody comes unless they want to talk secrets.'

'Talk seduction, more like,' thought Sister Boniface. She disapproved of the garden. In her view the only purpose a garden should have was to provide herbs, culinary or medicinal. It should certainly not be decorative for decoration's sake, like this one.

The day had turned warm, as the Loire Valley's weather could in April, and the sun seemed centred on Eleanor's garden, speckling through the hawthorn trees' branches which had been interlaced over the walkways, and on the stream channelled to run alongside them into a carved basin where the cool, indistinct shapes of fish swam beneath the water, and on the lawns which were of camomile and mint, grown not for the properties of those excellent plants, but for the scent they released underfoot. The place was full of the twitter of hidden birds, and from an unseen arbour came the inevitable sound of a young tenor voice singing. Inevitably too, it sang of Eleanor: 'Gently swaying, rose and fell/Her supple form, while her feet/Kept measured time with perfect beat.'

Against one of the walls was a topiaried yew hedge with niches carved into it in which stood statues, not of saints, but of beautiful young men and women, only saved from total nakedness by a negligent stone drapery or figleaf. 'Aren't they fine?' asked Eleanor, 'Henry of Blois had them brought back from Rome and Fitzempress liberated them from his palace as a gift to me.'

Sister Boniface did not answer. The statues discomfited her, as did the fact that the women walking beside her was revealed to be heavily pregnant.

Eleanor sighed again. This was going to be more difficult than she'd been led to believe. She was unused to people who were proof against her charm for long. She sat the nun down on one end of a stone bench, another involuntary Roman present from Henry of Blois, and eased herself onto the other end to look at her. If the child did but know it, she was beautiful, with that strangely pale, freckled complexion she had, and those amazing eyes. It was a more arresting beauty than

24

Eleanor's own, which was of the blonde type. 'The trouble with you,' thought Eleanor, 'is that you don't know what to do with yours, and I do. On the other hand, you don't have to.' She wondered what line to take and decided on a sincere piety.

Sincerely she said, 'I beg that you will not isolate me from this enterprise of yours in Ireland. And God's,' she added hastily. 'You are so brave to be carrying the Church's banner into the end of the world as you are. I wish I were going with you.' And in that moment she truly did. Eleanor's enthusiasms, though short-lived, were genuine. 'So let me be a part of it by helping you. Tell me what you want for your journey for instance.'

Sister Boniface was coming round; she was not insusceptible to charm and, anyway, she found herself beginning to feel sorry for this woman who was so much less beloved of God than she was. In the sunlight Eleanor looked like a lovely golden pear but she also looked vulnerable in her pregnancy. The Queen was, after all, thirty-two years old – eleven years older than Fitzempress – which seemed to the young nun, who knew little about the reproductive processes, an incredible age at which to be bearing a child, and a dangerous one. She was not to know that Eleanor's appearance of vulnerability was one of her greatest assets: she actually had the constitution of a horse.

Nevertheless, Sister Boniface could think of nothing she needed that the vast resources of Fontevrault couldn't supply, 'I am grateful, my lady, but God has provided for me.'

'Well, there may be one or two little things He's overlooked,' said Eleanor, 'I have prepared a pannier of articles, a swansdown quilt against the cold, some wine, a cloak, for your journey. And there's this I should like you to take with my blessing.' The sun shone on a prettily-carved trinket box with an elaborate 'E' intertwined into the device of Aquitaine gilded onto its lid. Eleanor opened it to show that its interior contained six gold coins.

Boniface was overwhelmed. She had owned nothing in her life before; even her rosary, her crucifix, was the property of Fontevrault. She wasn't sure she should take the box, she had a sense of being bribed, but her puritanism gave way before the beauty of its present and the giver.

'I'm very grateful.'

'But perhaps it is when you have arrived at this Abbey of . . .' Eleanor had forgotten the name, 'that I can be of the greatest assistance. You may wish to build something – a house for the poor lepers, perhaps – do they have lepers in Ireland? You see how ignorant I am. And that's another thing,' she was getting to the point now. 'I should love to hear about these poor heathens you are going to help. Somebody said they had tails. Do you think they've got tails? Will you write

25

to me and tell me everything? Their quaint customs, how the local kings comport themselves, how big their armies are, all that sort of thing?' What else was it Fitzempress wanted to know? 'Who's fighting who? That sort of thing?'

'I can't write,' said Sister Boniface, sharply.

'Of course you can't,' said Eleanor, who could. 'Which of us women can? But you'll have scribes and things, won't you, and you must send me letters, and I'll send you letters, and it will be lovely.'

Sister Boniface frowned. There was more here than a desire for travellers' tales.

At that moment there was a convulsion in the hedge against which the two women sat and two hands appeared over Eleanor's shoulders, slid lasciviously down her chest and clasped themselves round the swell of her belly.

'Henry,' said Eleanor contentedly, without turning round.

'Better not be anyone else,' said Fitzempress, 'Hello, Sister Boniface, and hello, young Henry.' He vaulted over the bench, knelt down and pressed his ear to his wife's stomach. 'Young Henry says "Hello" back.' He got up and plonked himself down on the bench. 'All the old women predict it's another boy, a brother for William.' He smirked. The only child Eleanor had produced during her years with Louis of France had been a girl. 'Now then. Has the Queen told you about the horse?'

'What horse?' asked both Sister Boniface and Eleanor.

'The horse, *the* horse. The one I'm giving you to take to Ireland with,' He stretched out his legs so that he nearly upset the bench and the women backwards. 'She's a mare, a racer, from the best stud in Brittany. My good aunt says you can tell a fetlock from a farthingale. So, all right; I'm giving you a horse.'

'Thank you, my lord,' said Boniface, thinking hard.

'I'm not doing this for nothing. I want you to breed from her. About the only thing I know about Ireland is that they've got some sturdy horseflesh over there and I want a new breed of charger for the army, something stronger and faster. I'm experimenting with heavier armour for my knights and I want something that can carry it.' He beamed at the nun. 'Let's try for that.'

She would have liked to disapprove, have time to think, draw back into her experience as a protection from this young man, but he so eclipsed everything in her experience that all the rules were broken and she could not cope with him. She was being hoisted into his service for God knew what diabolical reason, and while she was infuriated she was exhilarated and helpless. As he sat there with his arm around the golden queen, she felt that he had harnessed everything, all the world's acuteness and all modernity, into doing what he wanted.

'It ought to be two horses, my lord,' she said, 'in case one dies on the journey.'

Fitzempress peered at her. 'I wondered why they were sending such a young one,' he said softly. ' "Does she know what she's taking on?" I thought. Now I think: "Does Ireland?" All right, two horses. Enough?'

'Enough.'

The king hauled Eleanor to her feet. 'Come on, old woman. You can't sit here all day; anybody'd think you were pregnant. Sister Boniface, my blessing on you. You're to stay here and wait for the Cardinal. He wants to give you your marching orders. Good luck.'

As they walked away, the king's red head and the queen's blonde one turned to each other so that they could converse and in that moment it seemed to Sister Boniface that there was an equality as well as sexuality in their marriage which turned it into a companionship such as she had not dreamed could exist between a man and a woman. She was glad to sit quietly in this scented, song-filled garden and reassure herself by telling her rosary.

But there was a pounce on the grass in front of her and she looked up to see that Fitzempress had come back. 'Say some Irish,' he demanded.

She had been dreading this moment, but coming on her so unexpectedly now, she was driven back on an unbidden memory which brought words into her mouth without knowing what they meant.

'Eochu had two sons, Nuada Declam and Mafebis. From Nuada are all the race of Eber. Of his posterity are all the Eognachta,' she said in perfect Irish, her tongue and her throat making unfamiliar moves as she spoke with an ease that was almost alarming. She knew she could have gone on at length, but Fitzempress was nodding, satisfied that what he was hearing had no root in any of the classical languages with which he was familiar. 'Outlandish,' he said, and disappeared again.

Sister Boniface sat down again to await the Cardinal, telling her rosary harder than ever. All this was extremely unsettling for someone such as herself who thrived on the regularity of things; nor was it conducive to one's own internal order to find that hidden cupboards existed in oneself which contained strange, and possibly suspect, tongues and that these same cupboards could fly open to let them out when one did not know one had the key. 'Please God,' she prayed, 'allow me to be in control when I take over this Irish abbey, if take it over I must. Give me power to make a routine so that I can be in charge and establish your rules. Give me monotony.'

She heard steps progressing along the walkway which ran behind the hedge against which she sat and was opening her mouth to call out

27

to the Cardinal that she was on this other side, when a young man's voice, obviously addressing someone else, asked the question: 'What do you suppose Ireland's like?'

Sister Boniface shut her mouth and listened.

'To hell and gone. North. Cold,' said a companion voice. 'Definite lack of dancing girls. No palm trees.'

'That's the impression I got,' said the first voice, 'How he expects us to blend into the background among a lot of woolly tribesmen in bearskins, especially as we don't speak the bloody language, beats me.'

' "Use your sodding initiative," ' said the companion in an imitation of Fitzempress, 'Anyway, they're not all woolly. I met one in Syria once. Perfectly good knight; looked just like you and me. Well, like you – he wasn't as handsome as me.'

'I suppose we'll have to be horse buyers again,' said the first voice wearily. 'Here we are, two well set-up young marshals in the service of a great king and we end up as a couple of horse-copers.'

'That's all marshals are . . .'

The voices faded as the men reached the top of the garden.

Although Fontevrault had remained untouched by the war that the Plantagenets had fought in England and on the Continent to acquire supremacy over both, it had not done so in ignorance of what battles for power entailed. Many of Sister Boniface's fellow nuns had brothers and fathers involved on one side or another. The nuns had been as up-to-date in who was about to invade whom, and the intelligence which had been gathered preparatory to that invasion, as any military headquarters.

'Spies,' thought Sister Boniface with anger, 'Fitzempress is spying on this Ireland I'm going to.' And she herself had been enlisted as an intelligence getter. That was what all the girls-together request for letters by Eleanor of Aquitaine had been about. And the gift of the horse.

'I'll give him horse,' thought Sister Boniface. 'Trying to embroil a daughter of God in his filthy politics.'

The men had turned and were now strolling down the walkway which passed in front of her. She fell on her rosary, moving her lips like a mad thing, but managing to take stock of the two men from under her wimple. They were in their twenties; one tall, handsome and dark, the other shorter with mousey-coloured hair and both dressed like huntsmen, as so many of Fitzempress' knights were in imitation of their king, though their leathers were less scuffed and more self-consciously worn than his.

They bowed as they passed her, to honour her cloth, but didn't bother to lower their voices. Nuns were everywhere and anonymous, acting as chaperones, attendants, comforters, piously treated but otherwise as disregarded as wayside shrines; 'Pray for us, sister,' said the tall, dark one, mechanically, and resumed what he had been saying to his friend: '. . . You can understand him, though. Strategically, it's important. And in the wrong hands . . .'

She watched them out of sight, and when the Cardinal eventually came she told him what she had heard.

The Papal Legate listened with fascination and, to her surprise, some amusement. 'I knew Fitzempress wasn't as uninterested in Ireland as he liked to make out,' he said.

'But will he invade Ireland, my lord?'

'Unfortunately, I don't think so yet.' He caught her bewilderment. 'Dear daughter, these are high matters and are not for you, who should concern yourself only with the good of the souls who will soon be in your charge.'

He told her to sit down while he took the place recently vacated by Eleanor. The warmth of the day and his velvet robe were making him perspire. His bulk, his smell and his obvious intelligence reminded Sister Boniface of the Treasuress, but to her he was the most important person she had met that day, carrying the authority of the Pope – the only earthly authority she recognised. The aroma that came from him was therefore holy, and to be accepted as such.

'My child, the situation in Ireland is complex, but for your purposes it is simple. You are being sent to take over the Abbey of Kildare at the invitation of one of Ireland's many kings, Dermot of Leinster, in whose kingdom it is situated. Why he has asked for a foreign abbess is unclear. I was surprised when I heard of it, for usually these Irish kings give such preferments to their own kin. But I have met Dermot and he is an unusual man; part barbarian, as all Irishmen are, but with many civilised traits. His kingdom is on the eastern side of the country and I think he has a wish to bring it into the twelfth century by allying it to the mainland of Europe and adopting modern customs. Anyway, he has asked the Pope to send him an abbess.' He picked up Sister Boniface's hand. 'We are sending him you, confident that we have found the right little person to fulfil God's purpose.'

He kneaded her hand all the time that he was telling her what God's purpose was, which made her uncomfortable and distracted her from concentrating. She gathered that she was to hold the same position at Kildare as the Abbess held at Fontevrault, wielding power not only over the nuns of the convent, but over the monks of the attached monastery as well.

'You are to be our little crucifer, carrying the cross of Rome's Church and her tradition into this abbey which doubtlessly has strayed so far from it. You will countenance no variation of the discipline which you have been taught, and should Dermot or anyone else prevail upon you to do so, you will oppose him and send word through me to the Pope, and we shall come to your aid. Is that clear?'

It was, though Sister Boniface was more concerned with the fact that her hand was being dragged in the direction of the Papal Legate's velvet-covered groin. She didn't quite realise what he was doing, but instinctively she didn't like it.

'Thank you, my lord, perfectly clear.' She tried to pull her hand away, but failed.

'We are being given an opportunity to establish a little piece of Rome in this Irish wilderness,' said the Cardinal, breathing hard, 'and if we succeed here, we shall have a chance to spread the True Church's influence even more widely and bring Ireland back into her holy embrace.'

Sister Boniface began to panic. Her knowledge of dirty old men was restricted to what other young nuns had whispered in the dorter and one occasion when she'd been goosed by a half-wit herder in Saumur market. But how could this distinguished, all-knowing, all-powerful prince of the church be put in that category? She was as bemused as she was appalled by what was happening. Two irreconcilable planes of existence seemed to be overlapping; one in which a Papal Legate, only a little less infallible than the Pope himself, talked of godly matters, and one in which he was being very fallible indeed.

She got up, to seem as if she wanted to stand respectfully in front of him, but found her hand still clamped firmly by his own over the lump in his lap. There followed a struggle in which Boniface, bent forward and feeling ridiculous, tottered in a 180 degree arc around the Legate's knees on the fulcrum of her own arm, while the Legate lectured on – his eyes exalted on the branches above his head – and puffed.

At last he gave a blissful 'Aahhh', brought his eyes down from the trees as if remembering she was there, smiled sweetly and blessed her. She could go.

She found herself curtseying on one plane and shaking with disgust on the other, as much at his confidence as at his masturbation. He knew she wouldn't report him. And she knew she wouldn't report him; not just because nobody would believe her, or that he didn't deserve it, but he had implicated her in some way she couldn't fathom. She had been used, as if she were no more than a handkerchief in the sexual equivalent of the Cardinal blowing his nose. She had done nothing wrong; she was as innocent of breaking God's rules on sexual matters as when she had entered the garden, but somehow she carried out of it a guilt that would remain with her all her days.

It must be the garden itself. That was it. The blame lay on Eleanor's garden with its languor and lasciviousness. It had put some spell on the Cardinal.

She was not just willing, she was now eager to get to Ireland and throw herself into God's work in order to cleanse herself from her guiltless guilt.

Altogether it had been a bewildering and disturbing day. Apart from the nastiness she had just gone through, instructions had been heaped upon her whereby she must re-establish the rule of the Roman Church in at least part of Ireland. She must introduce the Order of Fontevrault in Kildare and spread it to other convents. She was asked to gather military intelligence for the Queen of England (though really for its King) and breed a new type of horse for Fitzempress' army.

Faced by these many and, possibly, conflicting orders, Sister Boniface knew that the only ones to obey were those which came from the very top.

'Thy will shall be done, Father,' she promised

Chapter Two

If it was the swan-shaped Daughter of Lîr who had examined Sister Boniface so closely when she stood in the kitchen doorway of Fontevrault on that April day, as if knowing the girl was to be important in the scheme of things, her immortal eye also perceived the patterns of power as she flew homewards.

Everywhere it was becoming centralised. That clever, cold-blooded spider, William the Conqueror, had spun an iron cobweb out of his own entrails and pressed it down on England and Normandy, connecting every living soul in both countries to the middle, which was himself.

His son, Henry I, had reinforced the system whereby everybody, except the Church, owed either rent or service to somebody greater – ending in the king.

Joyless as the system was, the misery that ensued when it was ripped apart in the following, contested, reigns of Stephen and Matilda at least showed the one priceless advantage of feudalism – stability. During the anarchy of the Stephen and Matilda years, when God and his saints turned their faces away, the meanest serf who had suffered under the old regime prayed for its return.

It had therefore been a grateful people on whom the new king, Henry II, had reimposed the iron cobweb and extended it. Now he prepared to spin new filaments into it, this time of a justice which would by-pass the untidy plethora of feudal courts – barons' courts, manor courts, sheriffs' courts, county courts – and link his subjects directly to himself by a Common Law. It was a modern idea, a great far-seeing idea and, since the people paid for their justice, a very profitable idea.

But as the Daughter of Lîr passed over the gridiron of Plantagenet Europe and came home to Celtic Ireland, she left neatness and order and exploitation behind and instead saw beneath her a chaotic swirl of patterning which had not altered since the time of myth into which she had been born.

The trouble with the Irish, everybody said, was that they had never been conquered by the Romans and therefore had no conception of a straight line. Their roads, said everybody, were as convoluted as their thinking. They even refused to swaddle their children as mothers did in better-regulated nations where babies were put into strait-jackets as soon as they emerged from the womb in case their limbs had ideas of their own. Not, said everybody, that more could be expected from a nation where even women had rights enshrined into the legal code.

The Irish elected their kings and made them share their power with abbots rather than bishops (another departure from the custom of other countries) and with the Brehon judges, representing a law which had been old before the Dark Ages blotted out the learning of the rest of Christendom. In fact, the Irish were in thrall to only one thing – tradition. But their freedom and thralldom made them vulnerable.

No king, not even Brian Boru in the previous century, had succeeded in overpowering all the others. The swaying scales on which the Irish had established their civilisation could not be decisively tipped. There could be no centralisation, no iron cobweb, in a country where power ebbed and flowed as one kingdom spilled over into another and was then driven back, where alliances between states were formed and broken and where a member of an opposing clan was as much a foreigner as a Turk.

Even the Norsemen hadn't been able to conquer Ireland but instead opted for what little they could get and had settled on strips of land along the eastern and southern seaboards. Everywhere else the political pattern remained locked in its timeless, tortuous reflection of Celtic art, as careless of the rest of the world as if it did not exist.

But the Daughter of Lîr, sagacious fowl that she was, shed tears even as she trumpeted out joy on her return, because her travels had taught her that, for Ireland, timelessness was coming to an end.

Hostility between the kingdoms of Breffni and Leinster had ancient origins, like everything else in Ireland, but in 1152 it had become a personal feud between the two kings when Dermot of Leinster abducted Dervorgilla, wife to Tighernan O'Rourke of Breffni.

Breffni, however, was in alliance with Connaught and in the following year Connaught marched against Dermot of Leinster, who was getting too uppity for everyone's taste, and demanded the return of Dervorgilla to her husband, along with the vast herd of cattle that had been abducted with her.

By the time the new Abbess of Kildare set foot in Ireland the business was nearly over. It had been a small war, no different from a thousand others Ireland had seen in her time.

It was only later that it turned out to have been Armageddon.

Dermot Mac Murrough, King of Leinster, acknowledged the demands incumbent on a civilised man by explaining in person to a prisoner when he had to blind him. It was never easy. For one thing the prisoner rarely took the explanation in good part, and for another thing it was so difficult to pick one's words.

'Look at it this way,' for instance, is a phrase that can sound tasteless to a man whose eyeballs have just been pierced, and if there was one thing Mac Murrough prided himself on, it was his taste.

It was an example of it that, for O'More, lord of Leix, he had the blinding done in the highest room of his tower at Ferns, so that O'More could look out of the window and carry the memory of a last beautiful view into his darkness.

It went well. Enna, the Mac Murrough's hereditary executioner and blinder, had adjusted the irons to exactly the right width and heated them to the point where they cauterised the eyes and produced little blood, which Dermot always hated. Madoc, the priest, had been sober enough to intone some helpful prayers. And O'More himself had shown all the courage which had made him such a pain in the arse as a vassal.

'I so wish you'd realise my side of things,' Dermot told him and smote himself on the forehead – he'd nearly said 'my point of view'. 'It's a matter of progress. How are we ever going to bring Ireland into the twelfth century if sub-kings like you keep defying overlords like me. As one reasonable man to another, there's got to be one High King.'

'It'll never be you, you treacherous bastard,' shouted O'More. He was still struggling against the ropes; Dermot had to admire him.

'Ah well now, treachery,' he said, 'Could I not be accusing you? Didn't you turn against me when the O'Conor proved so troublesome and took away me darling Dervorgilla, not that she was any loss, God bless her femininity. But I want you to know that this unpleasantness is not because of your treachery so much as your lack of foresight – ah God now, I'm sorry.' He tutted with vexation at his lapse into tastelessness. 'You see – ah God again – but I'm the only one fitted to be High King because I'm the only one with the European outlook. . . . There now, I said "outlook". My apologies, O'More dear. All the rest of the boiling lot of you, including the O'Conor, are just a lot of tribesmen.'

'You treacherous bastard,' shouted O'More again, 'you guaranteed my safety to the Church, you bastard.'

'That's another case in point,' said Dermot. He crossed to the window and looked out, waiting for the bells in the church and castle to ring for midday. 'The Church is as backward as anything else in this country. We're going to have to do something to Europeanise that as well. In fact . . .'

'My clan will have your balls for this.'

'On the matter of balls now,' said Dermot, leaning out of the

35

window; from this height he could see the procession of monks, like black ants, leading across the abbey gardens towards the church for None. He turned back into the room and nodded to Enna to get the other instruments ready. 'Since we're on the subject, I'm afaid now we're going to have to ensure that there'll be no little O'Mores. Just in case they should grow up with their father's old-fashioned ideas.'

O'More started screaming but the bells began to ring one second after. In the middle of it, the sentry popped his head round the door and mouthed his message through the hubbub. Dermot raised his voice to apologise for not staying longer. 'There's herself just been signalled. Did I tell you I'd sent to Europe for the new Comarba of Kildare?' He tried to interest O'More in the part the new Abbess was to play in his, Dermot's, plan for the Europeanisation of Ireland, but the man refused to attend so Dermot left him in his ignorance.

As he shut the door on the noise and blood, Dermot shook his head sadly at the sentry.

'A grand man, O'More,' he said, 'but no vision.'

Dermot bowed low before the new Abbess of Kildare: 'The swallows are not more welcome nor the saints more blessed than the sight of you this day.' he said. He turned to her companion, Sister Clotilde, and bowed again: 'There is a double grace on us.'

Tired as she was, Clotilde simpered. Seasickness had slimmed her down somewhat, but she still possessed proportions which did not usually attract compliments.

It had been a desperate journey; five days of heavy swell from the mouth of the Loire to Wexford with Boniface having to spend most of them below decks, dividing her time between Sister Clotilde, who insisted that she was dying, and the horses, who'd seemed intent on it.

True to his word Fitzempress had provided her with two mares, though not from Brittany but from the Holy Land with odd, thrilling heads, aristocratic blood and even more aristocratic tempers. Reluctantly, she'd been forced to let them recover from the crossing in the care of whichever king it was who'd met her on Dermot's behalf at Wexford. She'd lost track of the kings and lords she'd met since landing – dozens, it seemed, had popped out of the forest to greet her during the long ride to Ferns, making it even longer with their insistence on speeches of welcome, interminable accounts of their ancestry and achievements, and introductions to the ranking members of their clan.

She had been shocked by their beards, their magnificent, barbaric jewellery, their trousers and their boasting.

There was no recognition, no sense of familiarity with these people from the childhood she could not remember, and she was glad of it.

She did not want to feel Irish. She gloried in being a foreigner, in being thought a foreigner, bringing the good news of civilised, Roman, Christianity to a country that had strayed off its path. She was polite, but she received their welcome with a remoteness which bordered on superciliousness.

Oddly enough, it was Sister Clotilde who, once she had found her land legs, reacted enthusiastically: 'A splendid-looking people. And the country's just like England.'

Never having been to England, Boniface was unable to pass judgment, but it was certainly different from Anjou. As with the people, the landscape struck no chord in her memory and remained alien, though her mouth watered to hunt over it.

She felt the same need to keep at arm's length the King of Leinster himself, although he was reassuringly beardless, dressed like the nobles back home, and spoke to her in good Norman French. Dermot Mac Murrough was in his forties. He was a tall man with a face as round as a moon decorated by an exceptionally small mouth which would have made him comic, except that when he opened it to speak a voice of such quality came out that, for the person spoken to, it momentarily altered everything – his own looks into beauty, a dull day, the truth.

His reception of them might have been accorded to royalty. There were several more kings and queens, bishops, abbots, abbesses, to be greeted, a choir of young girls and boys sang a paean in praise of St. Brigid, of whom Boniface was now the successor, flowers were strewn, welcome cups were drunk.

'Devastated. I am devastated that I could not meet you at Wexford.' Dermot told her. 'A little local difficulty.'

As they rode up the hill towards his castle, Dermot leaned over to the new abbess, and pointed to it. 'Stone,' he said.

Boniface who was tired, and in any case did not expect castles to be built of anything else, merely nodded. 'Very nice.'

Dermot was quiet for a moment. He did not make that mistake again. Boniface didn't realise she had made one at all.

The feast that night was noisy and magnificent. Clotilde kept gasping at the jewels on display, the food, the workmanship and design of their drinking cups. The gifts Fitzempress had sent with them for Dermot, addressing him as 'his royal brother' – allies were always useful – barely compared with them, but Dermot accepted them graciously.

'I have a gift of my own for you.' Boniface had decided it would be politic to present the King of Leinster with one of the mares. She told him about her plans for breeding. Despite the sense of alienation she could not shake off, she was charmed by Dermot's interest and by his knowledge. They spent the first two courses talking horses.

By the third she felt they had established enough of a relationship to ask him why he had sent to Rome for an abbess for Kildare, a foreigner – Dermot had not asked the Pope for an Irish nun, nor did Boniface enlighten him that the Pope had sent him one. She found it puzzling; already it had become apparent that most of such appointments in Ireland were hereditary, a barbaric custom.

'Ah now, madam, you do me too much honour. Sure, and it was a good idea of mine. We have become insular, looking too much in on ourselves, creating our great churchmen and women from our own people and not bringing in fresh blood, new ideas. But it was the Archbishop of Dublin who wrote to the Pope. At my suggestion. He is of the Hy Kinsella.'

'And who are the Hy Kinsella?'

She was rude not to know, he decided, and, if she didn't know, to probe into matters which existed so deep in the marrow bone they could not be translated into words, especially foreign words.

'My clan.'

He began to talk to her about his plans. 'We are wanting to modernise. We don't want the old backward ways. One king, one church, working in tandem for Ireland and for God.'

It dawned on Boniface that, just as the Roman Church was using her appointment to further its cause, Dermot of Leinster had brought it about in order to further his. She had no doubt who the 'one king' of Ireland was intended to be. But she still didn't understand why he had sent for a foreign abbess, so she persisted in her questioning.

'Well now,' he said, 'The Abbess of Kildare has always carried such prestige, representing the great St. Brigid. With St. Patrick and St. Columkille she forms the most powerful holy triad in Ireland. So the various clans have always wanted to have one of their own relatives in the post, backward tribesmen that they are. It was time to bring in an outsider, someone away from tribal politics, who could help with our great reform.'

'Someone who could be influenced by you,' thought Boniface. 'Well, I am God's creature, not yours, not anybody's.'

Actually in this she did Dermot an injustice. Struggling in the sea of his ambition were moments of altruism and clear-thinking which rose to the surface now and then like drowning swimmers. He had indeed wanted a European abbess because he had thought she would prove neutral in the warring of the clans and would help to bring the Irish Church closer to the Church of Rome. In their relief that he wasn't going to try and impose one of the Hy Kinsella on Kildare, the other clans had agreed to his plan.

To show Boniface how impolite it was to get information by direct questioning, Dermot set about procuring his more subtly. 'While it was our gain, it must have been a loss for your abbey to lose its abbess.'

'Me? I wasn't an abbess. I was kitcheness of Fontevrault.' She gathered by his incomprehension that if there was an equivalent post in Irish convents, it was known by a different name. 'Don't you have kitchenesses in Ireland?'

'We have slaves to do the kitchen work, you cannot mean that,'

And Boniface was so shocked by the mention of slaves that she never did get round to telling the King of Leinster that her position had been a high one. Which was her second mistake.

'Slaves? You've still got slaves in Ireland? But slavery is banned by the Church.'

'You see how necessary it is that you come to teach us. Being a modern man, I do not keep them myself, of course, but I fear that the usage is widespread elsewhere.'

'What a night,' said Sister Clotilde, when they got back to their room. She weaved unsteadily towards a magnificent bed. 'Did you see the linen some of those ladies were wearing, the bracelets? And what a charming man. Boniface, if this is barbarism, it may not be so bad after all.'

Boniface grunted. She would be relieved when they got to Kildare and could begin work. 'Did the Queen talk to you? She only addressed a brief word to me.'

'There's been a quarrel between the Queen and the King I gather, but I don't know what about. They can talk all night, these Irish, and not tell you a blessed thing. And they're all devoted to the King. They said she was an O'Carroll. Everybody else seemed to be Hy Kinsella, whatever that is, or related to the king in some way, or his foster-brother or something. No thank you, dear.' The serving girl who had been assigned to them was trying to undress her. 'Where we come from we say our prayers before going to bed.'

In the early hours of the morning, Boniface was woken up by a stab of pain. The spring moonlight came through the unfamiliar, cambered window, across the bed to the doorway where the serving girl was sleeping on a paliasse.

Boniface frowned. She had no pain. Yet pain had been around somewhere. She decided it had been in a noise of some kind. She listened to the sounds of the night outside, which were like those in the Angevin countryside, but not quite. The smell of the air contained forest, turf-fires and a not-unpleasant something she could not recognise.

She gave Clotilde a pinch. 'You're snoring,' and went to sleep again.

It might have been O'More, now deep in a room under the earth, that she heard. Or it might have been the King of Leinster who had called his chamberlain to his chamber, and said: 'Free all the slaves.'

'All of them, Mac Murrough? Now?'

'Tell them they're not slaves any more. They're free to go.'

'Go where, for the sake of God?'

'Nowhere. Where can they go? Wouldn't the bloody place collapse without them? Tell the buggers I'll flay them alive if they make a move. But tell them they're free to make it.'

When the door closed behind the chamberlain, Dermot began to cry. He beat his fists against the stone wall until they were skinned, to the consternation of his cousin, Urlacam, who was sharing his bed that night. 'Don't be doing that, Mac Murrough darling.'

He threw himself face down beside her. 'God crucify them,' he wept. 'A washer-up. They sent me a bloody washer-up.'

Sister Boniface breathed freer when they set out for Kildare a week later. She wasn't sure whether it was because she was on the last leg of her journey or because she was leaving Dermot Mac Murrough behind. She found him disturbing although she was at a loss to know why.

'Well,' said Sister Clotilde, 'they did us proud. Most attentive, they were. I enjoyed myself. What's the matter?'

'The King.'

'I don't see why you don't trust him. You owe him your post and you ought to be grateful to him for the chance to do God's work.'

'I'm grateful to God.'

'Well, I can't see anything wrong with him. I admire a man who's trying to bring Christian light into the darkness. And he holds you in the greatest respect. He told me.'

'Yes, but why isn't he coming to the inauguration?'

'He's busy I expect. The poor man is a king, after all. And he's sent us with a magnificent escort – look at it.'

'But half Ireland's to be there, apparently. Why not him, if he's king of so much of it? A little local difficulty, he said. Don't you think there are rather a lot of little local difficulties?' She tutted with irritation. 'Things are happening I don't know about.'

'Politics,' said Clotilde, 'Earthly concerns. Nothing to do with us. Look, there's an eagle.'

When they left the Slaney valley, the countryside opened up into illimited, rolling grassland broken only here and there by woods and dotted with gorse just come into bloom. The impression that it was deserted was dispelled by a small field or two, and an occasional pasture for cattle, marked off by wattle fencing. It was the herds of ponies which held Boniface's eye; apparently wild, shaggy but, she saw, in good condition. They couldn't be as wild as all that, she decided, because they didn't gallop off as her cavalcade went by.

'We're approaching the Curragh,' said Murchadh, who was Dermot's brother and who had politely, though somewhat silently, accompanied them so far.

'The Curragh?'

Murchadh's voice took on a sing-song tone: 'It is the racing place of great horses and great kings, overlooked by the kings of Leinster when we lived in the palace of Dunn-Ailinn. The nun herself, St. Brigid, would sweep over its smooth sward in her chariot. Her convent is on the edge of it.'

Boniface began to warm to St. Brigid. 'Do you still have a palace at this Dunn-Ailinn?' The thought of Dermot hovering over her nearby threatened the freedom she was beginning to breathe in the gorse-filled air of this open country.

'Not just now.'

'Another little local difficulty?'

And there it was coming towards them, a band of armed men trotting down a hill in the distance.

'Put up the flag of truce,' shouted Murchadh over his shoulder.

'Truce?'

'It is here that we leave you, Comarba,' said Murchadh. He looked at her hard. 'It is by the Mac Murrough's doing that you are here, and you will be remembering your duty to him.'

With a certain amount of ceremony and exchange of Irish, she and Clotilde with their pack horses and the Arab mare were handed over to the new troop and were sent trotting off to the north, while Murchadh and his men turned back to the south.

'What's all this about? Whose soldiers are you?' asked Boniface of their new captain, first in Latin and then French, but though he smiled and bowed he seemed not to understand her.

She became alarmed. Was she being kidnapped? Was this appointment of hers so political that it was being contested by some enemy of Dermot's?

She had spotted monasteries in the distance during her journey, perched on hilltops, but as she approached Kildare she could see that this one outranked them all. The hill on which it stood was just another wave in the grassland sea which, Clotilde had said uneasily, reminded her of their crossing, but the church at its centre was as high as a cathedral and beside it, higher still, was a tower, a strange, round narrow thing with a conical top which commanded the country for miles around. Piled around this core were buildings which, from her view, presented their roofs in untidy geometric variety, walls, ramparts and, stretching down from these, houses, streets and shops – the nearest thing to a city she had yet seen in Ireland.

And ringing the bottom of this city were the tents of what was obviously a sieging army. As sieges went, it seemed an amiable affair. The gates of Kildare itself were open, allowing traffic to go in and out under the watchful gaze of some soldiers. Other besiegers were trading with merchants from the town and yet others were carrying on some loud, cheerful backchat with townswomen who leaned over the ramparts.

Boniface and Clotilde were taken to a large pavilion not far from the gates where they were greeted by a young man who introduced himself as a prince of Connaught and the commander of this section of Connaught's army.

'I must apologise, holy lady, that my father is not here to pay his respects to you, and I apologise for greeting you in a tent. In fact, I apologise for everything. But I thought we ought to have a little talk,' said Ruairi O'Conor in fluent Latin, and grinned. He was a tall, red-headed young man of cheerful disposition and under different circumstances, Boniface might have approved of him. They were not, however, and she didn't.

'Am I being kidnapped? I warn you, my person is sacred and I refuse to be embroiled in any of your disputes.'

The young O'Conor said he was glad to hear it. 'In a little while you shall be free to enter Kildare where, I understand, they are waiting impatiently to welcome you. They've been without an Abbess since the old Comarba died two years ago. But there is one little matter . . . I suppose the Mac Murrough didn't tell you that the north of Leinster had been occupied by my father's army?'

'No,' said Boniface, 'He didn't.'

'Typical.' The pavilion, like the young O'Conor prince, was pleasant, with one side open to the spring day, well furnished and well supplied with wine and provisions of which, Boniface noticed with disapproval, Clotilde was partaking as fast as she could. She herself had refused all offers of refreshment. She felt tired, angry and humiliated by her ignorance of the situation. There had been no indication during her stay with Dermot of Leinster that part of his kingdom was under the occupation of his enemies.

'Actually,' said the young Ruairi O'Conor, 'we don't intend to occupy it for long. The main body of the army has already gone north on other business. What's left of us is only here until Dervorgilla has her baby.' He looked carefully at Boniface. 'The Mac Murrough didn't tell you about abducting the lady Dervorgilla either?'

'You may assume, young man,' said Boniface, coldly, 'that the King of Leinster has not enlightened us on many things. Supposing you do.'

'He's left us in the dark a bit as well,' said O'Conor. 'For instance we didn't know that the new Comarba of St. Brigid was going to be so young and pretty.' He caught her look, and hurried on with the enlightenment.

It consisted of so many hostilities between so many kings with so many complicated Irish names that Boniface's head began to ache but the up-to-date gist turned out to be that, in order to pay back a certain Tighernan O'Rourke the king of Breffni, for past grievances, Dermot Mac Murrough had abducted O'Rourke's wife, Dervorgilla. 'Now the King of Connaught, my father, is in alliance with O'Rourke just now and so we hosted into Leinster to fetch her back for him. And the cattle she'd taken with her. Are you sure now you won't have some wine?'

'Just get on with it,' said Boniface.

'Ah well, now.' The young man was suddenly awkward. 'It's difficult, don't you see, you being a holy nun and all, and so young.'

'I gather this Dervorgilla was pregnant.'

'Very.' Ruairi O'Conor was relieved. 'In fact, we were approaching the Curragh on our journey back when she began to have pains, though they seem to have stopped now so whether . . .' A tap of Boniface's foot hurried him on. 'Anyway, there was nobody in our army to act as midwife, and anyway it wouldn't have been decent, so we popped her into the holy convent here. And there she is still with no baby yet to show for it. And claiming sanctuary.'

'Sanctuary?' Boniface was on her feet. 'You mean to stand there and tell me that there is an adulteress, a pregnant adulteress, in my convent claiming sanctuary?'

Sympathetically, the O'Conor poured her out some wine, and this time she took it.

'There now, isn't that the advantage of having a foreign abbess? We were afraid you might be in the Mac Murrough's pocket and would be taking her side and that we'd have to go in and get her once the baby was born.'

Boniface was so horrified that the wine horn dropped from her hand. 'You were prepared to invade sanctuary?' Things were getting worse and worse.

'Ah well, sanctuary isn't what it was. Three hundred years ago we watched the Norsemen burst into our holy places, raping and stealing and we waited for the wrath of God to descend on their evil heads. But nothing happened.'

'They went to hell, that's what happened,' said Boniface, 'and that's what will happen to you if you dare to set one foot over my abbey threshold, adulteress or not.'

The young man smiled at her, though with less charm. 'She can stay until she has the baby,' he said, 'and then we take her back to her husband, sanctuary or not.'

It was evening by the time the discussion was over and Boniface was allowed back on her horse in order to ride up the long shadowed track to her abbey gates.

She looked around at the small number of men and tents and asked: 'Aren't you concerned that the King of Leinster might counter-attack and retrieve this woman?' The last thing she wanted was to be in the middle of a war.

Standing politely at her stirrup, Ruairi O'Conor shook his head. 'We've got his foster-brothers as hostages. Say what you like about Dermot, he's fond of his family. And it's my view he only took the lady out of revenge; he doesn't strike me as keen to get her back at all.'

'This is awful,' moaned Clotilde, as they went up the hill. 'That Dermot . . . we've been most cruelly deceived. What a beginning.'

'We are here on the command of the Pope, the Holy Church, and God Himself,' said Boniface. 'So sit up straight. God is with us even in this benighted land.'

And, although Clotilde was beginning to doubt it, He was. As they left the ring of the besieging army, the town erupted around them. It might have been Jerusalem welcoming Christ on Palm Sunday. Fronds and flowers were lain on the track for their horses to step on, men, and especially women and children, shouted out greetings to her with unmistakable joy. They were a factor Boniface had not envisaged and she was moved by them, even while she knew that the warmth of their welcome was not for her personally, but for the figurehead she represented. In this divided, tribal land these people considered themselves as belonging to the clan of St. Brigid and her successor was holy to them, whoever she was, because the succession itself made her holy. She was their luck and their protection.

The huge abbey gates were open and out of them now came more joyful people, this time nuns and monks – very peculiar nuns and monks, as Boniface's tidy mind noted. The nuns had too much hair and nearly all of it showing, while the monks had too little from the outlandish tonsure which had shaved the front of their heads rather than the crown, making all of them, even the youngest, look bald. And they leaped about, making happy yippee noises, in a fashion not at all according to the dignity of a religious. However, their hearts were undoubtedly in the right place, and she could correct their appearance and mannerisms later. Their eighteen-year-old Abbess whipped her sleeve over her eyes so that she could bless them with propriety, and allowed herself to be led inside to her destiny.

Only one person seemed displeased at her arrival. As they crossed

the outer courtyard she heard shouting from a rooftop and looked up
to what appeared to be a gargoyle perched on its ridge, waving a
leather bottle and giving vent to words which needed no interpreter to
tell her were rude.

'Who on earth is that?'

Sister Gormlaith, the senior nun at Kildare, glanced up. 'Ah now,
Comarba, don't you mind. It's only Art.'

'And who is Art?'

'The *echaire-ri,* the head of the stable boys.'

'The head?' What could the others be like? Was she expected to
entrust her precious Arab mare to such a one?

'Ah now, he's a lovely man with only one fault and that against
himself – he's subject to a bit of liquor. Just now he's scared you'll
not be appreciating his handling of things. But he's of the *sidhe* – a
fairy man – when it comes to the horses. St. Brigid could have wanted
no better for the care of her stables.'

St. Brigid, Boniface felt, must have been easily pleased. She put Art
on her growing list of Things To be Dealt With, but it would have to
do tomorrow. Tonight she was too tired.

Rocking as if she were aboard ship, Boniface was carried into the great
abbey church of Kildare seated on a gilded throne carried by princes to
a fanfare of trumpets and cheering that out-crashed the noise any
storm at sea could have made.

'All hail, the heiress of St. Brigid.' The words were made massive by
the sheer force with which they were emitted by a thousand throats
and came hurtling at her as if they had taken material form so that she
nearly ducked.

The church was crazy with colour. Even when it was empty the
coldness which could have been engendered by the almost menacing
height of its roof was counteracted by the light from its many windows
bouncing off fiercely beautiful and comic paintings on the wooden
panels which hid the stone walls. What wasn't painted was carved and
gilded so that it seemed enveloped in a continual, glorious noise. But
now, packed with half the nobility of Ireland – the only great absentee
was Dermot of Leinster – decked in jewels and silks and with the
scarlet and blue cloaks of the common people who filled what space
there was left, some of them clinging to the vaulting and pillars of the
roof like brightly-coloured bees massed in a hive, it was shocking.

'This,' thought the centre of it all, clinging hard to the arms of the
throne as it advanced up the nave and trying to hold on to her senses,
'is sheer paganism.' The joy of all these people was pagan, God did
not want joy at the inauguration of one of his elect, He wanted order,
reverence – like the inaugurations back at Fontevrault – and above

45

all, quiet. 'But this isn't an inauguration,' thought Boniface, 'this is a coronation.' These people were not witnessing the installation of an abbess; they were seeing the most beloved female saint in their island return to earth in the form of her comarba, her heiress.

The European part of Boniface felt silly and improper as she swayed over the hands that reached to touch the hem of her blue, gold-encrusted gown. But an unacknowledged and ferocious vein throbbed to the stamp of a thousand feet and swelled with the indecency of power, confusing her so that she felt possessed by an alien being, 'I am St. Brigid,' said its voice.

They set her before the altar facing the congregation for the service, though what the service consisted of she never knew since she couldn't hear it above the tumult. She took in only part of what was going on around her, the words being said, the hymns, more like paeans, being sung, the prayers offered. She remembered more of it later, with disbelief; at one point the congregation had actually broken into a dance. At another the Archbishop of Armagh and the Archbishop of Dublin had become involved in fisticuffs as to who should proffer her St. Brigid's ring. It appeared before her on the pages of a St. Mark's Gospel – she knew it was St. Mark's because it carried his symbol, a winged lion – so beautifully illuminated that a rainbow might have collapsed, wriggling onto it. She put the ring on.

The Abbot of Kildare, old and shaky, was approaching her and kneeling. He ruled over the monks of her abbey. She found herself looking down at him. 'Compared to me, old man, you are nowhere,' she thought, St. Brigid thought.

There was a change. The shouting had stopped. The church had become silent so that the figures in it appeared carved, gargoyles reproduced in mass.

The palsied hand of the abbot put a pair of shoes in front of her bare feet, a tiny, ceremonial brass pair which had been made for St. Brigid herself, the Mary of the Gaels, seven hundred years ago. Knowing she must put on these shoes had given Boniface sleepless nights since her arrival. 'Supposing they don't fit?'

'Ah, sure now, they'll fit. Aren't you her very own Comarba?'

But if she wasn't? How could they take it for granted? But she had not been allowed to try them on in advance, it was not the custom and seven hundred years of custom was not to be broken. Would she be disgraced if her feet were too big? Would these strange people fall on her and tear her to pieces as an impostor? Anything could happen in this chaos, 'I am St. Brigid,' said the voice again, but it didn't sound as certain as it had.

Boniface flexed her toes and her courage, stood up and twisted her feet into the metal shoes. They were cold, her toes hurt with the constriction and the enamelled brass edge cut into the top of her feet – she saw blood trickle down the side of the right shoe and shook her gown down to cover it, lifted her head and face the enormous crowd in front of her. 'Behold the Comarba of St. Brigid,' shouted the Archbishops of Armagh and Dublin simultaneously in Latin, and then again in Irish: 'Behold the Comarba of St. Brigid.' If the cheering had been loud, it was as nothing to the roar that broke out now, so that it seemed as if it was sound and not the shoulders of Leinster princes that raised the new Comarba in her throne up into the air and carried her through the crowd to the hall for the ceremonial feast.

The only one who had nothing to eat at that feast was the Comarba of St. Brigid, seated alone on a dais, smiling blessings down on apparently limitless rows of tables at which churchmen and women, lords, ladies and, far down at the end, commoners began a marathon of eating and drinking, while her head ached and her feet were in agony. It wasn't that she wasn't offered food and wine, but that petitioners constantly knelt before her to 'kiss the blessed milk-white palm of you, Comarba,' and a milk-white palm couldn't bless and grip a leg of chicken at the same time. After the kiss each one had a petition.

'Will God and St. Brigid look kindly on my marriage to an Eoghanacht of Ara Cliath, Comarba? What day of the week would be best for it?'

'The Corcu Duibne have not paid their one thousand cow tribute, should we host into their land for it, or wait?'

'If I offer this chalice, will St. Brigid lift the curse on my family?'

'Can my son be baptised in the church of St. Brigid?'

'We are suffering insult from the clans of Meath. Should we make war on them now, do you think?'

She was dazzled by their certainty that she held the answer to their problem, while at the same time the European part of her felt that they were consulting her much as the ancient prophetesses had been by the ungodly of the past. What amazed her was that this certainty was unshaken by the fact that the question and its answer – sensibly, she told them all to wait until she was more cognisant with their situation – were made through an interpreter. There was not just complete lack of resentment that she was a foreigner foisted upon them, they ignored it altogether. Later she was to realise that partly they were relieved that she was an outsider, not some relative of Dermot's, and that anyway they had no sense of nationhood. To these handsome, rich men and women there was no such thing as 'Irish' or 'Ireland'. To the prince of Meath, the prince of Munster was as alien as a Frenchman. Their view of the country they lived in was not horizontal as a person who stood upon the land, it was vertical; the land was family, a tap-root that went back to a great ancestor. They might conquer somebody else's territory

47

for the riches it gave, but it remained just a place of hills and fields and cattle to them if their ancestor had not ridden over it, not true land at all. St. Brigid was not a national figure, she was universal, like the moon, and since her shoes fitted this particular woman then this particular woman was her heir, even if she came from far-flung Cathay.

It was then that Boniface saw how right she had been to conceal her Irish birth. They made it easier for her by not caring, and she realised that to reveal it would involve her in the maelstrom of Irish politics. By arriving among them from somewhere they had never seen and had hardly heard of she could remain remote, omniscient, a mystery in what was already a succession of mystery.

A mystery whose feet were in agony. By the time they carried her to an ante-room where Sister Gormlaith was waiting to take the shoes off, her feet had swelled over the edges of the enamelled brass and strips of skin came off with them. 'It could have been worse,' said Gormlaith, dabbing her feet with witch hazel, 'the poor dear Comarba before you had the bunions.'

It was an odd feeling to watch the terrible shoes taken away; they were used only for the inauguration and, since the Comarbship of Kildare was for life, the next time they were put on Boniface would be dead.

Up to this time she had slept in the senior nuns' dormitory, now she was taken to the apartment reserved for the Comarba. Sister Clotilde trotted along beside her. 'Sweet Mary, but won't I be glad to get to bed. Wasn't it wonderful? Of course, it was uncivilised, but it was wonderful.'

At the door of the room, Boniface turned to face her accompanying train of nuns. 'I thank you,' she said, 'and congratulate you. It went well. Now you can leave me.'

The Irish sister turned obediently, blessing her, and glided off down the corridor. Clotilde stayed.

'This is the Comarba's room, Clotilde,' said Boniface gently, 'I am the Comarba.'

'But . . .'

'Only me,' said Boniface, still gently.

Clotilde's face crumpled. In the days since their arrival they had never been apart. She bobbed a curtsey, wiped her eyes, turned and hurried after the sisters. Boniface watched her go, then limped into the room. For all the shouting and ceremonial, this was the true realisation of her high position, a simple thing. To be left by herself. Here was real glory for a woman who had never been alone in her life. She crossed the wide elm boards of the beautiful room to look out of the little window at a courtyard where a single pear tree stood by a stone-circled pool. Behind her was movement, but Boniface ignored it – it was only Ban, her serving woman, who didn't count as company, pouring water into a ewer for her to wash in.

As she snuggled down later under her swansdown quilt, the Comarba of Kildare remembered kindly that it had been given to her by a queen. A mere queen.

The sense of omnipotence lasted about a week, sustained by petitioners, high and low, and by the stream of invalids and cripples who were put in her path every time she went abroad so that her shadow might cure them. 'Oh High, holy nun, bless the track of our ways,' they called out to her. But gradually it began to dissipate.

'One of the O'Faolain princes wants to marry his wife's sister,' she reported to Father Flynn, the abbot of the monk's side.

'Does he now? Well, and she'll make him a fine wife – a lovely girl, a lovely girl.'

'She's his wife's *sister*,' screeched Boniface, 'It's incest. It's against God's rules.'

'That's a pity, because his wife doesn't seem to mind at all.'

Boniface went white. 'His wife's still alive?' She put her head in her hands. 'What am I to say to the Pope about this country?'

Father Flynn, very old, mild and ascetic, would have patted her if it hadn't been sinful for him to touch a woman. They had to hold their meetings in the church, the only communal ground on which the men and women of the abbey were allowed to speak to each other. They sat in two great chairs on opposite sides of the choir, the Abbot with two monks as his chaperones and the Abbess with two nuns as hers. Boniface despaired of understanding how a man who guarded so carefully against carnality in his own life could be so lax about its practice in other people's. But the anomaly was everywhere; not only were there separate entrances into the church for the nuns and monks, but the ordinary men and women of the congregation also had their own doors and, when a service was in progress, were separated from each other in different oratories. From the apparent exuberance of sin with which they mingled outside, Boniface wondered why the church builders had bothered.

The Abbot smiled sweetly at her. 'The Pope – that was a fine letter he sent with you. How is he?'

Boniface calmed herself with an effort: 'Well, thank you. Did you read the bit about incest?'

'So I did. I was forgetting. Well then, we'd better be telling the O'Faolain he can't marry her.'

'I've already told him.' Rome wasn't built in a day, she reminded herself, though whether it would ever be built here in Ireland if this gentle old dodderer was to be one of its bricklayers was doubtful. However, she was gratified to see that Father Flynn regarded her as his superior, just as the abbot of Fontevrault did the abbess there, and was prepared in his vague way to accept the new policy she brought with her. She had broached the matter of the monks' tonsures with him and he had agreed what he called 'St. Patrick's hairstyle', the custom of shaving the head from ear to ear and letting it flow down at the back, was now outdated and should be changed for 'St. Peter's', though he appeared to think that this was Rome wanting to be modern, for 'Didn't the poor dear Popes lose touch with us during their Dark Ages.'

Boniface moved on to the next item on her Things To Be Done list. 'Dermot of Leinster,' she said. 'I wish him to be publicly denounced. How can the sins of the common people be corrected when kings are allowed to flaunt their wickednesses unchecked?' When she'd learned of Dermot's adultery with Dervorgilla she knew that her initial distrust of the king had been vindicated.

The abbot shifted uncomfortably in his chair. 'Is this the little matter of the abduction?'

Boniface stared at him. 'Hardly a little matter, I should have thought.'

'Well, no. But do you see, Comarba, the fault lies with that temptress out there,' the old man pointed an agitated finger in the direction of the guest house where Dervorgilla was being lodged. 'I have chided him on the matter, and he tells me she set him on. She sent him messages that the O'Rourke was being cruel to her and inflamed him with her desires. She is Eve all over again, and it is shame on our holy abbey that she is in it.' His long white eyebrows jerked up and down in the nearest state he could get to anger. 'The Mac Murrough cried in his penitence as he told me, so he did. And he is seeking God's forgiveness with a substantial gift to our abbey here, and the promise to found a daughter house in Dublin.'

'So you won't denounce him?'

'A substantial gift,' muttered the old man, collapsing back in his chair, 'and a daughter house.'

'I see,' Dervorgilla was to get all the blame while Dermot bought his way back to the bosom of the church. Boniface shut her mouth tight. She had rarely been so angry. She held no brief for the trollop Dervorgilla, but neither was she going to let Dermot of Leinster get away with a flagrant breach of God's rule. This was just the sort of thing she had been sent to this country to change and, by the Lord, she would make an example of it. It appeared, however, that she would have to do so without Abbot Flynn. She sat still and silent for so long, the monks became nervous. Had she known it, she looked formidable – thin bones only just imprisoning a temper.

She moved on to the next matter on her list. 'St. Brigid's fire,' she said. 'It should be put out.'

The Abbot's thin body jerked in its chair and the accompanying monks and nuns jumped. 'Every night,' continued Boniface, 'one of my nuns leaves the dorter and goes up to the shelter by the round tower and tends the fire that burns up there within the hedge. It seems to me to be a pagan custom and I wish it stopped.' Irresistibly the fire reminded her of Beltane, heathen ceremonies, druids, leaping cattle and nameless pre-Christian rites. A babble of voices broke out around her. 'You can't be doing that, Comarba.' 'St. Brigid lit that fire.' 'It's been burning near seven hundred years.' 'It brings luck to the Abbey.'

Boniface nodded. 'Exactly. Luck.' Sacred wells were one thing, but fires, like so much in Ireland, were pure superstition. She didn't think she was going to win on this point, but she had to try.

The Abbot, having recovered from his shock, wheedled her again. 'Apart from the fact that it has been said there will be catastrophe if it ever goes out, we sell the ashes of it as a holy keepsake. Woman mix them into their bread to help conception.'

As far as Boniface was concerned that merely proved her point, but she could see she was getting nowhere. 'Then I wish it known that I do not mean to tend it.'

The Abbot smiled. 'You don't have to,' he said, 'Tonight is the twentieth of the fire's cycle. It's the night when St. Brigid herself sits up there and tends it.'

Well, she had won some and lost some. 'Take it slowly,' the Abbess of Fontevrault had advised her, 'Remember their tradition is as old as ours, in some cases older. You can't modernise them overnight.'

Boniface got up. The Abbot got up. They bowed to each other, blessed each other, and left by their separate doors to their separate convents.

That night, after her discussion with Abbot Flynn, Boniface stood at her window for a few minutes as she always did to drink in the solitude. Then she put on her outdoor shoes and went out. She walked towards the glow of the fire which, with the round tower, was the core of the Abbey, and looked over the hedge.

So much of the abbey's life, and therefore its Comarba's life, was dominated still by the customs and personality of the long-dead saint whose spirit was worshipped here. Encrusted as they were with legends, a whiff of a real, strong-minded, warm-hearted, quirky woman came out of them and here, tonight, was added a scent of horrifying ancient holiness.

The wattle shelter in which the nun, whose turn it was to tend the fire of St. Brigid, usually sat was empty. The heart of the fire under its covering of peat bricks sent up a straight line of white smoke against the dark, early summer sky. There was no sound but she felt herself to be watched. Boniface looked up and saw that the barn owl which made its nest in the highest opening of the round tower had its eyes on her. A conviction came that if she watched any longer, a peat brick might detach itself from the creel by the shelter and put itself on the fire. She walked back to her apartment.

'Does any sister accuse another?' asked the new Abbess of Kildare of her nuns, 'If so, now is the time.' She said it without expectation. Back home in Fontevrault at this point in the weekly chapter meeting accusations had come thick and fast – it was the duty of any nun to save her sisters from a fall from grace by bringing her sin into the open. Boniface had done it often enough herself. But either this peculiar Irish flock of hers were blind to their sisters' failings, or, which was more likely thought their Abbess, they weren't prepared to betray them to their new Mother Superior.

The silence in the chapter house remained absolute, apart from the sound of birds outside coming through the slit window high up in its walls. The building was narrow and deep and gave the impression that its congregation was seated in the bowels of a ship.

The Abbess surveyed her nuns, their consciences as apparently clear as their complexions – all except Sister Acall, who had an outbreak of boils. They were happy enough to accuse themselves, she thought. The last half hour had been filled with nuns spreadeagling themselves before her to knock their head on the stone tiles with 'Mea Culpa's' for peccadillos, some of them so small they would have passed unremarked at Fontevrault, but accuse each other they would not.

'Very well,' the Abbess' voice sliced into the silence. 'Then I accuse Sister Cruimtheris of not cutting her hair as I commanded all of you to do. Does she admit her fault?'

Sister Cruimtheris could do little else. As she lowered herself full length on the floor in abasement, some of her ginger hair flopped forward onto the stones, the only colour in the black and grey of the chapter house.

'Well?'

'There, Comarba, dear. I knew there was something. And didn't I forget? You give me a nice penance now, and, sure as God, I'll have it cut tomorrow.'

'You'll have it cut now,' said her Abbess, grimly. 'Sister Clotilde, the knife.'

Cruimtheris' red young head was exposed to the chapter and Sister Clotilde began shearing locks off at ear-level with what Abbess Boniface thought was unnecessary reluctance. The silence intensified the rasp of the knife, but nobody moved or spoke. Boniface always tensed herself for their revolt at times like this, but none ever came, though she was, after all, dealing with women who all claimed to be descended from kings, and Cruimtheris actually was a princess of Meath. She was grateful to them for their Christian compliance with her changes of their tradition – what few she was able to implement. There was never any hostility; when they opposed her, they merely ignored her commands. On the whole, she thought, they had been remarkably generous in accepting a foreigner as their head, especially Sister Gormlaith, the senior nun, who had uncomplainingly carried so much of the work while she and Sister Clotilde were finding their feet, and was equally prepared to relinquish her position to Clotilde without rancour.

She was beginning to be fond of her Irish nuns, but she did not allow herself to show that fondness and it did not stop her doing her duty.

'And now,' said the Abbess, when the cropping was over, 'Sister Cruimtheris will beg her bread in the refectory for a week in order that she may reflect on the sin of vanity.'

The trouble was, she thought, that, although they conversed together in Latin, she and her nuns spoke different languages. To them it wasn't vanity to have their hair long. It was merely the custom of St. Brigid. 'Female hair is a net of the Devil,' she told her flock, 'God likes it as short as possible.' But, again, she made little sense to them. There was surprisingly little sexuality in their make up. She had expected from what she had been told about the Irish before she got here, that she would be combating raging promiscuity, but among her nuns at least, there was none. They had opted for the celibate life of their own free will and their passion was for God and His saints. They talked to male visitors on amazingly equal terms, but with little flirtation. As for intercourse between them and them monks, it was precluded by a physical and spiritual wall, not to mention a strong, anti-female asceticism among the brothers.

Sister Cruimtheris' hair lay curved on the stones like red weed abandoned by a tide. The Abbess allowed the silence to continue – she had another lesson to ram home – until it was broken by a metallic birdcry from the fields outside. She took her opportunity: 'What's that?'

'Don't you know it, Comarba?' asked Sister Acall. 'It's not heard until the hay is scythed. It's a corncrake.'

'I am aware that it is a corncrake,' said the Abbess, 'the point I am making is that today it is a corncrake and tomorrow, which is the Sabbath, it will still be a corncrake. But only this morning Sister Eithne informed me that any birdsong I hear on Sundays is not birdsong at all, but the rejoicing of souls from hell having a holiday.'

Sister Eithne covered her mouth with both hands.

'This Abbey must be rid of heathenish superstition,' continued its Abbess, 'When God sends souls to hell, He damns them for all eternity.

53

He does *not* give them a day off. Is that clear?'

It seemed that it was. Abbess Boniface blessed her congregation and dismissed it. 'Officers will stay behind.'

When the great carved door closed behind the main body of the nuns, the Abbess self-consciously relaxed, though not too much. 'Always be dignified, but never a tyrant,' Abbess Matilda had advised her.

She faced the women remaining, all of them older than she was. 'I wish to consult you on the matter of Lady Dervorgilla's expected baby. As you know, she has claimed sanctuary here, which puts us in a quandary. Sister Aine, perhaps it would be a good moment to serve some wine.'

Among Eleanor's of Aquitaine's lavish parting gifts to her had been a tun of superb red wine which Boniface had been bestowing on her officers on special occasions – usually when she wanted her own way. 'Cosset them,' Abbess Matilda had said, 'make them feel part of a team.'

The team grunted appreciatively into the beakers Sister Aine passed among them. 'Isn't this great?' said Gormlaith, 'Them Norman grapes must be kissed by God, by God.'

The Abbess sighed. The grapes were actually from Bordeaux, but her nuns laboured under the belief that anything not Irish was Norman. She had given up trying to disabuse them. 'Well?' she demanded, 'The O'Conor besieging us at this minute is becoming impatient.'

'Comarba dear,' said Gormlaith, 'There's not a lot of "well" about it. The damned woman's here, still as pregnant as MacCarthy's old cow and we can't violate sanctuary and chuck her out, not even though she is an O'Melaghlin.'

'And what's wrong with the O'Melaghlins?' asked Sister Maire, who was one herself. Since Gormlaith seemed disposed to tell her, the Abbess said quickly: 'I should like to hear Sister Aine's view.' She had quickly learned to nip tribal disputes in the bud, besides she was beginning to have a great regard for Aine, who was tall, thin, and reflected to some purpose.

'Gormlaith's right, Comarba,' said Aine, 'We can't violate sanctuary, for sure, even if she goes on claiming it after the baby's born.'

'The minute that baby's born, O'Conor says he'll come in and get her, sanctuary or not,' the Abbess told her. 'He is a godless man, but there's nothing we can do against violence. Besides, I intend to see that she goes back to her husband then, willing or not. I am not sheltering an adulteress here forever. The question is, does the baby go with her?'

'Oh no, Comarba,' Sister Acall cried out. Her carbuncled face flamed with infection and pity. 'If you send her back to O'Rourke with her baby, he'll kill it. He will.'

'Kill a baby? Nonsense. Don't be so emotional, Acall.'

'I'm afraid he will,' said Aine, and the other nuns nodded their heads.

'O'Rourke's a pig of a man, so he is,' said Gormlaith. 'He'd kill a baby as soon as look at it. Quicker, as it's Dermot's.'

'He beats her,' said Sister Acall, 'Ochone, the poor mavourneen,' she relapsed into a moist Irish lament.

'It's true,' said Gormlaith, 'I despise the woman, but I'd have left the swine myself.'

'I see,' said Boniface, 'Thank you for your guidance. I know now how to deal with the matter. You may return to your duties.' She blessed them. Sister Acall was still sobbing.

As they went out, Gormlaith said 'Isn't it a pity about those poor souls in hell now. Mustn't they need a holiday.'

In rare leisure moments between her duties, Abbess Boniface had taken to walking the ramparts of her Abbey. She did so now, with Sister Clotilde, taking deep breaths of fresh air. It was always like coming up on deck. The sprawl of the Abbey buildings and the town below them resembled a flotilla of Noah's Arks which had been stranded on an Irish Ararat, washed around by the heaving waves of grassland which stretched to the horizon.

Clotilde, who had a forgiving nature, had become friendly again after her rejection as a room-mate. Together they rested their arms on the wall and enjoyed the view. Boniface was trying to sort out the confusion in her mind that her encounters with the Irish always engendered. It had seemed so straightforward back at Fontevrault; she had to venture into a barbarous country and bring it civilisation, a vast undertaking but comprehensible. Now that she was here she was bewildered by the fact that elements of barbarism as she understood it existed side by side with great learning, horror with beauty, customs that shocked her mingling with others that contrasted well with conditions back home.

'Is it an uncivilised country?' she found herself asking, 'or is it just different?'

Clotilde interrupted her musing. 'This is a wonderful land for game, at least,' she said, 'There's something under those trees over there, but I can't make out whether it's deer or boar.'

Her Abbess didn't bother to look. 'I'll tell you what it isn't,' she said, gloomily. 'If it's native to this blasted place, it's not what it seems.'

Clotilde grinned, partly in sympathy – Boniface was being sorely tried – but partly because cheerfulness insisted on breaking in. She hadn't wanted to come to Ireland. Indeed, when the Mother Superior of Fontevrault told her that Boniface had chosen her to be her companion on this venture to the end of the world, she had been both frightened and angry. 'Why didn't you ask me first if I wanted to go?' she had demanded of Boniface, 'It isn't as if we've ever been particularly friendly.'

Boniface had stared at her. 'What's friendship got to do with it? I'm going to need someone who'll tell me the truth, and you are the most honest person I know,' – an answer that had sent Clotilde back to the Mother Superior to say that she would go after all.

And now that she was here she was enchanted – still frightened, but enchanted. 'And so are you, young Boniface,' she thought, 'for all that you've bitten off more than you can chew.'

Boniface, too, was thinking that she would be more careful with her entreaties to God in future. He had answered her prayer for power with almost more than she could cope with; in fact she wasn't coping with it. Like everything else in this weird country, it was eluding her. Back home at Fontevrault this had seemed an important, but provincial, appointment; yet here, in the middle of it, everything was on a scale undreamed of by those who had wanted her to lick it into shape.

As Comarba she commanded a diocese as large as Leinster itself, with an influence which stretched far beyond. Strictly speaking the Abbot of Kildare was its bishop – she had been shocked to find that an abbot could also be a bishop – but Flynn's progresses weren't interrupted at every step by petitioners begging to have their wrongs righted – hers were. It wasn't Flynn who was consulted by kings, queens and princes – she was. Every time she rode out it was to find her route lined with crippled, afflicted men, women and children who had travelled long distances in the conviction that a glimpse of her countenance would cure their every ill.

Her power over this shambling, beautiful Abbey was absolute, yet its manipulation escaped her.

'Are they laughing at me, Clotty?'

Touched by the use of her old nickname, Clotilde said: 'The sisters? I don't know.' She was here to give her honest opinion and she honestly didn't know. She supposed they were not worse and not better than the nuns back home, they must share the same goodnesses, the same neuroses, the same hopes of Heaven, yet they didn't correspond to the women she had known. The context in which they existed was too different. It was like trying to recognise familiar landmarks in a fog. 'I can't grasp them yet,' she said, 'I suppose it'll take time.'

'I can't grasp anything,' said Abbess Boniface. The people, the whole country, had an avoiding quality. They were like their own weather which, when it was obviously going to be a sunny day, and you'd made up your mind to it, would rain out of sheer perversity. And then, just as you'd accepted: 'This is a rainy day,' the cloud would slip away and land you back in sun.

Laziness, she had decided quickly, was the besetting sin of these Irish Celts. Now she was beginning to think it wasn't laziness so much as a dislike of routine, a love of leisure. Work didn't get done – you could see it not getting done – and yet the place functioned. The wild horses roamed the grassland apparently at will, yet the quality of their pasture showed that it was grazed exactly right, neither too much nor too little, which argued management.

The cattle down in the watermeadows shone with a fat health which seemed to be achieved independently of their herdsman, lying on his back with a straw in his mouth. Further away there were hills which the people here called mountains, and they never stayed where they were put, sometimes advancing as a purple menace, at other times fading away in an innocent blue. Everything seemed one thing and proved another. Deception was in the air she breathed, and she was at a loss to analyse why it smelled so different from other air.

She concentrated all her frustration at this shape-changing on the arch-deceiver, Dermot of Leinster, who had seemed the essence of sophisticated Christianity, who had tricked her. 'I'll give him charm,' she promised herself.

'The people seem to like you, mind,' interrupted Sister Clotilde, who had been considering the matter, 'they call you Ann-something. It sounds complimentary.'

'It isn't. "*Anbobracht*". It means no-fat-person. They think I'm a living skeleton.'

'You should eat more. Gormlaith says she can see the stars twinkling through you. Why don't you tell them you're beginning to understand what they say?'

'Oh for goodness sake,' said Boniface, irritably, 'We've been over that. My position here depends on my neutrality. That's why they welcomed me in. Besides, it's useful to hear what they're saying without them knowing I understand it.'

But she knew that was not the only reason. Ireland had abandoned the child she once was and she could not surrender herself to it because of that abandonment. Perhaps one day, when her power over its souls was complete. . . .

'Crafty,' said Clotilde. 'As your truth-teller I have to inform you that you're becoming crafty. Incidentally, there's something I must show you.'

'Is it important? I have to see Dervorgilla.'

'It's frightening.'

57

It was still a hit-and-miss adventure to find their way through the Abbey and they still enjoyed it. A couple of paces could take them from their own twelfth century into the fifth, or seventh, from the cavernous, painted, modern church into the now rarely-used chapel which was thin and steep-roofed and built of a peculiarly Irish many-coloured stone and attributed to the founding saint herself.

'Perhaps St. Brigid was like that,' Clotilde said, 'Tweedy, and sort of fun.' Their feet passed over tiles, each one of them a work of art, to stone, to brick to beaten earth, out of shadowed archways into speckled, trellised walks, into gardens, down terraces, steps, past colonnades so carved with nightmarish animals and fiends that they hurried along them into cloisters where the perfection of shape calmed them again.

Everything led to the centre in which burned the sacred fire and where the round tower stood.

On their way to wherever it was Clotilde was taking her, they passed St. Brigid's oak, another of Boniface's headaches, though it was also a considerable source of revenue since a mere twig or acorn from its venerable branches was considered to contain some of St. Brigid's holy properties and fetched a good price from pilgrims and visitors. Nobody dare cut it with a knife or axe but St. Brigid's Custom allowed people to break off pieces with their hands, which led to contention between the Abbey, which regarded the oak as its monopoly, and the townspeople of Kildare who, being allowed to wander in and out of the grounds at will, kept stealing bits to sell on their own account.

Two small and very dirty boys were sitting underneath it today, whistling with innocence. Angrily, Boniface made shooing gestures at them. They got up to bow with the courtesy of princes before moving off, but as they did so she heard one tell another in Irish: 'Let's be waiting till she's gone and then fill our pockets.'

When she'd first arrived, the language of the common people had been a miasma of sound but lately more and more of their words came through clear and comprehensible, as if her ears were unblocking. Sometimes, as now, she could understand whole sentences.

She called in Latin to a passing nun. 'Would you come here, Sister Brigh, and tell these urchins that if they come back when I've gone, let alone fill their pockets, I shall have them whipped.'

As the message was retailed, the Abbess saw with some satisfaction that her stock had gone up in at least two young Irish minds.

'Where are we going?' she demanded of Clotilde as they passed over the hill and down towards the wall which divided the nuns' convent from the monks'. They were in an area she did not know, a maze of stone passages that led to cells like large beehives which were now used for storage.

'Here.'

58

It was a courtyard, very old, and with moss and valerian sprouting between its cobbles. The ivy overhanging its walls muffled sound and made the place oppressive on the ears.

'What?'

'Here,' Sister Clotilde lifted some ivy on an inner wall and stood back.

'Well . . . oh my God.'

It jumped out at her, shrieking. She'd fallen back before she could comprehend that it hadn't moved or sounded at all, that it was violence in stone, an ossified attack on the mind. The mouth was open as if it was braying, showing a rampant tongue. But it wasn't the face you looked at. The squat body was crouched and its hands were between its legs, fingering open a swollen labia, as if it would drag everything outside itself into the gaping hole of the exposed vagina.

Boniface retched. 'Oh God, what is it?'

Clotilde let the ivy fall back. 'I've asked. Discreetly. Of the sisters, only Aine will even admit its existence. She thinks it might be Eve.'

'Eve? Eve was a woman.'

'Well, it's undeniably female.'

'But Eve's in the Bible.' Whatever her faults, Eve was part of the Christian tradition, a fitter-in; she'd got used to Eve. But this carving on the wall belonged to no recognisable world except Hell. 'It's a demon.'

'Sister Aine says the townspeople call it St. Brigid. Boniface, I'm afraid women come here to . . . well, touch it. So they can conceive apparently.'

'Not any more they won't. I'll have it smashed. How can they think it's St. Brigid?' St. Brigid might be an interfering and often inconvenient saint, but she was in heaven with God, clean and beautiful. 'If no one else will do it, I'll wield the hammer myself.' But she didn't even want to come back here. To obliterate the thing would give it recognition. She felt polluted, that it would be lodged in her mind forever like a pustule, like Eleanor of Aquitaine's garden.

'What perversion carved that?'

'A devil. Or a man. Actually . . .'

The claustrophobic womb which the courtyard had become was lanced by singing coming from the other side of the wall behind them, disciplined, aseptic chant, as if God was reminding his nuns of his purity.

'What's that?'

'It's the monks. We're close to the monastery here.'

'Lord, we're late for None.'

'Gormlaith will take it,' said Clotilde, 'But that's what I was going to say. The thing was put here, facing the men's side as a sort of warning to them against you-know-what. In case they felt like coming over the wall. It's a warning against women. Who could hate us so much? Or fear us?'

'Us?' Boniface saw no relationship between herself and the thing. And she knew Clotilde was wrong. Whoever had perpetrated the carving on the wall was female, a demon probably, but a female demon. Its message was the hideous final triumph. 'Look into this,' it said to the male. 'Abuse it, enslave it, set up your masculine God over it. But this hole is what you come out of and this is what you disappear into. This is the final profundity.'

She was then as horrified by herself as the Thing. What bestial cupboard had opened in her mind to let that thought out? No doubt its evil was infecting her. 'I must go to my prayers,' she said.

They backed out of the courtyard, taking care not to touch each other. When they were outside they turned and ran, skittering back to the safety of the God they knew.

Boniface put off her visit to Dervorgilla until another time. She'd encountered enough sexuality for one day.

'I don't think Fitzempress himself has better housing for his horses, or better horses for that matter,' Boniface dictated to Brother Flan, her scribe, in one of her letters to the Abbess of Fontevrault. 'Should you ever visit us, Mother, we can promise you excellent mounts here at the end of the world.' (It was a little joke between them that she and Abbess Matilda addressed their letters from and to *In fine mundi in partibus Hiberniae*: Ireland at the end of the world.)

She looked suspiciously down at the membrane on which Brother Flan's goose quill had left those irritatingly mysterious shapes. Her relationship with Flan was not warm; Brother Flan disliked women, which was possibly why he had been designated as her secretary by Abbot Flynn in the first place, but just lately it had become distinctly cold because Boniface was beginning to suspect him of doctoring her letters, especially those reporting to the Pope and to the Mother Superior at Fontevrault; altering phrases of which he disapproved and even, occasionally, of suppressing matters over which she and the Abbot were at loggerheads. She had not been able to prove it, but there was a certain lack of response in parts of Mother Matilda's replies which made her wonder. He'd even objected at first to her describing Ireland as the end of the world, saying that it was the world which was at the end of Ireland.

'What have you put?' she demanded angrily. The thought that this pipsqueak of a monk might be thwarting her sent her nearly mad with fury.

'I don't think Fitzempress himself has better housing for his horses,' the monk said tonelessly.

'You'd better have,' Because she knew he disapproved of her interest in horseflesh, she went into a long description of her stables.

Unable to credit that stables in the charge of the drunken gargoyle, Art, who had greeted her so rudely on her arrival, could be anything but a shambles, she had discovered them to be not only on a magnificent scale, but an example of cleanliness and good management which any king would have envied as they would have envied her in having Art to run them, once they'd got over his occasional descents into drinking, and his ugliness. This, the ugliness, was unusual among a race that had so far turned out to be good-looking. Art was incredibly, agelessly, ugly; his pointed ears stuck out at right angles to his warty face. He was dark, squat, bow-legged and ill-tempered, especially to those ignorant in the way of horses. On his good days he tolerated fools with monosyllabic grunts. On his bad days, when he was drunk, he reviled them in lengthy, obscene tirades.

Since he had suspected this foreign abbess to be one such fool, their initial relationship had been bumpy. On the first day she had required him to produce a horse for her – she'd been going hunting with the nobles of a local clan, the Hy Tuathail – the mount had been an insult. Boniface had dismissed it with a glance and demanded that alternatives be brought out into the stable paddock for her to try. When she'd settled eventually on a high-spirited but soft-mouthed, chestnut mare called Dilkusha, she'd seen Art raise his eyebrows in surprise at her good taste. But he still didn't trust her. To Boniface's annoyance, he joined the hunt on his own pony to follow her progress. Whatever she jumped, however fast she galloped, Art was behind her. She'd tried shooing him away but Art had stuck to her as if attached to an invisible leading rein. Eventually the glory of the day and the sense of comradeship which comes to riders in a chase had cleared her bad temper. When they jogged back into the stables that night, Art had stood at her stirrup to help her dismount, muttering.

'What did he say?' Boniface asked of Sister Aine, who had come with them.

'He says you may be a Norman on two legs, but on four you're an Irishwoman. It's his version of a compliment.'

Boniface had taken it as such. Later, as she'd got to know him better, she wondered whether Art's almost mystical perception with horses extended to human beings, her in particular. When, through Aine, Boniface had explained her plan for breeding from the Arab mare, Art had approved. He treated the horse when she arrived as if she were royalty, fed her on a secret formula which put her in perfect health and found a stallion for her mate which, he said, came from Connemara and with which even Boniface could find no fault. He'd supervised the covering himself and Finola was now in foal.

'What's that he calls her?'

'Finola. She was the swan-daughter of Lîr, of the second sorrow of story-telling. Why?'

'Nothing.' But it was an odd coincidence. Art, without knowing – because nobody knew – had, out of all the names he could have chosen, picked on Boniface's real name, her Irish name, the one which she had been given by the parents she could not remember.

Of all the Irish she'd met, Art was the one to whom she was almost, but not quite, tempted to reveal her nationality. Despite the horror of his appearance, she felt comfortable with him. He was connected through the smell of horses, manure, liniment and even strong drink, to a forgotten time in the past, as if there had been someone like him in her childhood. As if not all her early childhood had been unhappy. This sense of security allowed her to lower her dignity by quarrelling with him as she would with no one else. Their disagreements were conducted through an appalled and amused Sister Aine, though more and more Boniface could understand what he said.

'Ask this maniac why there are gorse bushes tied to Finola's stall if you please.'

'Tell herself the bloody mare's becoming a stall kicker which is an evil habit as the Lord knows and brought about by boredom as I've told her till I'm sick of it.'

'Tell him I know what he's doing, him and his boredom. He wants to harness that poor thing to a plough because he's a serf who doesn't know how to treat a noble animal and if she's kicking it's because she lacks the right exercise. The *right* exercise, tell him.'

She visited Finola and Art and the stables every night when she could. They were among her happiest hours. Still smarting over Brother Flan, their familiar smell calmed her as it always did though, unusually, tonight they stank strongly of horse urine. More unusually still, one of Art's stableboys was hanging by his roped feet from a hook in the rafter. He arched his back to lift his head and greet the Comarba politely, an action that set him circling.

'What's going on?'

Art's croak came from a stall in which there was much activity. 'Didn't the bloody little shitpot take his eye off Cruith and let him feast himself on foxglove?' Cruith was a red roan, hence his name, and one of Art's favourites.

'He said the lad allowed Cruith to eat foxglove,' translated Sister Aine.

'Ask him how he is.'

'How are you?' enquired Aine of the revolving boy.

'Not him. The horse. Tell Art oily purgative food with tepid water every three hours.'

62

Art's dreadful head appeared over the half-door. 'Will the woman teach her grandmother to suck eggs? What does herself think I'm doing here? And the horse piddling like a bishop.'

They went to speak to Finola, Boniface explaining to Aine that one of the symptoms of foxglove poisoning was excessive urination.

Eventually Art joined them, grunting that the roan would do.

'It has come to my notice,' said Boniface, coldly, 'that he was drunk again last night.'

Art spat as Aine translated. 'Who'd be telling her that?'

'Never mind who told me.' Assured that she was now fond of Art, the nuns were happily informing on him. 'Very drunk. He was overheard accepting a bet from the smith that he could jump the paddock wall on a horse that was blindfolded. Did he do it?'

Art sulked. It was the recently suspended stable boy, now righted, who said: 'They were both blindfolded, your honour, but God lifted them over as sweetly as a zephyr.'

'I'll give him zephyr.' Not for the first time Art was treated to a lecture on the evils of drink, breaking God's rules and risking a good horse. She was interrupted in mid-flow by Brother Flan with a message from Abbot Flynn, but she waved him away. 'Tell this drunkard if there is any such recurrence, he leaves this Abbey for good.' It was an empty threat and she'd made it before.

'I didn't think he could do it,' said Sister Aine, as they left.

'I knew he could,' said Boniface, 'That's two prayers you owe me.' They paid their bets by prayers for each other's soul.

The confrontation with Dervorgilla, which Boniface was dreading, could no longer be put off.

In the lovely chamber over the west gate which was reserved for guests, Dervorgilla was kneeling in prayer at a prie-dieu while her ladies embroidered. She hauled her bulk to her feet at the Abbess' entrance with eager politeness. 'It's so good of you to come when you're so busy.'

Like everything else in Ireland, Dervorgilla was unexpected. Boniface had envisaged that a married princess who eloped with her lover would be a Delilah, someone tall, dark, young and throbbing with ungovernable desire.

The woman who greeted her with outstretched arms – Dervorgilla's hands were almost invariably palm-upwards, as if in a plea – was dumpy and forty-four years old. As usual with Irishwomen, her complexion was clear and made her look younger than she was, despite her greying brown hair. Her eyes stared out of her face like large, timorous pansies, the only remnant of what must once have been a beautiful, but short, woman. 'Shall we have some wine?' she asked, 'would that be nice?'

Someone had educated her well though, it was impossible not to feel, harshly. Her fluent, unaccented Latin came mostly in questions, asking for an approval that was rarely granted; her diffidence elicited the protective instinct in a few and the bully in nearly everybody else.

'She's so gentle,' had been Clotilde's verdict.

'She's so weak,' had been Boniface's.

Under some vigorous questioning by the new Abbess, Dervorgilla had admitted herself truly penitent for her sin in running away with Dermot of Leinster, although Boniface wondered whether that was only because the idyll had turned out badly. The ease with which Dermot had handed her over when threatened indicated that he had quickly tired of Dervorgilla, even that he hadn't loved her at all but had only abducted her in order to get even with O'Rourke, her husband, for past defeats.

As they'd become acquainted, Boniface had grown less shocked with Dervorgilla but more inclined to slap her. The woman was a pawn, prepared to believe anyone who knew their own mind, vulnerable to romance, impulsive, never thinking things through. She had been shifted about so that two men, Dermot and her own brother, the O'Melaghlin, could wreak revenge on her husband.

'My brother, bless him, thought I'd be happier with Dermot,' she told Boniface and her little hands had pleaded for understanding for her brother. She would blame nobody for the mess she was in. 'He said I'd been destined for Dermot really. We had been betrothed when we were young, you see. He was wonderful then, Dermot. I'd always thought I was in love with him. My brother said God would understand if I snatched some happiness. But God didn't like it, did He?'

The Abbess accepted some wine sternly. 'It has been said that your husband maltreated you, Lady Dervorgilla. Is that true?'

Dervorgilla eased herself down to the window seat and looked out. Her dress was of soft, green linen and, with the light behind her, she looked young. 'Men get like that, don't they?' she said vaguely, 'And of course he's old and spends so much time on the battlefield. They're not very good, men, at dealing with all the feminine things, are they? I don't think he meant it really, do you?' In Dervorgilla's soft mind men never meant any harm really.

'Did he or didn't he?' The irritation Dervorgilla always provoked with her evasions made Boniface's voice sharp.

'Perhaps he drank too much, do you think? My brother and he never got on, I just don't think I was the right sort of wife for him, poor old thing.'

'You have to go back to him.'

The pansies turned on the eighteen-year-old Abbess in desperate appeal. 'Can't I stay here?'

'Indeed you can't.' If Dervorgilla had been a different sort of woman, thought Boniface, she could have insisted on her right to sanctuary, which would have made things very awkward, but during the talks they had been having she knew she had gained such ascendency over Dervorgilla that there was no question of it. 'You may remain here until the child is born, but then we must hand you over to the O'Conor. It would be breaking God's rules for us to stand between a wife and husband.' She added more gently, 'O'Conor would come in and get you anyway. You wouldn't want that, would you? He's promised to escort you safely back to Breffni.'

'And the baby?' Dervorgilla's arm were protectively round her stomach, 'O'Rouke would . . .' she couldn't say it, 'He wouldn't be very nice to it.'

'What do you want to do with it?' And even as she asked, Boniface knew that asking Dervorgilla what she wanted was like consulting a pig on its fancy for flying; the situation in which Dervorgilla could choose to please herself had never arisen, and never would.

Sure enough, Dervorgilla returned her question with another: 'What can I do?'

Boniface got up to take a turn around the room. Her plan to trade the safety of Dervorgilla's baby for Dervorgilla's acquiescence in leaving the Abbey's sanctuary seemed less perfect here than it had down in chapter. Well, she had asked for power, and here it was, complete with responsibility. Her first duty was to God and her Abbey. 'We could find a wet nurse for it, and see that it gets safely to your brother's family.'

'Ye-es.' And if ever there was proof that Dervorgilla's upbringing had been harsh, it was in her reluctance to relinquish her child to the same.

'I see. Well then, it could be fostered with good people until it was old enough to be raised here, in Kildare, either as a monk or a nun, according to what it is.' She was aware that celibacy was not what every mother wanted for her child; she was consistently amazed by how keen some were to deliver their poor little offspring into the world of the flesh. And she was being generous in making the offer. It wasn't every abbey, after all, which would take bastards in – but she disapproved of that outlook; several saints had been born out of wedlock. St. Brigid for one.

'Here? She could be away from men?' Perhaps because of its vulnerability, Dervorgilla always referred to her future child as a daughter. 'That would be nice, wouldn't it?'

'Yes.'

'Would you take her away immediately?' Dervorgilla had her own sort of courage; she was smiling as always, but the pansies were overflowing.

'O'Conor is becoming impatient,' Boniface explained gently, and then got cross. There was pain around again. 'I hope you're not going to be difficult, Lady Dervorgilla.'

'No. Oh no. I'm sorry. I'm grateful. Really.'

They prayed together, the long penitential prayers in which Dervorgilla seemed to find comfort and which the Abbess knew were good for her soul. Afterwards Dervorgilla said: 'At Mass tomorrow, could you ask the priest to read that bit I like? About the women taken in adultery?'

'Very well.'

'He was lovely, wasn't he? Jesus. He doesn't condemn me, does he? He said so.'

The story of the woman taken in adultery had always rather shocked Boniface who couldn't help feeling that her Lord had bent His Father's rules a bit. 'Apparently not. Not as long as you're truly repentant and sin no more.'

On her way out, Boniface astonished herself again. She paused at the door, turned, and, in a different voice from the tone of command she generally assumed to Dervorgilla, found herself asking: 'Why don't you fight?'

And Dervorgilla answered her differently, as if they'd changed to another level of understanding.

'I'd never win,' she said.

Chapter Three

Dervorgilla proved difficult at the end. She bore the birth well, considering her forty-four years. She'd been right: it was a girl – but when they took the baby away she screamed. Long after she had been given over to the O'Conor, the Abbey's stones held the sound and whispered it back like a diminishing wrong note.

Away in Connaught Turlough O'Conor, its king, died. The young O'Conor received the news just after he'd delivered Dervorgilla to her husband in Breffni. He rode like a mad thing to Connaught to begin the vicious and bloody in-fighting against his brothers for the throne.

With Connaught having its problems the pattern of power flickered and shifted. The scales tipped to the other great contender for the High Kingship of Ireland, MacLochlainn of Ulster, who now prepared for war with Connaught.

Down in the south-east of the island Dermot of Leinster saw his opportunity to win the High Kingship for himself and called a meeting of all the Leinster lords at the ancient site of Dunn Ailinn.

It was a fine day with a light breeze which carried Dermot's voice compellingly to his audience. He spoke of history, carrying the lords of Leinster back to the third and fourth centuries before the birth of Christ, to the elemental tales of the common ancestor of all Leinstermen, Labraid Loingsech, to the time when a powerful Leinster confederacy dominated Ireland. He didn't speak of himself, only of Leinster, Leinster and, again, Leinster.

'Jesus God,' whispered the O'Faolain to the lord of the Hy Murchadha, 'he's after the High Kingship.'

But even as he translated into political reality the great phrases that rolled from Dermot's lips, he wept at them, and the ancestry in his veins shouted for Leinster's rightful supremacy, and his love for his province overflowed in a torrent that swept over the Wicklow mountains to the east, flooded the plain to the bogland and hills of the west and divided in clutching fingers down the Slaney and the Barrow and the Liffey to the sea.

Dermot's own eyes spurted tears as he called up Finn and the Fianna to come to his aid, and huge tattered figures came racing across the sky from the Hill of Allen to stand by his side. By the time he reached his peroration he had a massed, half-seen army of dead heroes standing at his back.

'Now is the time, now,' he roared at them all. 'While Connaught and Ulster tear at each other, let Leinster march to her glory on Tara. From here, from the height of Dunn Ailinn, let us resemble Labraid and throw down the mighty of the earth.'

He threw out his arms to raise the mighty of Leinster to their feet. However, with bad timing, a flock of swans chose that moment to come flying over Dunn Ailinn from the west where Kildare stood, five miles away. The mouth of Dermot's audience remained open to cheer but its eyes flickered heavenwards, even as it stood up, to an undoubted portent.

O'Faolain remained in his seat, though he had to struggle as if against pulling string to do so, and the Murchadha and Donal MacGillacolmoc, chief of the Hy Dunchada stayed sitting with him.

'Now is not the time, Mac Murrough,' called out Donal.

'But it is, my dear. The opportunity is here, I can feel it through my blood.' And they could see that he did. 'You're not going to be petty about old scores on this glorious day.'

The 'old scores' had mounted up in 1141 when the North Leinster lordships had risen against Dermot and been put down with a ferocity unusual even for him. The three chiefs who faced him were all young – he'd had their fathers killed.

'It's not that, Mac Murrough,' said Donal. They were pragmatists, after all: these things happened. 'But St. Brigid is against a war at all. She asks if we haven't had enough of fighting, and indeed my people are still bled white after their sufferings at the hand of the O'Conor's army.'

'And who is speaking for St. Brigid?' asked Dermot silkily. 'Not that bloody kitchen maid.'

He shocked the company by his disrespect. 'She's the Comarba,' shouted the O'Faolain, 'and one you gave us yourself. She has the sight without doubt. She told me not to marry my wife's sister, and, sure enough, the woman died the next month, so that saved me a waste of time.'

Donal MacGillacolmoc nodded: 'Even though she hasn't got the Irish, she reads your mind. In front of her I said something in our own tongue to my standard-bearer, and she knew what it was. She is the true Comarba.'

The discussion spread. Other lords, now freed from the madness of Dermot's voice, remembered that they too had been advised against war by the Comarba at Kildare.

Dermot begged, pleaded, commanded, threatened, but slowly his chance at the High Kingship, which would only come once and was here, now, while the other two great kingdoms fought each other, blew away on the breeze out of his grasp.

It was all over when Donal, remembering his depleted wealth from the latest war, and overcome by religious fervour, leaped on his chair to quote the ancient 'Hail, Brigid.'

'When from its side I gaze upon the fair Curragh.
The lot of every king brings awe for each downfall,
O Brigid, whose land I behold
Upon which each one in turn had his being,
Thy fame outshines their fame.
Thou art king over all.'

The company bent its head in prayer and, unseen, Dermot went behind a hawthorn tree and vomited.

'No hard feelings, Mac Murrough?' asked the O'Faolain as they went down the hill.

'None, my dear. Why would there be? We've lost our chance and now we have to decide which to throw in with, Ulster or Connaught. Personally, I'm for Ulster. I'm against the O'Conors.'

'Why either?' asked Donal, 'Let's get strong again first. Let's have some peace.'

Dermot turned on him and grabbed him by the throat. 'There is no peace,' said Dermot, smiling into Donal's eyes. 'We can't stop and let the others fight. We are cats in a bag and we must fight until one of us is left. It is our doom, willed to us by our ancestors, God help them. Either it will go on for all eternity, or we will be invaded, or one of us will conquer all the others and start making a coherent state out of our anarchy. Do you see?'

He was pulled off and thrown to the ground. A bewildered Donal massaged his bruised throat. 'He doesn't see,' explained Dermot gently, sitting up. 'I am the only one who does. You should have followed me, my dears, not the kitchen maid.'

A realisation of the danger entered the O'Faolain's dogged mind. 'No reprisals, Mac Murrough. I know you. She's not like O'More. She can't be unfitted by blinding. She's the Comarba. She's inviolable.'

They left him rolling on the ground, tearing at the grass. Murchadh Mac Murrough lumbered up, knelt by his brother and held his head until the fit had passed, then gently helped him to his feet. 'Do you want them killed?'

Dermot shook his head. 'Not yet. It's not them. It's her.' He wiped the spit from his mouth. 'I'm afraid, my love, that she wasn't one of my better ideas.'

Murchadh thought it out, a process he found difficult. 'If we kill her we'll have every churchman in Christendom cursing our souls. She's inviolable.'

As they rode towards home, Dermot was quiet. Murchadh, used to silence, didn't break it. They were nearly at Narraghmore before Dermot looked up.

'Not quite,' he said.

Boniface had a dream. In it St. Brigid, stout, comfortable, motherly, stood in front of her holding an illuminated first page of a gospel in either hand. Boniface knelt before her, knowing that the saint was about to reveal a great truth to her Comarba. They were in an enclosed garden – Boniface could smell roses and herbs. 'Yes, mother?' she said, reverently.

St. Brigid smiled at her and held out her right hand so that Boniface could see the page of vellum it held. It was the St. Mark's Gospel on which the ring of St. Brigid had been proffered to her at her inauguration, but this time Boniface's eyes were able to probe even further into its beauty, into each faultless spiral in an inch of space which consisted of hundreds of interlacements, the innumerable hairs on the winged lion of St. Mark.

'The Word of God,' said St. Brigid's voice. Then the saint held out her other hand, and Boniface found herself staring at exactly the same gospel. Not quite the same. In the place of the winged lion was the witch, the Thing on the Wall, terrible, exquisitely drawn, with the gaping vagina spiralling into a hidden infinity.

'The Word of Man,' said St. Brigid.

Boniface was filled with a colossal understanding. 'Thank you, mother,' she said, 'I see. I see. I see.'

She found herself sitting up in her bed, still saying, 'I see,' with the scent of roses and herbs drifting through her window from the summer dawn in the courtyard outside, still understanding something desperately important, but unable to remember what it was, although the dream was still clear to her. 'I've had a vision,' she thought, 'that was no dream, that was a vision. But what did it mean?'

It had something to do with Brother Flan. Her loathed secretary had been loitering, unseen but irritating, on the edge of the garden while she had talked to St. Brigid.

She was beginning to achieve true power as the Comarba of Kildare now. She had used every influence she had with the nobles of Leinster – all excepting Dermot, whom she had not seen since her arrival in Ireland – to persuade them from war and it had been a great day when they brought her the news that they had voted against it at Dunn Ailinn and thwarted Dermot's plans to take over the High Kingship.

Yet she was still powerless in one important field – her correspondence with the outside world. Brother Flan was definitely censoring her letters as he wrote them. Only the other day she had received a letter from the Abbess of Fontevrault asking a question about the form of Irish church services which Boniface knew had already been answered by information in one of her letters to Mother Matilda.

She stayed in bed while her serving maid, Ban, set her bowl of hot washing water in its canvas cradle on the tripod. Suppose, suppose, he was also doctoring Mother Matilda's letters to her? Not reading certain things to her? Censoring, weighting, embroidering? He might be denying her knowledge of all sorts of things which were vital to her. Was a worldwide network of abbesses being thwarted in true communication with each other by a worldwide network of malevolent monks?

'*Kak*,' she said, shocking Ban. She was learning Irish swearwords from Art.

As she went about her business that day she pondered on the meaning of her vision and told her nuns about it at chapter.

They were thrilled. 'Aren't we the lucky ones,' said Sister Acall, 'to be blessed in an abbess who is visited by the Blessed St. Brigid.'

'But what did she mean by it?' asked Boniface, irritably, aware of the honour of the greatest saint in Ireland trying to tell her something, but wishing she'd made it clearer. 'She seemed to be implying that the Word of God was virtually the same as the Word of Man.'

'Well, we know the Bible was physically written by men, I suppose,' said Sister Aine thoughtfully, 'but at God's dictation.'

'Was it?' Sister Màire had obviously envisaged a celestial pen inscribing the original from which all subsequent testaments were copies.

'Now I wonder why God made women unable to write,' mused red-headed Cruimtheris. 'Wouldn't the Word of Woman be something?'

The other nuns smiled indulgently; Cruimtheris was so young and so fanciful.

'Women *can* write,' said Sister Acall unexpectedly. 'There was that Hypatia in Alexandria in the old days and even though she was a pagan they say she was a great scholar. And wasn't one of our Norman pilgrims telling us only last year about that sinful philosopher who taught his inamorata to read and write? What was his name now?'

Boniface put a hand to her head. 'Abelard,' she said, 'Peter Abelard.' She had forgotten until now the scandal that had rocked the clergy of Europe only a few years before. 'Her name was Heloise.'

'That was it sure enough,' said Acall, 'and there you are, though one was a pagan and the other a sinner, they show that women can write and even read if they're taught.'

Boniface stared at the inflamed face of her nun. Really, she thought, Acall was extraordinary; most of the time a liability, given to sulks at imagined slights; the censing at Mass had to be done crablike in order to shield her from the sight of the swinging censor since anything which oscillated sent her into hysterics; yet occasionally, as now, she could produce surprising knowledge, just as at other times she showed penetrating insight.

'Then why shouldn't we?' she asked, 'Why leave it to pagans and sinners? I shall tell Brother Flan to start instructing a couple of you right away.'

Boniface had no love of scholarship for scholarship's sake; she herself did not want to roam the sacred fields of literacy. To experience the excitement of the written word was not for her, though she was aware that it held excitement, but since her frustration at the hands of Brother Flan she appreciated the need to command its power. For the very first time she realised how powerful it was. And how it would enhance the prestige of her abbey, not to mention herself, if she could tell the Pope that it contained literate nuns.

She blessed the sister, especially Sister Acall, with unusual warmth and hurried away. She would set the project in train at once.

She began her letter to the Pope with a report of her achievements in reform so far. 'May you not be displeased, Holy Father, by the advance of God's rule and that of His handmaiden, the Church, in this land,' she dictated, after she'd listed them. She looked suspiciously down at the wax tablet on which Brother Flan made his notes to be transcribed later. 'What have you put?'

'May you not be displeased, Holy Father . . .' he read back in his sullen monotone. He did not hold with the Roman way though he had been forced to adopt its tonsure.

'We now intend to devote ourselves to enforcing the prompt payment of tithes, rents and first fruits which are so scandalously neglected here,' Boniface went on. 'Furthermore we would bring to your Holiness' attention our intention to have some of the sisters of our congregation taught to cipher and to letter.'

Brother Flan laid down his stylus and folded his arms.

'Write,' commanded Boniface.

'I shall not. The Holy Father must not be misinformed. Women are incapable of lettering, and no one here will take on the task.'

'They will. Write what I say or you'll be dismissed and I shall find someone who will.'

'You won't.'

'I shall.'

'Where?'

Her chaperone, Gormlaith, and Flan's chaperone, Brother Aidan, looked up in alarm; the exchange had risen in a rapid crescendo to screams. The 'Where?' was intolerable to Boniface who, if Abbot Flynn backed his monk, and he probably would, was helpless. She found herself gasping, as if she were suffocating.

'I am the Comarba of St. Brigid and you will do as I say.'

'You are still a woman and therefore inferior.'

She grabbed his ear and hauled him to the door, her anger and his surprise giving her the advantage. 'Get out.' She administered a kick to his backside which staggered him along the passage until he could recover his balance. 'I'll give you inferior, you little bastard,' she shrieked down the passage after him.

Abbot Flynn was obdurate in refusing to allow any of his monks to teach the nuns to write, though he was more avuncular about doing so. 'It would addle the heads of the poor ladies,' he said sweetly, 'to put such a nonsense into them.'

'Then I shall send to the Pope to ask for a monk to be sent over who will teach them,' shouted Boniface. But, though Brother Fintan was appointed in Brother Flan's place, this new secretary also drove Boniface almost to madness by refusing to write to the Pope about it.

The Irish nuns were discreetly silent about her physical attack on Brother Flan, though, surprisingly, they treated her with a new warmth. Sister Brigh was overheard to say, 'Didn't I tell you she had the Irish ancestry?'

It was Clotilde, her truth teller, who lectured her on handling the matter badly, which made Boniface cross because she knew it was true, although on reflection she was unable to think of any way in which she could have handled it that would have altered the outcome, and never until the end of her days would she regret the contact between the toe of her boot and Brother Flan's bottom.

There was a change in her after this. Outwardly, she held to a greater dignity, almost stilted, and flaunted her power as Comarba as if to compensate for the lapse of both during the encounter with Brother Flan. Certainly she seethed at the impotence the monks had imposed on this one vital area of her authority; that they could deck her with garlands, bow to her, pay her lip service as a figurehead and then rein her in like some processional horse that had got out of line, brought her to screaming point. The more she thought how feasible it was for women to wield the pen, the more determined she became that they should. She wasted a good deal of time in trying to find ways of escaping from the incommunicative prison in which she had been put. At one point she briefed Sister Clotilde to go to Rome as her personal messenger to the Pope, but dropped the idea realising, as Clotilde pointed out, that it would take years.

But underneath all this frustration, she was oddly invigorated. Suppose that in the shameful little episode with Brother Flan there had been a microcosm, a miniature representation, of a global conspiracy by men against her sex? How many other women had conceived good, great ideas and been thwarted by their inability to publish them abroad?

Communication, history itself, was in men's keeping and who was to say that they'd got it right? She glimpsed rows and rows of annalists and chroniclers and commentators and philosophers bent over desks arrayed in lines that disappeared into the horizons of the past, and all of them looked like bloody Brother Flan. Sullenly, wickedly, and sometimes out of sheer ignorance, they altered what they knew to be true, just as Flan had changed her letters.

'What have you put?' Mentally she asked them the same question she had asked Flan, but she got no answer.

By day her memory droned out the sermons she had sat through in which she, representing womankind, had been castigated, denounced, villified.

' "I am Eve" ' Abbot Flynn had quoted an old Irish poem in one such sermon, very nearly making her laugh at the thought of him as a seductress . . .

'I am Eve, great Adam's wife,
I wronged Jesus long ago,
I stole Heaven from my kin.
It is I should hang upon the Cross.

'There would be no ice, no snow,
No winter with its blasts,
There'd be no Hell, no grief,
There'd be no terror, but for me.'

By night, in her dreams, St. Brigid held out to her the left-hand illuminated page which Boniface was beginning to think of as 'The Word of Woman' as if trying to pass on some secret inheritance. The grimacing face of the Thing on the Wall drawn on the bottom of the page became familiar, no longer frightening, its terror directed past her to something else. To Brother Flan. One night she sat up and said: 'It's Brother Flan who's frightened of it.' That was it. It was men who were frightened of the Witch on the Wall and its lozenge-shaped, predatory orifice.

Was it fear, and not contempt, that made them withhold the skill of writing from women?

Her mind felt stretched by the accommodation of new thought. Sometimes she trembled with fear that she might be breaking God's rules by questioning the pronouncement of men who had been His servants. But she was exultant, with an explorers' expectation of wonder and adventure in undiscovered territory.

Alone she looked out on it, and yet she felt God's presence with her as never before, and something else which might have been other women who had arrived in this same country of the mind whose footsteps had been obliterated.

It was the custom before winter set in for the Comarba of Kildare to make a *cuairt*, a circuit, of the lands and churches belonging to the Abbey. Donal MacGillacolmoc and the O'Faolain and others told Boniface it was also the custom to take with her a small, but effective armed force. Behind her back, and with the help of Abbot Flynn and the Archbishop of Dublin, they got guarantees from Dermot for her safety.

Unaware that she was being protected, Boniface used the visitation to enforce and modernise the system of tithes and rents owed to her Abbey. She had been doing her sums and discovered that if she put into effect all the schemes she had planned for the future they would be considerably underfunded. 'This should be a rich establishment,' she complained to Sister Gormlaith, 'and here we are tightening our belts.'

'The churches collect the baptismal penny and the screpall of anointing, and they give us two thirds,' said Gormlaith, loyally.

'Not regularly, and not until we go and fetch it,' said Boniface, 'which wastes our time and also costs money. And what's all this about first fruits?' The system whereby the first sheaf of a corn harvest, the first basket of apples, every first calf and every first lamb and so on, was owed to the Church, was new to her.

'Ah well now, that's more in name than in fact,' said Gormlaith, 'they're also due to give the first son and the first daughter to the Church but, sure, if they did that we'd be knee deep in monks and nuns. And anyway, they've been having to give it to Dermot for his wars.'

'Well he hasn't got any wars now,' said Boniface, 'so they can give it where it belongs, to St. Brigid.'

'Ah, Comarba dear,' wailed Gormlaith, 'Don't let's be having any more trouble with the Mac Murrough.'

'I am not aware of having trouble with him in the first place,' said Boniface.

The *cuairt* went well. The new Comarba was received with lavish welcome wherever she went, and her strictures on the future punctuality of tithe-paying and the re-institution of first fruits were attended to, though it was more than once pointed out that what went to St. Brigid could not then go to the King of Leinster.

'Render unto Caesar the things which are Caesar's,' said the

75

Comarba, 'and unto St. Brigid the things which are Brigid's,' a phrase which was widely admired and equally widely quoted, not least to Dermot of Leinster.

Time and again she was warned that she had offended the King by her advice to his vassals not to go to war, and that she was offending him again by demanding tithes and rents which he had appropriated for himself. In Celtic fashion, none of the warnings were direct, just sidling references to the fact that 'Your man,' which was how the King was universally called behind his back, 'was dangerous to cross,' that 'Your man has his funny moods, for all that he's our own.'

Boniface, safe in the certainty of God, failed to see the problem. 'I have no quarrel with Dermot,' she said in answer to them all, and she really could not see that she had.

The adulation she received during the *cuairt* went to her head, or so she was informed by her truth-teller, Sister Clotilde, who accompanied her. 'You're getting all remote, and sort of stiff,' Clotilde complained, 'and you don't tell me things any more.'

Boniface smiled at her pityingly. How could she take Clotilde into the heady, terrifying regions of the mind she was treading now?'

'Dear Clotilde, you are a good soul, but God is showing me matters in which you, as yet, can have no part. Have no fear that I shall depart from His rule in the high office to which He has called me.'

'You're getting pompous and all,' Clotilde said, and rode to the back of the column in a huff.

It was winter on the night she returned to Kildare.

In the early hours of that same night there was knocking on the gates of the Abbey and a few minutes later, Sister Brigh woke up the Comarba with the announcement that a lady was in the guest house, asking to see her.

'Can't she wait?' Boniface was tired. The *cuairt* had been successful, but punishing.

'Comarba dear, she's not that sort of lady.'

Nor was she. Despite the plain cloak in which she was wrapped, and even if Boniface hadn't already been introduced to her at Dermot's castle of Ferns, she would have recognised the woman as royal. The Queen of Leinster was remote; dried up, as if all traits had been leached out of her, but command remained. Under her uninterested eye, stumbling nuns and servants, unbidden, brought candles, wine and cushions and then retired. Sister Aine stayed as an interpreter, sitting back in the shadows, leaving the Queen and the Comarba to face each other across the table.

'I have come to warn you,' said the Queen with the emotion of someone watching grass grow.

Boniface began her piece about having no quarrel with Dermot Mac

76

Murrough, but his Queen lifted her hand and stopped her. 'It has only been a matter of time before he came against you and he's picked today. I don't know why today. I don't expect he does. But I saw the decision happen to him yesterday in Dublin. Since it was a Monday he was prevented by one of his *geasa* from setting out, and I made up my mind to forestall him. However, at midnight he will have been released from his taboo and, I have no doubt, is already on his way.' She closed her eyes as if to mark off some dreary agenda, then added: 'He has a large force of Hy Kinsella with him, and among them are some foreign mercenaries.' She opened her eyes.

'*Geasa*?' asked the bewildered Boniface.

The Queen looked towards Sister Aine. 'Tell her.'

Aine said: 'They are the forbidden things of the King of the Leinstermen.' It shocked Boniface to see that her nun was shaking. She went on: 'To travel withershins around the Wicklow Hills on Wednesday. To sleep between the Dodder and Dublin with his head on one side. To encamp for nine days on the plains of Cuala. To ride on a dirty black-hooved horse across the plain of Mullaghmast. To travel along the Dublin road on a Monday.'

Until that point Boniface had been uneasy; the Queen's horrific impassivity had made her recital disturbing, but this farrago of superstition reduced the whole business to vulgarity.

'I see that you are amused,' said the Queen. 'That is your prerogative. I have done my part.' She rose, and one of the Abbey servants popped up as if emerging from the floor. 'Prepare three fresh horses,' the Queen told him.

'But you'll stay the night,' spluttered Boniface, 'It's dark. You can't . . .'

'I thought I had made it clear,' said the Queen of Leinster, 'that Dermot will be here soon. I have my own reasons for not wishing to encounter him since I too made a decision yesterday. It was to leave him. I am taking with me a somewhat large proportion of his more valuable jewels.' She closed her eyes, again mentally ticking off things that ought to be said. Her face was skeletal in the candlelight and Boniface realised she was looking at a woman exhausted not just by an unthinkable night's travel – it was well over thirty miles from Dublin and most of those had been achieved in the dark – but by years that had drained out of her almost everything that kept life in the body.

'Ah yes,' said the Queen and turned to Sister Aine. 'It occurred to me on my way here that I might be putting you all in extra danger if Dermot thinks that I am taking refuge here. It was too late to turn back. However, if I were you I should raise the Abbey to be ready for attack.'

Boniface watched Aine turn and run. She heard her screaming. She heard other screams. The hysteria and fear seemed to be happening in some dimension which left hers untouched. She disapproved of it.

The Queen's dull eyes looked straight into hers. 'Goodbye. We won't meet again. I have to say that I think you are a stupid woman. You have meddled in things you don't understand and I have taken the risk of warning you of your danger not for your sake but as an offering to God in the hope that in return He will allow me to find peace.'

Boniface opened her mouth to speak, but the Queen went on. 'I shall not tell you where I am going in case Dermot tortures you and finds out.' She might have been remarking on the weather.

She wrapped her cloak more tightly around her and went to the door, then paused. There was one thing more on her list and she turned round to deliver it. 'I don't know what Dermot plans for you, but it will be dreadful. He is a dreadful man.'

She considered with her head on one side. 'Odd, when you think he was so very nearly a great one.' She nodded to herself. That was all. She went.

Boniface stayed on for a moment to collect her wits in the room which was still stale from the previous day's use, quiet, but already vibrating from the terrified preparations beginning around it. 'Oh really,' she said, crossly.

She went on saying it, still crossly, in the hour that followed, an irrelevance of disbelief in the midst of an all-too-believing panic which set in motion emergency procedures on a scale that made her realise they had been expecting this.

The bell in the round tower, the bell in the two churches of the Abbey, the bell in the monk's chapel, all the bells in the town sounded out the alarm as torches flared through the streets and passageways until Kildare was a clanging lighthouse on the edge of the black Curragh sea. The horror was infectious, ancestral to the Christian Irish who had watched Norse raiders lope towards their wooden shelters, axes in hand. It clung to people's faces as they streamed in through the Abbey gates, carrying their children and possessions. Boniface watched it cause irrational acts; Abbot Flynn directing the carrying in of the books and manuscripts to the church, and then wasting time arranging them in neat piles; Sister Cruimtheris opening her linnet's cage at a window, freeing the bird to certain death from night predators.

Father Flynn, Gormlaith, everybody begged her to leave before it was too late. 'Too late for what?' she asked, 'Dermot is a Christian king, not the Devil.' Over her head, Gormlaith said to the Abbot: 'She'll stand a better chance here. If he caught her outside . . .' The decision was made and they went off. Boniface stamped her foot and shouted after them: 'I am the Comarba,' but a monk rushing past pushed her off balance so that she fell against the wall.

Well, there was one thing she could see to. She 'Oh reallied' herself through the jostling and walked down to the stables. Art, she was relieved to see, was having all the horses led out, Finola among them with her beautiful, lanky new foal. Dilkusha was saddled.

'Mount up,' said Art, 'we'll get out by the postern.'

'Not you as well. I'm not leaving.' She watched Art's hairy little hands reach out as if to grab her and throw her up on the horse, but he didn't touch her. 'This whole thing has been blown up out of proportion,' she went on, realising for the first time she was speaking Irish, and had indeed been speaking it for some time. '*If* Dermot comes, and I say *if*, we will talk like reasonable people. He may be upset because his wife has left him, but I shall explain . . .'

'And hens will piss holy water,' said Art. 'Will you get on that bloody horse?'

'No. If the worst happens, and it won't, but just in case, I want you to take the horses, Finola and Henry anyway . . .' she had given the foal Fitzempress' name, though Art had trouble pronouncing it, '. . . and take them out through the postern to somewhere safe. Go to the disert first and take Sister Mairenne with you. Sister Mairenne was an anchoress who lived a mile outside the abbey walls in an isolated spot known as 'the disert'. 'I don't suppose anybody's given a thought to that poor soul all alone out there.'

'She won't come,' said Art, and the tears rolling out of his eyes were the most shocking event of the night so far.

'Neither will I. Do it.'

On her way back she found activity going on at the foot of the round tower where a ladder was being placed so that the nuns could climb up to its door ten feet above the ground. Brother Flan was there and when he saw her he pushed her into the queue and gave her the tower's heavy key. 'When the last one's up, haul in the ladder and then lock the door.'

She gave another 'Oh, really,' and tried to break away, but he caught her and shook her, viciously. 'You've caused enough trouble.'

The tower smelled of urine and bird droppings. They crunched on twigs as they moved and sat down on the bench which ran around the windowless room, if it could be called a room, into which the door opened. There were too many of them for the space, but ladders led up to the circular platforms of the higher levels and some of the younger nuns with steady heads climbed up them. Cruimtheris went some hundred feet all the way to the top and remained there as look-out. Sister Acall's nerves got on everyone else's since they kept making her faint and moan, but they had the virtue of keeping the infirmaress occupied.

The nuns rapped out questions to each other: 'Did they send the

79

message to the O'Faolain and Donal?' 'Will they come in time?' 'Will they come at all?' In the hubbub both in and out of the tower, Boniface was ignored.

They heard the boom of the Abbey gate being closed and its great draw-bars being slid into their brackets. Gradually the stampede of preparation died down to be replaced by silence. The tower whispered with unsynchronised prayers. They could hear Sister Cruimtheris' shuffle as she moved round her four windows calling out 'Nothing yet' with such regularity that when she said: 'They're coming,' it took some seconds to realise the change since her tone hadn't altered. Then it did. She began shouting so that the entire Abbey could be warned. 'They're coming, they're coming. Torches. Oh Jesus, hundreds of them. The speed. They're coming.'

Sister Clotilde said: 'It might be help,' but not long after that they heard shouting along the ramparts. There was a crash that vibrated up the tower as a ram was hurled against the gates.

In that moment Boniface took in the truth. Until then she had believed herself caught up in some conspiratorial re-enactment of Celtic legend indulged in by an excitable people to feed their love of drama. Dramatic it might be, but it was happening, was going to happen, to all these people, to her.

' "It will be dreadful," ' droned her memory, 'Dreadful, dreadful, dreadfuldreadfuldreadful.'

She screamed: 'But it was Your rules.' The faces turned to her in the shaking candlelight shocked her into the knowledge that she had screamed aloud, and some self-possession came back. They *had* been His rules. She was right. Her soul was safe.

She remembered her imagining from another, unreal life of a Boniface being speared by the pagans before her church door. Had it been prophecy? Was Heaven to receive her so soon? Could she face it as that heroic, imaginary Boniface had faced it?

It was a bit quick. She felt ill at the quickness of it, her stomach heaving. But a summons was a summons, and better by far than the powerlessness and insignificance she had experienced in this last hour or so. These nuns, monks, those frightened townspeople out there, were hers. In protecting them and sacrificing herself she would attain sainthood. It was the bit in between now and then which made her legs tremble. She stood up and unlocked the tower door. 'Help me get the ladder down.'

They clung to her, holding her back, pleading. 'I'll only be a minute. There's still time. I've remembered something important,' she said, then looked at them with all her old power. 'I am the Comarba.'

Knowing her own mind gave her the advantage. They obeyed her. 'When I'm down, pull up the ladder again and lock the door.' She gave the key to Gormlaith and stood on the top rung of the ladder facing inward, impressing a last image upon them. Clotilde was crying. 'May God bless you,' said the Comarba.

When she was down she called to them not to take the ladder up yet; some women and children were clustered around the tower and the hedge of St. Brigid's fire, putting their faith in the protection of the holy places. Boniface sent them all up the ladder, slapping them when they slipped or hesitated in her impatience to get on with her sacrifice. When her soul had gone to Heaven all their danger would be over, but in the meantime they might as well be safe, though overcrowded.

The ramming of the gate took on a hollower note cracked by splintering and the howling round the Abbey intensified. The ladder was hauled up into the tower and the door closed. 'Just a minute,' said Boniface to God and hustled through the hedge opening to throw some peat bricks on the sacred fire. 'Mustn't let it go out.'

'Now walk.' She had to concentrate to do it, as if forcing her legs through thigh-high water. Hell was breaking loose somewhere down by the big church in screams, clanging steel, hideous noises. She waded towards it.

According to the annals some one hundred and seventy people, monks and townsmen, women and children were killed that night. Dermot admired their resistance, especially that of the monks, who fought like warriors to protect their Abbess and their abbey, and as a mark of respect to their valour he had them butchered quickly. He ordered that all wounded be brought to the cloisters to be killed, a neat contained area where he could make sure the Hy Kinsella, and especially the mercenaries, got it over with fast and didn't indulge in refinements. Madoc was in attendance so that they all got extreme unction, or as much of it as Madoc could perform, being drunk.

Before each stroke Dermot asked: 'Where's the Comarba?' or 'Haven't seen my wife, I suppose?' but the replies, if any, were unsatisfactory. He soldiered patiently on until a small voice with more breath than sound in it, said: 'Stop that, in the name of the God. I am here.'

Holding onto the doorway of the church at the far end of the cloisters was a thin nun. He had found the Comarba.

For a moment, one self-sacrifical moment, Boniface knew that she had to be there. Her own death, anything, would be better than that this slaughter should go on. 'Stop it, in the name of God,' she said again, and wondered that God did not step out of the sky to raise again the contorted bodies which were lying around the cloisters, His cloisters. It couldn't go on. How could He let it go on? She saw one of the bodies contort itself even more and rise up in an effort. It was Brother

Flan, bleeding from a wound in the neck as he staggered towards her to try and save her. One of Dermot's men raised his axe and with a sideways sweep of it cut Brother Flan's head off. She was sprayed with blood as the body collapsed on itself and Brother Flan's head rolled towards her feet, still showing a concern for her that it had never expressed in life.

She saw Dermot put down his sword and gesture to his men to stand back. 'So you are,' he said jovially, remembering to add: 'The swallows are not more welcome nor the saints more blessed than the sight of you this day. Where's my wife?'

The dead had been draped like washing over the low wall of the garth while the still-living rolled in its centre at the feet of Dermot's men.

She heard herself moan: 'Oh my God, oh my God,' It had not been like this when she had imagined her death at the hand of pagans. Nevertheless in a rehearsed gesture she found herself with her arms outstretched. She said more loudly, 'Stop this. Kill me, but stop this.'

Dermot sighed as if at the female capacity for histrionics. 'My dear woman, I haven't come here to kill you. As I've been saying, I'm partly here to find my wife who seems to have run off with some of my property. Have you seen her by the way?'

Boniface stared at him, unable to take in what he was saying.

Murchadh said: 'The only place now is the round tower, we've searched everywere else.'

She understood that. They would get to her nuns. She said quickly. 'She's gone. She was here but she's gone.'

'Came to warn you I suppose?' asked Dermot, 'How like her. Always thinking of others. I'll find her. Now then, the other reason I called in was to remonstrate with you, my dear, because you haven't really come up to my expectations; in fact, I'm afraid we're going to be forced to have you deposed.'

Still she didn't understand. 'I am the Comarba and always the Comarba, even if you kill me.'

Dermot sighed again, how they did harp on about death these women. 'Please,' he said, offended, 'it's not going to be that sort of occasion. We're going to have a happy time. We're going to have a wedding. You're going to be married.'

The incomprehensibility of his words added new madness to the insanity of this plane to which they had all been transferred, where hideousness was permitted by God. A man near her said: 'She knows. She'll enjoy it.' They were laughing, Dermot looked around his men to see which one it would be; not any of the Hy Kinsella – he loved them too much. One of the mercenaries, that big drunk over there, the

Englishman, he was a womaniser. He whispered to Murchadh: 'What's the name of that bastard from Bristol?'

'Eric?'

'Eric. How could I forget?' He took the man into a corner and explained the procedure, elaborating, using words as an aphrodisiac, giving him more to drink, flattering, promising reward, until juice ran out of the man's slack mouth and Dermot was afraid he would peak too soon. 'Go get her, my boy. She'll struggle, but she's gasping for it. Go and get the bitch.' Eric obligingly moved down the length of the cloister. 'Wait, we need respectable witnesses, Murchadh, get the Abbot. The rest of you get all the live ones here. Father Madoc. *Madoc*, what about some appropriate words for the happy couple?'

Madoc swayed through a fuddled memory, 'I marry you to each other. Good luck,' he said.

Boniface watched it all, saw the gestures Dermot was making to the big man and the way the big man looked towards her. She took in the realisation of an event so monstrous that the knowledge that those men could perpetrate it at all almost outweighed the fact that it was to be perpetrated against her.

She stood outside herself, seeing what Dermot saw, a posturing, silly girl who had been merely allowed to pretend. All courage gone, she prayed for time to reverse so that she could send all the nuns out of the tower to face this and leave herself safe inside.

Carefully, she backed into the church. Because it was nearer to them the men followed her in through the lower door, the monks' entrance, maintaining a perverse effect of normal procedure. The choir and altar were lit, and she knew herself outlined against brilliant colour.

People were being herded in through the western door to watch. She saw Abbot Flynn and Brother Fintan. 'Help me.'

Dermot gave the big man a push towards her but stayed still himself, between her and the audience. The big man came up the nave taking silly, tiptoeing steps, laughing.

Boniface snarled. She reached up to the flambeau above her head, tore it out of its socket and threw it at the man. He sidestepped and left it flaming on the floor. Father Flynn's idiotic pile of books was right by her, and she began throwing them as hard as she could at the rapist coming up the church. The Word of Men. Energy gave her release and she screamed and threw, and threw, and as he still came forward, ran up to the altar, howling, and hurled its crucifix, then its candelabra, the pyx. The pyx hit him in the chest and he growled, loosened the string of his trousers and leaped on her.

Much later she was to remember that although he ripped off the bottom of her skirts so that she was naked from the waist down, he took trouble to hold her with one hand while he made sure her veil was in place with the other. 'Nun, Nun, Nun,' he kept saying.

She fought all through it, though the pain between her legs was like being reamed. She *was* being reamed. She fought because she had a sudden image of herself as ridiculous, being jerked up and down like some puppet on this human pole. She saw Dermot watching. She felt her head snapping back at each lunge of the penis. There was a moment when she heard laughing and applause. There was another moment when she was rolled towards the reredos and saw the face of the crucified Christ looking pityingly down. 'Help me,' she yelled at it. 'Jesus save me.' That brought on the man's orgasm. 'Nun,' he roared. 'Nu-u-u-nnn.'

He withdrew, pulled up his trousers, smiled sheepishly at the congregation and went. They filed out after him.

Boniface lay where she was for a while, retching, and then hauled herself up to sitting position; no skirt, her collar and bodice torn open but her veil still firmly on her head. Again she saw herself as ridiculous, not that it mattered. 'Help me,' she said quietly, out of habit.

The church was empty. 'Help me.'

Dermot didn't kill anybody else after that, effecting an orderly withdrawal of his men almost immediately. But the ex-Comarba was left in the church until the nuns had been helped out of the tower because none of the monks wanted to approach her. When Clotilde and Gormlaith and the infirmaress, Sister Maire, ran in they couldn't find her at first until a trail of blood and slime on the stones near the altar showed that she had crawled beneath it.

'I suppose we should have acted then,' said the Archbishop of Cashel, looking back nearly twenty years from his room on the Rock. 'It was an atrocious act. We condemned Dermot, of course, but the political repercussions of excommunicating him would have been far-reaching, and he was quick to show penitence in practical form. Some tidy little foundations, gifts of land, that sort of thing. And we were very tied up with reform about that time.'

The monk, still looking out at the plain, nodded.

The Archbishop poured out more wine. 'And she really didn't help herself, you know. She went quite mad, demanding action, excommunication for Dermot, his denunciation in the chronicles and annals, that sort of thing. She was quite shameless about it. She actually wanted it published abroad. She even wanted to inform the Pope, but I don't think anybody would write the letter. After all, that was the last thing we needed just then. It would have completed Adrian's picture of us as barbarians.'

'Why didn't she go home?' asked the monk, though not of the Archbishop.

'That's what we couldn't understand,' said the Archbishop, heartily. 'She was so advised, I believe, but there was some tale of a promise she'd made to the Reverend Mother at Fontevrault. A matter of honour, she said. Honour, I ask you. I'm afraid by that time it was obvious she didn't have any left. She was pregnant, you know.'

'Yes,' said the monk.

'Hideously embarrassing. You know what that means, don't you? It means, I'm afraid that she'd, well, enjoyed it. It's a well known fact women don't get pregnant unless they do. Well known. I can't remember now what happened to the, er, perpetrator.'

'Dermot had him killed,' said the monk, 'He said he couldn't keep in his employ a man who would rape a nun.'

The Archbishop shook his head. 'Typical Dermot.'

'So the annalists didn't mention the rape,' said the monk.

'Well, one or two. Loch Cè did. But more or less in passing, not a big fuss like when Aedh MacRuairc and the Hy Briuin killed the Superior of Kells and his congregation in 1117. It wasn't really in the same class. In a way she'd asked for it. God have mercy on her soul.'

'Yes,' said the monk.

PART TWO

Chapter Four

They put Boniface's bed next to the window in her room so that she could look out on her courtyard, and from there she watched winter turn into spring and the pear tree develop into bud.

Sister Gormlaith came in with the look of agonised love that all her nuns turned on her, as if they would do anything for her but didn't know what. 'There's a deputation from the north Leinster clans, Comarba dear,' she said, 'Donal MacGillacolmoc, the O'Faolain and the others. They want permission to march on Dermot in the name of St. Brigid, all of them swearing blood and fire.'

Boniface kept her eyes on the pear tree, 'No.'

'Just a little war, Comarba,' pleaded Gormlaith, 'Sure the man's not fit to live.'

'No,' said Boniface, 'No more death.'

She heard Gormlaith weeping as she went out and say to Ban 'The Christianity of her, and the courage.'

'No,' thought Boniface, 'No Christianity, no courage.' She felt nothing, as if she had been wrapped in a cocoon through which her brain sent commands and words as if from a long way away and belonging to someone else.

It was not Dermot's physical death her brain demanded, but his soul's. He must be removed from the mercy of God by the only institution which had the power to inflict that eternal punishment. He must be excommunicated. But even while her brain made that its priority, the person inside the cocoon wondered that the brain could have the energy to feel hatred and demand retribution. She dreaded the time when the numbness would dissolve and the emotions waiting outside it crowded in on her. Greatest of all, she knew, would be the pulverising guilt at her responsibility for the deaths caused by her blundering unawareness of how dangerous Dermot was. She knew she must see the man brought down, not for herself but for the people he had killed while they had been under her protection.

'He must lose his soul,' shouted the brain through the muffling cocoon, but the person inside it wondered if there were such things as souls, Dermot's, her own; and in the act of wondering gave up and instead watched a blue tit swing upside down on a twig.

She heard the door open and Sister Clotilde's heavy step across the boards. 'Abbot Flynn refuses to meet you, Boniface.'

The cocooned spirit found that understandable. She had wrought too much destruction on his abbey, too many of his monks had died.

'He's afraid to denounce Dermot, or demand his excommunication in case he comes against the abbey again. And, oh Boniface, he says he cannot meet you now that you are . . . no longer a virgin.'

Wasn't she a virgin any more? How odd that she should be condemned for the one thing of which she was guiltless.

'He won't even let us write to the Pope.' The elm boards of the room shook as Clotilde rushed to the bed and fell on her knees beside it throwing her heavy arms over Boniface's body. 'Oh my dear, poor dear, I would do anything . . . We must go home, away from this dreadful place. Mother Matilda will take you back. We should never have come.'

Boniface stared down at her. Somewhere there was an instinct to go back to those sunny, regulated corridors and hide, creep back beneath the mother hen's wing, but it didn't permeate the layers around her.

'Take her back.' Like a chick that had ventured too far and got itself hurt? A vaguely ridiculous object of pity? And hadn't she, in another world, made a promise not to return without success?'

She saw quite clearly and drearily. 'You must go,' she said, 'You go back and tell them. Get Mother Matilda to write to the Pope.'

'But you must come too.'

'And leave Dermot victorious?' She stroked Clotilde's back, 'You wouldn't want that.'

Clotilde wept, clung, protested, but Boniface knew Ireland was now such a horror to her that eventually she would be persuaded. For herself, no change of venue could rid her of horror, she would carry it around with her for the rest of her life and beyond – if there was a beyond.

Two weeks later she stood at the guest house window to wave Clotilde goodbye, 'I love you,' she said quietly, and wondered why she had never said it to Clotilde when she had been in her presence.

Two weeks after that she set off herself, accompanied by Art and Sister Aine to attend, uninvited, the great Church Council of Ireland at Mellifont.

The countryside was responding vigorously to an early spring, leaf, grass, flowers and blossom popping out like escapees from a prison in which only Boniface remained and which was so timeless, so seasonless that it seemed natural for her monthly periods to have stopped.

Numbness had its advantages. Though the beauty of Mellifont abbey, a copse of stone trees among the living foliage around it, failed to move her, neither was she nervous as she pushed past the enquiring priests who tried to bar her way into the great hall full of gorgeously mitred and coped men. How could they intimidate her more, who had been undone by the expert of undoing? Well, she'd give him undoing.

She walked calmly up the centre of them to the dais where the Archbishop of Armagh was addressing this great assembly of Ireland's ecclesiastical establishment, climbed up its steps and spoke.

'I make no apology, my lords, for interrupting you. You know who I am and what has happened to me and my abbey. In the name of St. Brigid I call for the excommunication of Dermot of Leinster. I demand that his name be written in the annals as infamous, that he be cast down from his kingship.' She heard her voice echo under the great carved beams of the roof, felt it sink into the velvet and silks of the congress.

She had no doubt of their acquiescence; they themselves had made her heiress to the saint of Kildare, they themselves had told her how important she was. Why were they avoiding her eyes? Why were they whispering? Why didn't they answer? Had they excommunicated Dermot already?

'Let his wickedness be recorded for all time,' she said clearly in response to the command of that distant brain. 'That he had me raped, me, the Comarba of Kildare, heiress to the great saint herself. In the name of Brigid I accuse him.'

There was outrage in the assembly, but not for Dermot. She watched a hundred pairs of eyes turn away from her, heard the tuttings of irritation, saw a couple of archdeacons come towards her to lead her away and then stop, not wanting to touch her. She saw Abbot Flynn flapping his hands in desperate apology to those around him, then twist his forefinger against his temple as if to indicate that she was mad.

They were embarrassed.

For the first time an emotion pierced Boniface's numbness – incredulity. They didn't want to know. 'Don't you hear me?' she demanded.

Beside her, the Archbishop cleared his throat. 'Will someone remove this poor woman?'

The archdeacons came forward and took her arms. She tore away from them, hissing through her teeth. 'Listen to me.' She knelt down on the edge of the dais to where a young scribe was frozen in the act of writing the Council's proceedings. 'Write,' she demanded. 'Write what I have said.' He got up from his table and backed away from her. She saw the Archbishop signal to the gallery where abbesses and nuns were separated from the male body of the council. The cocoon was ripping apart and the reactions from which it had protected her came rushing in, tearing her to pieces with their violence. She struggled on her knees towards the Archbishop and tugged at his cope. 'Depose me, my lord, for the great harm I brought on my abbey, but at least let me hear you excommunicate Dermot first.'

The Archbishop tore himself away in alarm. 'Did nobody inform this person that she has already been deposed? Father Flynn?'

'Why?' begged Boniface.

Two brawny prioresses were advancing up the nave of the hall and the churchmen fell back, relieved that the situation would soon be dealt with.

'Why?' begged Boniface again. 'Because of all the deaths?'

The Archbishop looked down and his amazement at her ignorance forced a direct answer out of him. 'My poor child,' he said. 'You were unfitted that night. Dermot had you unfitted for the post.'

'Dermot had me raped.'

The Archbishop nodded. 'Unfitted,' he said, and then big, feminine arms seized Boniface. 'Take her back to Kildare,' said the Archbishop, 'Let the new Comarba make some arrangement for her. I am afraid the poor soul has gone mad.'

He was wrong. Up to that point Boniface had been sane, trying to stop the world going mad around her. It was then, as she saw that structure on which she had built her life and in which she had put her trust was insane, that she went mad. They were going not just to ignore her, but obliterate her. She would be a non-person. She began shrieking incoherence at them and fighting every inch of the way as the prioresses half-carried her out of the hall.

The churchmen could hear her screaming outside and the Archbishop signalled to the choir to cover the noise; in a minute a cool, sexless Nunc Dimittis was re-establishing the order and purity of God, helping them to forget the woman who had brought sex, like the disgusting intruder it was, into their company, reminding them of everything their foundation was in being to negate.

The Archbishop heard one very young monk whisper to his neighbour: 'What's "raped"?'. He sighed. There it was. How could she not have known? She had been deposed for that; not because her abbey had been attacked. Abbeys had been attacked before and would be again while the Devil reigned, but their abbots and abbesses were not deposed, however politically inept. Her real sin – and nobody should have had to point it out to her – was in being raped, and not just in the decent privacy of a field, but in full view before a high altar. She had literally displayed the hole in the virginal fabric this choir was now re-weaving.

Perhaps they should send a messenger to the Pope to express regret at what had happened to his foreign nun, but he confidently expected that when the Holy Father heard the delicate circumstances attendant on the matter, he would take no action.

And the new Comarba – he was going to appoint Mór, daughter of Donal O'Conor Faily, a sensible Irish virgin of mature years and a good apolitical choice – she would have to deal with the madwoman, stop her making a nuisance of herself. He didn't know how, but it wasn't his problem.

The chanting ceased, leaving the air peaceful. He knew just how to strike the right note now and put this upsetting episode behind them all. He strode back into the centre of the dais and wagged his finger at the assembly, his kindly old eyes twinkling at them. 'These women,' he said.

If the Archbishop didn't know what to do with a raped ex-Comarba, the new Comarba of Kildare didn't either. The best thing would have been to put her on the next boat back to France and forget all about her, but Mor had gathered the unspoken dislike of the Council for any more anti-Irish propaganda in Europe, and a raped nun shouting her wrongs from the housetops would certainly have provided that.

Anyway, the woman was pregnant and Mór was sorry for her. For the time being, and until the child was born, she hid her out of everybody's way in Sister Mairenne's disert outside the walls of Kildare.

Everything stopped. Except the rape, which went on and on and on. When flakes of snow came through the ill-fitting door of the disert, the big man came in with them and began it all over again. He clambered in through the window on the moonlight, wearing the smiling head of Dermot of Leinster, and, without waking Sister Mairenne, raped her once more.

'He's dead.' Sister Mairenne broke her vow of silence to comfort Boniface when she woke screaming.

But he wasn't dead, he was alive and ripping her apart. And the guilt – if she'd done this or done that it wouldn't have happened – was alive. The overwhelmingness of male strength was alive. The cancer the man had left inside her was alive, and growing. Only Boniface was dead.

And God was dead.

The living cancer which had been implanted in Boniface's body emerged out of it in August, still living, and was taken away to foster care before she could see it, in accordance with the wish she had expressed before her final madness. It cried as it was carried away and the thin sound answered that of Dervorgilla's crying still echoing somewhere in the stones of Kildare Abbey.

* * *

93

The jolly young Norman pilgrim who turned up at Kildare in late September was the answer to its Comarba's prayer. She had him brought to her apartments where Sister Aine acted as interpreter, since he had little Irish.

'Have you sinned, my son?' Mór asked him.

'Bless me, Mother. I'm afraid I have somewhat.'

'And you seek expiation in holy pilgrimage?'

'Yes I do. Actually, I was hoping to travel into Connaught, from Loch Derg, but every time I set off I keep getting turned back. Apparently there's a war on.'

The Comarba regarded him sternly. 'There is indeed terrible war between Connaught and Ulster and in the normal way I would advise you not to go, though doubtless your soul could benefit by it.'

Sir John of Sawbridge perked up. 'Do I gather this is not in the normal way?'

The Comarba took a turn around the room, making the floorboards creak. She was a massive woman. She was also a worried one; the misery of the poor soul, who now had to be tied up for her own safety, concerned her. She was receiving no help; as far as the male church establishment was concerned the woman no longer existed. She had prayed long and hard for an answer and had now received one.

She looked at the young man carefully. For all his robe and his scrip and his staff he didn't have the look of a pilgrim, he was too pleased with himself, too tricky; nevertheless the Comarba was no mean judge of character and she saw, beneath the arrogance, a decency which the young man himself probably didn't know he possessed. She shrugged heavy shoulders. One took what God sent.

'My son,' she said, 'as heir to the blessed St. Brigid I have the privilege to grant indulgence, and I can promise to absolve you of many sins if you will help me in a certain manner. I want you to escort a poor lady to Connaught. I cannot say that it will be a safe journey, but I can send with you a guide who has travelled the area himself, and who should take you through most of Nature's dangers and even, with God's help, those of man. Will you go?'

Sir John, thought Sir John, you've done it again.

Fulke had already returned to the Continent with their early report on the state of Ireland, but since he'd sailed John had been thwarted time and again in his attempt to go deeper into the west by the bloody war they were indulging in over there. He hadn't worried too much. God wouldn't let him down. Something would turn up. And here it was. He was being given the perfect passport. The lifting of sins off his soul was a bonus, considering how many these charmingly willing Irish girls had enticed him into committing.

The two godsends smiled into each other's eyes. 'Madam,' said Sir John of Sawbridge, 'I'm your man.'

'She is a lady who has been foully mistreated. Ask me not how,' explained the Comarba on the way to the disert. 'As a result she wanders in her wits – a temporary affliction so the doctors inform me. God has not deserted her, however, for out of her ravings we have discovered that she is a noblewoman of Partraige ancestry. A curious patronym, you will think, since none of our native words begin with the letter 'P'. Of Pictish derivation probably, and we have traced her sept to the shores of Lough Mask where, though it may be sadly diminished, we believe it to still exist. She is called Finola.'

Sir John nodded politely. He didn't give a damn what the woman's name was. 'This Lough Mask,' he said, 'in O'Conor territory is it?' The O'Conor king was a powerful but unknown quantity and Fitzempress needed to know more about him.

'It is.'

The stone hut held a withered female hermit with hairs sprouting from her chin and, chained round its waist to a ring in the wall, a sticklike scarecrow that cowered and muttered as Sir John entered and which, he presumed, was his charge. Of the two he would have preferred the hermit.

'How is she today, Sister Mairenne?' asked the Comarba. A shrug indicated that the patient was as usual. 'We keep knives away from her,' said the Comarba in an undertone. She led the pilgrim up to the scarecrow. 'Lady Finola, this gentleman is making a holy journey to the stations of Lough Derg and has kindly agreed to escort you to your own people. Will you go with him?' She spoke in the loud, careful enunciation reserved for the deaf. She shoved Sir John nearer, 'Say something.'

'Nice day.' Mentally he picked the creature up between thumb and forefinger and held it away from him; there were lice crawling in the tangled hair. He'd seen saner March hares. And he wasn't keen on the way its eyes flickered over him and away. 'This sept as you call it,' he said, 'You're sure they'll take her in?' He didn't want to get landed with her.

'I don't know the custom in Normandy,' said the Comarba with dignity, 'and it is true that they haven't seen her since she was a child, but the Irish look after their own.'

Nor was Sir John reassured by the sight of his guide, a gargoyle on legs called Art, although he was surprised and impressed by the horse which was to bear the loony's luggage, an Arab, if he wasn't mistaken, with her yearling.

'We are sorry to lose Art,' the Comarba told him, 'but he is devoted to the Lady Finola and insists on accompanying her.'

'Then why doesn't Art take the loony?' wondered Sir John.

As they stood at the postern and watched the ex-Comarba and her escort ride off down the track to the west, Sister Aine wondered much the same thing. 'Surely Art could have taken her.'

'I don't want her left alone with a man,' said Mór.

'But Art wouldn't touch a hair of her head, and the pilgrim looks harmless enough.'

The Comarba of Kildare sighed. 'Dear daughter, you don't realise what she has become. It's the men I'm afraid for.'

There was no Boniface; she'd been jammed down on a spike and the cracks held together for a time before shards whirled off into a void of primal terror. It was the imbalance of the world which stopped the pieces of the non-thing from joining up, the unruled injustice of chaos. If she could even it, inflict some proportion, the shards might come together enough for her to return to a lakeside where a small, clean girl called Finola waited for her to enter the only substantial thing there was, the blessed insubstantiality of water.

The ugly one was safe, but the new one was taking her into a forest where trees reached out to stuff jagged branches up that torn entrance into her body. His face and voice intertwined with sexual foliage; she had seen him before.

'Was. She. Oh what's bloody Irish for raped?' He wasn't really interested, merely trying to make conversation; if he could improve his Irish during this journey it would be something gained. But the gargoyle ignored him as he had for three days, pretending not to understand even when he asked where they were.

And where were they? He'd expected to reach the Shannon by now in which case Connaught would be on the other side, but, though they'd traversed some mountains, they'd encountered no river as big as the Shannon was reputed to be. All they'd seen was bog and forest. He'd never known such forested country, or such a deserted one.

They weren't making good time: the loony's weak condition was holding them back, and the Arab didn't like acting as pack horse, not that he blamed it.

And Art insisted on treating the madwoman like a queen, watching over her, standing guard when she went off into the bushes as if he, Sir John, might have designs on her. Which would be the day. She gave him the creeps with her skinny, dirty little body and her muttering. Doubtless she'd encountered something nasty in the woodshed at some time or another, the way she shrank from being touched, but she was making an unnecessary meal of it.

The gargoyle's ears were waggling. Sir John heard the sound of cantering horses behind them on the soft leafmould of the forest floor. Until then they'd been following some track through the trees which Sir John had believed to belong solely to badgers, but Art had them and their horse off it in seconds. Why the little bastard thought anybody'd be interested in a pilgrim, a gargoyle and a loony, Sir John failed to understand, and said so. Art hissed the Irish equivalent of 'Shut up', took the woman further back under cover and then crawled forward on his belly to watch, Sir John went with him.

The riders were warriors. Sir John was impressed, as he always was, by the completeness between Irish soldiers and their mounts which they rode without saddle or stirrups, though why they made life so difficult for themselves was a mystery; something to do with their bloody tradition. Ah well, all the easier to defeat them in battle if it came to that. He hoped the Connaught troops were equally uncivilised. Still, the speed with which they could cut through this damn terrain made them formidable.

Art lay like a log till they were well gone, then went back to report to the madwoman.

'Hy Kinsella.'

They were the first words Sir John had understood since they'd started. He said: 'Isn't that the clan of Dermot of Leinster?' He'd met Dermot during his first survey and thought him an interesting chap.

Art nodded to the woman and indicated that he'd track them and that she was to stay where she was. He nipped off.

They were in a glade and the shadows were lengthening. The evenings were drawing in and another bloody day had gone without anything achieved. Praying for patience, Sir John began to make camp, and behind him the non-thing took a knife out of Art's saddlebag.

The leaves of the trees turned gold and red in the long, autumn light like the colours of a painted church. *Dermot of Leinster*, he'd said, Dermot of Leinster, only this time he'd turned his back. She would balance the void by sticking the knife in his neck and haul herself up by it.

Jesus, thought Sir John, the loony didn't believe in travelling light. Under the top blankets in the pannier was a very nice swansdown quilt, a box such as women carried their jewellery in and . . . Good God, on it was the device of Eleanor of Aquitaine. What was an Irish madwoman doing with an Arab mare and a trinket box belonging to the Queen of England?

He'd lived with danger for the best part of his life, and when a breath whistled behind him he ducked down and sideways. The knife point perforated his earlobe and scored along his cheek.

Though Sir John's looks weren't beautiful, he was fond of them

97

and he struck the knife out of the loony's hand with all his force, putting her on her back and kneeling on her legs to stop her kicking. His intention was to explain his displeasure with the flat of his hand on her backside, but he found himself looking into her eyes and he stopped.

It cannot be said that his anger was gone; for Sir John and his like treachery by a woman was more horrible than treachery from a man since it threatened the natural order of things. But in the woman's eyes was an experience, a re-experience, of something so dreadful that it was outside the natural order. It outweighed the attack on him. For the first time in his life John found himself hanging over the edge of somebody else's hell.

In trying to relate it to something he could understand he likened the woman to a dog turned vicious by the cruelty of a previous owner.

Now, Sir John's defence against outrages of the universe was to impose neatness on himself and everything belonging to him in the hope that it would catch on by extension. He had the true Norman's mania for order and, like all Normans, such order had to reflect his own importance.

In that moment of connection between him and the madwoman, she stopped being a person he was travelling with and became part of his entourage; it was a difference he would have been unable to explain, but it brought the woman under his responsibility. That he was stuck with her was a misfortune, but since he was indeed stuck with her he would train her like any other vicious animal, mixing reassurance with discipline.

Her jerked her to her feet. 'I don't know what your last master did to you, young woman, but *we* are going to do it different. You'll be a credit to me if it kills you. *Credit*, you bitch. Damn, what's Irish for credit? Well, you'll learn.'

When Art came back he found a shaking ex-Comarba sitting on a log, her hands tied before her, with the pilgrim inexpertly and painfully pulling through her hair an ivory nit comb which had been given to him by his mother.

'And tomorrow,' the pilgrim said to him, 'you can heat some water and wash this female. *Wash*, understand? And it won't do you any harm either. See what she did to my face? *Face*? There's going to be some changes. This may be the back of beyond, but if you think I'm travelling through it with a couple of disasters like you two you've got another think coming. *Understand*?'

And, oddly enough, Art looked at his ex-Comarba, then at the pilgrim, and nodded.

An abnormally dry, hot summer had shrunk the Shannon; nevertheless the pilgrim's jaw dropped when he saw the width of it. He decided to cross further up the eastern bank where it was narrower and where holy men ran ferries under the protection of St. Patrick, Sir John couldn't swim and distrusted any water on a large scale.

The woman was making progress, or rather, had ceased to be dangerous; she had stopped muttering to herself and her eyes no longer slid about in the way that had made him uneasy, they had just become dull.

She was more presentable now and he was less ashamed to introduce her as his distant kinswoman. He didn't want anybody to think he was married to her.

While they were on the more deserted part of the Shannon bank, he grubbed about for leaves of mugwort, remembering vaguely that his mother had used it on her hair to repel what she'd called 'visitors'. He boiled them and then took the woman behind a wall and washed her hair in the decoction. 'And if you ever tell a soul I've done this I'll kill you,' he said to the interested Art. He made her put on a new dress he found in her baggage and complimented her on the result: 'Less ratlike.'

He slapped her when she slouched, making her put her shoulders back. He slapped her when she didn't eat but, as she still didn't eat, he was forced to spend time spooning food into her. 'One for Sir John, there's a good girl. One for Art. I said one for Art, you little devil. That's right. Art *will* be pleased. Now then, one for St. Martin. How the hell did I get into this? One for St. Patrick.'

Starvation, he decided, was her problem; lack of food had made her brain thin. 'And it's not going to get fat on your food,' he told Art, 'which would make a dog retch. We'll eat at monasteries along the way.' If she died he'd lose his passport. Posing as a pilgrim might get him to the various holy places in western Ireland, but if he was to gather the sort of information Fitzempress wanted he needed to infiltrate the wider community, assessing ways of life, battle strength, strongholds and the like.

That evening they arrived at Lorrha where the great monastery of St. Ruadan overlooked the flat, brown swampland of the Shannon. The place was packed with pilgrims and the students who flocked from all over Ireland to its schools. Sir John was told by a harrassed porter that women were not allowed in the guest house. He had to take the winding Road to the Holy Women, to the nunnery where, though reluctant to interrupt the regime he had worked out for her, he left the madwoman for the night.

'She'll need feeding by hand,' he said, handing her over to the porteress, 'Chopped red meat and red wine for strength.' He watched the limp figure being led away. 'And stand up straight,' he shouted after it.

That night before dinner, he joined the other pilgrims and went down to the lakeside to wash in its holy waters, repeating prayers during the ablutions. It was never wise to ignore a saint as considerable as St. Patrick and, besides, Sir John approved of him; a good, military saint, he thought him, like his own St. Martin. There was a quiet intensity about the shadows around him, some richly-dressed, others very poor, old, young, many crippled. But Sir John found difficulty in concentrating on his own prayers. He was worried about the loony being out of his sight; if she collapsed while at the nunnery, she would be kept in its infirmary and his passport would be gone. Anyway, like every owner of a dog, Sir John distrusted other people to know its ways. Perhaps, after all, he should make a sprint to Lough Mask, stopping as little as possible – but that meant riding.

Until now he had covered the ground on foot, more in keeping with his disguise than on horseback. He hadn't enjoyed it; no knight was truly comfortable off his horse, but as a pedestrian he had been able to talk to more people and gather more information along the way. It had also enabled him to save the money Fitzempress had given him for expenses – and Sir John had all the care for money of a man who had begun life poor. Sighing, he decided that the situation demanded the outlay of some of it. He told Art to buy two 'inexpensive' ponies and a pack mule. He'd be able to sell them later.

It was with relief that he retrieved his charge, still limp, from the porteress at the nunnery next morning.

There were boats in plenty taking pilgrims to St. Patrick's Purgatory, but the ferry between the east and west banks of the Shannon had been abandoned and Sir John had trouble finding a waterman with a barge large enough to take them and their horses over. When he did he had to pay what he considered an inordinate price. 'Is this how you treat poor pilgrims?' he grumbled in his halting Irish.

'Poor pilgrims aren't going into Connaught at this time of year and in the middle of a war,' he was told.

He would have liked to go on the trip to the Lough island where nothing female could exist. The monks had told him that even hen birds alighting on it had been seen to drop dead; he had no difficulty in believing it. He promised himself a visit on his way back.

There was an armed sentry at the landing place on the opposite bank and they were taken to a watchtower and questioned by a captain of the Hy Many. They kept the story simple – a pilgrim escorting an unhappy lady back to her own people.

The Captain's heart was touched by the sight of the madwoman and her blank stare. 'Undoubtedly, she is of the Partraige,' he said. 'They breed beautiful women – strange, but beautiful.'

Sir John looked at his loony, amazed that anyone should think her beautiful. 'She's strange, all right. And very sick.'

The captain nodded. That much was obvious. 'But she'll get well among her own,' he said. 'There is healing for women at Lough Mask, so they say. God bless the track of your ways, then. I shall send word of you to the O'Conor.' He looked carefully at Sir John. 'And he'd be glad of your courtesy to pay him the visit when you can.'

Sir John promised to report to the O'Conor as soon as possible, and took the road to Lough Mask, with the loony and Art on the ponies and himself on the Arab, since it was more befitting to his status.

Up into Galway it was a good road, classified by the Irish as a *ramat*, which meant those whose land ran alongside it had the duty to keep it clear and they reached Athenry in one day, though the ride took its toll of the unprotesting loony who was beginning to breathe badly.

But after that both road and weather deteriorated and each day Art protested at setting out at all. He said his mistress was too ill, but Sir John loaded her onto her pony, wrapped every rug he could find about her and rode alongside, pulling on its bridle to keep its pace up to his own. They passed more and more stretches of water, some large, some small and each time they did so, Sir John expected to hear Art say they'd arrived at Lough Mask, but he didn't.

The road got worse, more hilly, dirtier, the horses became unwilling and the weather turned colder. The woman started to cough. It was evening when they trotted down a slope and saw water dotted with islands.

'Lough Mask?'

Art nodded.

'Thanks be to Jesus.' The place seemed deserted except for birds, but there was a smell of peatsmoke coming from somewhere. They followed it along a path that threaded through bumpy land which was otherwise almost impassable from the trees and rocks that bestrew it.

'God forgive me,' said Art, 'but the Lough's been beside us for miles and I didn't see it. It's a hidden place, Mask.'

Sir John grunted. There was no doubt this was strange territory, with a stranger atmosphere, but he didn't care if it was the moon as long as they found shelter for the woman. She would die, and soon, if they had to spend the night in the open.

Then he saw a glow on a hillock and made for it. There were large walls in front of him, and dogs barking behind a gate. He hammered on a high, solid door and spoke the words which opened all doors in Ireland. 'In the name of God, we need shelter.'

Minutes later he was in a courtyard and a house was in front of him. He lifted the shivering bundle down and carried her into it. The inhabitants were in the middle of a quarrel in which dishpans, baskets, vessels and hens flew about the main room like enormous, angry bees, Sir John ignored it, strode to the nearest decent bed, put the woman on it and began the fight for her life.

Despite the expansion of clans like the O'Flaherties and the O'Malleys, the remnants of what had once been a great people, the Partraige, still clung to the upper shores of Lough Mask. And though they were great no longer, they comported themselves as if they were.

In his huge and crumbling *rath* at the head of the lake, Iogenán, their king, maintained a travesty of the state his ancestors had once kept, appearing on public occasions with his nine required and hereditary attendants, leading his tiny army to war when his over-king, the O'Conor, commanded him to, and doing no apparent manual work. (Sometimes it was necessary for him to help get in the hay, or round up the horses, but his people would politely ignore his company until the job was over and he could resume his royal persona.)

Once their summer lands had extended over most of Connemara, but now the encroachments of more modern, vigorous clans had confined the Partraige to thin stretches of fields on the east of the Lough and the mountains in the west which bore their name, and where they ran their herds of horses. Mainly they were lake dwellers, the people of upper Lough Mask, using its water as a thoroughfare and an inexhaustible larder, and its many islands as pasture and refuge.

They were strange because the Lough was strange – nobody unless they had been born and brought up on it ever got over how beautiful it was, how difficult of approach and how varied. It was over six miles long and four miles across at its widest point, but to walk its shoreline meant a scramble of hundreds of miles and probably a broken leg, because it went in and out in fertile fjords stacked with slabs of rock, especially on the eastern side. Every bay and inlet was different from the next and hidden from it so that the dwellers in each secretive fjord, usually one family, were a separate community unseen by all the others, only meeting up with the rest of the *tuatha* on the water, or at riotous feast days or assemblies in Iogenán's *rath*.

The word, *measg*, which had become Mask, meant 'a mingling' and outsiders thought the name derived from the mingling of the rivers which flowed into Lough Mask and thence into its lower neighbour, Lough Corrib. Perhaps it did. Or perhaps it had to do with the supreme tolerance of the Partraige, where Christian culture mixed indolently with a culture that had worshipped goddesses and had been old before St. Patrick climbed to the top of the great conical mountain in the distance and, fasting, had sent all snakes packing from Ireland.

They were a gentle, tolerant people, the Partraige, and a dying people.

It had been the driest summer anyone could remember and an

extraordinarily sharp winter had come early, but not by the flicker of an eyelid did Niall of the Poems and his chief wife, Blat, indicate to the gentleman who came bursting in through their gateway – and that in the middle of one of their more interesting quarrels – the inconvenience, not to say hardship, the presence of him, his patient and the man Art would cost them. Indeed, they gave the impression that he was just what they had been waiting for to fill their cup. They asked no questions, and beyond the fact that the sick woman was called Finola, Sir John gave them no information.

Blat and her servants rearranged the house, fetched and boiled water, saw to the poor lady's more intimate needs, got rid of the waste products, did the extra washing, cooked the extra food, first slaughtering or picking it, while Niall took the credit and composed one of the best poems he'd done for ages on the romance of the wasted stranger who took his bed.

Sir John barely noticed them. Crossly he watched over his change, taking turns with Art to sit by her. It seemed impossible to him that she should die after all he'd done for her. He pointed this out to her unceasingly, bullying her to stay alive. 'Fight, you ungrateful little bitch,' he repeated until his voice was hoarse. 'Concentrate. You can do it. Fight, damn you.'

If she heard him there was no indication. She became increasingly feverish, coughed and muttered without intelligence. On the fifth day the local priest, Baccaugh, limped in and put beneath her pillow a knucklebone of St. Adamnan, well-known for his care for women. But he gave her extreme unction as well, and the holy oil slid down over eyes that intended to stay shut forever.

When he'd gone, Sir John knelt by the bed and prayed. 'Jesu in your mercy, I don't know why this stupid woman is important to me, but I would very much like her not to die. If there are sins I have not yet accounted for, forgive them. Jesu in your mercy, as we live in your mercy, hear my prayer.'

He looked across the bed to Art. 'How the hell did this happen to her?'

Art sobbed. 'One of the great ones tried to destroy her.'

'Fight, blast you,' said Sir John hopelessly. For the hundredth time he wiped the small face that was setting into the lineaments of death, then gave up. He'd done what he could. 'Well, he's bloody well succeeded.'

Straight fight eat one for St. Patrick fight ungrateful blast you fight, the new one's voice floated down on dustbeams of incoherence which mattered less and less as the void became softer and darker. Then a string of sibilants that made sense reached some portion that responded. Irritated, because it was so tiring and most of her pieces didn't see the point of it, she reassembled enough to grasp the ladder the syllables made. Painfully and grudging every effort she began to climb up it.

The two men watching the body on the bed saw its lips move. Sir John bent over her face to hear and saw that sweat was breaking out on her skin. He looked up at Art.

'What did she say?'

'I think she said: "I'll give him bloody succeed". '

While she just needed sleep and food her bed was put up in the loft where she was kept warm by Blat's goosefeather mattress and Eleanor of Aquitaine's swansdown quilt. Now she was on the road to recovery it was demeaning for Sir John to wait on her, so Niall went with him up the lakeside where he took up residence with the king and they all went hunting.

When Blat told her to open her mouth, she opened it and, when Blat told her to chew and swallow the food spooned into it, she chewed and swallowed it, and she went to sleep when Blat said, 'Sleep now, and grow strong.' The effort of will which had brought her back to life had exhausted itself in the process, leaving her incurious and dull.

'She's a sad thing,' Blat reported to Niall's elderly mother, who lived with them.

'She bears a sad name,' said Niall's mother, and Blat sighed. Finola, the name of the Daughter of Lîr, carried more personal sadness for the Partraige than just the tragedy of the mythical swan-woman. 'Tomorrow I'll bring her downstairs,' she said, 'and sit her to look out on the Lough so she can heal.'

The woman's body was still pitifully light, but as Blat lifted it she saw with satisfaction that the dent it had made in the mattress was deeper than it had been when the woman arrived. She made her up a chair-bed downstairs and propped her up in it in the doorway, covering her with rugs, to look out through the open gate to the portion of Lough Mask which filled the western view.

'It has the healing property for women,' Blat said, 'though there's a dragon under its waters.'

Nobody ever agreed on how many islands were in the Lough because they altered shape and position in an ever-changing light. Sometimes there were big islands far out in it and at other times they were small; only the islands and *crannoghs* near the shore remained consistent, but even they varied so much – some being treeless, some covered in trees, a couple bearing buildings on their backs and a couple a stone tower – that it was impossible to count them because many of them hid themselves in the inlets and, anyway, though you might start to do so, you invariably became so interested in some feature that you never finished.

The woman looked out on a path which led down from the gate in the wall over the grass, between the rocks to a landing place where upturned *curraghs* were kept like beached porpoises when not in use, as now. A white otter emerged from the limestone slabs piling the side of the inlet, contemptuously avoiding the trap Blat had set for it, and fished for trout. From the house came feminine sounds, sweeping, the click of a loom, women's voices in conversation. The woman sat quietly, smelling the lake water and the warm depth of the thatch above the doorway, and watched, listening to the call of the lake's diving birds.

The imperative was to live so that Dermot of Leinster didn't win. She would make sure Dermot of Leinster didn't live when she'd worked out a few things, like who she was and how she could cope with a world in which all the accustomed planes had shifted. Having no God and no rules to hang on to made her giddy. She had to use left-over bits from the shattered Boniface to make a new woman to stand up in the new world, a patched-up thing with no illusions, no preconceived ideas and no caste. But she was too tired.

In her lethargy, and so stealthily that she didn't realise it, something was happening to her.

She shrank; the view became bigger and the rocks down at the shore grew to enormous castles of enchantment where fish and crustacea swam in moats of lakewater. Without physically moving she was projected unsteadily down the path towards them and clambered up onto the highest, where it hung out over the lake, knowing every handhold and the dip on its landward side in which pinks grew. She got to the top and turned to look back, unsurprised that the house, where she still sat in the doorway, was familiar; the peat stacks and the pigsty, the cow byre and the hayrick; she could have guided a stranger round the back of it, past the labourers' huts and the smoke house to Blat's herb garden and the stream that hustled down from behind the house to the Lough where a kingfisher watched the water from an overhanging branch.

'Look, Blat,' she called, 'Look at me.' Blat's dog came bounding towards her as she stood on the rock and she watched its advance with pleasure, like a friend. It put its paws on her shoulder to lick her face and its weight knocked her backwards into the water. Unafraid, she looked upwards as she sank down, enjoying the bubbles that streamed out of her mouth, the peculiar effect of reeds the wrong way up. She saw Blat above her, unlined, younger, but anxious, swimming down towards her to gather her up.

'Are you cold, Lady Finola?' came Blat's voice and Blat's older face was in front of her, 'Have some nice broth now.'

It seemed perfectly natural to be two people, one big, one small; sleepily still unaware of what she was experiencing, she asked Blat:

105

'What's the name of the dog? The one that pushed me in the water and you rescued me.'

The soup bowl fell onto the ground. 'Finn?' whispered Blat. 'Is that you, Finn?'

Just as they had dragged her up from the lake all those years ago, Blat's arms gathered her up from exile into the warm hug of home.

Her mother, Anhin, had been the daughter of Iogenán, King of the Partraige, and, said Blat, 'as beautiful as the dawn.' So beautiful that she had attracted, while he was visiting the lake, the attention of Aedh, a nephew of the old king of Connaught, Turlough O'Conor, and he had married her and become Finn's father.

'Often and often you stayed here in this house when you were little,' Blat told her, 'for Niall of the Poems is your first cousin on your mother's side, if that's any comfort to you, and I'm your second.'

As a prince of Connaught, Aedh had official duties and one night, 'one black night,' said Blat, he gave a feast of welcome to some important merchants who had arrived in the harbour of Galway to set up trade between Connaught and their home port of Nantes in Anjou. 'They were Gauls by nationality,' said Blat, who refused to differentiate between foreigners, 'and demons by nature.'

Their leader, a young man – 'he called himself Robert de Chêne' – had become besotted by the beauty of Finn's mother. 'Not a morsel did he eat all through the feast, though he drank enough for ten, and just stared at her like the pig he was.' Since he was a guest and a foreigner who knew no better, Aedh ignored the rudeness. Next day he and Anhin and the child Finola went down to the quayside to speed their guests goodbye as they left in the rowing boats that would take them out to their ship in the bay. Suddenly an armed party, led by Robert de Chêne, fell on Aedh and his unarmed courtiers, killing Aedh and two others, and dragged Anhin into their boat, with the child Finola clinging so strongly to her mother that they'd taken her as well.

The Irish leaped into *curraghs* and gave chase, but the rowing boat had reached the ship long before them, and they were forced to watch her sail out of the bay.

'Your mother's body came floating ashore at Barna three days later,' said Blat, weeping, 'and whether the bastard killed her, or she killed herself, we never knew. And only God knows what she suffered before that.'

It was her daughter who was finely qualified to guess. Kneeling in front of her with her hands in hers, Blat saw the impassive face crumple into that of a child, open its mouth and bawl with terror as if she were again the little girl flapping her hands in her powerlessness to stop her mother being hurt.

106

Blat held her until she was calmer, knowing it would help her to have her cry out, and wiped her face. 'Every ship in Connaught went off in search of you – even the O'Flaherties – and the O'Conors sailed to Nantes and questioned everybody they could find, but no word was there of you nor the devil who took you. And in time we came to think that you, too, had gone under the water, for who would have imagined the man had enough mercy in his soul to keep you alive?'

'She's Irish,' said Finn, softly, hiccuping from her sobs, 'She's been abandoned. Pray for me for I have sinned.'

'And wasn't that another sin with him to say that,' raged Blat, 'as if your own people would abandon you. And what's "Irish" when it's at home? You are a Connaughtwoman of the Partraige.'

'Yes,' said Finn, 'I know I am,' and went into the first sleep since the rape in which, though the dreams were still ugly, she did not feel alone.

Now that they had been restored to her, she moved within the parameters of her first six years, receptive to kindness, experiencing smells and tastes as if for the first time, and hearing music with ears that seemed to have opened after a long deafness, as obedient as a child. She grieved for her mother and father but, with the knowledge that they had not abandoned her, she laid them gently to rest.

Music was everywhere. Ceaseless droplets of pipe notes came from the herders on the hills and from the bells round the necks of the sheep and cattle. When the families of the Partraige clan rowed to the inlet to call in and embrace with tears 'little, lost Finn' they sang themselves home again, their voices coming back to her over the water in cheery, half-toned song.

Niall returned to say that he and 'The Pilgrim' had met the King of Connaught while chasing wild boar over by Lough Carra and that the king had invited Sir John to go on an extended hunting tour with him, and then he sat down to compose a poem in honour of his restored cousin, and sang it to his harp so beautifully that even Blat, though grudgingly, said, 'You'd go nine miles of a dark night only to hear him.'

Too polite, as the other members of the Partraige had been, to question a guest he privately asked Blat: 'Has she said what she's been doing these years?'

'She'll tell us when she's ready and not before,' said Blat. But when she knew Finn was ready, even if Finn didn't know it, she took her fishing out on the lake.

Lough Mask was still that afternoon, but gaudy, with bright blue water and varied green islands splashed with the red of the rowan trees. The herons along the shore had their exact doubles reflecting back at them in the surface of the lake. Blat rowed out to clear water in the leather *curragh* which rocked unnervingly as she plunged her spear into passing char.

'I'm going to divorce the bastard,' said Blat, conversationally, knowing that to receive a confidence you must first give one.

'Divorce?' The left-over bits of Boniface were shocked until the new woman reminded herself that God's rules no longer applied. But it was still a surprise, though the marriage was manifestly unhappy. Niall knocked Blat around when he was drunk. He made fun of her in public and imposed work on her that would have killed a lesser woman. But she had assumed that Blat was content with it.

'Are you jealous of Almaith then?' Almaith was Niall's second wife, who lived further along the shore to the south.

Blat snorted, stabbed down with her spear into the clear water and brought up a fat, flapping fish. The cormorants sitting on an overhanging branch at the lakeside made a poor attempt at looking uninterested. 'Her? The poor thing can't say boo to a blanket.'

'What then?'

'I don't like the man. Apart from he will keep gambling away all me hard-earned wealth, there's no curb to his tongue. I'm a figure of fun to his friends with his lampoons on me. Loyalty is only one way to him and all going in his direction.'

'Can you divorce him just like that? Where I was only royalty can get divorces.'

Blat shrugged 'That's a strange place, then, where you were. Do women have no rights there?'

'No.' It was true now she thought about it. Perhaps it was why there were so many nuns in Europe; women escaped into the convent out of a rightless world. Here among the Partraige women had a different attitude, looking out with authority, walking straighter. A more feminine world altogether. 'How will you manage?'

'Some way. The children are grown up now, and I'll take me dowry back.'

Two coots chased each other past the boat in a spray of quarrelsome pursuit. Each day there were more birds on the lake as the swimmers and divers came down from the north for the winter. Blat was worried about the winter, which promised to be hard. 'They say it's a judgement on all Ireland for the insult offered by damned Leinstermen to the Comarba of St. Brigid at Kildare.'

They had to know; they were her family. But she felt deathly tired.

'That was me,' she said. 'I was Comarba of St. Brigid.'

As she talked, the sun began to set, giving the lake a candied appearance so that its islands looked like frosted cakes set out on a polished table. She kept pausing, more out of the weariness she felt for the history than for any difficulty in its telling. And while she told it, Blat kept patting her and crying.

'That bloody Dermot,' sobbed Blat, when Finn had no more to tell, 'That crooked bastard. If he swallowed a nail he'd shite a screw.'

And, for one abrupt moment, Finn laughed.

Iogenán, Finn's grandfather and the king of the Partraige, had already visited her unofficially at Blat's and Niall's house, sneaking in somewhat shamefacedly because he hadn't been able to wait to collect his nine attendants – since they were attending to his and their herds at the time – when he received the message that his long lost grand-daughter had returned to her clan. Politely, since he was without his royal entourage and therefore not officially recognisable, Blat and Niall had ignored his presence and Finn had woken up to find a nice old man bending over her bed, weeping, and saying, 'Well now, and welcome home Finola of the Partraige.'

But later, etiquette demanded that she be formally presented to the king and received into her family, the *derbhfine*.

With Blat and Niall she was rowed to the north shore of the lough and disembarked before the great earthen ramparts that had once dominated it but were now falling down into dips where hawthorn bushes made havens for birds and foxes. Her hand held high in Niall's, Finn walked through ten foot gateposts so old that the carving on them had weathered almost smooth and up an avenue built for chariot races to what had once been an immense wooden palace housing two hundred people, but where now Iogenán and his queen camped out in the hall with a dozen family and servants.

Finn looked at it unmoved. The old numbness had come over her again in the last few days.

'Weren't we the great people in them days,' Niall said, partly to himself, partly to Finn, 'when it was us ruled over Connaught.'

'When was that?'

Niall was vague. 'Sometime after the age of Noah,' he said.

A trumpeter sounded their approach with a cracked fanfare, and then rushed inside the doors to take off his hat and receive them in his other role, as Iogenán's chamberlain.

The hall was pillared with columns around which curled carved gargoyles, beaked birds and monsters who seemed frozen in the act of looking at her. Along one side on a bench sat the women, on the other the men, all of them dressed in their patched best and displaying the remnants of their jewels. But it was the faces that commanded atten-tion: weatherbeaten, lined with hard work, but every one, both male and female, handsome. 'What a good-looking people we are,' thought

Finn, hardly realising that she had begun to think of herself and the Patraige as 'we'.

Green light from the overcast day outside came through the luxury of thick, ancient glass windows dulling the brightly-coloured robes of the men and women into old tapestry. The only candles stood in wrought-iron holders on the dais to highlight the importance of the man who sat on a canopied throne. She could hardly recognise Iogenán in his crown and holding a white, carved wand. Beside the king, in only a slightly smaller seat, was his *brehon* with silver collar round his neck that would magically tighten if ever he gave a false judgement, just as blotches would appear on his cheeks from the same cause. Moran's complexion, though old, was clear and the collar fitted with ease.

Niall led his cousin up the hall in a silence broken only by Blat, who had taken her place on the women's side and couldn't resist encouraging her with a cheer. Finn smiled at her. Niall hissed at his wife for spoiling the gravity of the occasion and Blat said: 'Oh shut up.'

'Recite your ancestry, my child,' said the brehon Moran.

Iogenán waved his wand to silence the women and then pointed it at Finn. His face was tortured with wrinkles as if he had been carved himself, though he was not an old man.

And so, to a different king in a different land, Finn found her tongue, mouth and throat again performing movements they had been taught to make probably in this very hall. Strictly speaking, she should have begun with Japhet, son of Noah, who came to Ireland after the Flood, but that would have taken the rest of the day, so she began with Muirgius, once High King of Connaught before the Vikings came, through names which, perhaps because she did not really care who she was, came unfalteringly, down side-branches away from the High Kingship into the backwater of the Partraige again and eventually to her great-grandfather, Flaithbertach, who was either the great-grandfather or grandfather or father of every man in the room.

The king nodded when she had finished, and the men slapped their knees in approval, but, typical *brehon* that he was, Moran wanted more proof of her identity. 'Has she any distinguishing marks now?'

'Will you listen to the old fool?' shouted Blat, and the other women protested with her. Banba, the priest's wife, called out: 'Are you blind not to see who she is? I'd know her as her mother's daughter with her skin hanging on a gorse-bush.'

The king muttered to his *brehon*, who shrugged and gave way. Iogenán called her forward and put his hand on Finn's head. 'You are of the *derbifhine*.'

Ther was a cry of 'Welcome' that shook the pillars.

Iogenán stood up. 'I receive this woman Finola back into the

Partraige after long exile. She shall have a seat by my fire for as long as her need runs. By her right as a member of the *tuath* of Partraige, she shall have one killing of a salmon in its every waters, a share in its wild garlic, the quick sweeping of every stream, a night's supply of kindling and cooking material and the nut-gathering from every common wood, and she may race her horse on the common green and run it on the common mountain.'

Feeling touched Finn for a moment, like the twitch of a paralysed hand. 'Bless them,' she thought. They were trying to make up to her the years after her abduction by giving her back her roots; she found herself blinking away tears, grateful not so much for the gift of rights, delightful as it sounded, as for wanting to link her up in the long chain of family that led down into the rich earth of Connaught.

'Ach, the old fool's forgotten the island,' muttered Melg, Iogenán's queen, from the women's side. 'Are we not giving her an island for herself, Iogenán-ri?'

'I know,' shouted Iogenán, irritably, 'Where was I? Now then, and for yourself you shall have the island in Lough Mask known as Swan Island, because it was where your father first beheld your mother, may God rest her sweet soul.'

But there was more. She had been raped and, by having her, a virgin of their clan, raped, Dermot of Leinster had offered an insult to the honour of her people. No matter that the Hy Kinsella could eat the clan Partraige for breakfast, vengeance was called for.

Finn was allowed to sit down with the rest of the women while her male relatives discussed the matter and tried to ignore such gratuitous advice as 'Cut the bastard's balls off,' from their wives. Cuddled between the ample hips of Queen Melg and the bony frame of Blat, with the other women reaching out now and then to pat her, Finn found the occasion oddly without sting. It appeared that among the Partraige there was procedure for everything, even to what had happened on that night in Kildare.

More candles had to be lit as the discussion went on and it grew dark. Finn watched new light flicker on cobwebs in the corners, felt a draught from a broken window, and saw that the pillar next to her was riddled with woodworm and had the gold leaf peeling off it. 'Bless them,' she thought, again, 'they are ridiculous.' They were a powerless people, clinging onto a remnant of ancestral land which diminished yearly under the growing expansion of clans like the O'Malleys and the O'Flaherties. Iogenán was only a king because the Partraige treated him as one, and because his overlord, the O'Conor, allowed him to be one out of respect for his forebears; in Anjou he would be merely the lord of a manor.

It was like receiving support from half-visible, half-believed fairy folk. They were as vulnerable as she herself. Boniface would have been amused by their presumption, might even pitied them and busied herself to take them under her wing; the new, patched-up woman was grateful but hopeless.

Whatever those men decided would make no difference to what she had to do; she had been isolated from the clan too long, educated away from it, ever to be dependent on it. The formula for dealing with Dermot would have to come from herself, but where she would find enough initiative in the emptiness of her soul she had no idea.

But her menfolk went on discussing the matter as if they were still a power in the land; it was the women who had a better idea of the realities. 'Should we go to war over it?' asked Orlam, who doubled as Iogenán's marshal and charioteer.

'Will you listen to the man?' screeched Melg. 'Isn't Connaught at war with him already.'

She was ignored. 'Would Dermot pay her honour price, do you think?' asked Nessa, another of Finn's male first cousins, anxiously, and there were more snorts of derision from the women's side. But the men discussed both possibilities with gravity, and Finn fell asleep against the queen's shoulder with the words *enech* and *eric* – shame and reparation – sounding in her ears.

She woke up to a sudden silence: 'Where have we got to?'

Blat hushed her: 'Niall's had a good idea for once. He's going to rhyme Dermot to death.'

'He's *what*?'

'Don't you be laughing. It's been done.'

Finn peered into the hall. Niall was lying on his back in the middle of the floor with his eyes closed and a boy was tenderly holding over his head the musical branch made of silver and decorated with bells which Niall carried with him on official occasions as the court poet.

'Can you do it, Niall, do you think?' Iogenán asked anxiously.

'To the death?' asked Niall, still supine and with his eyes closed.

'To the death or exile.'

'I'll need to work at nothing else.'

'And that won't be difficult for him,' grumbled Blat.

'And it can't be done on ale. I'll be needing the very best wine.'

'Wine,' nodded the king.

'And a new mantle. Swans' feathers with drakes' crests. I could be going to my death, after all.'

'Yes, yes, but can you do it?'

'I can,' said Niall and sat up, flicking the branch to make it ring.

The cheering and stamping that broke out couldn't have been louder, nor the feasting that followed more jolly, than if a messenger had knocked on the door with the news that the King of Leinster had just dropped dead.

'That'll fix the bastard,' said Blat, propping a piece of pork into Finn's mouth from force of habit. 'I never did like the Leinstermen.'

Finn swallowed. 'I don't understand.'

'Niall is going to compose a satire on Dermot,' explained Blat patiently, passing a chipped but still-beautiful glass cup to Finn, 'Put a drop of this at the back of your soul. And when he's composed it, he will go round the courts of the kings on the annual *cuairt* of poets and he'll sing it.'

'And?'

'Well, but Niall's satires are strong. Didn't he bring out boils on the king of the Hy Fiachrach after their cattle raid with just a little gentle one? It's almost a pity to be divorcing the bugger, so it is.'

Tenderly, helplessly Finn looked at her family who were going to avenge her rape with a rhyme. 'Thank you, Niall.'

'I have eaten of the five salmon and the nine hazels,' sang Niall, drunk, 'My satires are deadly spears, my word is a blister, my quatrain certain death.'

'Then that is settled,' said Iogenán. 'We have received back the Lady Finola, but is she healed yet? Lady Blat?'

All eyes in the glorious, decaying hall turned on Blat, who shook her head. 'She is not healed,' she said.

Finola wondered tiredly how she knew. How did Blat understand that she had not always been the way she was now, compliant, quiet, uncombatative, depressed, with the good days only good because they passed without hurting too much?

Iogenán nodded. 'Well, then, we must send her to Scathagh.'

There was a deep intake of breath, and reluctant nods around the hall. Blat put her arm around Finn's shoulders. 'Must she go?'

'If she consents.' He stepped down from the dais and crossed to Finn, stooping down to stare into her face. 'There is no light in your eyes,' he said, 'and God knows, good reason for the lack. We want you returned to us as a whole woman and it may be that Scathagh can make you whole, though I do not always like her methods. Will you go?'

She looked back at the old man, not wanting any further disruption, not knowing whether Scathagh was a person or a place and not curious to know; but they loved her, they wanted her to go, it would please them and she wanted to please them. Above all, she didn't have the energy to refuse. 'Yes, if you like,' she said.

After they'd all eaten and drunk that night, Iogenán escorted Finn to the doors. 'In case you were wondering,' he said, 'we've had a message from the O'Conor. He and your man, the Pilgrim, will be returning here in a day or two. Do you hear that, Cuimne?' A very pretty girl fluttered her eyelashes to show that she did. Iogenán told Finn: 'Cuimne has attracted the love of the king of Connaught, just as your sweet mother attracted the love of his cousin, and may more good come of it than came to her, poor soul.'

'The Pilgrim's no man of mine,' said Finn, 'I don't know who he is.'

'Isn't that the coincidence,' said Iogenán, 'for neither do I. No pilgrim, that's for sure; here we are a spit from the Croagh of the blessed St. Patrick and he has not been to pray. Ah well, the man is my guest.' It meant that Iogenán could not question him. He kissed his grand-daughter. 'You will have company when you go to Scathagh for the Hy Fiachrach were raided by Ulstermen only a little while ago and have asked permission for their damaged women to come here. This is the place for the damaged women.'

'Yes,' said Finn, 'it is.'

And even if she still was not sure who this patched-up woman was, or whether she could survive, she took away from the king of Partraige's hall that night the certain knowledge of where she belonged.

Chapter Five

Blat was worried about sending Finn to Scathagh and felt it necessary to warn her kinswoman: 'Women who go to Scathagh either come back better or they die.' Finn nodded. She would opt for that. In the torpor of depression that had once again enveloped her life wasn't worth living anyway.

She listened without much interest to what Blat could tell her of Scathagh. The woman was eternal. As far back as Partraige race memory went Scathagh had existed. Where she came from was uncertain – Scotland, some people said. She arrived and returned to nothingness, like migrating birds though without their regularity; sometimes years would go by without Scathagh being in residence in one of her stone keeps on the islands of Lough Mask, but eventually she would turn up again, usually in winter, bringing with her women from all over the world who had been mentally or physically wounded, accepting any women among the Partraige who needed her peculiar form of treatment, usually women who'd been raped and who had reacted so badly to the rape that they were useless to the clan.

'When Ulster invaded us,' said Blat, speaking of two hundred years ago as if it were last month, 'nearly every female in the *tuatha* was raped, and most of them were rejected by their men afterwards. But Scathagh took them and made them different.' How different Blat was unable to say, but so changed that their husbands and fathers had been forced to take them back – though some of the women had refused to go back and from then on had led independent lives on the islands.

'They weren't the same women,' said Blat. 'The men said they had become people of the *sidhe*.'

There had been an occasion when Scathagh died. Men had been called to her island and found a dead old woman in the keep and, despite opposition by the then priest, had buried her in the church-yard. But two years later another Scathagh, or maybe the same one, had turned up again.

For men she was a forbidden mystery, and they kept out of her way. But it was tradition that while she was in residence on Lough Mask the

115

Partraige supply her with whatever she wanted. Horses were kept for her use on either side of the lake, *curraghs* were put at her disposal and she was entitled to take what she liked from flocks and herds, while women rowed across to her island every week with gifts of bread, beer and mead, laying them on the steps of her keep as on an ancient altar.

The Church loathed her, and the bells in the monasteries that had sprung up around the southern end of Lough Mask had rung Scathagh out of her island strongholds down there, forcing her back into the pagan tolerance of Partraige territory.

On a blustery cold day Blat rowed Finn out into Lough Mask and headed north towards a stone tower apparently rising sheer out of the water. Its squat walls curved outwards at the base so that from a distance it looked like an abandoned boot. Closer, it could be seen that it rested on a foundation of limestone slabs lying at all angles, as if it had been built on some giant, petrified swans' nest. Its ninety-foot diameter occupied nearly all the island, except for a small area around which roamed some goats and two sheep. Its only entrance – apart from its top, which was cambered and open to the sky – was a door ten feet up in its massive side.

As the *curragh* approached a voice from one of the tower's narrow lights shouted: 'Who are you and what do you want?'

Blat's reply came pat, like a formula: 'The woman Finola begs admittance as a candidate to the school of Scathagh.'

'Does she swear to abide by the rules of this academy and to complete its training?'

Blat, feathering the *curragh* to keep its steady, turned to Finn. 'Do you? You don't have to go. You have a place by my hearth forever.' She had already arranged the matter with Scathagh but the sternness of the tower was giving her second thoughts.

Finn looked at the grey bulk in front of her with disinterest; it was so silly to give her choices, as if they mattered. As if this ridiculous place mattered, as if anything mattered. The impulse for her to enter it came from other people; they were propelling her towards it and her own intertia kept her on the course they'd chosen. 'I might as well,' she said dully.

'What?' came from the tower.

It was an effort to raise her voice. 'I swear.'

'Let her enter.'

A rope ladder came tumbling out of the tower's door.

Blat patted her shoulder and said good luck as if she were saying goodbye and held the *curragh* against the island's tiny holm while Finn clambered up the steps to the tower wall, took hold of the ladder and began to climb. It wasn't easy, but the real difficulty was the memory of the last time she had been on a ladder leading to a tower. Halfway up it overwhelmed her and she clung, shaking and retching, unable to move up or down.

'Oh, *kak*,' swore the tower, 'All right, hold on and I'll pull you up.' Her knees and knuckles were scraped against the wall as somebody hauled in the ladder with her on it. A hand like steel dug into her shoulder and helped her on to the eight-foot wide sill. She looked down into a big round courtyard. In its centre was a large beehive hut. Lean-to sheds had been built here and there against the circular walls of the keep with lines strung between them on which hung sails and fishing nets and underneath which were different-sized *curraghs*. Damp streaks of green ran down the walls and there were puddles on the flags of the courtyard from yesterday's rain around which some miserable hens picked their way. An ungainly wooden crane was there to explain to anybody who wanted to know how goods were got in and out of the high doorway, but Finn was incurious. Apart from the clash of pots and smell of cooking from one of the lean-to's, the place was not welcoming.

Neither was the woman standing beside her. 'Can you get down the stairs?' she asked abruptly, 'Or shall I lift you down those as well?'

She looked capable of doing it; though stringy she was muscled. A hard, skeletal fortyish face set on a boy's body dressed in man's clothes.

Finn went down lethal, open steps to the floor of the courtyard. The woman ran down, showing off, and went to one of the lean-to's. She flung into its uninviting interior Finn's rucksack, which Blat had packed for her. 'You sleep in here.'

She led Finn to the main beehive. 'And you eat in here.' Through the gloom and stale rushes, Finn was pushed to a stool at a large circular table around which other figures were sitting. 'This is Finn,' she announced, and to Finn she said: 'Those four over there are Niav, Tailltin, Muirna and Bevo. They're of the Hy Fiachrach clan. Don't ask me which is which – none of them has said a bloody word since they came yesterday. The only one who talks is that one I call Aragon . . .' a finger was pointed at a shape which, because of its olive complexion and black hair was almost undetailed in the murk, '. . . and I can't understand a bloody word she says.' She rapped on the table to get attention, 'The academy begins its term tomorrow. Scathagh will make herself known to you later. I leave you now to get acquainted and to eat. I am called Dagda and from the age of seven until I was thirteen my father used me as his wife.'

They assumed she was smiling because they saw her teeth. 'Scathagh's first rule is this,' she went on. 'Each candidate must know the reason why the others are here. You won't start healing until

117

you've exposed your wound to the Mother's good clean air. So start talking.'

She left them.

Finn, who was nearest the door, saw her return up the flight of steps to the doorway landing and then up another flight which disappeared into the trapdoor of a gallery running the circuit of the walls, its roof flush with the top of the tower, and which, she assumed, was where Scathagh lurked.

There was silence when she'd gone. Finn stared across at the Hy Fiachrach girls who, because of their fair hair and skin, were easier to distinguish, and they stared back. She recognised herself in their blank faces; de-sensitised bits and pieces of humiliated women.

It was the other one, whom Dagda had called Aragon, who spoke in a burst of indignant, foreign syllables. Finn understood one word in three – there had been a nun at Fontevrault who had come from the Pyrenees, speaking a similar language.

'What did you say?' she asked in dog Latin.

'Ah,' said Aragon, pleased to have found some communication, however limited. 'What that man-thing say?' Though not by any means plump, she was better fleshed than the rest of them and, whatever had happened to her, retained twice as much life.

As best she could, Finn translated Dagda's little speech. Aragon approved of it. 'Now I tell,' she said. 'But when we eat?' Finn shrugged. However, Aragon's need to tell somebody who she was and what had befallen her, overcame hunger and for the next half hour she did so. Finn comprehended enough to translate for the others. Stripped of Aragon's considerable elaboration, and the comic element introduced by her terrible Latin, the story was stark.

Soon after her wedding to an Aquitainian sea-trader, she had accompanied her husband on one of his regular voyages to Galway. (The town of Galway was so well known to the people of southern Europe that Aragon was still under the apprehension that Galway was the name of the country and Connaught merely one of its towns.) North of the Bay of Biscay her husband had fallen inconveniently ill and, equally inconveniently, died. Robbed of their master the crew which, according to Aragon, consisted of the sweepings of several nations, had decided to make both his ship and his widow their own. When Aragon wasn't having to cook and clean for the crew she was being forced to sleep with them. 'Not nice,' she said fiercely to Finn.

Aragon's late husband had not only been the master of the ship, he had been its one experienced navigator and without him its course was erratic and managed to miss Galway altogether. When they had found themselves in a storm and drifting nearer to the wicked west of Ireland coastline, the crew had panicked and thrown Aragon overboard, thus ridding themselves of any evidence of their crimes against her and, they hoped, placating the god of the sea who didn't hold with having women on board a ship and had probably caused their problems in the first place. One of the men, more human that the others, had also chucked a barrel down into the sea and she had managed to spreadeagle herself on it.

As it turned out the crew had done her a favour. Aragon heard later that the ship had turned turtle further up the coast with the loss of all hands, though the ship itself was later salvaged by local seamen. Mary the Mother of God, hearing Aragon's prayers, had brought her safely ashore where she had been discovered by some fishermen and put into the keeping of the King of Connaught who, somewhat at a loss to know what to do with her – there would be no ships returning to Spain until the spring – but bound by the laws of hospitality to do something helpful for his guest, had sent her to Scathagh.

In Aragon's recital there was an angry refusal to give way to dreadful circumstances and Finn felt honour bound to respond to her courage by saying in return: 'As for me, I was a nun until a raiding party came to my convent and I was raped, after which the Church rejected me.'

A frisson of horror ran round the table, not just for the rape but for the sacrilege of the rape. It shook out of Tailltin an account of what had happened to her and her companions when their homes had been overrun by an Ulster war band – the Hy Fiachrach were a Connaught clan. Three of them, Tailltin, Muirna and Bevo, had been badly violated in public while the fourth, Niav, had escaped by hiding under some straw. But Finn saw even then that there was more hope of recovery for the three raped women than there was for Niav whose in-laws, brother, husband and baby had been burned to death in their house. 'And all she does now,' said Tailltin, 'is to beg God for those minutes back again so that she doesn't go and hide but stays to burn with them.'

There seemed nothing more to say, and the table became silent except for the gurgle of Aragon's stomach and her complaints of hunger.

It was the pretty girl Cuimne, beloved of the King of Connaught, whom Finn had met at Iogenán's rath, who brought them their supper. From the look of the food she had other things than cuisine on her mind – she slapped down a piece of bread in front of each of them and ladled onto it a skimpy portion of white beans and fish. 'Scathagh's rule,' she said pertly to Aragon, who growled discontent.

Obviously Scathagh's rule did not apply to Scathagh herself and Dagda. They watched Cuimne surmount the stairs up to the gallery with covered pots leaving behind an aroma of wine, meat, onions and wild mushrooms that made the pallid mess they had to eat seem even paler. Nobody, except Aragon, had the will to protest.

There were no candles or rushlights in evidence so as it got dusk they retired to the lean-to where six board beds had been laid out with skins for covering. Finn lay on hers in the darkness wondering whether misery shared was misery lessened, decided it wasn't and eventually fell asleep. In the night Niav woke up screaming, jerking the others out of their own nightmares. Tailltin held her while the other four impotently patted her pillow and made noises of sympathy. The usual phrases of comfort, like 'Never mind,' 'It'll be better in the morning,' were inappropriate. Aragon muttered what sounded like a prayer, but prayer had availed them nothing before and it didn't look like doing so now.

Dawn seemed reluctant to heave itself over the edge of the tower roof and down into the courtyard but while it was still doing it, Dagda had hauled the academy's candidates out of their beds, given them a bucket of ice-cold water to wash in and told them to forage in the kitchen lean-to for their breakfast. Cuimne had gone – she only came over to the island in the evenings – and they found nothing but stale bread, stale ale and the remains of last night's beans and fish to sustain them. Aragon was still grumbling when Dagda lined them up in the courtyard.

'Scathagh's second rule is this,' she said, 'that all candidates be proficient at handling a *curragh*.' When Finn had translated this information, Aragon grunted: 'At least we sail off this damn place.'

But it wasn't as easy as that. First the *curraghs,* one larger than the other, had to be hauled into the centre of the courtyard and greased. When Dagda lifted the lid off the vat containing the grease, lanolin squeezed from sheep's wool, a new element entered their lives – its smell. It was appalling and it was to live with them in varying degrees of intensity for the next few weeks as if they had been joined by a loud, pestering, aggressive personality which accompanied them to bed, slept with them and got up with them in the mornings. They were made to scoop it out with cloths and slap it on to the oxhides which covered the frame of the boats and work it into every inch of the leather. When they'd done the outside they had to prop the curraghs upside down on blocks so that they could crawl underneath and do the same to the bone-white ash cagework of spars that were the boats' frail-looking skeletons, rubbing it into the wood and making sure that every leather tie which lashed the frame together was supple with it.

The lanolin permeated their skin, their hair, their clothes and, it seemed, their nostrils while Dagda's voice dominated their ears, urging them to work harder and faster, pointing out sections which remained ungreased. The five Irishwomen obeyed her because they were too spiritless not to; when she didn't order them they stopped moving and stared into space. Aragon obeyed her out of solidarity with the others and because even she was intimidated, not by Dagda, whom she loathed, but by the unseen presence that lived in the upper gallery. Each one of them had the unnerving feeling of being watched by some body or thing overhead.

None of them had worked so hard for a long time; even so, Niav screamed in her sleep again that night. It did no good to comfort her, yet to leave her uncomforted was against humanity. It was also against sleep, which they all needed. The next morning, fetching buckets of water from the lake, they found that some Good Samaritan had left bread and a pot of honey outside on the tower steps. As they breakfasted on it Finn said: 'Perhaps we should take it in turns. Each night we'll delegate one of us to sit with the one who's having bad dreams. Let's face it, it isn't just you, Niav – we all have them.'

It was the beginning of what became known as nightmare patrol, a simple holding of hands in the darkness. It was also the beginning, though they didn't realise it at the time, of a group identity.

The next day they hoisted the *curraghs* up to the tower entrance, manoeuvred them through it and down on to the lake, which was achieved without damage to the precious leather skins, despite the tendency of the boats to swing round in the wind as if intent on their own destruction.

'This,' said Dagda, 'is where you landlubbers become sailors.' They looked at her with what, if they'd had more mental energy, would have been dislike. There was something artificial about Dagda; her lofty way of treating them, her delight in her superiority, were like a child showing off. She swaggered her energy in contrast to their lethargy, over-acted her sighs at their obtuseness, shouted her orders unnecessarily loudly, all as if she were trying to gain the approval of that the unseen presence the gallery towards which her every move was directed.

For the next two weeks they were either cold and wet or, while they were rowing, hot and wet. Dagda drove them like a galley slavemaster up and down the lake as they tried to get the strange, bladeless oars of the *curraghs* in and out of the water in some form of unison. They caught endless crabs, falling backwards to hit their aching backs on the thwart behind them. If it hadn't been for the lanolin which permeated them and the oars themselves their hands would have been skinned. When they had achieved something like proficiency at rowing, they were taught to sail, raising and lowering the single leather sail of the bigger *curragh* at the mooring by the holm until they felt they could do it in their sleep, and then finding out that it was a very different matter to do it out on the lake with the wind bucketing them through the water at speed, the steering oar refusing to respond to their inexperience and the lakeside coming up fast. The boat would have been torn into scraps by the limestone rocks which surrounded the margins of the lake had Dagda not chosen a section of Lough Mask edged thickly with reeds which acted as a buffer, though it was back-breaking work to get the boat out of them once it had lodged itself in.

All this time the lake itself stayed aloof as if disassociating itself from these blunderers; remaining grey, blustery and without personality. Swans stretched their necks and paddled frantically to take off out of the *curraghs'* erratic progress, while ducks and geese lifted out of the reeds in their hundreds, squawking at the disturbance.

They were in a limbo, neither depressed nor happy, and too busy to care either way. They had no wish to win Dagda's approval by doing well, but they longed to spite her and so did as well as they could anyway, working as a team against her. Eventually they could bring a boat inshore between rocks, as long as the rocks weren't too close together. The day even came when, after they'd returned from the lake for the night, Dagda reluctantly announced: 'Scathagh says you can sail by yourselves tomorrow. And I say you can go and fetch the peat from the other side of the lake. Nice little job. Try not to capsize, we need to keep warm this winter.' She made a 'so there' face at them.

'*Non Scathagh est*,' said Aragon as they sat round the table waiting for food, and repeated in the Irish she was acquiring: 'There is no Scathagh.' It was a favourite topic of speculation that Scathagh was a myth, a ruse invented by Dagda to gain gifts from the local people and keep themselves as slave labour. They didn't really believe it – there was a terrifying authority radiating from the gallery – but it enabled them to be scurrilous about whatever-it-was up there that Dagda went to at nights.

'That bloody Dagda,' said Muirna suddenly. 'Personally, I can't understand what her father saw in her.'

For a second they were appalled, and then a release of guilt gushed out of them like water bursting a dam. Upstairs Dagda heard the screams of laughter and pouted, but she nodded to a huge shape in the corner which nodded back. 'They're ready.'

Having spent the next day in cold rain transporting enough turves to last the winter from the drying-stacks on the far side of the lake, the candidates were mutinous by dinner time, despite the sense of achievement brought on by having handled the *curragh* successfully without Dagda. The food Cuimne gave them at night had not varied since their arrival in either its constituents or its quantity, despite the enlargement of their appetites. Tonight, as ever, beans and fish was their portion, their small portion. 'Jesus, Cuimne,' said Bevo, 'there was a haunch of venison on the steps this morning. What happened to it?'

'Scathagh's rule,' said Cuimne, as she always did. They were kept from lynching her by a departure from the norm; this time, after she'd served them, Cuimne drew up a big, beautifully-carved chair from the shadows to the table, put another, slightly smaller, next to it and in front of both places set a large, covered pot from which steamed nutritious smells. 'Scathagh is joining you for dinner,' she said.

Now the moment had come they were reluctant to face it, and none of them turned round to see what caused the tower to reverberate from the footsteps coming down from the gallery. A shadow blocked out the doorway and a figure passed round the table to the carved chair, exuding such a crushing sense of weight that they ducked as it went by in case it should fall on them.

If some blinded, inept Titan had been told what a woman looked like without actually seeing one, he might have carved his block of stone into something like Scathagh; a ball of a head with one side flat for a face balancing directly onto a square body of which the protuberances were immense breasts and belly, all held up on tree-trunk legs. Grey, frizzled hair still striped with red stood up out of the head in a shock that was alarming. Eye holes had been gimleted into the face and out of them shone wicked intelligence which, at the moment, was concentrated on the tureen before it.

Dagda helped her into the chair, took her own seat and lifted the lid of the pot to reveal a rich stew of venison with dumplings floating in aromatic gravy. Reverently she helped Scathagh to a huge portion. Besides the giantess Dagda looked inadequate and masculine; for all her hideousness, Scathagh was feminine, or at least a travesty of the feminine. Finn was reminded of the Thing Boniface had once seen on the abbey wall of Kildare.

They forgot to eat in watching Scathagh eat. She speared a hunk of venison onto her knife and shoved it in her mouth. Their eyes followed the gravy as it dribbled down her chin, seeing it as human blood; there was something reminiscent of cannibalismin in the way Scathagh chomped.

When at last she spoke that too was a shock; her voice was a rich contralto and only accentuated the terror of her appearance, as if she'd ripped it out of somebody else's throat. 'Good evening,' said Scathagh, 'Are you enjoying your training?'

It was eventually Aragon who had the courage to say 'No,' and even she said it apologetically.

'You amaze me,' said Scathagh calmly, 'What's wrong with it?'

There was silence except for the sound of chewing from Scathagh's mouth; Aragon's courage had run out.

'Perhaps you don't like the food,' went on the beautiful voice, 'or you feel you are slaves?'

They could hear through the open door the whiffling wings of hundreds of white-fronted geese spiralling down to their night retreat on the marshes of the lake, laughing to each other as they descended.

'You're right,' nodded Scathagh, 'You are slaves, but not mine; you belong to the men who attacked you. For them the night they did what they did to you is over, long forgotten. But you don't forget. You go on paying them tribute, still serving them, watching the dead die, raping yourselves, mouthing the parts they put in your faces, loyally bleeding from the sword hilts or whatever it was they shoved up your private parts.'

Tailltin's hands clenched on the table and Finn put hers over them.

'Diddums,' said Scathagh, horribly. 'Have I brought it back to you then? Might it be that in these past weeks you have betrayed your masters and forgotten their crime for a moment? Did you dare laugh last night? How could you? Is that how you repay your attackers?' She put her head down to her dinner. Dagda, who never took her eyes off her, helped her to another portion.

'I see,' said Finn, slowly. 'Isn't there an easier way?'

'Probably,' said Scathagh with her mouth full, 'but I don't know what it is.'

As it got dark Dagda fetched candles and placed them so that Scathagh's face was lit from below, disembodying it, making pits out of her eyes. The lovely voice which seemed to come from elsewhere spoke in Irish but with an accent, though neither then nor later did any of her candidates try to work out what it was. Analysis stopped at Scathagh. She just was. None of them, not even Finn, ever doubted that she was eternal or a representative of the eternal. Had she dropped dead in front of them they would have waited for an exactly similar replacement to come from some reservoir in the earth that spawned Scathaghs, a place that had existed before God took over the world and would go on existing long after He was dead. She never explained anything about herself or where that place was and they never asked. It was irrelevant. Part of it was deep within themselves.

'Your real training begins tomorrow,' she told them. 'Would you like some nice meat for your supper afterwards?'

'Yes, Scathagh,' they said.

Scathagh heaved herself to her feet. 'Then kill it.'

'It's simple,' smirked Dagda. 'See that rock sticking out of the water? I call it Aragon. Watch.' She fitted a pebble into a leather socket which had been sewn between two thongs, held the ends of the thongs in her hand and whirled the sling faster and faster round her head. The

124

sound was lethal and instinctively the group ducked. One of the thongs was released from Dagda's fingers and almost simultaneously splinters flew out of the rock thirty yards away. 'Now you do it.'

Still puffing – they had already run five miles – they were stationed well apart on the lakeside so as not to kill each other. Dagda made them run to retrieve their pebbles from the water and run back with them. At midday they collapsed into despondent heaps for a meal of bread crusts and water before the afternoon session with the javelin which they had to run to retrieve after each throw and run back with. In the evening they ran five miles back to the *curragh*, leaving the Aragon rock untouched. And there were still beans and fish for dinner. 'Tut tut,' said Scathagh, as she carved into a goose pie.

On the third day Aragon lost her temper and rushed at Dagda screaming and punching, and found herself whirling through the air onto her back. 'When you can do that to me,' said Dagda, 'you can have sausage for breakfast.'

The runs to and from the training ground became longer, but on the other hand the Aragon rock was becoming pitted. The lake, too, was relenting to them, becoming a still freezing, but perky blue. Lough Mask now so dominated their lives that it, rather than the weather, seemed to have brightened. However, the nearer they got to the prospect of a good meat meal, the more terrible it became that they didn't get one.

One night Aragon screamed across the table: 'You are a wicked old woman to treat us like this.' She used her own tongue, but it was still a daring thing to do. Finn had pleasure in translating, with her own embellishments. Scathagh didn't look up from her trough. 'Dagda, open the door.'

The cold night air came in to the hall and they could hear the night sounds of the lake. 'Go, or bear it,' said Scathagh.

'But I have nowhere to go.'

'Then bear it.'

Two days later two stones, one from Aragon's sling and one from Bevo's, brought down a crane, 'because,' as Muirna said, enviously, 'it was too big for them to miss.' On their run home along the lakeside they carried it strung on a pole between them as if it were a full-grown stag. Scathagh gave them some of her own dinner and made the two slingers stand on the table afterwards to ululate in triumph. 'Louder,' she said to them, 'Gloat louder.'

The next day Finn and Muirna brought down a pelican. They scrambled into the water to spear it as it flapped its one unbroken wing. 'God I'm sorry,' Finn told it, 'but it's you or beans.' That night she and Muirna stood on the table and howled like banshees.

As their food improved the training became more intensive. They were running twenty miles a day, practising with the sling and javelin and now, as an evening extra, they learned combat – Dagda taught them wrestling and the rudiments of sword-fighting while Scathagh herself initiated them into a mystery she called her 'Ploys', which left them bruised but exhilarated.

Somehow Art was brought in as horse-master, and every second day he and six Connemara ponies were waiting for them at the training ground. In the races and jumping Finn was undoubtedly head of the class, but even she balked at the steed leap. 'It's a simple matter,' Art told them, 'You can all get up on a horse, so what's the difference if the little creature's moving while you do it?'

'The difference is we kill ourselves,' said Aragon. 'What is the use of all this?' For days the ponies cantered up and down with sad patience while the candidates, running, clutching, slipping, swearing, tried to thump themselves onto their backs until Finn managed a run and jump that swung her body up by her hands only. The ferocious competition which was beginning to prevail among them gave the others desperation and soon they could all do it. They swaggered into hall for supper as if they had personally overcome the Brown Bull of Cooley.

Only Aragon questioned the good of what they were doing, and that doubt emerged from her dislike of Dagda; she was afraid the end result would be that she'd grow to resemble 'the man-thing' as she called Scathagh's lieutenant. 'She is turning us into men,' she said. 'I do not want to be a man.'

'Nor do I,' Bevo told her, 'but I'm beginning to feel their equal.'

The other doubter was Niav, or rather it was the group that doubted on her behalf. Although she took a willing part in all the exercises and lessons, genuinely doing her best, the depression, which now left the others for days on end, still emanated from her. However hard she tried she never managed to hit anything with her javelin or slingstones and therefore never had a truimph. The others covered up for her as best they could yet the fact that Scathagh never remarked on Niav's deficiency in bringing back game, and doled her out as much food as the rest, was vaguely chilling.

Two riders breasted the hill above the upper end of Lough Mask and paused to look down on it. The taller and darker of the two said something in poetic Irish of which the other only grasped the words: 'Lake of my heart and my love.'

'It's pretty,' admitted Sir John of Sawbridge.

' "Pretty"'? Have you Normans no soul?' asked Ruairi, King of Connaught.

'Not a lot when it comes to swimming bloody freezing lakes just to get at a girl.'

'Have you seen the Partraige women? The eyes and skin of them? And this one's borne me a son I haven't seen yet.'

Sir John shook his head. The way Irish nobles accepted a baby as theirs just because the mother said it was never failed to amaze him, especially as the child then appeared to have equal rights with a legitimate heir. For him it'd be a damn good reason for swimming in the opposite direction. However, he liked the O'Conor. They were both of an age and the difference in their cultures had set up an exotic camaraderie. The days spent hunting and visiting various clans had given him valuable insight into the Irish mind. And the two of them had wenched on a scale which could well provide the young king with several more heirs. The sexual complaisance of Irish girls, even well-born ones, was another source of amazement, not that he was complaining.

Now Ruari had sent back most of the large retinue with which they'd been travelling – 'I have an agreement with Iogenán not to cess too many of my household on him,' – and had come, with only twelve men, the minimum with which an Irish king could travel with honour, for what Sir John thought of as 'a couple of days of rumpty-tumpty' with his Partraige girl, Cuimne.

'Will you take her back to court with you?'

'And lose the romance of swimming out to her island? And me with too many wives already, not to mention a queen riddled with jealousy?' Ruairi O'Conor shouted orders to the men coming up behind them. 'Tell Iogenán with my compliments that I'll attend on him later and will he forgive a young man's ardour.'

'I've got a call of my own to make first.'

'Ah, your loony.' The O'Conor rolled his eyes and made upward thrusts with his clenched fist.

'Nothing like that,' said Sir John, stiffly, 'I have a proprietary interest in the woman. You Irish pagans don't recognise Norman chivalry when you see it.'

'Forgive us. Where did you acquire her did you say?'

'Kildare.'

'And she speaks Norman French?' The king was reflective: 'Interesting.'

'As much as she speaks anything, poor soul. Why?'

'Nothing.' Ruairi O'Conor applied his spurs and turned to wave. 'Give her a bit of chivalry from me.'

As if glued together horse and rider galloped down the hill track, across the flat and into the lake. Sir John watched the young king lie along the horse's neck, urging him through the grey water towards one of the islands. 'Fat lot of use he'll be when he gets there,' he said to himself, 'with his balls frozen off. Buggered if I'd do that for a woman.' Sedately, he trotted down towards the house of Niall of the Poems.

Blat was standing outside her gate, spinning.

'God save the work,' said Sir John, who knew the form now.

Blat looked up. 'Is it yourself, Pilgrim? Come in and have a warm.' There was some element of respect absent from the way she treated him, Sir John felt. However, she was a good woman and hospitable. He lowered his head when he got to the door of the house and entered, encountering the remembered smell of hens, turf smoke, humans and herbs. He greeted Niall's mother and looked around. 'How's my loo . . . my Lady Finola?'

'Gone.'

'Gone?'

'Gone.'

'Where? Did she leave word for me?' Had the woman left no broken sentence of thanks? No tearful expression of gratitude for his kindness? All he wanted was recognition of what he had done for her; that he hadn't had it left him peculiarly unfulfilled.

'She's gone to Scathagh to be healed.'

'Where's Scathagh?'

Sir John spent the next days sulking. He went hunting, played chess with Iogenán and diced with the young men of Iogenán's household, refusing their suggestions that he join them in a game of hurling, considering it an over-energetic form of suicide. But mostly he watched the lake. In this he was not alone. Lough Mask was a mirror to which the hills and all those who lived on them were the Narcissus. Blat did her spinning facing towards it, children played on its edge, households looked out on it first in the mornings, the herdsmen of the flocks piped to it and the peat-cutters in the bogs leaned on their turf-spades in the direction of the beautiful time-waster. There were cold nights when wolves were outlined against the moon on the hilltops staring towards the water as if it were the floor of some great amphitheatre and they were waiting for a play to begin.

Sir John was impatient of mystery unless it was in church and he resented the lake for an enigma which was feminine and therefore pagan, for whatever rites women were performing on those scattered islands to which men swam out and did not return – the O'Conor hadn't been seen for two days. He especially resented his role as spectator; in the world he knew it was men who acted and women who watched and that was how he liked it. He wanted women on the sidelines, admiring men's prowess in tournament and war, binding up men's wounds, listening to male talk, laughing at male jokes, with no other return than having a roof kept over their heads, on occasional baby and a brief acknowledgement of their damned needlework. That's what women were – an audience.

But still he watched the lake.

*   *   *

Cuimne disappeared. 'Frolicking with her royal lover,' spat Dagda. The preparation of the food, of which there was now abundance, improved because it was taken over by Blat, who moved into the tower in preparation for her divorce. 'Is it yourself?' she asked in amazement when she saw the thin, weatherbeaten, athletic Finn. Finn picked her up and swung her round. 'I don't think it is.'

At dinner Scathagh said: 'We're being watched. Who is it?'

The group shrugged. Unusually, after the meal was over, Scathagh summoned Finn up to her gallery while Dagda was left, jealous, down in the hall. 'Who is the watcher?' she asked.

'How should I know, Scathagh?'

'You know. Who is it?'

Finn gave in; the woman was all-knowing. 'It's the one who brought me here to the lake. He watches when I go over to my island to see to my horses.'

'Are you afraid of him?'

'Yes.' It was a different fear from any other, but fear was what it was. Somewhere, long ago, she had seen him before.

'Then he's your challenge.' Each of the group was being set the task of facing something they dreaded. Scathagh said it was time for them to act as individuals. Tailltin and Muirna, who were scared of heights, were set a rock face to climb; Bevo had to leap through fire, Aragon to unleash the smith's dog, which was renowned for its ferocity; Niav, easily intimidated by the male establishment, was made to walk up to the house of Baccaugh and tweak the priest's nose. 'That child worries me,' said Scathagh. 'Keep an eye on her.'

Sir John gained some information, though not much, in Iogenán's hall from men who guarded the Scathagh mystery at second-hand. 'It's nothing at all, nothing at all,' they told him, easily, 'just an old custom that's nearly died out. From the old days.' And when they said old days, he discovered, they really meant old, long before history had begun in Europe. 'A sort of last resort for women who've been, well now, damaged in some way. No use to anyone, a healing place. Scathagh heals them. Just a custom. A thing for women.'

And as for Scathagh . . . 'Ah well, she's just a lady.' But when Aengus, Iogenán's hereditary story-teller, was recounting the legend of Cuchulainn, Sir John's ears pricked up at the name of Scathagh Buanand as the head of some Pictish military academy. Sir John leaned over to Iogenán: 'Is that the Scathagh down on the lake?'

The king's face wrinkled even more and he wheezed. 'She'd be older than God if it were. But an ancestress, I dare say. There's always been a Scathagh.'

About his loony he learned no more than Blat had told him. She had gone to Scathagh to be healed, though she now also had an island of her own on which she kept the two horses she'd brought with her. He knew they knew more than that; some knowledge about her had seeped through and been absorbed by those of her blood like a staining fluid to which he, an alien, was resistant.

The next day he asked the porter at Iogenán's gate: 'Which is Scathagh's island?'

'Are you meaning Inis Cailleach? That one,' and the man pointed to the island with the stone tower.

Sir John was puzzled by the word 'Cailleach' which had two meanings as far as he knew: 'a nun' and 'a hag'. The porter had used it as if it were some combination between the two.

'And Swan Island?'

'That one.'

Boats sailed or paddled by women left the one with the tower each morning and made their way to the opposite side of the lake which, being less hospitable than the east side, was virtually deserted, though what they did there was unknown. Every now and then, before it got dark, a single boat would leave Inis Cailleach for Swan Island, but he couldn't make out who was in it, except that she was alone.

On the third evening a horse with John of Sawbridge on its back galloped into Lough Mask and swam towards Swan Island.

It was as freezing as he'd thought it would be and getting the horse up the frosted steps from its tiny holm wasn't easy either.

The island was small and through some trees he could see a turf fire burning near a couple of huts. A thin figure stood between him and the light and a voice as cold as his feet said: 'What do you want?'

Sir John led his horse round the ungrateful bitch and towards the fire so that she had to turn to the light and he could see her face which, now that the eyes were more sensible and alive, was better than he remembered it. A familiar mare whinnied at him from a stable door. 'Can I put my horse in there?'

'No you can't. She's in foal and yours is a stallion and anyway you're not stopping.'

'Don't you remember me? I'm the one who . . .'

'I know who you are.'

'Then you're an ingrate. The poor beast's shivering and going back would kill him, not to mention me.'

She walked over to a straw bale and chucked some handfuls towards him. 'Rub him down with that and put him near the fire and when he's warm, leave.'

'That's the last time I get the nits out of your hair.'

As he rubbed the horse down, he watched her fetch water from the lakeside in a bucket and pour it into a cauldron over the fire. She was younger than he'd thought she was, and too thin for any kind of beauty and her skin had become brown with too much weather and when he'd finished rubbing down the horse he walked round the fire and took her in his arms and kissed her which, he realised, was why he'd come to the damned island in the first place.

She went stiff as a board and hissed at him. He heard her say: 'It's all right, Art,' and realised the gargoyle was with them on the island. He let her go. She stepped back, a look of concentration on her face, brought her hands palm together in front of her as if she were praying, and jabbed them into his sternum, bringing her knee up at the same time.

When he was next able to notice anything but pain she was standing over him, regarding her hands. 'It works. Wait till I tell them.' She smiled at him for the first time of their acquaintance. 'That was Scathagh's Ploy Number One.'

'Was it?'

With something like sympathy, Art helped him back on his horse and whacked its rump until it went into the lake. It was even colder on the way back, but his balls hurt too much for him to notice it.

It wasn't in him to think that he deserved her attack, and if there was one thing in the world he loathed more than any other it was humiliation, but the odd thing was that, when he'd recovered, he found himself thinking of the woman with what he regarded as Christian forbearance. 'She's still lunatick, poor cow,' he said to himself.

Later that night, in the stone tower on the lake, Finn stood on the table in barbaric triumph. 'It works. Scathagh's Ploy Number One got him. Hear me and the kisses I gave him.'

But afterwards, summoned to the gallery again, Scathagh told her privately: 'It didn't work. You're still afraid of him.'

The gallery was always cold because Scathagh, insulated in her layers of fat, refused to have the shutters closed. She liked, she said, to be able to watch the approaches to her island. Finn wrapped herself more closely in the cloak Blat had woven for her and sat in the recess of the outer wall, looking out through the arrow slit at the west side of the lake where the sun was going down.

She was deflated. You never could lie to Scathagh. 'I know I am. I don't know why.'

'Sex,' said Scathagh. 'You're attracted to him.'

Finn looked round sharply. 'You're mad. Don't you know why I'm here?'

Scathagh shrugged. 'They say that sometimes sex with a man can be beautiful.'

'Not in my experience.'

131

'Nor in mine,' said Scathagh, amazing Finn who tried to envisage her in the clutch of a man, and failed. 'But I think we must both realise that our experience was limited. Niav mourns her husband.'

'But I could never be dependent on a man for my life. I'm worried about Niav.'

The birds on the lake had settled down now that it was getting dark, just a moorhen called from its nest in the reeds. The silence of Scathagh's massive shape was magnetic, a one-way pull that attracted words towards her. 'It isn't that anyway,' said Finn, in response to the pull. 'The Pilgrim's instrusive.' Whether he was attractive to her or not, and she didn't feel he was, there was an extra maleness about him which belonged to the Continent, to Leinster, to all the world she had known, but which didn't belong here. 'He's, I don't know how to put it, he's a sort of conqueror, an owner. He wants to possess things. And here, it isn't like that.' Here, on the lake, was the epicentre of a female world, ringed about by the Partraige's regard for women, and outer-ringed by the tolerance of the O'Conors. Connaught, if it assumed a human persona, would be a woman.

She went on, trying desperately to express it properly, 'It's as if all of us, Aragon, Muirna, me, have been wounded in the front line of a war that's being fought everywhere else but here. It's a war by men on women, as if they hated us. But here Blat can gain a divorce because Niall doesn't treat her properly, I can be given land and a place in my clan that makes me independent. Sometimes I feel this is the real Ireland, a feminine thing. Perhaps I feel that because it's vulnerable.'

Scathagh heaved herself to her feet and looked down at Finn, then out through the arrow slit to the lake. 'It is the last place of the Mother,' she said, 'and it is vulnerable. One of these days somebody will come along to try and rape it.'

'Can't we protect it?'

'We must.'

Finn had another visit from a man during one of her trips to Swan Island. The first she knew of him was when a voice behind her said gently: 'Comarba?' For half a second she was back in an assured time when petitioners and God had hung on her every word. 'Yes?' she said, and turned round.

A dark and extremely good-looking young man smiled with satis-faction. 'I thought you were.'

So complete was the wall she had set up between the life of Boniface and this new life that, although she knew she'd seen him before, she had a reluctance to remember where. 'Who the hell are you? I warn you, I can protect myself.'

'So I hear. Actually, I was Ruairi O'Conor if you remember, and

132

now I am your *Rí Ruirech*, your overking, but don't bother to curtsey.'

'I won't.' Her nerves had been put on edge at being taken back to Kildare; the contrast between that life and this needed almost volcanic adjustment. Besides, in the time since she had first met him outside the walls of Kildare this young man had been fighting his brothers for power, and had won. She was out of sympathy with power.

'I ask your hospitality,' he said, and to that ancient command Finn responded. She ushered the king into her hut, seated him on a stool and offered him mead, a gift from the wife of her cousin, Nessa. And, despite everything, she found herself being charmed.

'I come to you incognito, if it is not against your honour,' he said, 'because I gather that you, too, are incognito. But I wished to pay my respects. Little did I think that day at Kildare that I was welcoming my cousin as well as the Comarba. After all, you are my kinswoman as well as the Partraige's and I look forward to the day when I can receive you into the *derbhfine* of the O'Conors. Just name the day and may it be soon.'

'Damn it,' thought Finn; she wanted to cry again. The Church had cast her out because she had been raped, yet these Irish of the west, also knowing she had been raped, were practically clamouring to claim her and show her honour.

'Shall I reinstate you as Comarba?' Either the king was drunk on her mead or his own youth and power, 'I can do it, you know. I shall beat Ulster and I shall beat Dermot of Leinster. And when Dermot pays reparation for joining in this war against me, he'll pay reparation to you, by God.'

'Would you excuse me a moment?' asked Finn. She went outside the hut, leaned against its wall and breathed in cold air. Go back? Reincarnate herself? Flaunt a greater power than Dermot's? Make everything all right again? She looked out on a prospect where she was in the church of Kildare again with Dermot in the congregation, beaten, because the filth he had employed the last time they had been there together had sprayed back on him and left her untouched, inviolable, immaculate.

But it hadn't left her untouched and the view wasn't Kildare, it was a provincial lake, a backwater, haunted by birds and a people who were so obsolete that they gave women rights. She slipped her feet out of the calfskin boots Iogenán had ordered his hereditary boot-maker, who was also his cowman and part-time cook, to make for her. She wiggled her toes which had splayed and become calloused underneath with all the running she had been doing. Her feet had grown these past months, along with her understanding of things. They couldn't again be cramped into the enamelled slippers of St. Brigid. They were too big.

Anyway, bless him, the O'Conor couldn't reinstate her. The Church would never let him; he just liked to think that he could, or wanted her to think that he could. But it had been a very nice offer, a very nice offer indeed.

She went back in the hut and poured the king some more mead. 'No,' she said, 'But thank you.'

'Moved on?'

She sat down opposite him. 'How did you learn so much about women?'

He grinned at her. 'I like them. I thought the first time I saw you that you were too good to be a nun.'

'Women should be in bed or in the kitchen?'

'What's wrong with that? But if I just thought that, I should shut down Scathagh's academy.'

'Why don't you?'

He gave a shout of laughter: 'Good God, woman, my army isn't big enough.' Then he sobered up. 'So what will you do? Marry? I can find you a good husband if you want one.'

'Thank you,' said Finn, 'I shall never marry.' Abruptly she told him what she had told nobody else. 'I have to learn two things, and then we shall see. I have to learn to kill and to write.'

The king of Connaught blinked. 'I gather Scathagh is teaching you the first; why the second?'

She leaned forward. 'On their way to the Council of Mellifont some of the churchmen from Leinster and Munster called in at Kildare. Among them were the annalists from some of the great abbeys of Southern Ireland. I asked Sister Aine to find out from the monks what they had written against the date when Dermot invaded Kildare and had me raped. Some of them mentioned the attack on the abbey, though they didn't mention me. The abbeys which were in Dermot's pocket didn't even mention the attack. The chronicle of Waterford, for instance, contained only the fact that the hazel nut harvest had been exceptional that year.'

Ruairi worked on it. 'They'd written you out.'

'Yes.' The Word of Man.

'I see.'

She was warmed that he did. Here, sitting in front of her, was a human being who encapsulated the spirit of the country which had given her refuge and which she had come to love. Whatever he did he was the supreme leader of all Connaught, whose luck was his people's luck, who brought good harvest with his own fertility, the bridegroom of his land. The fact that he was probably still warm from the bed of Cuimne, a plougher of that pretty little earth, reinforced his symbolism to Finn. 'He fought against his brothers like a dog,' came the far-off voice of Boniface. 'Nobody's perfect,' answered her Partraige ancestors, 'He is our king of kings. Right or wrong you're stuck with him because in him is two thousand years of this country's birth and death, earth and water.'

Finn felt herself surrendering herself to him as his subject, prepared, like a good subject should be, to fight for him and the great tolerance he stood for. But she applied a last test.

'What do you think of Cuimne's baby?' she asked. Against one of Scathagh's strictest rules, Cuimne had one day brought her baby son for the candidates on Inis Cailleach to see. Dagda had hustled them both out quickly, but not before Finn had glimpsed the child. As with some of the other candidates, she found the sight of babies distressing. Cuimne's was a fine baby boy, but flawed in having one of his hands completely covered by a birthmark as if it had been accidentally dipped in a mauve adhesive. Cuimne explained away the blemish as the result of ill-wishing by O'Conor's queen, who was jealous of her and her child.

If Ruairi O'Conor was a man whose children had to reflect his own pride in himself, he would be ashamed of it.

The O'Conor beamed. 'A son fit for a king,' he said, 'I shall call him Cathal of the Wine Red Hand.'

Finn went down on her knees and pressed her cousin's hand to her forehead. 'My lord,' she said, 'If there is any way I can ever help you, I shall do it.' In the end you opted for what goodness you could get.

O'Conor took her homage pleasantly. 'Regard the help as mutual. Are you going to see my friend the Pilgrim again, incidentally?'

'Don't you trust him, my lord,' said Finn. 'I've seen him before somewhere. I don't remember where, but he's not trustworthy.'

'I like him,' said the king, 'and he certainly likes you.' He was intrigued by how intrigued John was with this strange young woman who had once held one of the greatest positions in the land, not knowing who she was. He wished they could get together. Ruairi liked his subjects to be happy, their sexual pleasure enhanced his own, and an unsatisfied woman was an untidiness to be abhorred. He didn't believe in chastity.

Why it came to her then she was never sure, but Finn had a piercing and disturbing moment of perception into the O'Conor's character. He had fought for the kingship, but he lacked the statecraft necessary to to keep it in this modern world; his attention span on matters of importance would be limited, easily distracted by the minutiae of relationships, unable to concentrate on essentials. He would see things as he wanted them to be, just as he had offered her back the Comarbship without being able to deliver it. He was a light king, however lovely a man. Dermot was the bastard of all bastards but he was the weightier king.

135

It was an insight that made Ruairi vulnerable to her, just as the Partraige were vulnerable, but no less worth fighting for. He had come to her offering his protection, and they were ending up with her wanting to give him hers.

'Just take care, my lord,' she told him. She watched her king get into his *curragh* and row himself back to the island that contained Cuimne and her baby, taking with him much that was wrong and a great deal that was right with her country.

Seated in Iogenán's sweating-house in the bog, Ruairi O'Conor looked with interest at the pilgrim's chest. 'A nasty bruise.'

'I fell on a tree stump,' said John, carefully hiding other bruises, 'How much longer do we have to stay in here?'

'An hour.'

'Judas priest, I'll never stand it.' It was not only bloody hot, it was claustrophobic crouched here in stone hut which resembled nothing so much as a seven-foot coffin in which a fire had been burning.

'You'll never get the rheumatism. I'm away back to court, John. Will you come with me?'

'Wore you out, did she?'

Ruairi stretched. 'What a woman. But there's things to be done; Christmas court to hold, kingdoms to win and snow on the way. I can't afford to winter in Partraige country, pleasant as it might be.'

'When do you move against Ulster?'

'In the spring.'

'Can I come with you?' To observe an Irish war at first-hand would complete the information for Fitzempress.

The king of Connaught was touched. 'Pity on the poor MacLochlainn. We'll beat him by ourselves, the two of us.'

'I suppose I'd better stay here until then,' said John, casually, 'I promised Iogenán I'd Christmas with him, and I don't want to appear rude.'

'Nor would one want to miss battling with a mad woman.'

'Do you know what the mad bitch did yesterday? I happened to be trotting along the western side of the lake . . .'

'The bit where the Scathagh women go every day?'

'Near there. And she comes galloping up on that colt of hers – this is no word of a lie – and challenges me to a race. I have to say, O'Conor, that I am surprised at the way you allow your women subjects to carry on.'

'The Partraige have always been a law unto themselves. Did she win?'

'She certainly did not, though it was a bloody near thing. I had to go some. She rides like the bloody wind and the colt's got speed. I don't mind admitting, O'Conor, that one of the reasons I'm staying on is out of interest to see just how much madder she can get.'

'What other course could a sane man take?' asked the King of Connaught before being dragged into the grey outside air by his feet and thrown into a pond on which a film of ice was beginning to form.

The women from Inis Cailleach bowed to their Christian upbringing and filed up to church for Christmas Mass along a path that had been dug through snow. In his sermon Baccaugh the priest prayed for the people of Erin, and especially those of Leinster, to stop their sinning so that God would ameliorate this winter with which He was displaying His displeasure. John had already discovered that the people of western Ireland reacted with something like terror to frost and ice, as if they were not used to them – which, indeed, they were not. Their Hell was cold; eternal punishment for sin being not fire, but blocks of perpetual ice.

John kept his eye on the row of shawled heads which stood apart from the rest of the congregation. 'Which one's Scathagh?' he asked Niall.

'Ach, she won't be here. She never comes.'

'How can the priest allow that?'

Niall shrugged. 'Scathagh's a law to herself.'

An irritation with this Irish tolerance for aberrations of behaviour burst into anger in the breast of John of Sawbridge. It was an insult to God that some hag should be allowed to absent herself from His house, let alone teach women to fly in the face of their nature. Under the feudal system to which he belonged every man and every woman knew their place in the general good; they weren't allowed to wander at will out of the structure into some horrific cult left over from the Dark Ages. 'You're a decadent lot for all your charm,' he thought with contempt, 'and that's why we're superior to you and that's why one of these days we'll conquer you.'

He spent most of the Twelve Days of Christmas so drunk on Iogenán's mead that he missed the new development on Inis Cailleach in which Scathagh's pupils came ashore, carrying special spears and so wrapped in fur that they looked like bears, mounted the ponies that were kept for their use by the lakeside, and set off on expeditions into the Partraige mountains.

'Do you fancy a bit of wolf-hunting now?' Iogenán asked him, when the general hangovers were better. 'With this shite winter they'll be getting troublesome and we'll be needing to nip them in the bud.'

'I don't mind.' The wolf wasn't his favourite quarry but it might keep his mind off things for a bit, and he certainly owed Iogenán some return.

137

But just as they'd got their equipment together and were about to set off, Blat came running in through the gates and whispered something to Iogenán, who in turn whispered to his huntsmen, who spat and dismounted. John only managed to hear a couple of the words. Iogenán turned to him in apology: 'Maybe tomorrow,' he said, 'The wind's wrong now. Maybe tomorrow.'

John nodded. The wind was from the north as it had been for days. He watched the others return indoors and went down to the porter at the gate who, being tuppence short in the shilling, answered what he was asked.

'What's a *conoel*, Goll?'

'Wolf woman,' said Goll, crossing himself, 'and it's a hard night for it, a pity on the poor creatures.'

'Open that bloody gate.'

He charged through it on one of the ponies which still had wolf spears strapped to its side. He could see the small band trotting off from the lakeside and then fanning out to take separate paths because whatever it was they were going to do, they were going to face it alone like the empty-headed, half-baked, embarrassing bunch of amateurs they were. He knew his madwoman now, however she was dressed, and he kept under cover until she was well on her way and then followed. He could tell from her every movement that she was scared shitless, and well she might be.

After two hours along tracks which went higher and higher, he rounded a bend to find her in the middle of the way facing him with a spear at the ready. When she saw who it was she blew out her cheeks in relief and then straightened up. 'What the hell do you want?'

'If you're killing wolves you'll need somebody to watch your back.'

'One wolf. I've got to kill one wolf and I know exactly how I'm going to do it. Young man, you seem to be under the misapprehension that I need your help.'

'It's become a habit.'

'Well, break yourself of it. Go home.'

She set off and he set off – in the same direction. He heard her swear something disgusting in Irish and she turned round. 'If I let you come along, will you promise not to interfere? Just stay still?'

'Yes.'

'All right then.'

She'd gained confidence in the last weeks, he realised. That use of 'young man' had contained authority as well as being an attempt to distance herself from him. But he knew her; she was his quarry and, like a good huntsman, he was getting inside her – not as he wanted to get inside her, but it was a start – and he knew she was glad he was there. She'd been frightened on the journey up by the moaning of the wind, and the shadows. Her little superstitious Celtic brain had conjured up ice monsters, and her memory had resurrected whoever-it-was who'd sent her mad in the first place. Turning to face the steps coming up behind her hadn't been a bad example of courage.

They went on for another hour and then turned off the track into what, in summer, would have been a stretch of high pasture and was now a good place to break your ankle with hummocks and dips hidden under level snow. Towering above its north side was a crest of rock and nestling under the rock, with its opening to the south, was a beehive hut such as shepherds and herdsmen built for shelter. She took the spears out of the sheath on her pony and tethered its bridle under a stone. He did exactly the same. Carefully skirting the edge of the field so as not to leave footprints across it, and sniffing the wind, she made her way to a clump of small rocks which were within a short spear's throw of the hut door. He followed with some respect; whether this worked or didn't work, she'd certainly thought it out.

She threw a fur down under the rocks and sat on it, indicating a place for him. Pretending to stumble so that he could get nearer to her, he sat down.

'What now?'

'Keep your voice down. We wait. Put that at the back of your soul.' She handed him a flask, and he knocked back a fair bit of it. When she'd put her hand inside her furs to get the flask out he'd felt her body heat.

She began to whisper, telling him about the wolves which she'd been studying in preparation for this night; she said they weren't as dangerous as people thought they were, lived in family groups or some such nonsense. She wittered on while he went nearly mad every time she moved and he could smell her hair and skin. Whispering was evocative of bed. She must know what she was doing to him; all this lust couldn't be going in one direction – the good, male, red-blooded God wouldn't allow it. But he'd bide his time. He was a better hunter than she was.

'In bad winters like this one,' she was saying, 'they keep down their breeding by having only one she-wolf and one male mate in a family. The other males go celibate and suffer frustration.'

'I know how they feel,' thought John. He wasn't even put off her by hearing her talking in this detached way about such things.

'And that's why . . .'

From the rock crest, there came far-off sounds. When the man and woman turned over on their stomachs and looked up they could see flurries of snow and hear grunts. 'They're playing,' said Finn. 'In a minute they'll sing.'

And they did, three of them, outlined against the moon, sitting in a circle with their muzzles up in the air, howling to raise ancestral hairs on the back of John's neck.

Almost immediately there was a scrabbling inside the hut and a dog appeared in a doorway dragging on a rope around her neck to join in the howling.

'Isn't that Blat's bitch?'

'Half wolf herself, in season, and no better than she should be.' Finn's teeth showed in a grin that was lupine and John had a twinge of sympathy for the male beast that was going to come down from the crest in a minute.

It happened just as she'd planned it. A huge grey suitor came puzzling his way down the rocks in answer to the bitch's invitation, sniffing suspiciously, and made a wide arc round the western side of the field until he was some yards in front of the entrance with the bitch on heat pulling at her rope and egging him on every inch of the way.

Very slowly the woman stood up and raised her spear. The wind was in her favour and anyway the wolf was too interested in whatever the bitch was telling him to notice any other movement. 'Please, God,' prayed John, 'don't let her miss. For both our sakes, don't let her miss.'

The great, terrible shape against the snow sprouted a spear in its side, and John blinked. Somebody who knew how to do it had taught her to throw. The wolf rolled over and lay still, and the yelping of the bitch in the doorway turned into whines. The loony lifted her head and gave out the high, boastful, ululating yell he'd heard Celtic huntsmen vent when they'd killed. She ran forward, drawing a knife.

What wasn't in her plan and what she didn't see in her triumph was two slinking shapes coming towards her from John's side of the hut. He grabbed one of his own spears and threw it as he'd never thrown before, then bent down to pick up another, but the second wolf had run off. He went over and dragged his spear out of the body and stood between it and Finn, who was busy trying to saw her wolf's head off and had noticed nothing.

She looked up at him. 'Admit I'm a great hunter.' But her face was green-white in the moonlight.

'Never saw a better.'

She indicated her dead wolf. 'Can you do this? I've got to prove to Scathagh that I've succeeded, and the body would be too heavy for my horse.'

'Cut its tail off.'

'Of course.'

She boasted as they made their way home – the unfulfilled bitch running beside them. 'What a throw. Did you see it? Right in the heart. None of the Fianna could have done better, Cuchulainn couldn't have done better.'

Boastfulness was an unattractive trait in a woman, he decided, and he only wished it made her unattractive. 'What was this enterprise, an initiation of some sort?'

'An initiative test. And didn't I pass it?' She raised her arms over her head in barbaric acknowledgement of her own prowess, and then looked at him with patronage. 'You behaved well. Apart from one unfortunate lapse, you've been quite honourable. For a man.'

'Thank you.'

'I don't see why we can't be friends. Scathagh says friendship may be possible between a man and woman once the right terms have been established.'

'I'd like to meet Scathagh.'

They were nearly back at Lough Mask. She turned on her pony to look at him, and she actually laughed. 'You wouldn't. Believe me, you would not.'

Cold as he was, he stood on Iogenán's ramparts to watch her until she'd paddled her way to the island.

'We're to be just friends, are we?' he said to the dawn, 'Lady, if you think that, you're even madder than I thought you were.'

141

Chapter Six

Not all the candidates got their wolf on the same night that Finn got hers. Aragon and Bevo had both chosen Finn's method but the bitches they picked for the trap turned out to be seductive wash-outs, unable to tempt even the most sex-starved male wolf to his death. Bevo subsequently used Blat's bitch, this time successfully; Aragon resorted to the wolf-pit method that Niav and Muirna and Tailltin had decided on and, although it took time, there were eventually six wolf-tails ready to join the others won by previous candidates in the gallery of Hag's Island.

The celebration feast was uproarious. Iogenán had sent sides of pork and venison to the tower for Christmas, but with the wolf-hunt hanging over them none of the candidates had felt like eating, so the meat had been packed in ice to await this occasion.

Outside, the world had frozen hard. Blat had to crash a stave through the ice on the lake by the steps every morning to get water and to keep the ducks happy. But inside the hall there was warmth from peat fires, candles, good food and the knowledge that they had passed the second stage of their training with honours. Until Niav stood up and said: 'I'm sorry, it's no good.'

Scathagh, looking more horrendous than usual with a wolf's tail over one ear, stopped eating and the others put down their cups in the general dread of what the girl was going to say. They had become not so much a group as a pack, each one's welfare dependent on the others, able to sixth-sense what another would do under crisis circumstances – it had saved their lives more than once. Niav had always been the vulnerable one in it, but until now their group strength had managed to cover up for her. Their corporate mind had always contained in it the knowledge that the pack's increasing physical prowess merely reminded Niav that her baby would never grow up to know anything like it. Muirna put out her arms as if she would prevent Niav admitting what they all knew, but the girl moved away from her.

'It won't work,' she said. 'It nearly does, but then it goes again. I could manage everything if it weren't for my baby. Muirna killed my wolf for me. I didn't want to. I don't want anything except for this nothingness to stop.'

She went out. All eyes turned to Scathagh. 'What can we do?'
Scathagh shrugged and returned to her meal. 'Nothing.'

In response to a message from him Finn met her cousin, Nessa, on Swan Island – no man was allowed to visit Hags' Island, or wanted to.

Rare among the Partraige, Nessa was a worrier, a man concerned with correctness, who would pursue a detail until it dropped dead from exhaustion. He sat on a stool in Finn's hut, fidgeting and talking. She gathered, without him actually saying so, that war raged in his soul between pride that she had once been the Comarba of Kildare and shame that she had been brought so low.

He did not approve of Scathagh. 'Are you all right with her?' he asked, 'These survivals of the old days should be allowed to die out; it is not right that women should have to undergo such things. It gives them strange ideas.'

'Don't worry about me.'

'Would you be wanting to marry again, do you think? There are those who have approached me with a view to it.'

She was touched and amused. 'Really?' Then she paused: 'What do you mean – "again"?'

Nessa held out his long hands to the fire. 'We're not cut off here, Cousin, you know. I go to Dublin twice a year to trade hides for the *tuatha* with England and Normandy and, although I say it myself, I do not think that the Partraige have ever suffered through my dealing.'

'I am sure they have not.' His thin jawline was peculiarly muscled; Blat had once told her that Nessa believed food should go down to the stomach well masticated, and chewed each mouthful forty times.

'I hear things. And it is said – forgive me, Cousin, this is a matter of business and must be approached as such – that there was a priest present on that disgraceful night; words were uttered, there was a question of marriage . . .' It wasn't until he blanched that she knew how formidable she had become.

'I will not discuss this.'

'No, no, of course not. But, Cousin, rid your mind of the personal view and the circumstances. If it had been an ordinary rape . . . well, the man was an Englishman and I think, under English law, if we could produce the priest and prove the marriage – yes, I know you did not consent, but legally the man would be required to marry the woman. In the ordinary way.'

'Nessa, continue on this line and I'll take you by the neck and throw you into the lake.' The realisation that she probably could deflated some of her anger with the stupid little man.

But Nessa couldn't leave it. 'Don't you be distressed now; this is business. The man may have had goods which are rightfully yours.'

Nessa would lie awake at nights at the thought that any of his family were missing something to which they were entitled. 'I merely want to make enquiries on your behalf when I go to Dublin in the spring. I might even go to Bristol. He was a Bristol man, you know.'

'I don't want to know. Leave me alone.'

'But I think I must . . .'

'Oh, do what you bloody well like.'

Muirna and Finn were practising Scathagh's Ploy Number Six, only to be used in extreme circumstances, because it was lethal. Both of them were wearing iron collars. The others were practising wrestling with Dagda, who was being infuriating and saying things like: 'Can't you attack harder than that? When I want to be tickled to death I'll let you know.'

Then she said: 'What's the matter?' All five of the candidates had suddenly become still because they were only five.

'Where's Niav?'

'She was here a second ago.'

They moved, running for the steps to the tower door, which was open. Finn slipped and clawed to the top on her hands and knees. 'Please don't,' she was begging, 'Please don't.' She was saying it as they climbed down the still-swinging rope ladder. They saw Niav for a second standing on the steps which led directly to the hole in the ice before she went into it.

They flung themselves down, plunging their arms into the water to grab her when she should bob up again but Niav had kicked herself under the ice. They could see the green-white, blurred shape of her hands pressing against its underside to walk her away from them. Aragon ran for Blat's stave and began thudding it into the ice, following the movement underneath but the hands pressed determinedly on until they slowed and fell away and there was just a dark shadow, like a seal, rolling to show what might be a face and then rolling again in a current that took it deep into the lake.

The bell on the roof of Hag's Castle hadn't rung for help in ten years, but it rang now. 'There's one of the women under the ice,' reported Goll and Iogenán laid a hand on John's arm, though his own face was white. 'There is no need to rush, my son. She is dead at this minute.'

They knew the lake so well that after they'd questioned the man who'd brought the news, who'd had it shouted at him from the tower, they could estimate which current had taken the body and where it would be debouched. They gathered down at a backwater inlet a mile away under overhanging alders which striped it in the moonlight, and hammered at its ice until they had uncovered a long, black finger of water. After that there was nothing to do but wait. More flares were brought, somebody handed round ale. Baccaugh joined them, carrying his box of holy oil. 'Was it an accident?'

Niall of the Poems turned up with his small harp and sang quietly a song of mourning for a drowned woman. 'The crabs have your eyes,' he moaned, 'Fish swim through your white arms.'

Iogenán tried to comfort the Pilgrim. 'There, don't be worrying. It won't be her. She's strong. It's only the weak ones who go, and them so damaged that they'd be no use to anyone anyway.' The pilgrim didn't seem to hear him so Iogenán left him alone.

On the Maumturks Hills some wolves were howling as if for a dead enemy.

'There's something,' shouted one of the men further out on the ice, as an indistinct darkness travelled slowly below their feet. John saw a white face streaked with black hair, which was what he had been expecting to see. Baccaugh began muttering the prayers as the body was lifted out of the water.

'Leave it,' said a voice, and a woman shouldered her way into the crowd. 'She's ours. We'll carry her to the church.'

Baccaugh looked up. 'Not until I know about it, you won't. How did this woman die? I'm having no suicide in my church.'

Dagda stared him out. 'An accident. She slipped on the step.' The other women from Inis Cailleach were with her.

Baccaugh asked them: 'Do you say the same?'

'Yes,' said Finn.

The priest sighed. 'God have mercy on her soul and yours.'

John unfolded his arms and flexed fingers which had gone numb, he had been standing still for so long that he staggered briefly as he moved. He watched the women wrap their dead in a cloak and carry her away.

Later that night, just as the priest was getting off to sleep at last, with the comfortable shape of his wife fitted against his back, he was woken up by the Norman pilgrim and hauled out of bed. 'I want to talk to you.'

'Has the world gone mad this night? Put me down, you foreign bastard.' Kicking and swearing, Baccaugh was carried out of his house and into the comparative warmth of his cowshed and the smell of ruminated hay. Across the lane the light of candles flickered in the church where the hags were keeping a vigil over the body of their companion.

'Now then,' said Sir John, 'Regard this as confessional and shut up about it. I want you to exorcise me. I've been bewitched. Spelled. Possessed by some demon.'

'Serve you right,' said Baccaugh, 'Show me the demon that did it

146

and it'll have my blessing.' But he was intrigued. 'Who bewitched you?'

John jerked his head towards the church. 'One of them, the crazy one I brought here. She's bound me with a magic which means I can't think of anything else. It's unnatural. I thought it was her under the ice just now . . .' Baccaugh saw that the man was trembling, '. . . It's unknightly to feel like this and I want it done with. I want her out of my mind.'

' "Ah Corydon, Corydon, what is this lunacy you're possessed by?" ' quoted the priest, who was a romantic. He got up from the straw and fetched a bucket and began milking his cow; he might as well use this hideously early morning to advantage. 'It may not be a spell, my son. There are natural explanations for feelings between a young man and a maid. If you could win her . . .'

'The name's John,' said John impatiently, 'and just between ourselves, Father, I don't want to win her, I want to screw her. It's all I think about. If I could do it I'd be happy to undergo my penance, but since that doesn't seem likely, her being as mad as she is, the church will have to intervene. I want rid of her, finished. And don't tell me it's bloody natural – I've never felt like this in my life.'

The priest's hands moved rythmically up and down and milk hissed into the bucket. His head was against the cow's side and he hummed as he worked. 'Scathagh has the old power, no doubt about it,' he said, 'and the good God knows what she teaches those who fall into it. Well, my son, there are procedures against witchcraft which the blessed church has laid down and it may be that we could try some as a protection against this Galatea of yours.'

'Finola.' Sir John stood up. 'When can we start?'

'After that poor creature is buried,' said the priest firmly. 'Until then I have a lot of praying to do.'

John afterwards blamed the failure of the anti-witchcraft exorcism on the priest's love of Virgil. Himself, he followed all the procedures to the letter, drinking the disgusting purges Baccaugh concocted for him, patiently enduring the sprinklings of holy water, repeating uplifting psalms and St. Paul's thunderings to the Galatians against the witchcraft of the flesh. But what stuck in his mind were the words the sentimental old fool would utter softly, almost helplessly, as they looked out on the lake together, weaving the enchantment it contained closer about him than ever.

'More sweet than thyme, more fair than pale ivy,
more white than swans you are to me.
Come soon, when the cows through the meadows are homing,
come soon, if you love me, my nymph of the sea.'

When the thaw began and warmer air from the Atlantic raised mist from the ice of the lake so that John could no longer see it, the priest said: 'Are we doing any good here, do you think?'

'No. The moment the roads are open I'm off to join the O'Conor in his war.'

'Have you ever thought of marrying the woman? There's nothing like marriage to kill an enchantment.'

Sir John looked down at Baccaugh, appalled. 'Marriage is business,' he said. 'The future, my whole advancement rests on marrying for advantage. If you think there's any profit in marrying a penniless madwoman from some swamp, then I don't.'

'Our boys marry for advantage too,' said Baccaugh calmly, 'but they have another wife or two for pleasure, though it's very cross my bishop would be to hear me say so.'

The gulf that lay between the Irish and the stern, upright Christianity of the Norman way of life yawned before John and shocked him into the realisation that he not only must, but wanted, to leave this place with its mist and its sensual siren harps which could cling to a man's soul like weed to his legs and drag him down. It did him good to recognise it. His sinews were stiffened. He would go off to the Irish war and then return to the clean, clear, masculine thinking of Fitzempress' court. 'I'm joining the O'Conor,' he said, 'I won't be back.'

' "Soft meads, cool streams you would find here, and woodlands, dear Lycidas," ' murmured the priest, ' "A paradise where we could have grown old together." '

'The name's John,' Sir John told him, 'and shut up for Christ's sake.'

A week later he left Lough Mask for the O'Conor court at Tuam. Iogenán's household and Baccaugh saw him off. He thanked them all courteously and tried to urge his horse into a trot though the mud brought about by the thaw sucked at its hooves. He didn't look back.

' "But I'm a soldier," ' completed the priest, ' "forced by insensate zeal for the War God to go where weapons fly and the foe's in battle formation." Ah the poor lad, the poor pilgrim.'

The hopelessness which waited to ambush them at every set-back seeped through the Inis Cailleach tower as did the mist, rotting mental and material fibre. The Hy Fiachrach girls keened for Niav until the place reverberated like a bell-chamber. Aragon and Finn grieved more quietly, and Dagda went off on a lone hunting expedition into the mountains.

Scathagh let them wallow for a week and then called a council of war: 'Training begins again tomorrow.'

'I'm not beginning again,' said Aragon. 'There is no point any more, there never was.' She had the courage from knowing that all the others agreed with her.

Scathagh's awful head swivelled towards her. 'How interesting. What are you going to do?'

'Go home. The seas will be open soon and the O'Conor said he would pay my passage.'

'And what will you do when you get there?'

Aragon shrugged: 'What can I do? Marry again, I suppose, but what man would have me without a dowry . . .' her head went down into her hands as she envisaged the sort of man he would be.

'A man, though,' said Scathagh, 'we all must have one of those to protect us, mustn't we?' She was making them nervous. 'What would you *like* to do?'

Aragon pushed back her thick, black curls. 'Like? I would like to go into the shipping business. There's money there, and possibilities to build up a fleet of traders and . . .'

'Then why don't you?'

Aragon stared at her. 'I have no money. I am a woman. I have no ship.'

'You had a ship, or your husband did. You are owed its salvage at least. Get it. There are laws – man-made laws I grant you, but they can be made to work for us if we know how to use them.' She spat onto the floor. 'Now listen to me. Niav failed the course because she couldn't survive what men had done to her. Men are the enemy. Never forget that. When eventually you leave here you will be going into enemy territory, but if you finish your training you will be equipped to survive in it because you will not be weak and you will not be afraid.'

'We'll be misfits,' said Tailltin.

'Misfits can survive. Well, what will it be?'

'Survival,' they said.

In the early spring Iogenán took his pitifully small army to swell the ranks of Connaught. Men useful to the community like smiths and horse trainers and tanners and poets overnight turned into boastful warmongers brandishing newly-polished spears and galloped off with them.

The women on Inis Cailleach went on with their training, perfecting the skills they had acquired and learning new ones. Scathagh gave them lessons on law, not only Irish law, but Norman and how to manipulate it to their advantage. She also taught them duplicity. 'If you're going to flourish among the enemy,' she told them, 'you must learn to lie, cheat and steal.'

They were taught to disguise themselves, and had to go to the

149

aenacht at Cong dressed as old, male, pedlars – the fish glue with which Scathagh stuck on their goat-hair beards smelled awful, but nobody seemed to expect pedlars to smell of violets and they got away with it. While Scathagh kept a look-out from the top of the tower they had to invade it from the shore without her seeing them, swimming, lying still under water and breathing through a reed stuck up through the surface when she looked in their direction. If she spotted one of them they had to go back and start again. This wasn't as difficult as the assignment to steal Iogenán's favourite hunting spear from the wall of his hall, although even that wasn't as tricky as Scathagh insisting, when they got back, that they should lie to her about how they'd got it and then cross-examining them on their story.

Finn, burdened by Boniface's convent upbringing, found this exercise particularly burdensome. It seemed to her that although she was no longer answerable to God she was still answerable to her own honour and that she was telling too many lies. She had lied to the priest when she'd said that Niav's death had been an accident. What bothered her most of all – and puzzled her – was that she had lied to the pilgrim when she'd told him Scathagh had said that friendship could exist between men and women. Scathagh had said no such thing. What Scathagh said was that men could be used and exploited if possible, or avoided and fought if not. You could sleep with them to gain your own ends when necessary, but you could never, never be friends with the bastards.

Irritated, Finn discovered that she was waiting.

With so many of the men gone to the war, the Partraige women were working twice as hard as usual, but even as they whisked through the fields, and in and out of the houses, their heads turned most frequently not to the lake, but to the road that ran down to Lough Corrib where news would come from. To her chagrin Finn found herself in a similar state of suspension.

'Are all men the enemy?' she asked Scathagh privately, and Scathagh had answered: 'All.'

One beautiful spring day, she walked up to where Baccaugh was weeding ragwort out of his donkey's paddock. He looked up nervously at her approach. 'If it's tweaking my nose, or stealing things that you're after, you can tell Scathagh I've had enough of it.'

'I'm off-duty.' She put her arms on the top of the wall and loitered, feeling the sun on her back, wondering why she had come. Strictly speaking she should have been on the other side of the Lough, practising knife-throwing under Dagda's tuition, but she had rebelled; it just wasn't a day for knives, it was a day for smelling grass and passing under the various shades given by budding trees and watching nice little priests weeding in hats made of rushes.

She was a whole woman now; physically fitter than she'd ever been so that she had an adolescent compulsion to run even when there was no reason; to jump a gate rather than open it. And today, particularly, she felt adolescent, with an excited longing for something, but she didn't know what.

They talked horses, leaving long gaps in the conversation to be filled in by blackbirds in the hawthorn tree and the unexpected heat. The Fitzempress colt had turned out well, slightly shorter than his dam with her well-balanced neck and head but with his sire's compact back, a good cavalry horse. She had arranged with Iogenán to take some of his mares out of the herd and keep them separately serviced by her stallion when he was ready to go to stud.

After a sufficient interval, she asked casually: 'Have you had any news of the Pilgrim?'

To her surprise Baccaugh turned on her: 'Now don't you be pursuing that poor lad. Didn't he have enough trouble getting free of you and your enchantments as it is? If he dies fighting for the O'Conor it'll be on your conscience, and him a guest in this land.'

Finn stared. 'I didn't enchant him.'

Baccaugh savaged another root of ragwort. 'Maybe you didn't and maybe you did, but he left here as if all the devils in hell were after his blood, swearing he'd never be back.' He glanced up at the young women leaning on his wall watching him with eyes that were a deeper blue than any eyes had a right to be, and the poignancy of all springtimes caught at his throat so that he added: 'But I'd put money on it that he will be, the poor bastard.'

The young woman was still for a while and suddenly she stretched, raising her arms into the warm air as if she reached for the sun, unconscious of anything but the well-being of a young body in tune with the spring, and sending the priest back to his weeding as if his soul depended on it.

Finn turned to look down on Lough Mask, idly hitching her elbows over the wall and squinting against the brightness of twinkling water. Beneath it were Niav and Boniface and a dragon. And dragons were always dangerous. But not today. Today it had let her off its hook, restoring a circulation through which swam a fish blowing bubbles that exploded in every extremity she had.

From the trees behind Blat's house came the first summer call of a cuckoo and the priest swore because he had heard it while standing on a patch of bare earth, which meant that his crops wouldn't flourish this year. Finn turned her head to smile at him: 'Don't worry. It wasn't a cuckoo.'

'What else was it then?'

'It was a soul on holiday from hell.'

*   *   *

151

The Irish rules of war were beautiful, rigid and archaic, like those for every other Irish ceremony. Men died as nastily as in lesser countries, but while they watched their arteries spurt or wiped their brains out of their eyes they had the comfort of unalterable tradition behind them.

John of Sawbridge had meant to act merely as a detached observer, but the inefficiency he saw around him offended his sense of order. Even at the last minute, before the decisive battle at Ardee, he was still begging the O'Conor: 'At least give yourself the edge; let your cavalry use stirrups.'

But the Ruairi he'd known in Partraige country had gone, to be replaced by a regal and, in John's view, idiotic stranger who forgave his guest's vulgarity by smiling gently at him and quoting the old Brehon saying: 'To hold any new thing fair – this is the way of folly.'

There was no ambushing of the enemy, no use of spies – a deserter who came over with information from the Ulster side was instantly beheaded for ungentlemanly conduct. Instead the O'Conor sent a herald to MacLochlainn giving him his army's position and inviting him to meet it in pitched battle.

As the Flemish mercenary captain, who stood watching with John and other foreign guests on the rise outside the O'Conor's pavilion, said: 'It's not war, but it's the most elegant way of killing people I've ever seen.'

A herald with a voice like a bull-roarer gave out the identity of the Connaught clans marching onto the field as if he were announcing arrivals at a banquet: 'The O'Flannagan, the O'Mulrenin, the O'Finaghty, the Mageraghty, the Partraige, the O'Flynn, the O'Hanly, the O'Fallon, the O'Beirne, the O'Concannon, the O'Heyne, the O'Shaughnessy, the O'Malley, the O'Flaherty. . . .' Thousand on thousands of men took up their positions, each clan almost dancing to the sound of its own trumpeter, and every man throwing a stone onto a growing pile of stones as he passed it.

'What are they doing that for?' asked John.

DeBoeuf, the Fleming, said: 'It's one of their better ideas. Every soldier puts a stone into that cairn; if he survives the battle he takes it away again. That way they can estimate their losses, and also have a monument to the dead.'

Half a mile away across the plain where other trumpets made a fainter counterpoint, John could see another cairn rising among the Ulster activity. He nodded towards it: 'That one looks bigger to me.'

De Boeuf shrugged: 'The O'Conor's outnumbered. I told him, but he wouldn't listen.'

Defensive armour was another vulgarity Irish armies dispensed with; the minority wore leather helmets with iron bands round them, but the majority had their hair flowing as free as their beards. John, who'd spent the night in the O'Conor's pavilion and had seen him dressing, happened to know that he was wearing a metal box strapped over the parts, 'which,' he'd said, 'I would most hate to lose,' but other than that the commander-in-chief of Connaught, like the commander-in-chief of Ulster, was going into battle wearing linen and silk.

Sir John, objecting to nakedness in battle even as an observer, had borrowed an iron helmet and a mail corselet from De Boeuf, as well as a saddle with stirrups.

What they lacked in protection, the hosts gained in colour. Tunics and battle standards were clashes of rainbows. Each clan carried a shield of the same colour so that it could be recognised. John could see the small contingent of Partraige standing out with shields that had been freshly limed into a dazzling white.

As the marshals of both sides rode to the front of their armies, the ranks behind them looked like hundreds of lines of washing hung out to dry in the breeze of a fine day. It seemed a pity to spoil it.

'We proclaim Ruairi O'Conor,' roared Mac Dermot of Moylurg, O'Conor's marshal, across the distance which separated him from the roaring Ulster marshal, 'descendant of the elder brother of Niall of the Nine Hostages, flood and dignity of Erin . . .'

While he elaborated on the perfections of his king and the slimy unworthiness of his opponent, and the marshal of Ulster did the same, a small contingent of priests, led by the Bishop of Tuam, was carrying the lovely, jewelled Cross of Cong, which contained a piece of the True Cross, round the Connaught army to provide it with an invisible ring of Christian protection.

'This'll take hours,' said De Boeuf, 'Let's go and have a drink.' They chose one of the pavilions at random and found a hogshead of good Bordeaux standing beside a table on which goblets had been laid out in full assurance that their owner would come back for a victory celebration.

'What annoys me,' said De Boeuf, pouring generously, 'is that this won't change anything. They're just fighting over the title of High King. If the O'Conor loses, and the probability of numbers says he will, all that'll happen is that he'll prostrate himself in submission in front of MacLochlainn with a sword in his teeth, give him a few hostages, pledge that he'll be a better boy in future, and go home. MacLochlainn will go home and call himself High King of Ireland for a bit until somebody challenges him again, and nobody will have won any ground. Or lost it. When I win a battle I want some land out of it, with rents and loyal serfs and permanent possession for me and my sons. Give me good old feudalism – but they don't see it like that.'

'They're a funny lot,' said Sir John, 'I like them, though.' He held out his goblet for a refill.

'Oh charming, charming,' said De Boeuf, 'I could settle here permanently. I could. The women alone . . . but it's the land thing, I'd never really own it. They just don't see land as something you can own. And they're such bloody amateurs about war. I've persuaded the O'Conor into having a small detachment of my mercenaries for emergencies, but he seems to think we're not really playing the game. "Look," I said to him, "have a standing army of mercenaries who can be summoned immediately, without having to wait until they've put their bloody crops in, and who won't go home for the bloody harvest." But would he listen?'

'That's one thing about Fitzempress,' said John, filling up again.

'Now you're talking,' said the Fleming with enthusiasm. 'Fitzempress is a professional and he understands professionals. He's a bloody marvel. Now I've seen. . . .'

They swapped Fitzempress war stories and drank more wine, deaf to the change in tone of the trumpets and the shouting from the great plain outside, until a spear pierced the roof of the pavilion, caught in a tent rope and hung downwards, circling over their heads. De Boeuf finished his goblet, 'Nice talking to you.'

Staggering slightly, John followed the Fleming out. From the look of it the battle wasn't going to last half as long as the ceremonies which had preceded it; everything was in full swing and a square mile of air whirred with arrows, missile stones, battle cries, death howls, the rubbing of drums and the calls of trumpets, but the Ulster army was bigger even than he and De Boeuf had estimated and it had pushed the Connaughtmen nearer the O'Conor's tents, leaving the middle ground where the two hosts had first rushed on one another a deserted ploughland of mashed earth and bodies.

John did his best to stuff away mental notes into his brain to report to Fitzempress; the accuracy of the stone slingers, even more deadly than the Majorcans he'd once seen fighting under Fitzempress' banner; the unusual string handle on the spears of the spear-throwers; the small amount of cavalry. And if the Irish lacked professional tactics, there was nothing amateur about their courage.

But he'd been brought up to fight, he was drunk, his pulse beat to the coughing drums and he could see, far off on the right flank, little puffs of powdered lime like smoke signals coming off the shields of the hard-pressed Partraige and even while he was telling himself: 'You're an observer, John, so observe,' he'd weaved over to his horse and was galloping off to get the stupid buggers out of the mess they'd got themselves into.

When he sobered up, the Connaught lines had been torn down and their wonderful washing had fallen into dirty heaps in mud made by mixing earth with blood. Ulster had won. Ruairi O'Conor was in the

MacLochlainn's pavilion on his belly with a sword between his teeth. Sir John himself was surrounded by wounded Partraige. Niall of the Poems was already composing an edited version of the battle, and some of the others were gently singing a lament for the dead they had already lost, and for the Partraige lad who was coughing blood as he lay across Sir John's knees and whom they were about to lose.

While they waited the sun began to go down; doctors and stretcher-bearers moved quietly over the field, rooks flapped in the sky, hoping it was safe to come down to feed on the open eyes below them and a couple of golden eagles circled on warm thermals watching the crawling wounded, being sporting birds who liked to eat prey that moved. The long shadows and the scent of bruised grass remembered other, completed days.

The Fleming, De Boeuf, lumbered through the fallen washing in search of his Norman drinking companion, and squatted down beside him. 'Well, it was a good battle if I only knew what it was for. Pity about our side. Is he dead yet?'

John looked down at the Partraige boy in his lap. His name had been Dubthach; they'd gone hunting together. 'Nearly.'

'Are you hurt? There's blood on your face.'

He put up his hand to his cheek where an Ulster dagger had reopened the scar the loony had given him. 'You ought to see the other fellow.'

De Boeuf's face, blank like everybody else's, did its best to smile. Out of Dubthach's young, adam-appled throat came the last sigh and his hold on John's hand went limp. The other Partraige lifted him up and took him away. 'God rest his soul,' said De Boeuf, automatically, 'I don't what it is, Sawbridge, but at times like this I want a woman. I don't mean to screw, though that as well, but I just want to hold one, if you know what I mean.'

'I know what you mean.' The lament the Partraige had sung had reminded him of the night he'd waited for the drowned hag, when he'd thouht it was the loony who was dead.

'So shall we go off and find a couple, you and I?'

'Another time,' said Sir John. 'It's a kind thought, De Boeuf, but I've already got one in mind.'

A news vendor brought the announcement of the Connaught defeat to Lough Mask. He was one of the unwashed, curiously-dressed little men who did juggling on the side. Since he couldn't tell them the names of the survivors or the dead, the women paid him the minimum, sent him off and redoubled their work.

'If that bastard Niall is going to be killed, now's the time for him to do it,' Blat said angrily, 'before I divorce him, so I can get widow

155

status,' and she kept going to the window of the tower which over-looked the shore. She no longer loved him but, as she said, you couldn't rid yourself of twenty years of worrying about a man just because of that.

Two days after the news vendor had been and gone, Finn played truant again. 'If you don't mind, Scathagh,' she said, and took the small *curragh* to the shore. She tied it up, nodded to the women who were fishing from the holm, and walked up the track until she was out of sight of the lake and had reached the road. She sat down under a rowan tree on the verge where sheep were cropping the grass.

There had been an interval of rain between spring and summer, but an unusually hot sun was drying out the earth again. She picked some stones out of the roadway and practised throwing them at a clump of foxgloves thirty feet away; she stripped a flower off every time. 'I needed a day off,' she said to herself. A couple of Partraige sheep watched her nervously. She considered them and decided that their legs looked like black knitting needles stuck into a ball of wool. There was no reason for her to feel as gauche and out of her depth as she did: she had a perfect right to sit by a roadside to look at sheep if she wanted to.

'It's nice, just sitting here. He may be dead. And what if he does come? What are you going to do then, you stupid woman? Where does he fit in with killing and writing?' But the adolescent longing that had come to her so late persisted and she stayed where she was.

The first sound of hooves was Baccaugh and his horse, bringing back fresh supplies of communion bread from Cong. 'Do you think they'll be back today then?' he asked her, 'it takes longer than that from Ardee.'

'How do I know?' she shouted angrily at him, 'I'm taking a day off, that's all.'

The second set of hooves carried a tired young man who looked as if he was expecting to see her. There was no greeting; John dismounted and put his arms round her, rubbing his face against the top of her head. 'Don't you ever let me do that again.'

Even if they'd known that the next eight days were all they were going to have together and that the memory of them was going to have to last the rest of their lives, they wouldn't have done anything different. They went to Swan Island and made love, swam, caught fish, cooked it over the open fire and ate it with stale bread because they couldn't be bothered to go and fetch fresh, and made love again. It wasn't so much that time stopped for them as changed its shape, no longer demarcated by meals or work that had to be done, or the bells of the monastery down the lake which uselessly tried to regulate it. Instead daytime went into night time in a spiral in which they could slide back and recapture the high moments, most of them spent on the pile of skins in Finn's hut, or profitably wasted in inanities.

'Call these breasts?' John said, 'You should have seen the woman I had in Brittany – Bertha the Bosomy.'

'Big were they?'

'Big? My dear Loon, they were pillows, waves of pearly foam breaking into headlands of coral. Compared to Bertha's these are acorns.'

'What are you doing that to them for, then?'

'If there's nothing else one has to make do with acorns.'

Or: 'Did I tell you about Anita the Athletic, what I had on Crusade?'

'Tell me about Anita the Athletic.'

'Madly in love with her, I was. Still am. Breasts like mosques. Together we swung from minaret to minaret, humping to the seductive call of the muezzin.'

'Sounds tiring. What's a muezzin?'

'Something like a camel, and you wash your mouth out with soap. People who belittle Anita the Athletic have to pay the price.'

She paid it.

She was so grateful to him for making sex funny, she could have cried. The jokes severed any connection between the nightmare act at Kildare and this amiable, magical, liquid coupling that took her into a dimension she hadn't even dreamed could exist, where stars intermingled with skin textures.

There had undoubtedly been a lot of other woman and, equally undoubtedly, he had told them he loved them. It didn't bother her. It might have done if he'd put her in the same category by saying that he loved her, but he never did. Laughing her into bed was a protection for both of them. Once, after a climax, he still kept her clutched to him.

'What's the matter?'

'Damn you, you bloody woman.'

He wasn't joking; it was the nicest thing anybody had ever said to her.

Eventually they were both so hungry that fetching supplies became a necessity. Even so, they sat for an hour in the sun on the island's tiny beach, burbling, before they could bear to break the spiral.

'I'll go. It'll give me a chance to dally with Almaith the Amorous; she's been beckoning to me every night when your back's turned.'

'Does Niall know that?'

'Certainly not. It's a secret between us. I'm the only man who can satisfy her voracious appetite.'

'All right, you go. My lover on the other side of the lake has been waiting for the chance to swim over.'

'More fool him. What's that dirty little grebe doing to that lady grebe?'

'Same as you were doing most of last night.'

'Filthy little beast.'

It was high summer, a day to begrudge wearing clothes. The water was so still that she could see a brown trout resting in the shade of a rock as clearly as if it had been in the same element as herself. The replete sound of wood pigeons cooed from the trees on the hills and dragonflies shimmered over the rushes.

'Let's both go.'

As they clambered up onto the holm of the inlet leading to Almaith's house, Finn knew it had been a mistake to come back to civilisation. There were people about and her conscience was stricken to remember that there were Partraige families still grieving for a pile of stones left at Ardee. 'You go,' she said, 'and while you're dallying remember to ask Almaith for fresh bread, and some bacon if she'll trade it for trout – oh, and some cabbage.'

'What am I, a bloody housewife?'

'I can't go, Pilgrim. I'll get drawn in, or they'll separate us somehow. Please.'

It was ridiculous, he thought, that he had the same feeling as when she'd been mad and he'd left her at the convent overnight and had worried until he got her back; he should be getting free of her by now. 'God save me from loony women,' he said, and strode off. He flustered poor Almaith into giving him the supplies quickly, and was returning to the pier within half an hour. The sense of menace dissipated as he saw that she was still there, sitting in the sun with her back to him, her bare feet dangling in the water. She had been talking to her cousin, Nessa, who was walking away from her along the holm and coming towards him. A dull man, but he supposed he could afford to give him a minute or so's chat.

'How's trade, Nessa?'

They stood under the trees to talk. Nessa's jaw muscles moved fascinatingly as he droned on about his success with the hides at Dublin, and what a bad season the eastern side of Ireland was having. 'I have just been telling my cousin some news to her advantage which I learned there. Doubtless she will tell you of it.' Nessa disapproved of their liaison on Swan Island, he could tell; well, he disapproved of it himself if it came to that. Sooner rather than later, he'd have to get back and report to Fitzempress. He'd take her with him, put her in the context of the real world and see if he'd be free of her then.

'. . . somethingsomethingsomething Bristol,' intoned Nessa.

'Ah, Bristol,' said Sir John, 'Earnest little town, definite lack of dancing girls. You like it, do you? Well, better be getting on.'

But Nessa refused to let him go and expounded at length on Bristol and its trade.

Finn had listened reluctantly to what Nessa had to tell her; it would reconnect her to the real world's time and give her decisions that she didn't want to make, apart from the fact that thinking about it made her sick. But he was inevitable and she was forced to hear him. As he left, she kept on staring down into the water where weed flowed backward in the almost imperceptible movement of the lake and then pointed forward in branches like parallel roads which never met.

She heard with relief the familiar voice challenge Nessa and sat there listening without turning round, enjoying her lover's awareness of her as he was forced to make small-talk. Their conversation came to her, slightly echoing on the heavy summer air. 'Bristol . . .' she heard him say, and grinned because he was getting impatient, '. . . definite lack of dancing girls.'

Somewhere else, somebody else had said that. In the same voice and he was saying it on another warm, scented morning. In a garden. Eleanor of Aquitaine's garden. 'Definite lack of dancing girls,' the voice she knew was saying, and there had been two of them.

Desperately, she turned round and looked at him afresh with Boniface's eyes. He was the shorter one, with mousey-coloured hair, the one who wasn't quite as good-looking as the other. They'd both bowed to the nun who sat anonymously on the garden bench. Now he winked at her. Quickly she went back to staring at the water.

She couldn't remember exactly what else they'd said but Boniface had been left in no doubt that they were going to Ireland as spies for Fitzempress. She could fool herself by pretending that she didn't remember, but she couldn't fool the clear-minded, unloving, unloved Boniface. He was a spy. It made sense of his being here at all, a fact that she'd accepted because it had suited her and the Partraige hadn't questioned because they were too hospitable.

Boniface's ideals had been affronted by Fitzempress' underhandedness, but Boniface hadn't really cared, being the citizen of a concept, not a country. It was Finn who cared now that she belonged to Ireland; not Dermot's Ireland or the Ireland where women were raped, as they were raped everywhere else, but the Ireland of a lake and an easy-going freedom so sure of itself and so deep-rooted that it could allow some of it to spill over to its women. Fitzempress came into her mind clearly with his genius and his energy and his administration, able to pick up this lazy country of hers any time he wanted and attach it to his modern empire, imposing his own law on it so that it became indistinguishable from anywhere else.

Fitzempress' Common Law treated women like chattels while providing justice for everyone else. Women married who they were told to marry under Fitzempress' Law. It would not allow Blat to divorce Niall because he was unkind to her. It might suit other countries, but not her Ireland. It would wipe out all the eccentricities and kindnesses. Scathagh would have no place in Fitzempress' Ireland, nor would Blat and nor, for that matter, would there be any feudal position for Niall of the Poems. Everybody in their place was how it would be, every blade of grass owned by somebody, no liberal sharing of the salmon and the wild garlic, no quick sweeping of every stream.

She saw quite clearly the potential for her country if it could only think of itself as a country and not a collection of inimical states. If there was one king of Ireland (as long as it wasn't Dermot) if it could cohere, it could leap ahead of the modernity of Fitzempress to an even newer and better civilisation where women were recognised as partners . . .

In that moment she took on the king of the most powerful empire in the world as her enemy. Dermot became a side issue; she would rid Ireland of Dermot because he wasn't fit to live in it, but if Fitzempress put his clever, interfering fingers on her country, she would fight him.

She looked at her bare toes in the water. 'I'll give him spies,' she said.

The complicating factor was her love for one of them. It was a complication that made her so vulnerable that if even now he said: 'Look, I'm a spy for my country, but what do countries matter to such as you and me?' she was terrified that she might reply: 'Nothing', and chuck Ireland overboard like a cherrystone. She resented being that much in love. But he hadn't said it and wasn't saying it now. As he took the oars of the *curragh* to row back to the island, he was just concentrating on being funny at Nessa's expense.

She watched his face as he rowed, which he did with self-conscious care because he knew she could do it better. It wasn't the best-looking face in the world, and she hadn't improved it when she'd caused the scar along its cheek – a fact he pointed out every time he shaved. But it was nice; people took to it because it was confident and amusing and open. And behind its openness was a closed compartment of calculation.

How could he look out on Ireland, and on her, for God's sake, from those honest Norman eyes, all the while weighing up strength and weaknesses as if they were pieces on a chess board? She felt sick. She had been tricked. The understanding she had thought to exist between their bodies and minds had been an illusion.

If he was going to put his country first, then she must do the same. But first she'd give him a chance because she loved him so much.

As they carried the provisions out of the boat, he said: 'Should we eat first, or should we . . .?'

'Eat,' she said, 'I want to tell you something.'

160

She raked off the turves they had left covering the fire to expose the red-hot core and put the pan on them to heat up for the bacon. She always began what little cooking they did because, he said, that was what a woman was for; but he always finished it because she was so sloppy – her sense of order had died with Boniface.

The afternoon was too hot to sit by a fire, so they took the cooked bacon to eat between hunks of new bread, and sat under the alders at the edge of the island, their feet in the reed bed, and she began telling him the story of Boniface. Her hands shook and, hungry as she was, most of the bread and bacon went to the ducks. It was very much worse telling him than an assembled gathering of the Partraige; partly because she had to go into more detail and partly because they had achieved such intimacy as they were that to introduce a new element would inevitably change things.

He was flabbergasted by the beginning. 'A nun?' he said, and jerked his head back to the hut. 'You and me. A nun?'

'Oh do shut up,' she said wearily, 'We've got a long way to go.'

She told him how and why Boniface was selected as Comarba of Kildare and of the interview with Eleanor of Aquitaine and Fitzempress. The only thing she suppressed was that the interviews had taken place in Eleanor's garden at Chinon on the day two young agents for Fitzempress had been walking along its paths.

As she talked, she could feel him adjusting his image of her, turning it this way and that to fit the unfamiliar roles she had once played. Her estimation of him went down because his estimation of her went up. 'I'd no idea you were so important,' he said with surprised respect at one point, and she nearly hit him. Boniface, seen from this distance, was a diminished, deluded figure for whom she felt contempt and genuine pity.

Dermot, on the other hand, had grown to awe-inspiring proportions in his savagery. She thought very little more of the English mercenary he had set on her that night at Kildare than she would have thought of some instrument used in a sexual assault. Dermot's face watching the rape was what she most remembered; it was Dermot who had raped her by proxy. As her story approached that night when so many people had died at Kildare along with Boniface, she became reluctant to go on. The contrast between that obscene travesty and what she now knew should exist between a man and a woman was too great. Her voice petered out.

She heard the Pilgrim say: 'If you're going to tell me you were raped, you needn't bother. I didn't think you'd gone mad because you'd lost your handkerchief.'

She grabbed hold of him and kissed him.

*　　*　　*

161

By sundown the mosquitos and midges which were always a factor at Lough Mask in the summer became a menace, especially to a man without trousers, so the Pilgrim put his back on – he dressed like an Irishman, but kept his Norman/English identity by refusing to grow a beard – and they sat near the fire's peat smoke to afford them protection from insects.

She was right. Telling him her story had altered their relationship. The rape had made no difference, except to make him speculate with some energy on which, among a variety of painful deaths, he would inflict on Dermot of Leinster if he ever caught up with him. What worried her was his pleasure that she had held high office and had once been sought after by Popes, cardinals, queens and kings. It had enhanced her value to him.

'I've done well for myself, haven't I?' he said, 'An abbess, by God. Not bad for an innkeeper's son.'

'If you're estimating my worth,' she told him icily, 'you've forgotten that I am also a princess of the Partraige.'

'Ah well, yes, but it isn't the same.' It was only his world that counted, and the strangest thing of all was that he believed it must count most with her, as if she were just sojourning in this fey, foreign land temporarily, like he was. He seemed to think that she was his ally, and that by outraging her Dermot had turned her against all Ireland; that she was only here, at Lough Mask, because she had nowhere else to go. 'So you're an Angevin really,' he said, patting her on her head, 'Not quite as good as Norman, and not nearly as good as an English Norman like me, but one of Us.'

She was Us and the Irish were Them. 'And Fitzempress sent you over as an informant for him, did he?'

She went still, waiting for him to say 'Like me,' but he didn't. 'We could use your new breed of horses,' he went on, 'they're ideal for Fitzempress' cavalry.'

'Do you know him?' Please, please, blast you; I've given you practically everything I can. Give me the truth about you.

'Of course. I was his marshal. I told you. I suppose when I get back that I will be again.' He yawned. 'Tomorrow we ought to make plans about getting home.'

And that was the other development in their relationship. Since she was Us, his home was now her home; he didn't even ask her if it suited her to go.

'Pilgrim,' she said, 'what are we going to do?'

'Well, I thought we'd go into the hut in a minute and take off these clothes and . . .'

'What are we going to do in the future. What will I be?' She sounded him out. 'Are you going to marry me?'

162

He was shocked. 'Marry you? Of course I can't. All land belongs to somebody in Europe, so the only way a king can reward a landless man is to give him an heiress. Good Lord, Loon, you've lived there. You know.'

Suddenly she was sorry for him; his ambition to better himself was impelling him on an inflexible, foredestined road which allowed no diversions, however happy they might make him.

She said: 'So what do you intend to do with me?'

'Keep you in sin,' he said, heartily, 'Build you a bower where we can rumpty-tumpty to our hearts' content; a secret, flower-scented bower, like the Fair Rosamund's.'

'Won't your future wife mind?'

'She hadn't better. Besides, she won't know. Eleanor doesn't know about Rosamund.'

'Who is this Rosamund?'

'She's Fitzempress' bit on the side. One of the many, but apparently she's something special. He's got a place for her down at Woodstock, near his hunting lodge and he goes chasing down there whenever he can. He's besotted with her.'

For a moment she remembered Eleanor of Aquitaine in her garden and the couple who had seemed so suited. Every man in the world, then; highest, lowest, best, was treacherous; it was built into the male system.

'And what do I do all day in this bower when you're not there?'

'I don't know. Needlework, rock the odd cradle, sling a few spears at passing wolves. Whatever women do.'

But I'm not that sort of woman, she thought. You love me but you've no idea of the sort of person I am. How Rosamund bears the waiting I don't know, but I'd go mad. I don't even know how to do needlework.

'It sounds delightful,' she said. She had begun her own betrayal.

His love-making changed that night. He was more commanding, as if he were more sure of her, less fun. She felt that he was squeezing her not only physically but mentally, making her into a more conventional shape. If you fitted me into that bower of yours, she thought, you'd be tired of me within the year. He'd fallen in love with her because she was unlike any woman he'd met, but now that he'd got her he was prepared to take away the individuality that had attracted him in the first place.

But she couldn't bear to let him go. She gave him chance after chance. As they lay watching the moonlight, she said: 'You're no pilgrim. Why did you come to Ireland?'

She felt him tense and then give a deliberate yawn. 'I most certainly was a pilgrim, until I got led away by mad abbesses.' He leaned over and nuzzled her ear. 'Let's do it again.'

The next morning she persisted, desperate to make up her mind one way or another, not wanting to make it up against him. 'Do you think Fitzempress will invade Ireland?'

She was burning the bacon, and he snatched the pan away from her. 'How could you be a kitcheness and such a bloody awful cook?' As they ate he said: 'Fitzempress? I shouldn't think so. He's got enough on his plate. Which is more than I can say for mine.'

'But he might?'

And then he said: 'Best bloody thing that could happen.' He saw her face. 'Come on, Loon, face it. They're a lovely people, but they can't go on like they are, continually warring between the tribes, all these backward customs. I mean, that's why you were sent here. You can't tell me you approve of that little priest over there having a wife.'

She looked across the water towards the smoke behind the willows which came from the louvre in the thatch of Baccaugh's house. 'I like his wife.'

'So do I, but that's not the point. Priests shouldn't have them. Honestly, somebody's going to invade them sooner or later because they're such a bloody shambles. You ought to have seen the battle at Ardee. And look at how the poor old Partraige are preparing to avenge you on Dermot – with a poem. I ask you.' He hissed in his breath. 'What Dermot needs is a touch of the castrations, not a bloody poem.'

On and off for the rest of that day, in between making love to her, he cited the weaknesses of the Irish. On one level, she realised, he had a genuine affection for them and on the other he was perfectly prepared to betray them. All his friendship for the O'Conor, the kindness he had received from Iogenán, from Niall, from Blat; all that was in one compartment of his soul and had no connection with what he saw as his duty to Fitzempress. During the battle at Ardee he had charged in at the risk of his own life to save the Partraige contingent and yet he would take their country away from them without a second's thought.

'When I was at Tuam,' he told her, 'there was a peasant draped across Ruairi O'Conor's threshold; he'd been dispossessed of some cattle or something and wanted Ruairi to get them back for him. And do you know how he was doing it? He was starving himself. It's a custom. You fast against somebody.' He jerked his head and tutted. 'If they fasted against me they could starve themselves to bloody death, but Ruairi righted his wrong for him. Said it was against his honour to be fasted against. I ask you.'

She watched him as he revealed more and more of his contempt, watched his long, thin feet when they went paddling, watched his hands as he did up his boot-lace, watched his mouth as he chewed a reed, unable to imagine what it would be like without him, listening to him leaving her.

'And this Scathagh business. I said to Ruairi I couldn't understand how he could allow it.'

'She healed me,' said Finn, gently.

He was affronted. '*I* healed you. Look at you,' He ran a hand down her flanks and tweaked her bottom. 'Not a bad-looking woman, considering the wreck you were when I found you. You can thank sex for that. That's what women need, not roaming about killing wolves and kicking young men in their prospects. If I had my way Scathagh and all the rest of the hags would be thrown off that island, lock, stock and whatsit.'

It was getting dusk again, the clear evening light gaining a bloom.

'God,' he said, leaning back, 'but it's lovely here. I give you that. I could do wonders with this place.' He looked reflectively towards the north bank of the lake where shadows were making untidier the untidy shape of Iogenán's *rath*. 'That'd make a wonderful site for a castle. You could dominate the country for miles around if you built a castle there.'

She built it in her mind; a tall, grey, geometric, unforgiving entity like the castles back in Anjou. Around it was not the pastoral, communal countryside that existed now but fenced, arable fields, each one docketed and calculated. Lough Mask would be accountable, so many eels to be trapped and attributed, so many fish and no more to be caught for the lord who owned them. The deer out there in the forests wouldn't be the clan's any more, they would be the king's and anyone who took one without the king's permission would be a poacher in his own land and subjected to the terrible punishments of feudalism. There would be a block outside the castle for the cutting off of poacher's hands, a gibbet with Partraige bodies swinging from it.

This would be a Scathagh-less place, with the priest's wife and his children cast out of it, and a bewildered Partraige subject to laws and taxes they'd never heard of; the women marrying whom they were told to marry, and lumping it if they didn't like it. Military keeps on the more strategic islands of the lough. Mailed soldiers keeping a different peace from the lazy, amiable peace which permeated the very earth. Her earth.

Not for you, not for anybody, she thought, is that going to happen here. I won't let it happen.

And that was that, the end of the only love affair she'd ever have. He didn't notice.

In the night she said: 'When do you want to take me to this bower of yours?'

He was pleased. 'Tomorrow?'

'The day after. I've got goodbyes to say.' She sat up abruptly, dislodging his arm: 'Where's Art?'

'Oh my God, who?'

'Art. Where is he? I haven't seen him in days.' The island had seemed to float off into some summer-filled time of its own, leaving the rest of the world to disappear, but now she had to re-connect.

'Sloped off because he couldn't stand seeing us together, I expect. Worships the ground you walk on, poor little sod. I saw him lying in a corner at Almaith's house today, pissed as a newt. Almaith seemed less than delighted to have him there under her feet, I can tell you.'

She was amazed. 'Does he? Worship the ground I walk on?' She got out of bed and wrapped her shawl round her while she went to the window to look out at the lake. Perhaps the celibates had got it right after all; there was too much pain in this business of love between men and women. Now that she had begun to feel agony in advance for the separation she was going to impose on herself and the pilgrim, her heart ached for the pain of any other human being.

'Seems to. Can't understand it myself, but I can't see any other reason for him to throw up a good position at Kildare to go traipsing Ireland with a loony.'

From his view he could see the ouline of her head; her hair was darker than the light which was suffused by the reflection of a full moon on the lake. The confidence with which he'd gone to bed, when he'd thought he'd got her labelled at last, was less assured now. He wanted her away from here and in his home surroundings so that he could get used to her, and so that her particular assembly of features – and God knew he'd seen more beautiful women, and had them too – wouldn't keep thrilling him down to the marrow every time he looked at her. It was so bloody un-knightly to be obsessed by a woman. He wanted her domesticated, like a water supply, his own well that he could dip into when he needed to and would stay put when he didn't.

The next day they made visits to the same people, but at different times and with different objectives. Sir John was bidding a final, and truly regretful goodbye to Iogenán, Baccaugh, Blat, Niall and all his Partraige friends. Finn was saying *au revoir* and a lot of other things.

She went to see Nessa. 'Where did you say that priest was?' She spent a long time at his house making arrangements. Then she went back to Inis Cailleach where she entrusted everything she knew to the women who had become her sisters.

The Academy's course was as good as over. Aragon was preparing to leave and begin her legal fight for the ownership of her late husband's ship. Bevo was going with her. 'I've decided I like boats,' she said.

Tailltin and Muirna were still trying to think of an alternative to going back to their clans and being married. Muirna was considering joining one of the strolling bands of actors, jugglers and acrobats which went around the country giving entertainments.

Finn looked round the hall at all of them, her beloved fellow-hags, the pretend-man that was Dagda and, finally, the great female who sat like a troll in her carved chair.

'We're all misfits,' she thought, 'Tailltin was right.' It wasn't just the rapes but Scathagh who had changed them so that they were disqualified from, and no longer wanted, the conventional role of a women. Perhaps the Pilgrim was right. If it hadn't been for Scathagh she might have gone off to his damned bower and been contented.

'You made us independent,' she suddenly shouted at Scathagh in accusation. 'What are we going to do?' She had made an absurd decision which would lead her into loneliness such as she had never known, not to mention hardship. It wasn't too late.

'Don't talk to Scathagh like that,' Dagda said, outraged.

'Why not? If I'm independent now I'm independent of her as well.'

Unexpectedly, Scathagh lumbered up from her chair and over to where Finn sat and looked her in the eye. 'Applaud the first graduate,' she said to the others. 'Dagda, get some wine.'

Finn nodded. The Pilgrim's bower wasn't for the woman she was now, even if she ever had been. She was a fighting Connaughtwoman, and she was going to have to fight.

As they drank Finn's health, Muirna said: 'Admit it, you haven't made our lives easier.'

Scathagh looked around the table. 'I see women fit to live their own lives. If you ask me 'fit for what?', that was never my problem.'

'So we're on our own,' said Tailltin.

'That's a condition of life,' said Scathagh. 'Certainly you won't have me; I am leaving here again. I am needed elsewhere. Whether you have each other is up to you. I gather Finn has a plan so I suggest you listen to it.'

Finn told them. After they'd discussed it Scathagh took Finn up to her gallery. The floor shook as she heaved herself over it to a chest which she opened and, after some rummaging, took out two leather bags containing powdered substances. 'These should do the trick.' She told Finn their properties, how and in which quantities they should be used. 'I gather you don't want to kill him.'

'I should,' said Finn, 'if I were a proper patriot. But I love him.'

'Don't,' said Scathagh, 'and don't love your country either.'

'What else is there? Outside the church, Ireland is the only country I know of which gives women some rights of their own; even in Leinster their rights are written into the law.'

Scathagh took her round to the other side of the gallery, a portion of it that Finn had never seen. On their way they passed the big, shambling double bed which, Finn realised, Scathagh shared with Dagda. Past that the gallery was virtually empty, only rolled up rugs and hangings lying on the floor among packed baskets and chests.

167

Scathagh was preparing to leave and Finn knew she would find the world even less safe without her. In one of the window lights, standing on a sill was a figure in stone only nine inches high and yet with a density of mass that made it seem larger. At one and the same time it was like the Thing on the wall at Kildare, though without its violence, saddle-backed, crouching over its open labia, but worn into a gentler gravitas. 'The Mother,' said Scathagh, 'the oldest thing there is. The only non-betrayer. Love her.'

Behind the figure's bald head the window framed a piece of the lake which had turned opal under the setting sun. 'I love you,' said Finn, temporising, 'if that will do.'

Scathagh's face made no change. 'We are all Her daughters,' she said, 'and while you're about it, extend some of your affection to Dagda.'

When she came to Dagda as she said her goodbyes, Finn kissed her: 'Thank you, Dagda, for all you've done.' Scathagh had been right; in her own awkward way, Dagda, more mentally crippled than any of them, had given her students everything she had.

Dagda was ungraceful. 'Well, I hope you remember it.'

With the four others Finn stood for a moment in a circle, their arms linked round each other's shoulders. 'It's not goodbye, hags. Thank God.'

Finally, as the long dusk of the summer evening set in, she went to find Art.

She rowed back, pulling as savagely at the oars as her emotions pulled at her. 'What happiness has there been in your life that compares with the happiness you've known with this man?' they asked her. But her adolescence was over. She knew, as surely as she knew anything, that the idyll they'd known on Lough Mask couldn't survive transplantation. 'One of these days,' said the mature Finn, 'that same man and his master will try to rape my country as surely as Dermot and his man raped Boniface. Could I sit in some English bower while they did it?' She looked around at the darkening lake and its enfolding shoreline. 'No, I couldn't. And I'm not going to.'

Swan Island was casting a long shadow over the water and the Pilgrim was pacing up and down. 'Where the hell have you been?'

That night she said: 'Would it be all right if we stopped off at Glendalough on our way to Dublin? There's a priest there that can prove my claim to some property.'

'You won't need any property.'

'It's always useful.'

It wouldn't have been any sort of life that he offered her, she thought; it would have had to be lived entirely through him, cut off, dependent on his visits, his interests, his financial support. She was right to be ending it, but that didn't help the pain.

'Pilgrim.'

'Yes?'

'Art's coming with us. He'll be waiting with horses at first light. Iogenán's lending us some of his horses and keeping mine for a while.'

He grunted. He was outside the hut by the light of the fire trying to wrestle her swansdown quilt into a pannier, while she packed by rushlight in the interior.

'Pilgrim.'

'What?'

'I'm grateful. This time with you has been the only youth I've ever had.'

She was departing from procedural banter and making him uncomfortable; her voice held a note that added to the elegaic quality of the lakeland summer night.

'Plenty more where that came from. This bloody quilt has got a will of its own.'

She put Scathagh's powders into the box Eleanor of Aquitaine had given her and packed that round with her leather sling. There was no more youth to come. She told herself she'd been lucky; some people didn't have eight such days ever.

When he came back into the hut, he found her stretched face down on the bed, her hands clutching the bedclothes and holding them against her face and body as if she would absorb them into herself.

Chapter Seven

The Wicklow mountains were typically Irish in being unexpected; the innocent traveller set off from Dublin into the gentle hills of its south and was suddenly embroiled in dizzying granite. It was like finding the Lake district just outside London, or the Pyrenees on the edge of Paris. They were so wooded with oak, ash, rowan, alder, holly and yew that from the depth of one of their few passes it was impossible to see their tops, which reinforced the impression that they were not so much rising up as swooping down, great blocks of leafy, celestial rubble tipped out by God to remind man of his insignificance.

St Kevin's Road which ran through the pass leading to Glendalough pursued the track the saint had taken in his search for a womanless, temptationless solitude. It had been built over his holy footsteps so that vast numbers could follow in them on a winding, empirical road which dealt with hazards as it came to them; logs laid over the bogs, a stone bridge over a waterfall, cobbled ramps to assist horses up inclines.

Sir John was physically and mentally feverish, querulous at this delay in catching a boat for home, and unwell. The smell of bracken when they were under trees would overwhelm him so that he was semi-conscious for minutes at a time. His back had developed a rash that itched abominably but the effort of scratching it made his limbs ache. Alarmed, he insisted on being helped down from his horse to pray at every wayside shrine. His mortality commanded his attention to his sins which seemed enhanced by the vibrations of holiness coming from the monastery even before he had reached it, and by the obvious and enviable state of grace of the other travellers on the road, pilgrims, sick and troubled petitioners, churchmen high and low.

If he died now with eight days of thorough-going sin on his soul . . . and he hadn't thought to confess before he left Lough Mask because it hadn't seemed like sin . . . his loony kept offering him some herbal drink which she insisted would make him better but didn't at all.

A lake . . . a great sheet of cool water . . . Glenn dà Locha, the Glen of the Two Lakes . . . St. Kevin had pushed an importuning woman into it . . . his loony was importuning him to drink again . . . her face wavered in front of him: 'I love you. Remember I love you.' . . . Bees

171

and insects buzzed into collective sound: 'Have we overdone it?' 'No, he'll be all right.'

'Take him into the shade until I get back.'

'. . . Remember I love you.'

Scathagh had assured her he wouldn't die, would, in fact be as right as rain in a day or two; nevertheless Finn wavered as she walked down the road towards the monastery gates. Nothing, no country, no way of life was worth this; where did it end if you returned betrayal for betrayal?

But her feet carried her on to the stone gateway. No woman was allowed in beyond the walls and the porter was even dubious about letting the Abbot know that she wanted to see him, but her professional Latin and the Queen of England's device on Eleanor of Aquitaine's box eventually persuaded him to send a message. She sat on a stone bench under an oak tree by the river opposite the gate, just able to see over the wall of the monastery the steep roofs of its many churches and the priapic round towers which rose up in puny rivalry to the surrounding mountains with their ogreish names, Lugduff, Poulanass, Derrybawn and Coomaderry. An angular, crucified Christ hung in stone outside the gate with his flat, nailed hands palm-outwards and his little head sunk on his right shoulder. She averted her eyes from the thing; it had watched Boniface's violation at Kildare and done nothing. The sound of a choir chanting a Laudate interspersed with the trilling of sandpipers from the lake. Butterflies chased each other in aerial courtship. She felt isolated by this male powerhouse of sanctity and learning, lonely for another lake where the coming together of men and women had reflected the natural order about them.

'How can I help you, my daughter?' asked a voice. Like all the men of his clan, the Hy Tuathail, Abbot Laurence O'Toole was tall and bony. A childhood spent as a hostage at Dermot of Leinster's court had given him a wider view of life than was usual among monks. One of its few advantages had been to make him, like Dermot, aware of the world outside Ireland.

He also knew a distressed woman when he saw one, and immediately sent one of the monks attendant on him for a restorative glass of nenadmim, the crab-apple cider brewed on the premises. For a moment, Finn wondered if he would know who she was – he had been in the congregation which had witnessed the inauguration of Boniface as Comarba of Kildare – but few monks looked closely enough at any woman to recognise her again, and he didn't. Suffering and sexuality had changed her, and she was wearing a red dress and cloak lent to her by Meld, Iogenán's queen.

The woman's distress was genuine enough, but the story she told him was a lie. 'My lord, I am the wife of Sir John of Sawbridge, a knight in the service of Henry, the King of England. I myself was a lady-in-waiting to his Queen, Eleanor. We have been visiting the shrines of Europe and it was while we were returning from Kildare that my husband fell ill, and is even now back along the road in a fainting condition.'

'My dear daughter, why did you not bring him in? We have infirmaries here and doctors who are skilled in all complaints.' He was a kind man.

'My lord, I fear that the most excellent infirmary may not meet his case.' Her voice faltered. Here we go, she thought. 'I fear he may be a leper.'

Into the river-cooled, bracken-scented air came the whiff of corruption. From the darkest corner of the monastery gateway a rag-ridden spectre gibbered at them and shook the wooden clapper in its decomposing white hand. As one man, the monks crossed themselves. Abbot Laurence told one of them quietly: 'Fetch Brother Clyn.'

'You won't put him in with lepers yet?' Finn asked, 'I may be wrong.'

'No, no,' Abbot Laurence reassured her, edging back along the bench, 'There is a quarantine house for such cases. He will be kept there for a week until Brother Clyn has diagnosed what it is – there are many conditions of the skin which give rise for alarm, but which turn out to be something quite susceptible to cure. And Brother Clyn is very skilled, a son of the O'Hickeys, who are the hereditary physicians to the O'Briens of Thomond, and has translated the authority of Galen into Gaelic, as well as the Book of the Prognostics of Hippocrates. Your husband will be in the very best of care.'

If she hadn't known that this was the procedure, she wouldn't have brought him. 'You earn the gratitude of King Henry, my lord, as well as my own.'

Even abbots destined to be saints were not immune to the possibilities of having a friend in Henry II's class, and Abbot Laurence O'Toole smiled at Finn. He would have patted her head, but the spectre in the corner gibbered at him, so he desisted.

Brother Clyn was thrilled at the prospect of another real live leper for his lazar house which just now was low in patients; all respectable Irish infirmarians liked to maintain them in memory of St. Patrick who had once accommodated one in his house. On their way to the place where she had left Sir John he explained to Finn that people were inclined to believe any skin ailment was leprosy, 'when in fact it may be caused by the *bolgach*, which can be as serious in a different way, or by a demon, or merely by eating salmon out of season.'

By the time they reached him, Sir John was completely unconscious, having been given a last draught of the laced mead by Art. Of Art himself there was no sign, though Finn nodded her head in the direction of a clump of bracken which nodded back. If everything went according to plan, Art would be going into the monastery later on, and she didn't want him associated with herself in the monks' minds.

While Finn held him, Brother Clyn lifted Sir John's eyelids and then stripped off his tunic. He frowned at the angry rash raised by the powder made of rose-hip pips and various noxious substances provided by Scathagh and with which Finn had secretly and liberally dusted her lover's shirt. 'Extraordinary,' he said, 'I've not seen its like before, but I don't think it's leprosy.'

'Thank God then.' Finn cradled the pilgrim's head in her arms.

'But I think, madam, that your husband should be quarantined until this affliction has been safely diagnosed. There are pestilences abroad this year brought upon us, I fear, by the wickedness of our own king and this may be one of them.'

He was relieved when she said that she would be staying at Cill Brigid, a small nunnery in the foothills, for the duration of her husband's illness. 'Return in seven days, madam, and I am sure I shall have good news for you.'

They loaded the pilgrim onto an ambulance cart. She scrambled up to kiss him for the last time and then stood watching it rock away towards the gates of the monastery.

When it was out of sight Art joined her with the horses. Neither of them spoke as they took a track up to the mountain tops.

The plan was to disappear. If they left for Dublin before he did – once he had recovered, and persuaded the monks to let him go – he might be able to pick up their tracks. Besides, they still had business at Glendalough.

They were searching for a site which overlooked the monastery where they could wait and watch for the Pilgrim's departure – at least, Art was looking for one; Finn just sat her horse and followed Art. They had provisions for a week and there was no lack of water in the Wicklow mountains, even during the drought which was turning the eastern plains of Ireland into concrete.

Brushing through overhanging branches, they followed a goat track going upwards until the trees began to thin and they were increasingly treading tracks of heather through which broke lichened outcrops of granite; to their right was more mountain, but to their left there were occasional glimpses of tree-lined drops and of lakes reduced to twinkling ponds by the distance. Along the steeper edges ancient shepherds had planted hawthorn hedges to stop their flocks plunging to their death, and in their effort to cling on to the soil the trees had developed muscled trunks as thick as wrestler's arms. It was when they had passed one of these hedges that Art, speaking low, said: 'Mistress, there was a hand back there.'

174

As the words penetrated a miasma of misery, heat and flies, she looked at him carefully. Poor old Art had taken a lot lately. She must use him more kindly.

'Not a dead hand, either. It moved.'

They retraced their steps quietly, each drawing a dagger they carried. Outside the benificent influence of Glendalough, this was country which belonged to outlaws.

Sure enough, out of one of the hawthorn clumps stuck a hand. It was a left hand resting on a smooth section of branch, cupped palm-upwards as if waiting for alms to be put in it. A small, once-smooth hand with well-shaped nails but now grubby and marked here and there with scratches and hard work. It was attached to a wrist of which the arm disappeared into the hawthorns' interior. They stood still and listened, but no sound came from within the thick wall of leaves.

There they were and there the hand was; expectant, possibly magical, impossible to ignore. In the circumstances Finn was thrown back on her manners and did the polite thing. She extended her own hand to the one in the bush and shook it.

'Oh my God,' said a high voice from the hawthorns.

With difficulty Art parted the spiked branches and they peered in. Between the mountain edge and the hawthorns was a patch of thin grass and on it, with his right side to the drop, sat a very small monk next to a large wheel of cheese and keg of water. There was a manuscript on his knees. He was patting his heart from the shock, and when he saw Art's face he patted it harder, but even then Finn detected an artificiality, as if by over-acting his fright he was, as it were, earthing it.

'Don't *do* that.' He came crawling through the tree roots at them and stood up, a very small monk indeed. The artificiality was not just in his manner but extended to his looks which were so perfectly handsome, apart from a balding head, and so miniature that they seemed unreal; he might have been carved from a less-than-lifesize piece of soapstone. He could have been a child playing at monks, but he was not a child, though whether he was in his twenties, thirties, or even forties, it was impossible to say. His long lashes blinked at them: 'Well, and what are you two dears doing on my mountaintop?' He was shaking from shock still, but playful.

'What are you doing?'

He wagged a finger at them. 'I asked first.'

'Looking for a place to stay.'

'Ooh-er. Please yourself. I'm not curious.' He used his shoulders as he talked, shrugging, lifting one, then the other. 'Well, I'm Brother Pinginn. My mother gave me the nickname and it's stuck.' – A pinginn was the smallest denomination in Irish currency – 'And since you ask, I was trying to do a St. Kevin. "Pinginn," I said to myself, "Pinginn, see

175

if God has forgiven your sins and sends a blackbird to lay eggs in your hand, like He did to the blessed Kevin.'' I was quite prepared, you know; I'd have stayed still until she'd hatched them, bless her, like St. Kevin did. But He seems to have sent me you.'

He peered upwards at Finn and added naughtily: 'Comarba.'

Art was still holding his knife and instinctively tightened his grip on it. Pinginn held his hands up to his throat in part-feigned, part-real terror. 'I can't help it if I know who she is. I was at Kildare for a while, and I like studying women's faces, especially hers. You could kill me but it wouldn't stop my knowing and if I know something I have to say it. I think the whole world would be better if we all said everything to each other, and I know it's got me into trouble beforeandwillagainbut- that'sthewayIam . . .' He spoke faster and faster, babbling himself into a frenetic spiral which Finn began to fear might end in a fit. She shook him by the shoulder. 'Stop being silly.'

Immediately he stopped. He blinked at her gratefully. 'You could stay with me. I won't tell anybody,' he said.

He lived in a cave opening out onto the mountain's face, just below the patch of grass on which they had found him. A path safe only for goats led down to its mouth, which was screened by bracken and bramble. Brother Pinginn shepherded Finn down it with officious gallantry, putting himself between her and the drop – 'Heights are about the only thing I'm not afraid of.' Tenure of the cave would have been dreadful in winter, but in a summer such as this it was attractively cool; a perpetual trickle of water ran down its back wall where ferns grew in the fissures. Scratched on its walls with considerable artistry were outlines of a hare, two wrens and a jackdaw, drawings of creatures which Brother Pinginn had found wounded in some way or another and had tried to help. 'But I'm not going to do that any more. I'm not. It hurts too much when they die.' From an iron spike driven into a fissure three rolled manuscripts hung on strings to keep them from damp. 'These are my three best friends, Virgil, Homer and Boethius. Say Hello nicely.'

It was more than big enough for three people – and by peering over the brambles at its mouth it was possible to see the portion of St. Kevin's road that led to and from the monastic city of Glendalough.

Brother Pinginn took them back over the mountain to where there was pasturage for the horses, and shocked Finn to the core by refusing to go near the animals. 'Nasty big things,' he said. He was afraid of horses, the only person Finn had ever met who was. But he helped them carry their panniers to his cave, staggering on ahead in his eagerness to give them hospitality.

Finn was having trouble fitting the little man into the scheme of things. 'Is he a fairy man, do you thing?' she muttered to Art.

Art spat: 'He's a fairy right enough.' And Finn realised that for the first time, to her knowledge, she had encountered the phenomenon known as 'effeminacy' which was whispered about in convent dormitories with ill-informed discussion on Leviticus Chapter eighteen, verse nine, as to how one could lie with mankind as with womankind and what exactly one did that condemned it as 'abomination'. She was still unsure but, of all people, she had the least reason to unquestioningly accept the Church's condemnations. The little man didn't seem vicious to her, just odd and vulnerable.

He flapped impotently with a blanket, trying to string it from the cave roof in order to screen off a sleeping compartment for her, until Art snatched it from him and did the job himself, and then pointedly made up his own bed of bracken as far away from Brother Pinginn's as possible. Through her fatigue that evening as they fed from his wheel of cheese she listened to his babbled account of how Abbot Laurence had told him he was more fitted to the life of a hermit than that in a community, and she heard pain more clearly than the words. 'A misfit,' she thought, as she drifted off to sleep on a bed of bracken, 'Like me.'

In the middle of the night she woke with a familiar ache in her back and wetness between her legs. She was menstruating. As she fumbled in her saddle-bag for the linen cloths and the harness which kept them in place, she began crying at the cruelty of the non-existent God who allowed her to conceive from rape but not from love. The Pilgrim's baby would have been an inconvenience in her life verging on disaster, but now that all chance of having it had disappeared she knew how very badly she had wanted it. Once she'd begun weeping she found it difficult to stop and stumbled, holding her hand over her mouth to stifle the sobs, out through the bushes of the entrance, and felt her way up the goat track to the grass at the top where she could weep unheard for the woman she might have been and now would not be.

The night around her went comfortlessly on about its business, exuding the smell of gorse and far-away trees, emitting a scream of terror from a leveret as a fox carried it to its earth, carrying the infinitesimal chant from the valley where a necklace of tiny lights wound its way to St. Kevin's church for night office. She was crying into an abyss.

But not alone. A humped little shape a few feet away was crying with her. 'I'm sorry,' sobbed Brother Pinginn, 'I'm so sorry for you.'

There were times to come when this little man would embarrass and exasperate Finn almost to violence but however frayed their relationship became it held through the generous strand woven on the night he, a stranger, grieved for her. She marked the beginning of her long and laborious march back to faith from the same moment.

He had earned the right to know something about her so for the last time in her life she told him her story which earned her the right to hear his. He kept it short but very much to the point. He was an Ulsterman from one of the poor branches of the Clan Sinach and while he was a child his father – 'Not a nice man at all; I couldn't tell you what he did to my darling mother.' – offered him as a novice to the abbey at Armagh where one of his few happinesses had lain in applying his talent for illustrating. When the monastery of Jumièges in Normandy, which had close links with Irish monasticism, had appealed to Armagh for a first-class illustrator, Pinginn was the one chosen to go. 'They didn't tell me there was a war on. Stephen, the king of England, was fighting Queen Matilda all over Normandy and hell was loose.' He and his companion had been caught on the road by a band of roving cut-throats such as war throws up. His companion, who was in charge of their money, had been killed for it. He had been lucky to escape with his life, 'at least, I suppose I was lucky. They used me as a woman.'

He turned to look at her. 'Men can be raped too, you know.'

She hadn't known.

'And, well, it might help you though it doesn't help me, but you ought to know that there are worse things than being raped.'

'Are there?'

'You can enjoy it.' He began to cry again.

Finn looked over the valley into new complexities of horror in the human condition. He shouldn't have told me, she thought; he shouldn't tell anybody.

The monk wiped his eyes. 'I didn't want to hide from you that there is a lot of filth on my soul,' he said, 'But I want you to know that Jesus and I are working on it. He knows I couldn't help it.'

Being the sort of person he was, he had confessed what had happened to him and his reaction to it when he got to Jumièges. They had sent him back to Armagh at once. Once there he was again totally honest and Armagh, too, had decided to get rid of him and had sent him to Glendalough which at first, thanks to the humanity of its aboot, had been prepared to tolerate him.

The monk shifted. 'Are you still talking to me?'

She was overwhelmed by his guilt and his courage. Who was she to condemn anybody? 'Yes.'

'Good.' He had no defences at all, either in his honesty or in his empathy for another's suffering, as if what had happened to him had exposed his nerve endings to vicarious pain, so that a grieving human being or an injured animal could cause him agony. Partly because of what he described as a nasty incident with another monk, and partly because he kept bursting into tears every time he passed the figure of Christ on the cross, Abbot Laurence had sent him away to be a hermit. 'But I get so lonely,' he said, 'left alone with my sins. If somebody doesn't need me, I'll die.' There was no doubt he was in earnest.

'So eventually,' he went on perkily, 'I had a heart to heart with God and I told Him straight: 'Lord,' I said, 'Unworthy as I am, if You don't send at least a blackbird to nest in my hand, like You did to St. Kevin, I'm going to chuck myself off this cliff, even if I do end in Hell because at least Hell has some company and I can take water to other thirsty souls or something.' And I would have done, you know.'

Finn believed him. 'And you got me instead.'

'A portent,' said Brother Pinginn, 'that's what it was. And don't tell me you don't need me for something or other, because I don't believe you and I shall help you anyway. So there.'

Obviously she had acquired him, or he had acquired her. 'Can you teach me to write?'

'Oh, that,' said Brother Pinginn, 'Consider it done, dear.'

A week later three pairs of eyes watching from a mountain top saw a rider take St. Kevin's Road towards the north at breakneck speed. Even as miniaturised by distance, they could tell that it was a bitterly angry young man who rode as if in pursuit of something or someone.

'And that's that,' said Finn. 'Now we can get on with the plan. But first I'm going for a walk. I don't want anyone with me.'

Brother Pinginn came toiling up the track to where Art and Finn waited for him under the trees. It would have been cooler to wait in the cave – the heat was becoming ferocious – but Finn was impatient and insisted on going to meet him.

'Well?' she said.

'Do you mind?' asked Brother Pinginn, going to a trickle of a stream and dabbing his face with its water. 'It's hot. I'm a very hot person.'

'Well?'

'Well, he's there all right, like your cousin said. And he really is a priest, though who ordained him I can't think, because he drinks, God love him. Perhaps he's got a secret sorrow.'

'I'll give him secret sorrow,' said Finn, 'Go on.'

'Well, my friend – the kitchen porter, you know – my friend says that he – that's the priest, not my friend – got so unreliable with his drinking that even Dermot got fed up with him and chucked him out of his household, and he sought sanctuary at Glendalough.'

'We know that,' said Art roughly. He couldn't stand Brother Pinginn. 'What did you do?'

'Well, I told my friend the kitchen porter to take him a message, not saying who it was from of course, to say that if he can climb over the wall tonight while the others are at night office, he'll find some people waiting for him who know something to his advantage.'

'He'll be suspicious,' said Finn, 'God in Heaven, it even sounds suspicious to me. He won't come.'

'Well I didn't know what to do,' said Pinginn crossly. 'But I also said that these same people would give him a flask of wine if he came. And that was very clever, you know, because Abbot Laurence has forbidden him all alcohol except communion wine, so he hasn't had a proper drink for ages. I know drunks. I bet you he comes.'

'How much?' asked Finn automatically. 'All right, we'll pack up and be ready in case it works. Did you ask about . . . the pilgrim?'

'Yes, I did. The poor leper. Well, he was very bewildered at first when he came round. He kept saying there'd been a mistake and that you would come and explain everything.' Pinginn's small face distorted with pain, because Finn had squeezed her eyes tight shut. 'I'm so sorry. But it's all right; he got angry after a bit, especially when Brother Clyn kept trying to give him herbal baths and such. In fact, he threw Brother Clyn into the river and knocked down the monks who were trying to restrain him, and stole a horse and rode off saying that he was going to England and that if you ever crossed his path again he'd kill you. So that's better, isn't it?'

'Ideal.' It was what she'd planned; there was no point in whining over her success being a desolation.

'And I also told my friend to tell Abbot Laurence that I'd received a visitation from St. Brigid saying I must take the world for my pillow and go off to serve her.' He crossed himself. 'Well, you were her Comarba so it's true in a way, isn't it?'

The processional that night was Psalm 37. 'Fret not thyself because of evildoers, neither be thou envious against workers of iniquity,' sang the monks on their way to church, 'For they shall soon be cut down like the grass, and wither as the green herb.'

Sitting on the bench by the stream on the other side of the wall from the chanters, where the oak tree shaded her from the light of an August moon, Finn experienced a longing to go back to the purity and ritual of Mother Church which made everything so simple. She was tired and scared at making decisions on her own authority. 'But what else can I do?'

'Trust in the Lord, and do good,' sang back the monks, 'so shalt thou dwell in the land, and verily thou shalt be fed.'

It had been a problem persuading Brother Pinginn to get on a horse though eventually, shaking with fright, he had persuaded himself: 'Well, if it kills me perhaps it will cry, like Achilles' horses did for their dead charioteer,' though who his friend Achilles was he did not explain.

The chanting faded, commending Finn to commit her way to the Lord and He would bring it to pass, and as it did so a stone from the monastery wall rattled into the roadway, and a figure hung from its arms for a moment then dropped itself down.

Finn got up and walked towards it.

'Hello, Madoc,' she said.

They had laid plans for practically every contingency when Dermot of Leinster's priest recognised her . . . if he attacked, if he ran, if he shouted . . . in the event he did none of these things because he didn't recognise her. The bloated face which had presided over her rape at Kildare just stared sullenly back into hers and the voice which had blessed the assault into a marriage said: 'What do you want?'

All that blood and pain, the baby, the madness, her exile from the normal world, and he didn't even know who she was.

'This,' she said, and gave him Scathagh's Ploy Number One. When he was on the ground retching she kicked him. 'That's for Boniface.' He was dealing with a hag now, not a nun. She kicked him again, 'And that's for all the dead people,' and once more, until Brother Pinginn, protesting, dragged her away. 'That's not going to help us.'

'It helps me.'

A grinning Art bound the man's hands, stuffed his bridle-cleaning rag into the open mouth, and got him up on a horse.

Then they headed for Dublin.

Brother Pinginn babbled nervously as they waited on Wood Quay where, they'd been told, most of the ships plying between Dublin and Bristol tied up.

Finn shook him. 'Stop that silliness. We'll have to take whatever boat will take us.' And there won't be too many of them, she thought. Most common sailors were superstitious about women, priests and monks as passengers and here was her party containing a representative from each of those unlucky categories. Two sea captains had already turned them down, and Art had gone off to try to find one prepared to take the risk. She could have taken passage in one of the high-class ships which served the monasteries, but she was afraid they would ask questions about Madoc who at the moment was sitting comparatively quietly beside Brother Pinginn on a pile of planks in the semi-comatose condition induced by a dose of Scathagh's laced mead, but who would become troublesome when it wore off. He had developed a horror of Finn and when conscious kept trying to escape from her as if from some dreadful thing in a nightmare.

Finn was tired, flustered and hot, lovesick for Lough Mask. Behind her the open gates in the walls of Dublin city spewed out people, sewage, and the effluent of its tanneries, butcheries and iron foundries down tiny alley ways lined with shops selling everything from women to whelks. The summer was drying up Dublin's water supply so that instead of being swept down the open drains on either side of the streets and into the River Liffey, the sludge accumulated in them to the delight

181

of a large population of flies. The knowledge that of her own free will she had opted for this place made her even sicker than its smell.

As they sat there, however, she became diverted, and Brother Pinginn became entranced, by the entertainment of Dublin's quayside which was so busy and so noisy with such a polyglot mixture of tongues and nationalities that the Devil puffing sulphur and wagging his tail could have passed through it virtually unremarked. His representatives on earth were there; Finn and Brother Pinginn watched with appalled fascination as the entire crew of a very strangely-shaped ship with a crescent on her mainsail unrolled mats onto the deck, knelt on them facing west and began a complicated series of obeisances and mutterings.

'Saracens,' squeaked Pinginn. They waited to see if God would strike them dead but, apart from shrieked imprecations from a St. Patrick's monk who was overseeing the unloading of oakboards from a *curragh*, nothing happened to them. 'But you can see that their idolatry has affected their complexions, poor things,' said Pinginn, 'they've gone very dark and one of them is quite black.'

The St. Patrick's monk was having a bad time; while he was voicing his protest against the presence of a Saracen ship to the quaymaster, he caught sight of a party of merchants disembarking from a French fishing boat, and held up his crucifix as protection. 'Jews,' Finn heard him shout, 'is this port to be overwhelmed by the ungodly?' The quaymaster shrugged; as long as the ungodly paid their harbour dues it was all right by him.

In many ways the indigenous traders, seafarers, shipwrights and workhands who strode the quays of Dublin were as compelling as its foreigners. The few women who were among them were as proportionally large as the men, who were tall and mostly fair, like their Norse ancestors who had come over in their dragon-prowed boats and made Ireland hell until it had domesticated them, its soft air dissipating their icy energy. Now they bellowed their greetings, bargainings and quarrels in the liquidity of the Irish language.

'Aren't they the big men,' commented Brother Pinginn, wriggling with pleasure, 'They make me feel weak. Ooh-er, look at that giant.'

A truly enormous blond man, at least six-foot four in height, was standing in a rowing boat, sculling it upriver with one oar over the stern. As he reached their section of the quay, he moored it to one of the bollards, clambered ashore and leaned down into his boat to pull up a passenger in it with one hand so easily that for a moment he held him in the air before setting him gently on his feet. The passenger was Art.

'Your man's name is Hjörlief something,' said Art as if his enormous companion were deaf, 'He's a *Finnghoil* but he's left his land for this one and he trades mostly between Dublin and Bristol. He'll give us a passage if he likes the look of us.'

182

Finn looked mistrustfully at the Norwegian, finding masculinity on this scale bothersome: 'He's overlarge,' she said.

'Will you hush?' hissed Art, 'It's taken me an age of trouble to find him.' Finn saw that Art had done most of his searching in taverns.

At that moment Madoc, who had been coming round unnoticed while their attention was diverted, screamed at the sight of Finn beside him and bolted round the woodpile behind them. Finn bolted after him and found him trapped in a cul-de-sac formed by the stacked planking. Madoc shrieked when he saw her coming after him and began fighting. For the second time Finn gave him Scathagh's Ploy Number One and followed it up by a modified version of Number Four, which cut off his air supply just enough to quieten him down without killing him. 'The mead,' she shouted to Pinginn on the other side of the woodpile. As she looked up she saw that the Norwegian, the only man tall enough to see over the stack, was watching her with interest. 'Pinginn,' she shouted again, and spoke upwards to the Norwegian: 'I'm taking him to England as a witness in a property case. It's all right. He just gets funny turns. He won't be any trouble on the boat.'

'Yust a property case, sure.' The big man nodded calmly.

Madoc was drugged and half-dragged back to his place, peacefully leering. 'He thinks he's drunk again, poor lamb,' said Brother Pinginn.

Finn was ruffled. 'Will you take us or not?' she demanded of the Norwegian. He nodded. 'Ya. Three shillings each.'

'Twelve shillings?' Finn was appalled. 'I could buy four horses for that.'

'Could they yump from here to Bristol?' asked the big man. 'And property case maybe, but abduction we call it where I come from.' His accent dipped and rose, but he was obviously no fool.

It was like bargaining with a mattress; behind the Norwegian's vast, stolid exterior was a vast, stolid implacability which infuriated Finn. However, by reviving some of the old skills from Boniface's marketing days, she eventually won concessions. It would make a large hole in Queen Eleanor's gold, but the twelve shillings was to cover the return trip as well. They were also given permission to camp out over the nights in port on board the Norwegian's ship, which was a relief since putting up with Madoc at a tavern on the way to Dublin had been an experience which shortened Finn's life.

'Where's The Noes inn?' she asked when it was settled that they sail on the next dawn's tide.

The man looked down at her. 'You don't want to go there.'

Finn's temper snapped. 'Don't you tell me where I want to go, you overgrown pirate. I'll go where I want. Are you going to tell me or not?'

The lips of the colossus twitched under his gold beard. 'Yust along, by the Stein.' He nodded downriver.

Pulling a somnambulistic Madoc between them, they skirted the western walls of the city towards the Dame's Gate Bridge. Brother Pinginn said: 'What got into you? You were very rude to that man.'

Finn turned on him. 'I'll tell you what got into me. I'm sick of being pushed about by men. I'm sick of sailors, and priests, and pilgrims and kings. I'm sick of loving them and hating them and being exploited and betrayed and buggered about by the bastards. Well, it's finished. I'm going to do what *I* want from now on and if you don't like it you can get out of my way.'

Brother Pinginn blinked. 'Ooh-er. I thought he was lovely.'

They crossed the bridge over the River Poddle just before it widened out to enter the Liffey, and immediately they were in open country again. The noise of the city behind them dwindled to just another buzz among the buzzing of bees crawling into the foxgloves on the banks of the track. Flocks of sheep cropped common pasture that spread for miles with the occasional interrruption of a church and its out-buildings. Black-headed gulls skimmed along the Liffey to their left where cockle-gatherers stooped to get in their harvest from the mud-flats before the wading birds beat them to it.

The building of Dublin and its continued building of boats had cost the land its big trees for miles around, but there were plenty of silver birches scattered over the common, and alders along the banks. The air was sunny and scented with a tang of salt. Finn breathed it in deeply as if into new lungs. She had a feeling of enlargement; the pieces which had been flown apart on the night Boniface died had come together, scarred, welded, but at least and at last a whole. Ever since that night she had been reacting to what had been done to her, by Dermot, by the Partraige, by the Lough and Scathagh. Even her affair with the Pilgrim had been a reaction to an unbidden emotion. She had been responding to disaster, hate and then love until she hadn't known what was going on or what character was going to emerge out of it all.

Well, now she did. That encounter with the over-large, over-masculine Viking might have been petty, but it had been the latest in a long line of oppressions. She had felt daunted by him and when she had fought back and insulted him a new woman had exulted inside her, just as she had when she'd downed Madoc. Not a nice woman, perhaps, but a woman who was no longer prepared to be manipulated by laws – God's, society's, or anybody else's. From here on she was going to make her own.

A little further on Brother Pinginn caught sight of a line of people being offloaded from a boat moored out in the middle of the Liffey and hauling themselves through the mud-flats to a point on the bank where a group of armed men were waiting for them, away from the dis-approval of the Dublin churches. As they got nearer they saw that the line was made up of pallid young men and women, some of them little more than children, strung together by a rope which passed round each one's neck. Muddy and exhausted, they waded to where the slave-traders were waiting for them.

Finn found Brother Pinginn dragging her arm. 'Use one of your ploys. Let's go and rescue them. I can't bear it. We could buy them and set them free.' She shrugged him off: 'Don't be silly. We're going to need what money I've got left.'

'But we must help them.' He was crying. 'Please, please. They're going to be *sold*.'

'That's their problem.' From now on she would concentrate only on her own. While Art coped with Madoc, she pulled Brother Pinginn on until they were well past the scene. He suffered all the way. 'You've grown hard,' he sobbed.

She looked into the depth of the mended soul. He was right.

The Noes Inn stood at the end of a line of battered warehouses and shacks on a wide stone quay which served the small river Stein where it entered the river Liffey just before the Liffey itself widened out into its own estuary. Behind it, a neck of land protected it from the sea before rising inland into a hill on which stood some tumuli overlooking Dublin Bay. Above the tumuli, exposed to all the winds, was a church hospital. 'That's a leper house,' said Art, 'The locals call it Lazy Hill, but it's really Lazar Hill.'

'We'll check the water supply,' said Finn, 'I'm not using water a lot of lepers have been bathing in.'

On the west side of the creek, facing the quay, was a mill, but what commanded the eye in the green, blue and mud-coloured view was a vast standing stone which stood guard just outside the Stein's mouth. Plain and stark, it towered about sixteen feet above the water. 'Who the hell put that there?'

'The Norsemen,' said Art, 'to mark their first landing place. This is where they first landed when they came to Ireland. In Irish it's "The Long Stone" but Lief calls it "The Stein". It's what the creek and the whole area get their name from.'

'Who?'

'The sea captain,' said Art. 'He said I was to call him Lief.'

'Huh.'

The bridge over the creek was made of wattle hurdles, like its much bigger counterpart over the Liffey further upriver, and had a disturbing flexibility. While crossing it warily they heard a shout from behind them: 'Don't go over there, lady.' They looked round to see a powdered figure whom they presumed to be the owner of the west bank's mill gesturing for Finn to come back. 'It's no place for you, lady.'

'Perhaps he knows something we don't,' said Brother Pinginn, nervously, then added a look from Finn, 'But he doesn't know you either.'

The Vikings might have made their first settlement at this, their first landing place – they had built a defensive stone tower at the point of the peninsula, and buried their dead warriors where their wraiths could watch over it and the sea from their tumuli – but they had quickly turned their backs on it to dispute and win from the indigenous Irish the area round the Liffey's ford where their city now stood, and if the Stein settlement then had looked anything like it did now Finn didn't blame them. The place was a waterside slum. The only building in good repair was the tower itself, ancient as it was, and the stone quay that served it. Against the tower, actually leaning against it like an over-familiar drunk, was the inn, though the tubbed bay tree which stood outside it as a sign had gone brown from thirst. The clap-board of the inn's two storeys was rotting, its thatch was going severely bald and such of its rubbish that hadn't been thrown into the creek to wash against the quay piers littered the quay itself. From its loft window a couple of skinny girls dutifully displayed their braceleted ankles to any passing trade – obviously the innkeeper catered more than food and drink to his customers – but not as if they were anxious to attract it.

The other buildings along the quay went socially downhill from that; dirty, collapsing, indeterminate structures which might have been warehouses, shops, even dwelling places; all of them looking as if they had lost the will to function. One open door displayed the dispirited basics of a ship-chandlery. But to whom? No boat bigger than a rowing boat was tied up at the quay, there were no cranes for unloading cargo, no inducement for the larger ships passing up the Liffey to call in. The place's nearest neighbour, the miller, shunned it; the lepers from the hospital on the hill were banned from all public places, and even a dump like this would be off-limits to them. So who used it, the inn, the warehouses, the girls?

'Smuggling,' said Art, which had been Nessa's opinion, when he'd described the place to her; and now, as she looked towards the place, became Finn's. The upper lights of the tower, for instance, were high enough to have a panoramic view; upriver towards the city, northward over the Liffey estuary to the other bank, westward over the rise of land which sheltered the other buildings at their back and inland to the south. A candle in any of the seaward lights could guide a ship towards it at night, carrying the commodities of trade on which the King of Dublin would otherwise insist on levying a tax, which was practically everything that passed through his port. She was disgusted, not by the probable illegality of this place she had come to see, but by the fact that it manifestly wasn't making a profit out of it. Nobody would live

186

in such a slum if they were making gains, however ill-gotten.

'We'll see,' she said to herself. New horizons were opening to the new woman. Crossing to the bank she did not at once turn into the quay but skirted the buildings to view the land at their rear. It turned out to be a dip of ground in which previous husbandmen had cultivated gardens to judge from the herbs growing wild among the weeds between the fencing and a cluster of choked apple trees. Her concern was the inn's water supply. She traced it to a spring issuing halfway up the hill – she was pleased to see that it retained some vigour even in this drought – which twirled its way through a course in the grass. A leper from the hospital was dabbling his feet in its unprotected source while he washed his bandages and, further down, some cattle trampled its edges as they drank. By the time it reached the back of the inn it had been dispersed and merely oozed into a pond in the fly-blown backyard. As Finn watched a serving man emerged from the inn's backdoor to plunge a ewer into the pond and return inside with it. She rejoined Art, Brother Pinginn and a still-dazed Madoc, who were being solicited with much vulgarity by the girls in the loft window.

'We're going in,' she told them, taking a deep breath, 'Don't drink anything.' They had to squeeze through a door which had so dropped on its hinges that its access must have impeded any fat customer.

Inside the place was mercifully dark, lit only in parallels by the sun coming through the slits of the closed shutters, but their noses informed them that the interior lived up to the exterior's promise. Slumped figures clustered round tables in the shadows glanced up like disturbed dogs at their entrance. One of them actually snarled. The demeanour of these customers suggested that they were here only because they'd been chucked out of everywhere else.

'God's blessing on you all,' called Brother Pinginn, brightly.

'Out,' a figure loomed up from a corner, 'Get her out. No women allowed.'

For a second Finn's knees sagged. The voice was the same as the one which had ejaculated "Nun" on the night of her rape and the face and shape were the same as the body which had covered hers before an altar. Nessa had warned her – 'The twin,' he'd said, 'from the same dark womb in the same dark hour' – but she hadn't been able to prepare her stomach.

She swallowed. 'If you're worried that women will lower the tone,' she said clearly, 'who are those ladies upstairs?'

There was a guffaw from one of the shadows.

The man was in front of her now, illuminated by the crack in the door and she looked him straight in the eye. She might feel sick but she wasn't afraid of him; she had the ability to kill him if she wanted, and through him the spectre of his dead brother. She was going to take

187

away his inheritance. She saw him falter and become puzzled, like a guard dog with an intruder who acts unexpectedly. He swore and shrugged, as if he couldn't be bothered to turn her out and instead said to her companions: 'Are you going to drink or not?'

'Order some beer,' she told them and began her circuit, wading through the filthy rushes to the back door to look out into the back-yard, peer into barrels, crick her neck to the tantalising door at the top of the steps which was also the door of the tower.

'What you doing?' demanded the innkeeper. She took the proffered pot of beer from his hand, paid for hers and those of the others, and ignored him.

'Their father was a considerable merchant,' Nessa had said, 'with property in Bristol and Dublin and a ship to trade between. But the sons were gamblers and after his death they lost nearly everything except the inn and the ship – and they've mortgaged even those to the Jews in Bristol.'

It will take money, thought Finn, but Nessa was right: the place has possibilities.

'What you want?' The rapist's brother was becoming aggressive again. 'You going to drink that beer or not?'

Finn was lighthearted by her relief of compunction to such a pig. She lifted her pot of beer and emptied it so that it sprayed his feet. 'Not,' she said. Ushering the others before her she emerged into the sunlight to catch the boat for Bristol.

The English Church had been trying to abolish slavery for years, with more effect than its episcopal counterparts in Ireland, but it hadn't succeeded with Bristol. Bristol had been a trading port before there was a church; a great castle had been built there because of the impor-tance of the town rather than, as was usual, the other way round. It wasn't that Bristol was wickeder than other cities, more that it had been supplying demands so long that the process had become compul-sive. If there was a market for slaves in Ireland, Spain, Iceland or Niji Novgorod, then Bristol felt it had no other course but to pack men and women on offer in the poorer parts of England into boats and send them off, just as it sent off wool and iron in return for tallow and skins, apes and ivories. If there'd been a demand for grandmothers, the Bristolians would have shrugged their collective shoulders and shipped them out as well – nothing personal, but trade was trade.

Under the anarchy of the Stephen and Matilda war, Bristol had either the good luck or good judgement to back Matilda which meant that, added to the peace and stability engendered by her son's reign, it had his gratitude as well in the form of a favourable charter. So the port of Bristol, which boasted that it could accommodate a thousand

188

ships in its harbour, prospered and allowed its community of Jews to prosper because Jews had money and were prepared to loan it for expansion.

So the Jews prospered, but such profits as they were allowed to keep after giving the king of England his rake-off – all Jews belonged to the king or, as they put it, acted as his milch-cows – they invested in building themselves thick-walled, high-windowed stone houses close to the king's castle in Bristol where they could take refuge if the prosperity ran out. For it had been forced on Jewish attention that when times were bad Gentiles had a tendency to look round for a scapegoat and remember that it was the Jews who had been responsible for crucifying Christ and must therefore be the cause of God sending the flood/drought/murders/pestilence/financial depression that was afflicting them at the moment. They would then inflict their righteous anger on the Christ-killers in very unrighteous ways.

Until she landed on its soil, Finn had forgotten that there would be people in England who actually spoke English – unlike every other member of her party. To her dismay she discovered that such people were in the majority in the vast rabbit-warren of a market that was Bristol. Though traders shouted out their wares to her, African birds in cages, samite from Syria, sea-coal from Yorkshire, apples from Gloucester, they might have saved their breath for all that she understood them. At last they discovered a clerk keeping tallies who spoke Norman French, though with a Bristolian glottal stop. 'The Jewryl? Straight up to the castle and turn right along Matildal street.' He winked craftily at them. 'But if it's usural you're after, my duck, there's Christians who'll advance you money at less interest.' Since usury was not forbidden among the Christian Irish, as it was elsewhere, Brother Pinginn and Art did not realise how illegal his proposition was. Finn did. Even so, she would have preferred to deal with him if she could; Boniface's superstitious horror of the unnamable rites which, she'd been taught, were perpetrated by the Jews in the secrecy of their temples – the dismembering of Christian boys, spitting on the cross etc – weighed oppressively on her. But it was the Jews who held her future and it was from the Jews that she would get it.

The Jewry, when they found it, looked closed. It always did. Jews locked their front doors and made entrances and exits by secret ways. The only sign of life was behind a huge iron barred gate like a portcullis. Behind it, in a passageway leading to a closed door, sat an old man surrounded by a collection of artefacts made odd by its range. There was a cooking pot, several books, a good hauberk, a ploughshare that had seen hard service, two rabbits in a hutch, a pile of assorted cloths, a skirt, three hats, a reliquary and a pile of hay. 'Poke it through the bars, whatever it is, lords and lady,' he said, 'and we'll

see how much old Bundy can advance on it. Good terms. Good terms.'
After a shrewd look at them he'd spoken in French.

'I am looking for a certain Berechiah ibn Daud,' Finn told him.

'Let's call him Benedict,' said the old man nervously, 'a good Christian name and what for do you want him?'

'Business,' said Finn, 'mine.'

They'd have had less trouble being admitted to the Tower of London treasury; it was only when Finn spoke the two words, 'court case' that the old pawnbroker agreed to call somebody else, the somebody else heard "court case" and agreed to call the Rabbi ibn Gabirol, and it was when the Rabbi, who had silky black curls flowing from under his black hat, heard the words "court case" that the gate was unlocked and the door beyond it unbarred to allow Finn and her party to pass through, once Art had been persuaded to leave his dagger in Bundy's possession for the duration. Finn's dagger was under her cloak and she was glad of it, though the only massed Christ-killers she saw were a group of small boys glimpsed through an open door sitting at benches and chanting. Elsewhere, at first, it seemed almost disappointingly prosaic; as she proceeded along passageways, Finn heard women calling to each other from their overhead windows and saw washing being draped on lines between them, just as if they were normal people. But when they reached the centre of the labyrinth the Jews had constructed she could see she was in alien territory.

It was a large, square courtyard paved in white stone with pillared archways on its four sides forming a walk above which was a gallery where more archways led off into rooms behind a fretted ironwork balustrade. In the centre of the courtyard a fountain was playing water into a marble basin.

It was a beautiful place and totally unsuited to the climate. Later, when Finn's knowledge of Jews had advanced, she was to understand better. The Jewish community in Bristol was Sephardic, still longing for the home in Cordoba from which they had been driven by the Berber invasion, still remembering the sharply-divided light and shade of Iberia under another sky which left them perpetually cold. Though bee-eaters and hoopoes had been replaced by sparrows and chaffinches in the courtyard's sweet chestnut tree there were rare moments when the English sun, as now, shone just enough for a melancholy pretence that they were not here at all.

'*Pulchrissime, magister*,' said Brother Pinginn in his best Latin to the Rabbi, enchanted, as they seated themselves on benches, but the place made Finn nervous and her French harsh. 'I've come to give you a chance to avoid a court case I intend to bring against a certain Harold of Bristol, whom I understand to be in the debt of one of your people, Benedict ibn Daud . . .' The Rabbi raised one thin, yellow-white hand to stop her. 'His chirograph must be checked, forgive me a moment.' He left them.

'What's a chirograph?'

A servant brought them refreshment while they waited, dried figs and almonds and sherbet to drink, which sent Brother Pinginn into ectasies but which Art, who was as nervous as Finn, pronounced to be "fizzy piss". 'Will we be giving him some?' he asked, nodding at Madoc who swayed on the bench beside Finn, his dull eyes staring at his boots, 'Isn't this his big moment after all?'

Finn nodded. How much longer they could keep the priest under sedation without killing him was worrying her. On the other hand, trying to economise with Scathagh's fast-dwindling draught, they had given him none for the sea journey over, and that had nearly brought disaster. For Madoc, waking up from drugged confusion to confused reality, had broken free from Art's grip, screamed at Finn and, in trying to get away from her, had fallen overboard. A second later Brother Pinginn had jumped in after him, a noble act which might have proved more effective if he'd been able to swim, which he couldn't, though Madoc could. Shouting instructions and horrific Scandinavian oaths, Lief threw a raft over the side and had his men turn the ship round in an amazingly short distance. The sea was calm, luckily, and they had soon hauled both men aboard relatively unharmed.

From that moment Madoc transferred his horror from Finn to Brother Pinginn, spitting and punching at the little monk whenever he came near him.

'There's gratitude for you,' said Finn, crossly, 'when you tried to save his life,' but Brother Pinginn shook his head.

'He's fighting himself. He's me. One of me, and he loathes it. He won't admit it to himself. I expect that's why he drinks.'

When the Rabbi returned he had someone with him, a Jewess whose appearance underwrote every prejudice the Gentiles depicted into the caricatured Judensau they scrawled on walls. She was fat, middle-aged, hook-nosed, and outrageously bedangled with every form of jewellery – a sharp contrast to the Rabbi who was thin, cultured and aesthetic – as if she had made herself into her own walking safe deposit. The loveliest thing about her was her smell. Finn, who was used only to dabs of rose- or lavender-water, sniffed appreciatively at a new, exotic, olefactory experience. The woman wheezed with effort and moaned at her feet, which were squeezed into tight, high-heeled shoes, but her flat, black, kohl-rimmed eyes gave the impression, as Art said later, that if she shook your hand you should count your fingers after.

'It is as I thought,' the Rabbi told them, 'the debt has now passed to

191

the Lady Belaset and she holds Harold of Bristol's chirograph. She should hear what you have to say.'

'And get on with it,' said the Lady Belaset, 'because these seats put the cold in my bum.'

She embarrassed the men, even her Rabbi obviously felt she was letting the Jewish side down, but Finn's hostility became tinged with admiration. 'That's it,' she thought, 'to become disgraceful, where you don't give a damn.' Aloud she said: 'This Christian priest here is witness to the fact that he performed a marriage between myself and Harold's brother, Eric of Bristol, and therefore it is me, and not Harold who should have inherited his property. I am prepared to produce this man in the King's Court to prove my right, but I have come to you first to see if this procedure can be circumvented.' She felt queasy and ashamed that even in the mind of Jews she should be bracketed with the rapist. 'But this is survival,' she thought, 'I'm owed.'

'That's a good word that circumvented,' said Belaset, 'you want to explain it?'

'Foreclose his mortgage,' said Finn, 'Basically you own his inn and his ship anyway . . .'

'No Jews don't own nothing,' said Belaset, 'the Christian god and king don't allow it. Christians own things, Jews just lend the money to buy 'em.'

'. . . and put me in as the owner instead,' finished Finn.

Belaset stood up, rubbing her backside, to peer at Madoc. 'That a witness?' she said, 'I seen livelier corpses.'

'He'll talk,' said Finn, praying hard, 'when it's necessary.'

'Now it's necessary.'

All the way over on the boat Finn had been training Madoc for this moment, telling him that if he ever wanted to see Ireland again and end his present purgatory, he had to pronounce three words. 'When I ask you, Madoc, all you have to say is: "I married them". It was a joke to you, you bastard, wasn't it? Remember? But the joke's home to roost, Madoc. Say it. Say: "I married them".'

Madoc hadn't wanted to remember. He had screamed and spat and shouted – it was during the enforced rehearsing of his lines that he had jumped overboard.

Now Finn said, 'Father Madoc. On the Octave of St. Brigid in Ireland, did you or did you not pronounce words of marriage over me and Eric of Bristol?' Was it worth it? Yes it was. She was owed. They'd landed her with the rest of this life to fill, they could fill it. Madoc stared fixedly at his boots but Finn's training and threats brought the reflex, 'I married them.'

Art audibly whistled with relief.

'Not very convincing,' said the Rabbi, but Belaset, scratching her armpit, was looking at Finn. 'What a lady like you could do with an inn and a ship?'

'A lady like me,' said Finn, grimly, 'can do anything.'

Belaset nodded. 'You come and talk with Bela. Let's the men stay here.'

She took Finn's arm and hobbled her towards the other side of the courtyard where steps led up to the gallery. Again Finn's nostrils twitched, intrigued and delighted by the sophistication of artificiality. No flower she'd ever come across smelled like this. 'You like the scent?' asked Belaset.

Finn nodded. 'What's the flower?'

'Never mind the flower,' said Belaset, 'mostly it comes out of the whales' heads.' Her room was a riot of tapestries, foreign carpets and cloths of which the colour bewildered the eye. Delving into a chest underneath a pile of mouth-watering silk she came up with a piece of oiled silk wrapped round something the size and shape of a ball which turned out to be a grey, waxy substance. 'See that, Irish? That's from a whale's head.'

Finn regarded the ambergris. 'It looks disgusting.'

'Never mind disgusting, that make scent stick. You ever get the ship, you look for whales and get that stuff out their heads, we're in business. I got perfumiers in Spain make smells court ladies sell their virtue for if they got any. I send some to Eleanor of Aquitaine and her ladies go crazy for it. Eric of Bristol didn't have no wife.'

The tone hadn't changed but Finn jumped. 'He killed the wife he had,' went on Bela, 'pushed her downstairs for nagging, only nobody could prove it so the property stayed in the family. But he went to Ireland to join Dermot so her brothers didn't get him, but he don't marry no more, not that I heard and if I don't hear, it don't happen. Raped a few women maybe.'

Their eyes met. 'It would still be valid,' said Finn, carefully, 'If he raped a woman and a drunken priest had said the marriage words beforehand.'

Belaset nodded, 'Maybe, maybe not.'

'And rape is an offence for the King's court,' said Finn, repeating Scathagh's law lessons, 'and a woman is entitled to compensation for it and a royal judge might give her the man's property as compensation, especially if she'd been made the rapist's wife, and he might rule she wasn't responsible for the debt run up by the man and the man's brother. There's justice in England under Fitzempress, they tell me.'

'Sure,' said Belaset, 'if you pay for it. But that Fitzempress owns the Jews and his share of the money owed them and he don't give it away so easy. You got money?'

'No.'

'Then how'd you pay a mortgage, always supposing some damn fool transferred it you?'

'I wouldn't,' said Finn, 'not at first. In fact, I'd need to borrow more.'

'You like the clothes off Bela's back?' asked Belaset, twitching one of her many shawls off her shoulders, and proffering it, 'the skin of her teeth, maybe? Where you learn to bargain like that?'

'In a hard school.'

'Hard, maybe,' said Belaset and her spurious rage dropped away as she looked carefully at Finn. 'You suffered, certain. But you ain't suffered like Bela. You ain't suffered at all until all your children die before you do, like Bela's. You got children maybe?'

And lancing through a chink in her mind she had kept stopped up until now, barely knowing it was there, Finn experienced a pain so sharp she thought for a moment it was physical. It paralysed her. She found herself enveloped in the Lady Belaset's fat, scented arms. 'Your god and my god,' Finn heard her say, 'they're male, sure for certain. Neither got no pity. You want a drink?'

Finn shook her head and Belaset resumed her seat. 'All right, I tell you what. I like Ireland. You people tolerate Jews and only kill each other. That's nice, refreshing. Maybe I take a chance on you. Tuppence interest in the pound per week, coming down to a penny when we got mutual confidence and Bela's a fool.'

Nessa, the only Partraige in the entire clan who understood percentages, had briefed Finn. She pulled herself together. 'Not that much of a fool,' she said, 'that's over forty per cent per annum. A penny interest in the pound per week will be all I can afford, and that won't be for a bit either.'

'You want to ruin me?'

'It's better than nothing a week, which is all you're getting now. The inn is a pit and the ship's laid up.'

'Who says so?'

'Lady Bela, I'm going to make money. I'm going to run the best inn in Ireland. I'm going to use my ship for trade and earn a fortune. I'll kill whales with my bare hands and get that stuff out of their heads, if that's what it takes to get more money. And I'm going to get information so that not a leaf drops in Christendom but I know about it, by God I will.' She stopped, shocked at what had been formulating in her head and only just crystallised into intention by words.

Belaset was slowly nodding. 'Bela better get in on this empire early, eh? What for you want it? You don't want no jewels and fancy men. Pretty girl like you can get them any day.'

'Power. I'm going to need power.'

'Power yet. It don't keep you warm nights. And I tell you about

194

power. You get it, you keep quiet about it, or sure as certain some man'll come and take it away from you.'

Finn smiled. She was beginning to like the Lady Belaset very much. 'You and I can beat them.'

'You got charm, you know that?' said Belaset. 'But the job you got, it'll take more than charm.'

When they rejoined the others Belaset put on another show of rage. 'That Harold, I'm finished with him. He reneged on his payments long enough. This lady can take a message to Moses Maimonides in Dublin to foreclose and take seisin legal. Harold can go to hell, and this Irish lady can take over. We make a new chirograph, she and I.'

'Is that wise, Lady Belaset?' asked the Rabbi worriedly.

'How do I know from wise. It's a chance. So poor old Bela's a chancer.'

When, some hours later and after many signings and transactions, the Gentiles were leaving Jewry, the Rabbi remembered to ask. 'What about the ship?'

'Sure,' said Belaset, 'Who's to be the new master so's we know the name when he calls to collect?'

'It's a mistress,' said Finn, 'Her name's Aragon.'

Bemusedly the two Jews let them out of the gate and watched them go down the street. 'Rabbi,' said Belaset in Hebrew, 'the next time old Bela says she'll take a chance, just slit her throat. Save time. Cut out the middle man.'

'Middle woman,' said the Rabbi.

Five days later, as mysteriously as he'd left it, Madoc was returned to Glendalough. The monks found him wandering outside its gates in a dazed condition. When they questioned him on where he'd been, his answers were confused and they could make nothing of them. Thereafter there was a change in the man, though Abbot Laurence wondered whether it was for the better; true, Madoc voluntarily gave up drinking, but he seemed to have become vicious and when he talked, which wasn't often, he swore revenge on someone whose name he could not remember.

Three weeks later, as she prepared to become landlord of the inn at the Stein, Finn produced a piece of board and asked Brother Pinginn to paint an inn sign on it. 'New owner, new name,' she said. 'It's to be called "The Swan".' But when Pinginn proposed to draw just a swan on the board, she stopped him. 'There can be a swan in the picture,' she said, 'but I want a lake scene. The Swan doesn't mean a bird.'

'What does it mean then?'

'An island.'

Chapter Eight

The 1160's had promised to be good years for Dermot Mac Murrough but they didn't live up to it. He'd started the new decade as undisputed King of Leinster – or as undisputed as a king of Leinster ever was – as king to the King of Dublin, and with the High King of Ireland, MacLochlainn, as his ally. All that stood against him was a defeated Connaught and poor old Tighernan O'Rourke of Breffni, still raging with humiliation from Dermot's abduction of his wife, though she had long been returned to him.

But as time went on Dermot became haunted by voices, as if his conscience had become externalised and acquired the gift of speech and song. Several times when he was out hunting he heard the *bean sì* calling his name from the woods. 'Dermot, Dermot,' it keened, 'Remember Kildare.' When he went hosting into Meath, it called to him from the mists on the road to Tara, 'Remember Kildare', and though some of his men went plunging after it, all they found was bog and an echo. At night when he was in sore need of sleep, the wailing woman flew to his window and pressed her terrible lips against its bars to whisper, 'Remember Kildare.' While he was looking over his cattle at the *macha samraid* a tiny fairy man in the robes of a monk appeared on a hilltop and chanted 'Remember Kildare,' before he vanished. A herd of his horses galloped by him in the Barrow valley and one of them shouted 'Remember Kildare.'

He thought he had lived down Kildare, for he had regretted it as an impolitic move and had given penitential money to the church as well as founding new convents in Dublin, plus rebuilding into a beautiful abbey the monastery at Ferns. But the trouble with a vociferous external conscience was that it not only reminded him of his sins, but it reminded everybody else as well. It seemed to Dermot that those who were with him when the voice called whispered to each other afterwards and avoided his eye.

He could have lived with it; he had lived with his conscience for fifty years and it hadn't bested him yet, just as he had got along without anybody's good opinion but his own. It was the poem he couldn't live with; the country wasn't big enough for both of them.

197

It was well known that the best of Irish poets, the most respected people in the land, could, if angered, use a satire to kill or, at least, inflict shame and disgrace, which was worse. A poet could compose an *aer* to blight crops, dry up cows and raise blisters. Senchan Torpest in the seventh century had been put in an ill humour on discovering rats eating his dinner and had uttered a line which killed ten of them on the spot.

Who composed the satire on Dermot Mac Murrough was not discovered. Dermot traced the source to Connaught but was unable to pinpoint it further. Pride in his satire had warred with cowardice in the soul of Niall of the Poems and, not unreasonably in view of Dermot's lust for revenge, cowardice had won. It seemed to have been sung first by the bards, who every so often went *en masse* round the kings and chiefs of Ireland delivering their latest compositions, during their great circuit of 1160. Even among Dermot's allies it was well received, being both funny and vicious and conforming to all Irish rules of prosody; his enemies heard it with joy.

It loses nine tenths of its sting in translation, of course, but its refrain went something like:

> 'Sing of great King Dermot,
> Leinster's worthy son,
> who bravely marched his army,
> against a single nun.'

In no time it was being sung at the *aenachts* and markets, even in Leinster itself.

The Irish could respect a bastard, but not a ridiculous bastard. Suddenly it was recalled that though he had cuckolded Tighernan O'Rourke, Dermot himself did not know where his own wife was since she had run off with part of his treasury.

Dermot knew he was being laughed at; the very air of Ireland sniggered behind his back, but he could find nobody with the courage to sing the poem to his face. Eventually it was Murchadh Mac Murrough who, first disarming his brother in case of accidents, repeated it to him, then held him until he was out of the fit.

Perhaps, even at that moment, Dermot was defeated though, being the man he was, he faced it out. His allies and sub-chiefs were bound to him by loyalty in some cases, fear or bribery in others, but Dermot knew that all those bonds would not hold them to a laughing-stock. The satire combined with the voices was rotting the links and at the first real test they would snap.

Finn personally took only a small active role in the persecution of Dermot, though she mastermined it. The work was done, and done brilliantly, by Brother Pinginn, Niall of the Poems of course, Art, Blat and the hags of Inis Cailleach until a groundswell of anti-Dermot laughter arose all over the nation and made their encouragement unnecessary. For Finn, getting rid of Dermot was now merely one objective; she also had to watch out for Ireland.

On a wet autumn day Moses, the Dublin Jew and agent for the Lady Belaset of Bristol, turned up at the Noes Inn with several Dublin constables and the necessary writs, and evicted Harold of Bristol from it. Harold protested, kicked one of the constables on his shin and spat at Moses, but there was nothing he could do about the foreclosure which was legal and long overdue. Out of their charity the Jews paid his passage to England and, swearing revenge, Harold took it, enlisted as a mercenary and disappeared into the maelstrom of European war.

It was still raining on the next day when Finn and Art carried their saddlebags over the wattle bridge to the Noes quay. Finn stopped in its swaying middle and looked at what was now, if she could pay the mortgage, her property. Not only was she the new landlord of the inn but she had also used part of Belaset's extra loan to buy cheaply the crumbling buildings that ran inland from it along the quay. In themselves they were too derelict to be worth much, but ownership of their site gave her the entire Noes peninsula, apart from the leper hospital further away up the hill.

The prospect was not edifying. Rain made even meaner the deserted, crumbling collection of buildings. It dripped off balding thatch into drains blocked with filth and, even as she watched, a flake of rust responded to one raindrop too many and one of the hinges holding a shutter broke off so that the shutter swung down and sideways, drooping like a creature given way under ill-usage.

Finn turned round to look at Art. Art looked back. Finn picked up her saddlebag and walked onto the quay. As she did so a tall, sallow-faced man in bright cloak and headgear stepped out of a shed doorway.

'Lady Finola? My name is Vives and Lady Belaset instructed me to welcome you, watch over you and give you the keys.' He looked at her carefully to see if this Gentile would mind the protection of a Jew; he had come to Ireland from East Anglia where anti-semitism had broken out into pogroms and had still not got used to the general lack of prejudice among the Irish lay community.

Finn thanked him gratefully. His presence gave official sanction to what increasingly seemed a mad enterprise, his welcome made the day less grey, and she needed all the protection she could get. The keys, however, proved redundant. The inn was about as secure as a cheese. Not only were the shutters rotting, but so was the door which anyway had been kicked in. They went inside.

Harold of Bristol had taken his revenge with an axe. Every table,

199

chair, stool, every beaker and jug had been smashed. The earth floor was an undergrowth of splintered wood and pottery shards.

Vives said impassively, 'I am sorry.'

Finn shrugged. 'I was going to burn it anyway.' While it retained objects that the rapist's brother, and perhaps the rapist himself, had touched the place was abhorrent to her. 'I'm going to tear down the walls and begin again.'

They walked out into the back garden, which Art called 'the bawn', to find more ruin, smashed barrels and water butts. But Finn's interest was in the water supply. They walked across the flat, weedy garden, through a neglected orchard and up the slope to where the stream emerged out of a fault in the hillside. Despite the drizzle, another leper, or perhaps the same one she had seen on her first visit, was sitting on a stone beside it, gloomily watching the run of water through the slit in the bandages which covered his face.

Finn felt revulsion overcome the compassion which Christ enjoined should be extended to lepers. 'Get away from here,' she shouted at the wrapped figure. 'Haven't you got a stream up at the hospital?'

The figure turned to her. 'I like this one.'

'Well, it's mine. And you keep away from it.'

There was a wooden clapper in the suppurating hand and the leper shook it at Finn before he limped off up the hill. She was aware that this was not a good beginning among neighbours, but she couldn't help it. Even as Boniface she had always dreaded the ceremony at Easter when the nuns of Fontevrault had accompanied the Almoness to the lazar house at Montsoreau to distribute alms which, even though they were proffered on long, shovel-like alms plates, involved a contact that made her own healthy flesh crawl with digust. She was able to feel pity for lepers only when they were out of her sight.

The next most important place was the tower, about which Finn felt considerable curiosity. The lower part of its south wall formed the north wall of the inn and its only apparent entrance was up the inn's rickety staircase, which also led to the gallery that served the inn's sleeping quarters.

They climbed up to the landing in front of the door and Vives presented the keys for Finn to try in its formidable lock. He too was obviously curious about the tower and intended coming in with them. Finn didn't dispute his right – the Jews were her mortgagers, after all. She tried first one key and then another, but none of them fitted, then Vives tried, then Art. 'Damn the man,' said Finn, 'he changed the lock.'

They scoured the inn for its key without finding it and reluctantly Finn sent Art down to the saddlebags to get an axe with which to break it – the lock was big and made of excellent brass, the only thing of quality in the place. As they waited on the landing for Art to come back

Vives said: 'We always used to think that Harold of Bristol used this tower for smuggling.'

'Well he didn't make any money at it,' said Finn irritably, upset at having the cost of a lock added to her already horrific outlay.

Vives coughed. 'We never felt it in our hearts to condemn him too strongly,' he said tentatively. 'The King of Dublin charges heavy duty on goods brought in through the port. We have to import our own particular wine from Spain and the king takes advantage of the fact.'

Suddenly Finn realised what the Jew was saying. 'You mean if I did some smuggling myself you'd come in with me?'

Vives winced. He liked a more subtle approach to such matters. 'I am sure we could reach accommodation on business of mutual interest,' he said.

Finn nodded. 'We'll see.' If things went on getting more expensive, she might indeed go into the smuggling business.

It was easier to smash the door, which was old, than the lock, and after Art had swung his axe a few times, they managed to manoeuvre themselves through the splintered gash into the room that took up the middle floor of the tower, a fairly ordinary, square, unlit, plank-floored room, but immediately Finn knew what it was to be dead. Not a premonition of death, but a realisation of it. The coffin lid was tamped down on her and life blanked out, annihilation, no sense with which to realise there was no sense. Every particle of her body absorbed the moment, which was all it lasted, so that while able to see she was also blind.

Art noticed nothing and went over to the trap door which led to the undercroft. The hand that went under her elbow to steady her was the Jew's. She turned her head in his direction. 'Is that it?' she asked. 'It can't be that. Where's God?'

Vives looked down at her and saw suffering; he knew suffering. 'God is everywhere,' he said, very gently, 'but it may be too soon for you, whatever you have been through, to realise it.'

He took her up to the top floor of the tower. It was better up here, though the dimensions were exactly the same as below. But air came through the four long lights and with it the smell of the sea. Finn walked to the west window and looked out. From here the river opened up into its estuary and the bay. Today, in the rain, it was a grey-brown view of mudflats and cloud and unbounded sea. She was wracked with home-sickness for other water, for the enclosed, colourful, reeded security of Lough Mask. 'What the hell am I doing here?' she wondered, 'when I could be home.'

But this was still Ireland. It was the door to Ireland. She could only watch out for her country from here. From here she could face the island across the sea that threatened hers. She saw herself as a porteress with the Pilgrim and Fitzempress and the entire Norman army advancing up to her door. 'You can't come in,' she said, and slammed the door in their faces. She grinned at herself for being so ludicrous, and then swore at herself because, once the Pilgrim's face was recalled to her mind, it stayed there.

Art's ugly head popped up through the trapdoor. 'Will you see what I've found in the undercroft,' he said and added, as Vives moved forward, 'It's private.'

'It's all right,' said Finn, 'He's a friend.' The few words the two of them had exchanged in the middle room had covered a deeper communion; she felt an understanding with Vives and with Belaset that had its root in some mutual physical and mental exile.

Art lit a lantern and they negotiated the steps which followed the curve of the wall down past the middle room and through its trapdoor to the undercroft.

It smelled of damp, and of liquor from smashed vats of beer and wine, but among the detritus of broken wood, sailcloths, rope ladders, masts, oars and rusty anchors, they found three untouched barrels of red wine, which Harold had either overlooked or hadn't had time to destroy. Finn tapped one of them, holding the beaker attached to it up to Art's lantern with a hand that still shook. She smelled it, then put her finger in to taste it, unwilling to drink from the beaker. With the benefit of Boniface's training by the Cellaress of Fontevrault, she pronounced the wine excellent Aquitanian. 'From the Bergerac, I think.'

'Will you stop boozing,' said Art, 'and come and see this.'

'This was another trapdoor. The heavy stone square that usually blocked it was lying to one side and a chain which ran through its ring was still attached to a pulley on the wall, showing how it had been lifted. They smelled fresh water and when Art held the lantern over the hole they saw below them the brown, peaty water of the Stein trying to enter the bigger force of the Liffey further out. Little whirlpools made sucking sounds which reverberated through the undercroft.

They dropped down one of the rope ladders and each one in turn climbed down it to see. Trying to steady the ladder into facing north Finn found that behind her and to her right and left were the solid, barnacled, weeded foundations of the tower, but ahead of her two massive piers held the tower's base where it overlapped the foundations, so that there was a shallow tunnel under this north-east corner of the undercroft and a roofed mooring for small boats bringing goods to Ireland.

'Here's your smuggling route,' said Art.

Finn was delighted. Here was her own secret back door. It was ideal for smuggling. A ship could moor out in the estuary, as if waiting for the tide, and load its cargo into a rowing boat. From upriver it would look an innocent enough procedure, a small boat rowing into land. But it wouldn't land; it would disappear into this hidden harbour and unload.

Vives bowed to Finn. 'When you have settled in,' he said, 'we shall have much to discuss.' They went on exploring. It was Vives who found the well. They heard his voice echoing from the other side of the undercroft and the scrape of a cover being lifted. 'You could stand a siege.'

It was a terrifying well; small in diameter, but when Finn dropped a piece of wood down it they had time to count their fingers before they heard the whispered splash. It would take so much labour and time to wind up the bucket that it would be easier to carry water into the tower from the inn, but Finn was glad the well was there. When you were in the business of stopping an invasion, you never knew what would happen.

Shivering with cold they returned to the slightly warmer desolation of the inn and Vives, offering hospitality at his home but being refused – Finn intended to live on the premises from this day forward – bade them goodbye. 'Who will design the new inn?' he asked.

'Art,' said Finn, 'and me. But Art's the expert.'

The Jew looked down at Art's squat form with new interest. 'He knows about buildings?'

'He knows about stables,' said Finn, firmly. She had planned this out; fundamentally, she reckoned, there was not much difference between the feeding, watering and wining of human customers and the stabling of horses. Both should have light, airy but draught-free accommodation on floors that were crack-free and suitably drained, with easily-cleaned feeding surfaces. 'Besides, he's spent more time in inns than most men.'

Art ignored the slight. 'And we won't be having rushes on our floors either,' he said, 'Apart from they shelter fleas, they absorb damn-all. We'll be needing sand or sawdust, easily swept out and soaking up spills and blood.'

'What blood?' asked Finn.

'Sure, you've got to expect fights.'

'Not in my inn, I don't.'

Vives looked at them both. 'Whatever else this inn may be,' he said, 'it should be interesting.' He bowed and went.

Like a good host and hostess, Art and Finn waved him over the bridge and past the mill. The moment he was out of sight, they rushed into the inn and began the work of clearing it. Finn was struggling to get a broken bench out through the back into the bawn when she heard Art swearing upstairs. She went up. Along the room at the back of the gallery was a communal, raised bed of slats and underneath it was a row of chamber pots, all of them full. Art was pointing into one of them. Holding her nose, Finn peered. At the bottom of it, shining like a fish in yellow water, was a large key such as would fit a large, brass lock. 'That bastard Harold had a nasty mind,' said Art.

By nightfall the rooms in the tower had been scrubbed, Finn had a bed made up in the top room, Art had his in the middle room, and the inn had been emptied of its wreckage which was lighting up the sky on a bonfire in the bawn. They sat by its glow, too exhausted to contemplate the stairs to the tower.

A white figure advanced across the grass towards them. Finn groaned. 'Get away from here,' she shouted.

'It's not a leper,' said Art. It was their nearest neighbour, the miller, still white from his milling. He was bellowing welcome and proffering a flask of excellent ale. 'The name's Molling,' he told them, as they passed round the flask, 'and glad I am to see the end of Harold of Bristol. Do you know that his customers used to frighten away mine? Will you be wanting to buy flour?'

He was Dano-Irish and a typical miller, being large, jolly and unscrupulous. Finn was glad to see him and told him about her plans for the inn – at least those she was willing to admit to a stranger – and her worries about the lepers and her stream and her scheme for its supply to the inn.

'Water?' he said, 'we millers know everything about diverting water. How else would our wheels go round? Leave it to me. And what do you intend doing with the girls?'

'Girls?' asked Art and Finn.

'Come with me,' said Miller Molling. He took them through the inn, along the quay to the disreputable warehouse. They followed him up its ladder to the loft and there, curled up on some straw and sleeping like exhausted children, were the two prostitutes who had propositioned Brother Pinginn, Madoc and Art on the day she had first set eyes on the Noes Inn.

'Been here for days,' roared Molling, 'couldn't or wouldn't go with Harold of Bristol – not that I blame them – and nowhere else to go. I sent them over food, Christian duty, but I won't be having them in my mill, for I am a Christian man and clean-living though my dear wife is dead, God rest her.'

Disturbed by his voice, the two girls woke up and looked back at them out of sullen eyes.

'Strictly speaking, I suppose they're now your property,' said Molling, as if the girls were deaf, 'since Harold bought them on his mortgage. Will you keep them?'

Finn looked with dislike at the two, thin bodies. Boniface's upbringing had taught her that prostitutes were as bad as lepers, and for all Finn's liberation from convent ideas, she could not fight off revulsion. 'No,' she said, 'it's not going to be that sort of inn.'

But she was not capable of turning them out into the night, nor of letting them remain in the cold of the warehouse in their dirty, tinselly and extremely scanty clothing. 'Oh, get over to the tower,' she said, 'Take some straw with you. You'll find blankets in a saddlebag. Make up your beds there until I decide what to do with you.'

Unspeaking, coughing, the two girls gathered armfuls of straw and crept away. When Finn reached the tower it was to find that they were in the middle room which meant that, if the proprieties were to be observed, she had to sleep there while Art took his bed to the top room.

Tired as she was, she found sleep difficult that night. Although she'd put her bed as far away from the prostitutes as she could, she was disturbed by their continual coughing. Even in the dark the room maintained its peculiar oppression, and from the trapdoor to the undercroft came the suck and moan of the waters beneath the tower. She covered her ears, but the noise came through her fingers transmuted into the crying of a child, which was how she heard so many sounds nowadays.

With sacking on her back to keep out the wet, she worked in the rain like a dog, stripping the old thatch off the inn, walking into Dublin to order supplies and new reed for roofing – reed was more expensive than straw, but it would last longer – chipping away at the old plaster on the walls and thanking God that her time with Scathagh had given her muscle and endurance and hardened her hands. Art had persuaded her not to pull down the basic structure of the inn. 'The lathe and wattle is sound,' he told her, 'it just needs re-plastering, and the wall at the back is stone. All we need to dismantle is them out buildings.'

Miller Molling was a great help; not personally, though he made frequent forays over the bridge to encourage them, but in lending them his servant-of-all-work, Gorm, a silent weasel of a man who could turn his hand to anything. Together he and Art pulled down the warehouse and outhouses, burning such wood as was rotten and using what was not to extend the new inn.

For the next ten days it seemed as if life would never again consist of anything except wet and hard work, but slowly a Swan Inn assembled fresh-smelling bones out of the corruption of its predecessor. There was only one interruption, when Finn and Art tried out the system which they believed Harold of Bristol had used for his smuggling.

Finn put a lantern in the north window of her tower's top floor, first closing the shutters on the other sides so that the light could only shine out onto the Liffey, virtually unnoticeable to anyone who wasn't directly north. Candle in hand she went down past the bleak middle floor to the undercroft and waited. It wasn't nice.

Odd how the dimensions of a building had confirmed to her that God did not exist, was just another misrepresentation of male history. It had been one thing not to believe in Him when she was insane, quite another to be of sound mind and without hope. She was suddenly overcome by the fatuity of what she was doing. This emptiness was insupportable; perhaps she should run after the Pilgrim and beg his love and pardon, perhaps she should go back to Lough Mask, live a quiet, Partraige life and let Ireland look out for itself.

'I'm damned if I do,' said a voice of sheer courage from the only human presence in the dungeon. And Finn smiled at herself, for if she could not go to heaven, neither could she be damned. The tower was reality; she would stay in it and face it. In one sense it freed her of responsibility except to those she was responsible for, this eccentric entourage she was collecting, and Ireland, that most eccentric of countries. For them and for herself she was going to fight with no sins barred. The rest of the world could look out.

An oar batted the underside of the trapdoor. Finn freed the counter-weight they had attached to the chain to make it possible for a single person to open the trap, and pulled. Art's face was framed in a black square. 'That lantern up top's no bloody good except as a general guide,' he said, 'on moonless nights we'll be needing another hanging on the piers. And the ship that brings the cargo will have to show a light or you end up rowing all over the Liffey to find the bugger. If Lief hadn't got worried and shown a lantern on his port side I'd have finished up back in Connaught.'

'Did you bring that blasted Viking into this?' Finn was furious. 'Why not invite the King of Dublin while you're about it?'

Unperturbed, Art scrambled into the undercroft. 'If this was a trial run, didn't I need a trial ship to get a trial cargo off, you stupid woman? He's brought us in some nice Gloucestershire wool so the lord and lady customers can sleep warm and a nice iron cauldron and the devil of a job we had getting it into the *curragh*. And not a drop of duty to pay on any of them. Your man's a fine sailor, and a better smuggler.'

Finn sighed. It seemed that a Viking giant had joined the Swan Inn and its fight for Ireland.

On the tenth day, unbelievably, it stopped raining and on the day after that Finn heard a call from over the bridge, dropped her plas-terer's board and ran, yelling, along the quay to welcome the people she most wanted to see in the world. Brother Pinginn, Blat, Tailltin, Aragon, Muirna and Bevo had arrived at their new home.

Muirna pointed at the tower. 'Inis Cailleach all over again,' she said.

Finn kissed her, kissed all of them. 'Now you've come it will be,' she said. She gave them no time to explore but hauled them up to the top room of the tower to feed them and, with Art, to hear their news. They were full of it. Thanks to all of them, except Aragon who had been seeking the salvage of her ship, Dermot was a haunted man who now

206

heard the words 'Remember Kildare' in every bird call, every creak of a door. 'Muirna even managed to get into Ferns and hiss it through his window,' said Bevo, 'Blat and I shouted it in the market when he rode through, and other marketwomen took it up. He's not a well-liked king, and everybody in Leinster is worried he's brought bad luck on them. Brother Pinginn was wonderful, kept shouting it on hilltops and then scampering off. But the best thing is Niall's poem. Everybody's singing it.'

Finn looked at her king-wreckers with tears in her eyes. 'Thank you,' she said.

'Ach,' said Muirna, uncomfortable, 'We've got a purpose at last. Tell us about the inn.'

She told them, drawing her and Art's plan in the dust of the floor.

'Basically the Swan will be three inns,' she said, 'one for the sailors and common people because we're going to need their information, especially the sailors'. But if we're to attract good-class trade we must have a separate section with better sleeping quarters.'

'What's the third?' asked Brother Pinginn, fascinated.

'That's for special visitors,' said Finn, 'the secret ones. They'll come to the tower.'

She told them about the undercroft, told them everything in her pleasure at being part of a group again; of Miller Molling, the lepers, of her scheme to literally stream-line her inn, with a water supply that would lead into her kitchen then out again to a washing trough, and would be well away from her house before leading into the privies.

'That stupid man there,' she said, nodding at Art, 'wanted the privies next to the kitchens, but I'm going to have them sited like at Fontevrault.'

'If it's a bloody convent we're building,' grumbled Art, 'we can save our bloody trouble, for nobody'll come.'

Finn ignored him. 'And I'm going to have fireplaces and chimneys in the wall like they did at Fontevrault, so the smoke goes up the chimney and doesn't choke us to death.' Every other inn she knew of, even on the Continent, kippered its customers by having the smoke from the fire in the middle of the floor trying to find its way out by the louvre in the roof. The Swan, thanks to Fontervrault's example, would be the most modern inn in Christendom.

'And Gorm is making sure our stream is out of reach of those damned lepers.' The strange little man had come up with the idea of enclosing the source in a shrine on which was carved the totally unwarranted shamrock cross of St. Patrick – 'to discourage vandals,' he said, winking – and piping the water through buried hollow tree trunks joined together with pitch straight down the hillside to a cistern in the inn.

'The Swan's inherited two problems from the Noes Inn,' Finn said, 'one's the lepers, as I told you, and the other is those two girls downstairs. Harold bought them as slaves. They were the inn's prostitutes.'

The hags gasped. Only Aragon, who was wider-travelled than all of them, had ever seen a prostitute. 'Poor dears,' said Brother Pinginn, immediately, and trotted off down the stairs to talk to them.

'I just don't know what to do with them,' Finn explained, 'I'm not going to keep them here, that's for sure, but at the moment they seem too ill to move. I'd hoped I'd get some work out of them after a bit, but they're useless for anything.'

She'd unwillingly learned something of their history. They were like enough, to her undiscerning eye, to be sisters, though they were not related; they were fair-haired, skinny, very young – they reckoned their ages about fifteen – both had been sold by poverty-stricken parents, and been shipped into Ireland from Bristol some two years previously.

Brother Pinginn came back into the top room. 'They're sick,' he said, as if it was Finn's fault.

'I know that.'

'Very sick. They've got blood in their sputum when they cough. They've got the *serg* – the withering disease.'

'They say the *serg* is rife in England,' said Aragon.

'Perhaps they got it from one of Harold's customers,' said Tailltin.

'However they got it, they can't stay here,' announced Finn, and Aragon, who hated illness in herself or anyone else, agreed with her.

'But where can they go, poor things?' asked Brother Pinginn. 'They haven't got anywhere else.'

'Back to England where they came from.'

'Back to slavery.'

'Well, then, a convent.'

'Sure, a convent would be lovely and understanding to a couple of foreign harlots,' drawled Bevo, surprising Finn who had been sure all the hags would agree with her. And Tailltin joined in: 'It's no way to begin the fight for Ireland and its women by sending away the first couple of waifs we come across.'

'But they're not Irish, for God's sake.'

'*Non Angli, sed angeli,*' quoted Brother Pinginn.

'Oh, shut up.'

'I won't. I think you're being stinking. It doesn't matter if they're Irish or not, it's just Ireland's shame that they landed up here. They didn't choose to become prostitutes, poor dears. It was a sort of rape, and we, of all people, should know about that.'

There was a silence. 'He's right, Finn,' said Muirna, gently.

'Oh shut up, I know he is. I just don't know what to do about it.'

'If they stay here we'll all get it,' said Aragon.

'Not necessarily,' said Pinginn. 'There was a monk had the *serg* at Glendalough and Abbot Laurence cured him.'

'A miracle I suppose?'

'Sort of. He had the loft of the old stables cleared out so that the patient was well above damp ground, and let the wind in to blow away the contagion – like it might be in this tower room – and kept him warm and rested all the time and fed him the best food with milk and some wine occasionally and offered up prayers to the Holy Mother and St. Mochua and St. Kevin, and he was cured. So it was a miracle; it just took longer than most.'

'How long?' asked Finn, suspiciously.

Brother Pinginn became interested in some dust on the window seat. 'About a year.'

'A *year*? You want me to entertain a couple of foreign whores in this tower for a year?'

'This top room would be best,' said Pinginn, 'because of the air, you know. I can do the praying for them.'

'Not here, for God's sake. This is my room.' The moment Gorm had finished thatching the first section of the inn, Art had moved his bed into it and, with enormous relief, Finn had left the prostitutes and the hated middle room for the top floor. She sighed. 'Jesus.'

Brother Pinginn nodded. 'That's just what he would do.'

A voice in Finn's mind demanded: 'Where's the profit in it?' A charitable act on this scale would have earned her merit points in Heaven under the system Boniface had believed in; in this new realism it would gain her nothing but trouble and expense. Nevertheless, these people, her friends, were here because they loved her and loved Ireland. The Swan was a democracy or it was nothing. And in this instance she was outvoted. 'All right, help me take my things back down, and a pox on the lot of you.'

Next day two coughing, ex-prostitutes snuggled their abused bodies into the first clean, warm beds they'd ever had to themselves in one of the finest rooms they'd ever seen, and fell asleep.

Finn found that sharing the middle room with her fellow-hags alleviated some of its nastiness, though the moan from the confluence of waters at the base of the tower still disturbed her.

Aragon stayed only a fortnight; when the seas were free from winter gales she took passage with Lief, the Norwegian, on one of his trips to Bristol to collect the ship that had once belonged to Harold of Bristol now that it had been made seaworthy.

With the remaining hags at Finn's disposal, work on the building of the Swan speeded up and became a pleasure to all of them. Art taught Bevo the rudiments of carpentry and she began to make the simple furnishings the inn would require. While Art and Gorm completed the

209

new sections of the extended inn, Blat started digging and planting the vegetable and herb gardens. Finn, Tailltin and Muirna dismantled a stone wall in the bawn and built a kitchen. Using her memory and commonsense Finn constructed two chimneyed wall fire-places, one in the nobles' parlour and one in the new kitchen.

'What's them?' asked Miller Molling on one of his inspections.

'So's the smoke can get out,' Finn told him, sucking her bleeding fingers.

'Funny looking things.'

They were definitely not beautiful; both having a drunken tendency towards one side, but they were, she knew, not bad for an amateur stonemason. She plastered the fireback of the grates with clay mixed with cow manure to make it tensile and, offering up a prayer to her non-existent God, lit a fire in each. Watching the flames from the shavings and off-cuts direct themselves up the chimneys was one of the most beautiful sights she'd ever seen.

There was a shout from outside. 'Smoke.' Modestly, Finn went outside to receive an applause which couldn't have been greater if she'd built Chartres Cathedral. Only Gorm and Art were unmoved; they couldn't see the point of chimneys.

Finn looked round: 'Where's Pinginn?' The little monk was of no use at all in the building processes; he ran about investigating everything with interest, contributing no practical help whatever and generally getting in people's way, but his delight in everybody else's achievement was warming.

Blat pointed to the orchard. 'Down there.'

She went through the sopping grass to find him. The winter had been mild, if extremely wet, and looked as if it was giving way to an early spring. Blat had pruned the apple trees to within an inch of their lives, but they would soon be in bud.

Suddenly she realised she wasn't unhappy. She couldn't say she was happy – happiness was what she'd known with the Pilgrim and unlikely to be repeated – but her depressions were becoming rarer, giving way to a prosaic but satisfying sense of achievement. She had lost a lover, but she had found a cause, a family and a new home. There was no point in longing for the old one; she had to find contentment here. She *had* found contentment here.

'Pinginn,' she called, and then she saw him, surrounded by bandaged figures to whom he was doling out some of the ale they had bought from Miller Molling. 'God damn it,' she said; the lepers had been a growing nuisance to the building workers, sometimes ringing the site altogether, shouting abuse, threatening Finn because she'd piped their favourite stream, leering at the hags and demanding free beer with menaces.

210

She was so angry that they ran off, leaving Pinginn to face her. 'But the poor things deserve some kindness,' he said, miserably, 'they have little enough.'

'They've got a hospital up on the hill,' said Finn, 'and I'm going to see they stay there. How many customers will we get while we're infested with lepers I'd like to know?'

She stormed up Lazy Hill to the lazar house and found the hospitaller examining his apple trees, just as she had done. She'd already encountered him a couple of times; a gentle, completely ineffectual old monk.

'Can't you keep your lepers under control?' she shouted over the hedge at him.

He looked round, mild and apologetic. 'I'm afraid not, God love them,' he said. The trouble with lepers, thought Finn as she stormed back down the hill, was that the biblical status of their disease and the general tenderness with which they were treated gave most of them airs. "Uppity as a leper" had entered the language. Nobles and kings frequently had their progresses interrupted by a bandaged, suppurating figure rapping a wooden clapper and shouting for alms with considerable rudeness. Gritting his teeth into a benign smile, royalty would chuck over a piece of silver both to mark his charity and to stop the nuisance coming any nearer.

She passed a sheepish Brother Pinginn. 'I'm seriously thinking of getting a dog that'll attack monks and anything in bandages,' she shouted at him.

Blat heard her and looked up from her digging. 'Get geese,' she said.

'Geese?'

'Geese. The poor men only approach from the hill, not the quay. Put geese in the orchard; good watchdogs, good eating, and a brave leper who'll come near them.'

Finn patted her cousin on the back, and put geese on her list of animals to be acquired when the inn was finished.

And at last, on March the 5th, the Feast of St. Kieran, one of the twelve Apostles of Ireland, it was. Silently the staff of the Swan gathered in the middle room of the tower to make a ceremonial procession round the inn they had built, with Brother Pinginn leading the way and giving blessings.

'Can the girls come too?' he asked, 'It's mild and a little outing would do them good.'

Finn was reluctant; processing her inn with a couple of prostitutes, however much they had put their past behind them, would, she felt, bring it bad luck. She resented the fact that the rest of them had been working so hard while the two girls had just idled about in the top room eating their heads off, but Brother Pinginn had refused to let her use them, other than to give them a little light sewing. The taller one, who had brown eyes, struck Finn as one of the stupidest girls she'd ever met – and she was never given any reason to change her mind. The other one, with blue eyes, had wits as sharp as her nose. Her name was Elfwida. That of the dim one was Wulfraitha but to the Swan establishment she had quickly become known as Perse, short for Persingly, which was how she began almost all her pronouncements. 'Persingly, I like sunny days better than rainy ones,' she would say, or, 'Persingly, I think lambs are sweet,' or, 'Persingly, bad food makes me sick.'

Well, they had assumed personalities and become part of this odd establishment of hers. 'Oh, all right,' she said.

The staff of the Swan Inn went down the staircase into the first section, the nobles' parlour. It smelled of fresh mortar and sawdust. In its middle stood a long oak table, which had been shipped down the Liffey from Naas in Kildare, and had cost five of her fast-diminishing shillings. Settles, benches and rush stools edged the walls. The back of the room was open stone and contained Finn's fireplace complete with trivets, gridiron and spits, though this was mainly for cosmetic purposes since the bulk of the cooking was to be done in the communal kitchen at the back connected to the nobles' and common parlours by separate doors.

In silence the staff looked at their handiwork, Bevo passing her hand over a chairback, then progressed to the kitchen. This was a wonderful place with an enormous fireplace next to which was the cistern. Pots, ladles, choppers, skillets and carving knives hung in neat rows on the walls, herbs from the ceiling. Blat, who was in charge of it, was secretly afraid of its modernity, but Finn knew there was not its equal in Ireland, nor in England for that matter. Hams were curing in the smoke house. Bins were full of flour, oatmeal and salt. A peat stack stood outside the back door near the newly-planted herb garden, and fires were laid ready to heat the stones of the sweat-house and the bath. Ale was brewed.

They moved out into the bawn and stood to admire the herb bed by the door, soon to sprout parsley, rosemary, thyme, mint and sage, then on to the vegetable beds planted with cabbage and beans. Animals had been bought and there was a cow with a calf in the byre, and a she-donkey in foal cropping the pasture. As they passed under the budding apple boughs of the orchard, a dozen geese came honking towards them and Brother Pinginn skipped to Finn's side for protection. Blat had gone into Dublin to bargain for them and come back driving them before her, ferocious strong-necked birds with loud voices and a loyalty only to those who fed them, which the Swan company took care and turns to do, all except Brother Pinginn who was intimidated by them.

The apple boughs were in bud as they passed under them and up the hill to see the unwarranted shrine of St. Patrick which enclosed the source of the stream.

There was no water in sight, except the view of the Liffey to their left; the stream now ran underground through wooden pipes – not a complete success, since they had a tendency to burst in cold weather, but adequate. Reverently the staff followed the new turves which had covered the pipe back down to where it emerged to pour its water into the cistern in the kitchen. The overflow was conducted by a tiled gulley through a washing trough outside, and they followed it, past the sweat- and bath-house, and then to where it returned back into its natural course and a pond for horse and cattle, which was also stocked with fish.

Finn took the lead. The next bit was her pride and joy. The stream left the pond and flowed on into the trees to disappear beneath two wooden huts, one larger than the other. Just as in the best monasteries, the water, having served every other need, could now serve the most basic. She threw open one door and then the other to display the larger, first-class privy which had two individual cubicles containing a seat in which was a carefully-sandpapered hole, and the second-class privy which contained the more usual communal bench with holes of varying sizes to fit various-sized bottoms. Sheep wool, for the wiping of those same bottoms, hung on little hooks.

The staff stood in admiring silence, listening to the stream which would take impurities away into the Stein which would take them into the Liffey which would take them out to sea.

'Gawd,' said Elfwida, admiringly, 'what a shit-house.'

'And your sailors'll still piss straight into the Stein,' said Art.

From behind them advanced the geese, who seemed to regard the privies as their special area. Pinginn complained: 'They're ruining my health.' The geese rushed him every time he came, so that his trip to the privy were fear-filled and infrequent scampers, 'I'm getting constipated.'

Muirna asked Finn, 'What will happen when the customers go to the privy and the geese attack them?'

'Oh hell,' said Finn wearily, 'like Iogenán used to say, we'll burn that bridge when we get to it.'

They returned to the second-class parlour; much the same as the nobles' except with the more usual centre fire – Finn had run out of stone and couldn't afford to buy any – and a deal table, passing by the inn's oiled, clapboarded frontage which gleamed in regular horizontals broken by the carved doorways and shutters along a swept quayside. A new bay tree flourished in a pot.

For a moment, before going in they looked up at the sign which was set between the two doors. Pinginn had painted it well – a lone swan flew over an island on a lake so familiar to most of them. Instinctively the hags clasped each other's hands.

'This is home,' said Tailltin as if defying a statement nobody had made. 'It's Ireland.'

'Dermot's Ireland,' said Finn. Dublin, for all its autonomy, was still part of Leinster. 'But, God help us, not for much longer.'

That night they opened for business.

And nobody came.

Well, Miller Molling and Gorm came, and the miller sat in solitary state in the first-class parlour and Gorm in less state, but equally solitarily, in the common room. Both were entertained with more food, drink and attention than they could cope with, but the occasion lacked sparkle. The staff kept looking towards the door. 'What's the matter?' asked Tailltin, 'Why won't they come?'

Finn shook her head. She didn't know what to do. With two of her few last pennies she had hired a crier to shout the news of the wonderful inn through the streets of Dublin, but new inns were being opened every day in that flourishing city and, with the weather still wet, nobody wanted a muddy ride or a damp boat trip to visit yet another.

They were up against stiff competition as far as travellers went. The monastic houses had excellent accommodation for guests, and Irish hospitality laid on its kings the duty to provide free public hostels for anyone needing lodging and food, though, as none of these was in the Dublin kingdom, Finn had hoped they wouldn't affect her business.

The next morning Muirna and Bevo rowed out into the Liffey and shouted out the attractions of the Swan to passing boats but all that did was to give a crew of a Manx traders the idea that the place was a brothel, and their disappointment on finding that it wasn't led to a nasty scene which ended in the hags having to throw them out.

It was in the middle of this fracas that Belaset arrived to see what was happening to her loan. A crazily-coloured figure against the dull blues and greens of the Liffey landscape, she hauled herself out of Lief's longboat, which with its shallow draught could navigate the Stein, and up the steps of the quay, watching with interest as a protesting trader thrown by Bevo splashed down into the creek. 'You got so many customers you can throw them away?' she asked Finn. She hobbled into the first-class parlour and stood near the fire taking off her shoes and rubbing her backside. She refused Finn's offer of refreshment and looked round. 'Nice place.'

'It's good to see you,' said Finn, 'but I thought you'd be coming over with Aragon.'

'Nothing personal,' said the Lady Belaset, 'but I should experiment at my time of life? If that girl don't sink her first few trips, then maybe, but I got other business here in Dublin can't be done forty fathoms down. Now then.' Despite her fatiguing trip she wanted to meet everybody and see everything. She disapproved of the ex-prostitutes still wan and coughing in the tower chamber – 'Charity's one thing, maybe: millstones is something else' – but she was delighted by the smuggling route which she thought might prove useful to the Dublin Jewry on occasion.

'Nice place,' she said again when they were once more back in the parlour, 'Pity the clientele's invisible.'

'I don't know what to do,' confessed Finn miserably.

'You got to give the place personality. Get it known for something definite, something the others don't got. Swan's a crap name, anyhow, too pure and who wants pure? The monastries got pure. More like ''Amazon'' the way your girls handle men. Now, Bela, you got an idea.'

She chewed the rouge off her lips while the Swan staff sat and watched her much as the ancient people had waited for the pythoness to speak.

'You remember Eleanor Aquitaine went crusading with that pissy first husband of hers, Louis of France? Dressed her ladies like Amazons, bare boobs and all?'

'I'm not baring mine,' said Bevo, firmly.

Belaset didn't hear her. 'You up in crusades?' she asked them.

She left shortly afterwards, still refusing wine or food. 'You want Jews to drink here you got to get kosher wine,' she told them.

They all stood on the quay to wave her goodbye as Lief's rowers took her on towards Dublin city to pursue her other investments. 'Even she won't eat here,' said Finn, 'and she owns it.'

But after such a long, dull winter the nobles of Dublin had become bored, and they pricked up their ears as word mysteriously spread of a strange inn down by the Stein run by strange women who had sworn to remain virgin until Jerusalem was freed and had actually gone on crusade to the Holy Land where they had learned strange skills from the Saracens. The intriguing rumour came to the ears of Asgall Mac Torcaill, the King of Dublin, who was sick of the sight of his own city walls and was in search of somewhere new to drop into after hunting trips.

Vives hurried over the Stein to warn Finn. 'The king intends to pay you a visit,' he told her. 'He will pretend it is on impulse – he cultivates the Viking virtue of spontaneity. Open-handedness, drinking bouts, quick to anger, that sort of thing.'

Finn could see he disapproved. Like her cousin Nessa, Vives was a careful man but whereas Nessa's carefulness was natural to him, Vives had learned it in a hard school. It was his survival.

'How did you get the information he was coming here?' she asked after she'd thanked him.

'My people depend on advance information; forwarned is fore-armed. We are a network all over the world. We exchange it. Sometimes it saves our lives, sometimes it doesn't.'

Finn nodded. 'After I've got this inn established, Master Vives,' she said, 'you and I must have a little talk.'

'We saw your welcome-light,' boomed King Asgall, 'and were drawn by thought of mead-foamed cups.'

Mead-foamed cups were ready, silver-shoaled herring browned on oil-spluttering griddle, venison cuts from antlered forest-runner stewed in iron-bound cauldron in flame-flaring fireplace. 'And if they don't stop shouting,' grumbled Blat, 'they'll get thin-bladed onion-chopper up leather-clad arseholes.' The Dublin-Norse mode of speech was catching. For days afterwards the staff of the Swan referred to the Liffey as "Stag of billows, peatland courser." To have guests at all was thrilling, especially such exalted ones as the king of Dublin and eleven of his jarls, but there was no doubt they were wearing.

'When are they going home to their night-linened wives?' asked Bevo, exhausted, after seven hours of running back and forth with pitchers of ale, mead and wine. 'Not till rise of dawn-breaker from the looks of it,' said Finn, putting the sixth batch of bread into the wall-oven.

The Dublin Norsemen looked like Vikings, ate and drank like Vikings, boasted like Vikings and, by the end of the night, were belching and farting like Vikings, but Finn decided that three hundred or so years of Celtic influence and inter-breeding had made an uneasy mixture. Instead of being benign it had robbed the Vikings of their confidence and made them curiously effete. For all his back-slapping geniality, King Asgall's eyes flickered about to see what impression he was making. He and his fathers had long ago adopted Christianity, but he liked to confuse it with a little paganism and replied to Brother Pinginn's grace with: 'Thanks be to Balder. I mean, Christ.'

There was a forced quality in the way he and his jarls insisted on putting Norse speech patterns into their now Irish mother-tongue, as if they were clinging onto the time when dragon-prowed ships had sailed the widow-maker and terrified the world. They still thought of themselves as terrifying, and there was defiance in the way they remembered that they had risen against Dermot of Leinster's father and killed him, as if it had been a great deed and not just another tribal assassination which had caught him by surprise. There was insistence on how any man could speak his mind to the king on the Thingmount, the great man-made hill which stood midway between the Stein and the city, but Finn noticed that his jarls fawned on Asgall and praised his prowess in a way that would have sickened Irish nobles. Certainly their democracy

216

did not include inviting their servants in to eat with them; it was only at Finn's suggestion that they were taken into the common parlour to eat at all. And once they'd elaborated on how brave they'd been on their hunting trip, 'kiss of thin-lipped axe on wolf-pate,' the hunters fell to swapping gossip.

Art was disappointed. 'Lief's a better Viking than any of them,' he said, and Finn saw that the huge Nowegian was watching the feast from the kitchen door. As she pushed past him to get more ale he said, 'You take care. They get dangerous now.'

The jarls were getting restive as they got drunker. Finn had managed to recruit some entertainment – a harper, a sword-swallower and a couple of acrobats – but hadn't had time to find anything special, and anyway the jarls had seen them all before; a couple of them began banging on the table calling for women. 'Where's Amazons?' shouted somebody and the banging became concerted with a cry of, 'We want Amazons.' A large red-headed jarl stood up to make a grab at Muirna, the gentlest-looking of the hags which was probably why he picked on her. 'You an Amazon? Let's see your tits,' and began trying to tear her dress front down with a hand made clumsy by drink.

Lief reached for his dagger, but Finn's hand clamped on his arm. 'You dare,' she said. The last thing she wanted was a knife-fight. 'Leave it to Muirna.' They saw Muirna smiled in kindly fashion at the Norseman as she gave him Scathagh's Ploy Number One. The sight of their companion rolling and gasping on the floor as he held his testicles so amused the rest of the jarls that their humour was restored. King Asgall was still laughing when he eventually left, and in a grand gesture scattered enough silver on the floor to pay for the food, drink and breakages twice over. 'Come again, my lord,' called Finn as her guests lumbered onto their horses and headed for the city.

The Swan's reputation was made, though from that moment on both the inn and its female staff were given the generic name 'Amazon'. The ladies of Dublin insisted their lords bring them to look at the women who had the fighting skills of the mysterious east and asked questions about the crusades which the hags couldn't answer. They adopted Belaset's advice, saying they were under a vow to reveal nothing of what they had seen and learned, thus making themselves even more mysterious. One lady looked up at the sign Brother Pinginn had painted and which hung above the door. 'Is that what Outremer looks like? What a pity. No different from Connemara.'

The new inn became popular and the sight of boats tied up at the quay and the sound of cheerful feasting attracted the big ships coming up the Liffey so that it became a regular thing for their crews to row over and spend the night there before going on to the city to discharge their cargo. Finn began spending most of her nights serving in the second-class parlour listening to the sailors' talk, asking questions and building up her knowledge of events in the outside world.

The drawback to the Amazonian reputation was that it became a matter of honour for some young drunk to challenge one of the hags to a fight and become sufficiently objectionable until he got it. Much of the clientele came in anticipation of seeing one of their number thrown out. Behaviour was considerably better in what became known as the sailors' parlour.

'It's wearing me out,' complained Bevo. 'It took two of us to chuck out that bloody Ragnar last night. Eleanor of Aquitaine has a lot to answer for.' But as a result they made sure they kept fit and did the exercises Dagda had taught them up in the tower room in their spare moments before a fascinated audience of two ex-prostitutes.

There weren't many spare moments, and as spring advanced they became fewer. Once the wreckage of the previous night's feasting had been cleared up there was a day's work preparing for the next; there was brewing, baking, broth-pastry-sausage-cheese- and pudding-making, vegetable-peeling, butchering, salting, curing, saucing, spicing, pickling, herb-fruit-fungi- and egg-gathering, fish-catching, shellfish-collecting (these last were Brother Pinginn's department), to say nothing of marketing, putting fresh straw into the used palliasses upstairs, emptying the baths and chamberpots, filling cauldrons of water and preparing the fires. They worked like slaves, though afterwards they all remembered that period as one of satisfaction. Ten times a day Finn wondered what they would have done without Blat whose generalship in the kitchen and whose ale, marrow-pudding and honey-salt pork glaze attracted their own admirers to the Swan/Amazon. It was also a pleasure to see Brother Pinginn in his element; though by no means the most useful member of the staff, he derived joy from the tasks he had to do and said he had never been happier in his life. He was occasionally a worry at nights when he could not resist batting his eyelids at some of the beefier Norsemen. More than once a hag had to step in and save him from somebody with homosexual tendencies who wanted to take Pinginn up on what seemed to be an invitation.

'Will you stop it?' said Finn, 'I'm trying to make this a respectable inn. Did I or did I not see that sailor pinch your bottom?' Brother Pinginn was contrite. 'They always go too far,' he said, 'I don't mean them to.' And Finn knew he didn't; the little monk was not out for a sexual encounter, he just couldn't resist flirting. 'Save it for Lief,' she said. Perhaps knowing that he was safe, Pinginn was outrageous with Lief, mincing across the big man's path whenever he came in, nudging him in the waist with his elbow and pretending to cry when the Norwegian merely picked him up and put him outside the window to get rid of him.

The drain on supplies during that first flush of the inn's success was so great that Finn had to borrow money from Vives in order to buy more. But she was able to pay it back with its interest within a fortnight, and a month later began the repayment of Belaset's loan, which Vives called every week to collect. It was Aragon, on her return with Harold of Bristol's former ship, however, who raised the possibility of paying it off quickly.

They were having a meeting in the tower-room discussing Aragon's forthcoming maiden voyage, when she said, 'That stuff of Belaset's, Finn. I think I can get more.'

'What stuff?'

'Ambergrease is it? She showed it to me. I've seen lumps like it before, only much bigger, some this big.' Aragon spread her arms.

'Jesus, where?'

'When the O'Conor *brehon* and I were trying to get my ship money out of those stinking O'Malleys on the west coast.' O'Conor's judge had awarded Aragon the right to some of her ship's value, but the Ui Maille, who had salvaged the ship, were delaying payment and earning Aragon's wrath. 'They call it "whale shit", foul-mouthed pigs that they are. They find it floating on the sea and each of their boats carries some as magic. The O'Malley chief has this much in his house, like a boulder.'

'Does he know what it's good for?'

'For scent?' Aragon raised her heavy black eyebrows. 'Have you smelled the O'Malleys? But if he thinks it's valuable he'll raise his price. I'd rather deal with Belaset even. You want me to get it when I go back and see if the O'Conor's got my money out of them?'

They discussed it. The seas were opening for trade and Nessa was due to arrive with the Partraige hides and furs which Aragon, and a crew Lief had picked for her, were going to carry down to the Aquitaine where, it was thought, they could get a better price for them than in England. She was to bring back wine and any other commodity she judged saleable.

'I'll go to Connaught and get your money,' said Finn, 'I've got an idea I want to put to the O'Conor anyway, and I'll get the ambergris from the O'Malley while I'm about it. I'll teach him to owe a hag of Inis Cailleach.'

The absence of two hags from the inn would require the hiring of extra staff in their place. Finn cast longing eyes towards the consumptive girls who were still confined to the tower and eating their heads off. 'They look better to me,' she said.

'And they're going to stay better,' said Brother Pinginn, firmly. 'The year's not up.' So two members of Dublin's proletariat, a boy and a girl both lumpish and big for their age, were taken on as scullions.

When it came to it, Finn was reluctant to leave the inn, partly because she was sure it would go to pieces in her absence, and partly because it had become a home. But most of all she hated taking leave of Aragon, realising at the last moment, the hazards of storm and current and robbers the hag would face on her voyage.

They renamed Harold of Bristol's ship *St. Brigid* and poured a jugful of the Bergerac wine over her prow for luck. The stain looked like blood, which earned them respect among the Dublin seamen who still secretly sacrificed a goat or a lamb over the figurehead of their ships at the beginning of every voyage, much to the rage of the Church.

Finn and Aragon stood on the Stein quay and looked out to where the *St. Brigid* rode at her anchor in the middle of the Liffey. To Finn's anxious eyes she looked frail, an uneasy cross between a rowing galley and a sloop.

'Will you be all right?'

'I want to go and I can manage it,' Aragon reassured her, 'She's a sound ship and that's a good crew Lief has found. They're terrified of me.'

The inn staff lined up on Lazy Hill to watch the *St. Brigid* row out to sea and set sail. On the same day they climbed to the roof of the tower and waved as Lief rowed Finn and Art to the north bank of the Liffey where horses were waiting for them. 'Damn,' thought Finn as they watched their figures dwindle into articulated matchsticks, 'I'm going to stop this getting fond of people.'

However, now that the inn was established, she had to begin to watch out for Ireland.

'She going to make this journey all right?' asked Lief of Art.

'Yes, *she* is,' said Finn crossly, 'and what are you going to be doing while *she* is away?'

'I got business in Iceland,' said Lief. 'More ambergris there than you ever seen.'

Finn rounded on Art. 'Do you have to tell him *everything*?' Part of her anger was because the Norwegian would be away from the inn, where he had taken up semi-permanent residence. 'He irritates the hell out of me,' she thought, 'but he's safe.'

Chapter Nine

The Great Hall of Woodstock was only a royal palace because Fitzempress said it was. It was big, but it was still a hunting lodge. Antlered heads, the smelly masks of wolves and boars, spears and bows lined its otherwise plain walls. Though its stools and benches were finely carved there were no chairs. Dogs were everywhere. The breeze that ruffled the branches of Oxfordshire's forest came through the wide windows and open doors, as if the hall were a temporary interruption in a landscape which had no intention of letting it stay.

Even the courtiers in it dressed like huntsmen in imitation of their king and thereby grossly wrong-footed the jewelled kings and princes who, summoned there against their will, had done their best to look impressive.

Nevertherless, one by one, the kings and princes approached the dais, ground their teeth, sank to their silken knees and swore loyalty and allegiance to the shabby man who stood on it.

'King Malcolm of Scotland,' called the chamberlain. The King of the Scots knelt.

'Prince Owain of Gwynedd.' Owain mumbled his homage.

'Prince Rhys of Deheubarth.' Rhys knelt. Aware that his defiance against Henry II and his subsequent defeat had brought about this humiliation of his Celtic fellow kings, he was forced to make his submission more placatory than was good for his pride. But after he'd made it, typical Welshman that he was, he stood up and saved his face with eloquence and grace. 'It is to me no small source of pleasure that I have lost my lands to no mean or laggard clan, but to a king of rare fame and distinction.'

Fitzempress was less graceful: 'It was *my* land in the first place.' he said. Up in the gallery, a travel-stained watcher groaned. 'Llandovery was *my* castle and you keep your hands off it in future. I thank you, I thank you all; let us hope that we can live in peace from this day forward. Anybody want to go hunting?'

The man in the gallery turned away. Fitzempress had done it now; to anybody such a dismissal would have been unwise; to these particular princes to whom, if they were like their Irish compeers, courtesy was an immutable law, it was an insult that could only be wiped out by death – theirs or Henry's. Sir John of Sawbridge found it difficult to understand how his master could be a wizard of diplomacy in his dealings with other lands and so ham-fisted with the Celtic nations. He wished he'd got back from Ireland sooner; he would have advised another approach altogether.

He waited for his king in an ante-room which had walls of roughly planed tree trunks, so that it was like a glade in a wood. Why the hell had the king insisted on the princes submitting to him here? Why not at one of his rich, stone palaces? For that matter, why did he consistently refuse to have Woodstock modernised?

Then it occurred to him. It was to keep Eleanor of Aquitaine away, to make it his own, uncomfortable domain, because somewhere in the vicinity was the scented bower of the Fair Rosamund. The words 'scented bower' went from his brain to his gut, and twisted. Damn all women.

The king stamped into the room without greeting. 'You're thinner.'

'Pleased to be back, my lord. So are you.' He was shocked; without gaining a single line on its skin, the king's face had aged. The first thing he'd been told on landing in Bristol was of the quarrel between Henry and his Archbishop of Canterbury. At Westminster the justiciar, Richard de Luci, had warned him: 'You won't find him as easy-going as he was. He can face anything but the defection of a friend; he trusted Becket, which was why he made him primate against the wishes of the Church. He thought he'd found the man who would help him forward his reforms. Instead he created his own stumbling block. Becket is fighting every move, however reasonable – and they *are* reasonable – which will take away the slightest privilege from the church.'

'Wants to become a saint?' John had asked.

'Wants martyrdom,' De Luci said. 'He's lucky, or unfortunate, in that he's opposing the one king in the world who won't give it to him.'

'Tired?' Fitzempress whistled for a page who came running. 'Give Sir John wine.'

'Thank you, my lord. No, not tired.' He was nearly dropping, but you didn't sit down if the king didn't sit, and Henry never did.

'All right, tell me about Ireland.'

Sir John was a first-class spy. He detached his contempt, his anger, his admiration, all the personal feeling he had poured out to Finn, from his report to his king. 'You have to think differently to understand it,' he said, 'It has no political system we would recognise, no centralisation. It works on a social, almost family basis, tipping this way and that with wars which to us would seem like anarchy, but which keep a fine balance and have kept a fine balance since time began. However, it's a balance that wouldn't survive invasion.'

'What would happen then?'

'To be honest, I don't know. The clans might combine against the invader or they might regard him as just another clan to fight, or to make an alliance with against the others.'

'Let's go outside.' Henry was getting interested and he did his best thinking in the open air. There were no gardens at Woodstock, just grounds with fine oaks and sheep nibbling the grass smooth about them.

John breathed deeply; it was good to be in England again, sniffing air he could understand, where there was no magic, no strange lakes . . .

'Can it be conquered?'

John detached himself again. 'Not in the sense that William conquered England. It's too elusive. There's no standing army to beat, no real capital to install yourself in. The clans would slip away into the trees and the bogs and emerge somewhere else. I suppose if you cut down all the forests and starved the population into submission . . . oddly enough, I think you could conquer it without it knowing it had been conquered.'

'Creep up on it?'

John looked at his king. 'Well, yes. They'd probably accept a High King from outside who had no clan affiliations. No show of force, just sweet words.' He said meaningfully: 'You have to be very careful with Celtic honour.'

'And you think I offended it just now? I saw you watching.'

'A trifle brusque, my lord.'

The king kicked a twig into the middle distance. 'Bloody right, I was. These sodding Celts get on my nerves. Did you know that bloody Welshman attacked Llandovery? Had to come all the way back from fighting in France to take it away from him.'

Odd, thought John, that the king attached so much importance to France and so little to the lands which were his nearest neighbours and could cause so much greater trouble in the long run. Oh well, he was an Angevin, born in the very heart of Europe. It had given him a different perspective.

'I was wrong, wasn't I?' said Fitzempress, unexpectedly. 'Well, I'll tell you what we'll do. I'm extending my Ferrets. It seems to me that an inch of secret intelligence can save an "ell" of a lot of warfare.' He grinned at his own joke. 'I'm going to put a lot more spies on the royal expenditure. And you, my son, since you understand the Celtic mind so well, are going to be my chief of intelligence over the section devoted to Brittany, Wales, Scotland and Ireland.'

'No!' John had shouted before he could stop himself and remember he was in the presence of an emperor.

223

'Let's walk back,' said Fitzempress. 'Why not?'

'My lord, I'm not . . . fit for it. You know I'd lay down my life for you, but . . . Can't I serve you some other way? I don't like them. They're an awful people, treacherous, untrustworthy. They enchant you and then they stab you in the back.' All detachment gone, he knelt. It was when the king walked on past him that he realised what he was doing. He was throwing away all chance of the advancement for which he had hankered; Henry didn't make alternative offers. It was the Celts or nothing. 'Oh God,' he said, and ran after Fitzempress and took his place by his side. 'I'm sorry, my lord. Of course, I am yours to command in any way you wish.'

Henry nodded. He knew that.

Back in the ante-chamber, the king said: 'I've found you your heiress, John. And she's pretty. But we can't have her marrying a mere knight.' He whistled and the page appeared. 'Pour more wine for my lord baron of Llanthony.'

Overwhelmed onto his knees again, John calculated his gains. He'd got his advancement, his heiress, his lands. All he lacked was the pleasure which should have gone with each. Well, it would come. In time he'd start feeling joy in things again. 'Thank you, my lord.'

Fitzempress looked down at the bowed head of his chief of Celtic intelligence. 'She must have been quite a woman,' he said.

As Finn and Art moved into the west they caught up with cavalcades of gorgeous lords, *brehons* and abbots of the clans of Connaught heading for a gathering with their king at Tuam. It wasn't the usual *aenacht*. Something was Up. It was spring, the season when young men's fancy turned to thoughts of war; in between showers there were stirring smells of new grass, new flowers, new blood. 'The O'Conor's wanting another try at the High Kingship,' said Art.

Locating the king was therefore not a problem but, as Finn began to realise, getting to talk to him would be. In the first place she was reluctant to appear at Ruairi's palace on a well-attended and notable occasion; there would be enquiries as to who she was at a time when she should remain in the background. Then again, O'Conor's queen was notoriously jealous and would not welcome a lone woman who wanted private audience with her consort.

'I'll take him a message,' said Art, 'and he can meet us at Lough Mask. It's only twenty miles on from Tuam.'

'He won't be able to leave all those guests for so long,' said Finn. Lough Mask was another place she was reluctant to visit, though she had messages to deliver there on Blat's behalf.

Eventually she put up at the ferry house at Corofin, telling the ferryman and his wife that she was on a pilgrimage to Croagh Patrick but needed to rest. She had to wait there for three days which she spent staring out of the loft window at the rain, fighting another depression and a sense of worthlessness, which she thought she had conquered.

She was well into her twenties, she had found a grey hair in one of her plaits. She was an ageing tavern-keeper. A dowdy, ageing tavern-keeper, an unnecessary woman. Her only commitment was to a country, and countries didn't keep you warm at nights or gather round your knee. 'And am I only committed to give myself something to live for? Am I making myself ridiculous in this activity to give myself some importance? And does it bloody matter anyway?'

She missed the hags. Most of all she missed Brother Pinginn. When she was with Pinginn, irritating and silly as he could be, she lost some of her certainty in the godlessness of the universe. Without him the lid of the coffin came down. On the third day Art practically had to drag her out of the loft in order to keep the appointment he had made.

They rode up a river path through a dull, rain-soaked empty countryside to an ash tree which had been split in two by lightning. One half still sprouted black-tipped buds, the other half was dead. After an hour they were joined by a truant young man on a breathless horse.

'I told the hunt I'd join them later. They think I'm wenching.'

'Huh.' Some wench. In her misery she barely had the energy to curtsey to him.

'And if they saw those eyes of yours, they'd know I was,' said the king of Connaught.

Droplets of rain twinkled on a bunch of small, pale daffodils growing out of a cleft in the dead trunk. On the soft, westerly breeze came a scent that for a second carried a memory of Lough Mask. Dear,. dear, she thought, one compliment from a handsome man and the sun comes out. She was ashamed of her invigoration. They walked beside the river as she talked with energy, telling him what had happened since they last met and what she had been about. He liked the stories about the hags and the inn and Brother Pinginn. But especially he wanted to know what had happened to the Pilgrim.

'He has gone back to Henry of England, who sent him,' said Finn, 'My lord, I warned you. He was a spy.'

'I liked him,' said Ruairi O'Conor. 'We got on.'

'That's beside the point,' said Finn harshly, refusing to remember how she too had got on with the Pilgrim. 'He was an agent of Fitzempress sent to gather information about Ireland, and the only reason one country wants information about another is if it intends to annexe it. We are in danger, O'Conor.'

'Not necessarily. Our brother England may merely wish to trade with us.'

225

Finn counted to ten. 'Your brother England is gobbling up countries like a pig with acorns,' she said, 'Wales, Normandy, Brittany, Scotland, Touraine, Maine, Anjou, Aquitaine. If your brother France doesn't look out, he'll go the same way. Fitzempress owns more of Europe than he does.'

'Then he's got more than enough to keep him occupied,' said the O'Conor comfortably. It was a point that Finn had already considered. If Fitzempress was kept busy enough quelling the revolts of the many dukedoms, baronies and principalities which had never belonged to the Angevin Empire before and didn't want to start now, his mind and resources could be kept away from the little island off Britain's west coast. She began telling the O'Conor what the Jews with their network of information had told her of the international situation. Of Louis of France's jealousy of Fitzempress, the man who had married his divorced wife, Eleanor. Of Eleanor's duchy, Aquitaine, which was in a state of uproar against its new duke – Finn had hopes of Aquitaine being a perennial thorn in Fitzempress' flesh.

The O'Conor listened politely and let his eyes stray. He knew some of this but found global politics uninteresting. He perked up when Finn began on the quarrel between the Archbishop of England, Thomas Becket, and Fitzempress – personalities were what fascinated him.

'The Jews say that Fitzempress and Becket loved each other when they were King and Chancellor but, as Archbishop, Becket is a changed man. He has given his love solely to the Church, and resists every change Fitzempress wants to make.'

Finn had hopes of Becket as another distracting thorn. Since she was trying to impress Fitzempress' villainy on O'Conor's mind she did not point out that in the Jews' view it was Becket who was the villain.

'Fitzempress is a reasonable man,' Vives had said, 'He uses Jews well. He milks us for all he can get, but he's clever enough to know that only contented cows give good milk. Becket . . .' Vives deliberately made his voice non-commital . . . 'Becket is an anti-semite. He would have us all exiled or worse. He is a man of passion, some say unbalanced.' In the Jews' opinion Henry II was fighting the crime wave in England left over from the civil war by introducing laws of commonsense. Among them, all clerics were to be subject to that law and, if they committed a crime, were to be handed over to the civil courts for punishment. 'At the moment,' said Vives, 'any villain with a tonsure can rape, steal, murder and get away with it because the Church courts cannot punish him. All they can do is reprimand him, perhaps strip him of his clerkly status and send him out to sin again. But Becket is refusing to recognise the right of the king in this matter, and is opposing the Constitutions of Clarendon as if they were an attack on God Himself.'

226

'I think what I shall do,' said Ruairi O'Conor, 'is to send my brother England some friendship gifts, to establish good relations. Then, when I am High King of Ireland, as I shall be, he will know that he has nothing to fear from us.'

'He knows that, for God's sake,' said Finn. She was appalled by O'Conor's inversion of the situation. He had absolutely no idea. Ireland was the entire world to him and he could not set it in context with any other world. It was impossible to transfer to him her awareness of Fitzempress' quality because it had no parallel in Ireland; the greed for power of the Irish kings stopped at Tara: Henry II's was limitless. For all his youth, Ruairi was aged by the weight of the culture behind him: Fitzempress was a raw, fresh, vulgar upstart to whom everything was possible. Even the blindings and murder with which Irish kings got their own way was provincial stuff compared with the Angevin's global criminality in blinding whole countries out of his conviction that they would be best under his rule.

'O'Conor,' she said, 'you once asked if you could do anything for me. You can. Give me permission to be your agent, your watcher. From my inn I intend to spin a spider's web of information, so that if the King of England or anyone else makes a move against you I shall know it.'

He smiled at her, not because she was a woman making a fantastic suggestion, but because he just didn't understand the urgency with which she made it. 'Now why would anyone want to invade Ireland?'

'The Vikings did.'

He became less complacent. Though the Viking invasion had taken place three hundred years ago, it had burned a scar into the Irish soul. 'It's an idea,' he said.

'A very good idea.'

'What would you want me to do?'

She moved quickly. 'I want some money for the web, to pay other agents. And when you send those gifts to Fitzempress, send one of my hags with them. Send Muirna, say you would like one of your relatives to learn the ways of a European court. She's fourth cousin to you on your mother's side, after all, and she sings like a lark. A good ambassadress. They'll think it's one of our customs. They know nothing about us.'

Ruairi O'Conor frowned. 'I don't want her spying. It would be against my honour.'

'She won't spy,' lied Finn, 'she'll, well, just watch your interest. Please, my lord, indulge me. Remember who I was. I know these foreigners, I was brought up among them. Everything I do now is in your interest.'

He smiled down at her. 'My little watcher by the sea.'

All right, you amiable, vulnerable young bastard, thought Finn, patronise me. But do it.

'And you really think it's necessary?'

In that question Finn saw the reason why he infuriated her nearly to madness and why she gave him the loyalty of her heart and soul; he was politically childish enough to doubt the value of having a spy network, but he was more mature than any man she knew in being prepared to take the advice of a woman about it. There, in that one question, was Connaught. There was the Ireland she intended to defend. 'Yes.'

'In that case, my spider cousin, spin your web.'

She kissed his hand. 'And, my lord, will you insist that the Ui Maille gives us Aragon's ship money? We're paying back every penny we make at the inn to the Jews, and I want to start a trading fleet. It's a good way of getting information.'

'The O'Malley is under my roof at this minute. But he'll probably pay you in fish from the smell of him.'

'Tell him to make it hides.' She could sell hides to England. 'And if that's the case, make him throw in the boulder of ambergris he keeps in his hall.' She told the O'Conor its potential, '. . . but let the O'Malley think Aragon needs it for good luck. What's happening up at Tuam anyway?'

As she'd thought, it was preparation for war. 'Even Ulster won't put up with the MacLochlainn for much longer,' said the O'Conor. 'Connaught's time is coming, and when it does a certain ally of MacLochlainn, namely Dermot of Leinster, will pay for what he did to a certain abbess.'

'Take care of yourself, O'Conor.'

'I'll be riding up to that Dublin inn of yours one of these days as High King with my conquering army behind me, asking for a drink.'

'You'll get it.'

They arranged that O'Malley should send for the ambergris – and Aragon's payment – immediately. 'Tell him to deliver it to Iogenàn's hall. I'll wait for it there.'

'I wish I could be with you. There's been no time for Cuimne and my son lately. Ah God, Finn, do you remember Lough Mask?'

They stood transfixed in the camaraderie of sweet times remembered.

Lough Mask was unbearable. From the ramparts of Iogenán's *rath* she watched its waters dimple in the showers and then clear to reflect the pale green edging of trees and rushes. After the first look towards the islands she turned her back on it, but every welcome, every face, tempted her into some self-indulgent pain. The absences were even

228

more dreadful. The door of the tower on Inis Cailleach swung open to display an empty courtyard. Scathagh had gone, nobody knew where. Finn left Swan Island unvisited.

She allowed herself to ride into the hills and, by accident, find the field where she had killed her wolf. She was puzzled by two wolf skulls being nailed to the door of the hut which had once held Blat's bitch. Somebody else must have killed one.

She was glad when the hides and the ambergris arrived and they could go.

Muirna went pale when Finn broached the plan to place her in the household of Eleanor of Aquitaine. 'It's Abroad,' she said. 'They're Galls – foreigners.'

'They won't eat you,' said Finn, impatiently.

'But you said that's just what they would do.'

'I said they'd eat Ireland. They're civilised when they're at home.'

It took time, but as Finn extolled, truthfully, the wonders of Eleanor of Aquitaine's court and, even more truthfully, the value of having a spy in it, Muirna was seduced, as Finn had known she would be. Muirna was in many ways the most sophisticated of the hags, certainly the highest-born, and though she was happy at the inn, she would be in her element among the excitement and riches of a European court.

Finn spent some of her profits on clothes, mostly for Muirna so that she could uphold Ireland's honour at the Plantagenet court, but also for the rest of them. In the rush of building the Swan she had overlooked the fact that its staff's robes were virtually threadbare.

It was Pinginn who supervised Muirna's wardrobe, showing an interest in ladies' apparel that Finn considered unhealthy. 'You lay people are so lucky being able to wear colours and all these lovely, lovely things,' he said, swathing himself in silk. He spent happy hours overseeing the sewing parties up in the tower room, and devised a headdress for Muirna based on the cap Irish noblewoman favoured which had a roll brim around the skull-covering, decorating it with pearls that he had collected from oysters. 'They'll think she's barbaric in that,' Finn told him. But Pinginn said: 'We'll start a new fashion.' And in that he was correct.

Nessa provided enough ermine to decorate a hide cloak for Muirna, and Gorm, Miller Molling's all-purpose worker, tooled some leather into very creditable slippers.

With what silk was left over, Pinginn, who had talked to real crusaders in his time, designed an outfit for the remaining hags. 'If they like to think we're Amazons,' he said, 'we'd better look like Amazons.'

A few days later the staff assembled in the tower room to inspect their new uniform as modelled by Tailltin. Finn's mouth fell open. Tailltin's top was a tunic of emerald silk with a jerkin of dyed scarlet leather – colourful but unexceptionable – her lower half, however, was in trousers, loose, thin trousers that gathered at the ankle.

'Well,' said Pinginn, bridling at the silence. 'I think it's really elegant. And it's just ideal for hags, what with the Ploys and all. We'll attract ever such a lot of custom in it.'

'Well, I'll not be wearing it,' said Blat firmly.

Finn said, 'And you're not either,' just in case Pinginn had been thinking in that direction. There was no doubt, however, that it was a novelty, and novelty was what attracted customers. Tailltin endorsed Pinginn. 'I'd have learned the steed leap a damn sight quicker if I'd been wearing this.' And Bevo agreed. 'Ragnar will positively enjoy being chucked out.'

Finn considered. The Church hierachy would condemn women for wearing trousers but the Church hierachy didn't patronise her inn.

'All right,' she said, 'Bevo and Tailltin can try it out to see what the reaction is.'

'Coward,' said the hags.

It took nearly a year for Ruairi O'Conor to act on the idea Finn had given him, but eventually he was ready to send an ambassador, some friendship-gifts, and Muirna, to the court of Fitzempress.

On a fine May day, the women of the Swan Inn wrapped Muirna's finery in lawn scented with rosewater and then packed it into a chest. 'Now, have you got enough warm clothes?' asked Finn. 'Remember that the O'Conor is to supply you with spending money but there's a gold piece in your purse just in case. Oh, and don't forget that the harpstrings will need tightening after the journey.' Niall had made Muirna a small Irish harp on which she could accompany her singing – they were banking on Muirna's voice, which was especially sweet, delighting the Queen of England's musical ear. 'And I've put a bag of dried sorrel in the chest. You're to put it in red wine and drink it for stomach upsets.' She pulled the ermine cloak more closely about Muirna's throat, unable to think of anything more to do for her but wanting to do it.

Muirna caught her hands. 'Finn, look at me. I'm all right.'

The guilt and worry that she was sending Muirna into dangerous exile had kept Finn in a fury of preparation until that moment. Now she looked into Muirna's eyes which were wet, but steady. 'You can come home any time you like,' she told her.

'I know.'

'And Bevo will be over in a while to see how you're getting on.'

230

'Yes.'

'And I'll come over when you're sure that he's . . . when there's nobody in court who's likely to recognise me.'

'I know.'

'Take care.'

They all went in the *curragh* to the far shore of the Liffey. Art was waiting with two horses to accompany Muirna to Galway where she would embark in the O'Conor's ship. They watched Muirna's elegant figure pass into the trees of the north bank and out of sight. 'She'll be so homesick,' grieved Finn.

Bevo shook her head. 'She'll love it. Think of her as another strand in your spider's web.'

The net Finn had been spreading from her tower on the Stein was not exactly a spider's web. For one thing she didn't want to trap anything in it, and for another its radii were cruder and had gaps that no self-respecting spider would have tolerated; nevertheless, as the months had gone on, she'd composed a network of informants which enabled her, like a spider, to be aware of the vibrations of disturbance within the range of its filaments. And the filaments went far and to some surprising places.

Ireland she covered in many ways. Discovering what Dermot was up to involved no effort since the whole of Leinster kept a wary eye on all moves its king made and the gossip about his activities was retailed in every inn within it, the Swan being no exception. She was kept in touch with Connaught by Nessa and Niall of the Poems and by the O'Conor himself who, when he remembered, sent her secret messages about his plans for war against MacLochlainn and Dermot Mac Murrough.

In his cups King Asgall was totally indiscreet and Finn was as up to date with what was happening within the Dublin court as if she were part of it.

Brother Pinginn turned out to have odd – some of them very odd – friends scattered about the Irish monastic community and when they visited Dublin they would send him a message and he would meet them in the city and garner their news. None of them visited the Swan, which was disapproved of by the Church because of its Amazonian reputation.

Niall of the Poems let it be known that any poet on his way through Dublin would get free board and lodging at the inn on the Stein, and though the stream of men, and occasionally women, who began to turn up there were mere harpers as oppose to the *fili* – the great poets – they were fruitful sources of gossip as well as providing entertainment for the guests.

Her contact with the world outside Ireland was maintained by sailors, none of whom needed encouragement to talk, and by the Jews whose own network spread to England, France, Spain, Germany,

Rome, Scandinavia and even Russia. Vives told her everything he knew on his weekly visits to collect Finn's repayments, though he was one of the few people who showed suspicion at her questioning, especially about Fitzempress – he knew her well enough by now to realise that she wasn't gathering information merely out of feminine curiosity. 'Do you plan harm to the King of England?' he asked. 'Remember, he is a good friend to us.'

Finn considered, and then took him partly into her confidence. 'Only if he invades Ireland,' she said, 'as I have reason to think he might.'

Vives considered in his turn. He, too, had no wish to see Ireland conquered, even by a king like Fitzempress who, liberal as he might be towards the Jews, still burdened them with a vicious taxation, whereas in Ireland the Jewish community was left virtually unhindered. Besides, he liked and admired Finn and hoped to make a considerable profit when Aragon brought back her consignment of wine from Aquitaine.

'Very well,' he said, 'You shall know what I know.' His knowledge was especially valuable because it was not only international but financial. Almost everywhere in Christendom – except Ireland – Jews, the Christ-killers, were forbidden to hold land and therefore practically the only occupation left to them was usury, which was forbidden to Christians. As a result no war could be fought, no great enterprise mounted, no castle built without borrowing from the Jews. Aaron of Lincoln, the Jewish financier for whom both Belaset and Vives acted as agents, advanced money to private individuals on corn, armour, estates and houses all over Europe. Even the Church was his debtor; he boasted that the great conventual church at St. Albans had been built entirely on his loan. Thanks to Vives Finn began to know who among the great was doing what in Europe, and how much it was costing them.

It was Scathagh who had provided her with her best sources in the Celtic lands of Brittainy, Scotland and Wales. At one time damaged women from all these countries had been healed in her academy and she had armed Finn with the names and whereabouts of ex-hags who were likely to be useful.

In July Bevo left Dublin for Anglesey, heading for the English court but taking a circuitous route through Wales to meet Gwenllian ferch Owen ap Griffith, an illegitimate daughter of the Prince of Gwynedd and named for an intrepid grandmother who had been captured while leading an army against the Normans and put to death with her men. She herself had been violated by the Norman lord of Kidwelly, 'and you will find,' Scathagh had told Finn, 'that the Normans are not her favourite people. She is a clever woman and, thanks to her training here, a forceful one who has the ear of her father, Prince Owen.'

Bevo's brief was to make contact with her and discover how relations stood between Gwynedd and England. 'At the moment they are peaceful,' Finn said, 'and Owen is behaving with perfect rectitude towards Fitzempress. But the Jews say that he nurses a grievance from the insulting way the king treated him and will move against him if he shows weakness. If Aquitaine gives Fitzempress trouble, if war breaks out again in France, if Becket becomes more of a nuisance than ever, if I can stir up the Bretons, he will be weak. Tell her to tell her father that will be the time to move.'

Tailltin was sent to Scotland with a similar brief to contact the favourite mistress of Malcolm IV, a lady delighting in the name of Gruoch.

It was an exasperating time for Scottish patriots; Henry Fitzempress had taken Northumberland away from Scotland and annexed it to the English crown. On Tailltin's return she reported that Gruoch had assured her the Scots would rise against him under Malcolm. 'But Malcolm is ill, and his heir, William, will need convincing that Fitzempress can be beaten. They hate the English king, all of them, but they've got a healthy respect for his fighting qualities.'

Finn had no doubt that Fitzempress could be distracted almost indefinitely from thoughts of an Irish invasion if his more immediate Celtic neighbours began to give him trouble. Her job was to orchestrate the rebellion which all of them threatened but which, without cohesion, could become an unsynchronised series of revolts that could be put down with comparative ease.

'You're inciting war,' her conscience told her. 'All's fair in it,' she answered back, 'for Fitzempress is inciting it already and it would come sooner or later. Besides, it will save Ireland.'

With Tailltin safely back home Finn decided to take on the next operation herself. Despite the absence of its hags, the Swan could run smoothly. Blat was the mainstay of the kitchen and the two ex-prostitutes were now on light duties, though Brother Pinginn still insisted they stay in bed in the mornings. Even so, she would have liked to leave Lief in residence as a safeguard, but it would make her assignment much quicker to charter his boat there and back than wait around for a merchantman to take her.

A week later she was in Brittany plotting with a witch called Jehane.

It was not an easy interview because Jehane kept going off into trances, occasionally screaming a prophecy and then reverting to perfectly ordinary conversation, as if she'd just left the room to put the kettle on. It was conducted in a tall, single tower on a deserted section of the Breton coast near Dol and the views from its top floor window gave Finn vertigo.

233

Jehane had staggered backwards when Finn had been ushered into her tower by a servant, rolled her eyes and frothed at the mouth. 'Burning,' she kept muttering, 'I see burning.' Then she'd come round: 'And how is dear Scathagh?'

'Well when I last saw her,' said Finn, bewildered. Jehane was obviously a woman of means, yet her room was littered with the paraphanalia of ancient witchcraft more usually found in the huts of eccentric beldames. It was clear that in Brittany at least, necromancy was still a profitable business. On the walls were strangely knotted straw dollies, black wax candles, cabbalistic incantations on strips of parchment which waved in the breeze from the windows. Dreadful smells came from stone jars on the shelving. Jehane herself wore the high, winged hat of the Breton and a cloak on which was embroidered the signs of the zodiac; she was thin, dark and intense. Her age was almost impossible to guess, but it wasn't young. Scathagh had not mentioned the circumstances in which Jehane had gone to her academy – nor did Finn ask – but she had said, 'Don't underestimate her, nor the power she wields over the great families of Brittany. The old faith still holds sway there.'

Vives had said, 'With its difficult terrain in the hinterland, Brittany is an almost impossible country to rule. Each lord thinks himself a king and wars against the others. But Fitzempress cannot leave it to itself because it holds Nantes, and Nantes guards the mouth of the Loire and, therefore, the access to Anjou. His puppet there is Duke Conan, an unreliable man.'

Finn decided there was no point in wasting time in subtleties. 'Lady Jehane, I am concerned at the inroads Henry Fitzempress is making into the Celtic countries.'

'Aren't we all, dear,' said Jehane. She went rigid and held out her grubby, long-fingered hands in the attitude of incantation. 'But the young eagles will tear out the innards of the old one, pecking at his eyes and bowels. Oh Henry, Henry, beware your sons. They will be our revenge.' She dropped her arms, wiped the sweat off the dark hair on her top lip and poured some powerful-smelling liquid from a jar into a chipped cup and gave it to Finn. 'Drink this, it will return your lover to you.'

'I don't want him returned,' said Finn, but a glance from Jehane's dark eyes made her drink it just the same. Coughing, she said, 'Lady Jehane, I am aware that Ralph de Fougères is preparing revolt against King Henry. He has borrowed money for it. What I want to know from you is whether Duke Conan will quell that revolt on the king's behalf or allow it to take place.'

'Do you ask me in the name of the Mother?'

'I do.'

'We are all her daughters. I must consult the runes.' Jehane fumbled in her clothing, brought out some carved stones and threw them on the floor. The mutterings and peerings at them took some time. 'This is ridiculous,' thought Finn. 'What am I doing here?' But she bore with it because Scathagh's opinion of this woman had been high, and Scathagh's opinion was worth noting. Besides, there was no doubt that there was real power in Jehane's mysticism; she made Finn uneasy.

At last the witch squatted back on her haunches. 'He will do as I tell him,' she said. 'for his soul is in my thrall. Especially will he obey me if I offer him money. His gambling debts have mounted up lately.' She began to sway back and forth, about to go into another trance.

Quickly Finn said, 'How much?'

Jehane scratched her armpit. 'Five hundred pieces of gold.'

Finn considered. It was a huge amount, but she could get it easily enough from the O'Conor. Since Irish princes counted their wealth in cattle and rarely used coin, the fine Irish gold which washed down their rivers was usually turned into ornaments, or made into ingots which mounted up uselessly in their treasuries.

'And two hundred for me,' said Jehane, casually.

Finn spent the rest of the day in that odd tower. But by the end of it she was convinced that Jehane could deliver the soul of Conan as and when she wanted to. And that when rebellion broke out in the marches of Brittany, its Duke would allow it to happen.

Jehane walked with her down to the beach where Lief was waiting to row her to his ship standing out on the flat, steel-coloured sea. As the day had progressed Jehane had become less and less witchy and more and more business-like. But in saying goodbye, she spat on her forefinger and rubbed it on Finn's forehead. 'You are in danger,' she said, 'Stay away from towers.'

She had learned to kill. She had spread her net, laid her plots. All she could do now was watch and wait for the time to act. And learn to write.

'. . .our friend "p" is a commoner, as in Pinginn,' chanted Brother Pinginn, 'so he goes below the salt on our table – that's the line – but he's a merry little fellow and he pops his head up to nod at lady "l", who sits above the salt. There, like that. Hello, Lady L.'

'Hello, Lady L,' mocked Elfwida, drawing a perfect letter "p" on her slate.

'Bugger you, Lady L,' said Finn, whose "p" had gone into spasm.

'Clerk Finn can wash her mouth out with soap,' said Brother Pinginn, 'and work on friend "p". Clerk Elfwida can go on to our little serving maids, the vowels.'

She had reserved the mornings for lessons with Brother Pinginn, imagining they would be oases of calm and erudition in which she would become a female wizard in that magical, male mystery, literacy.

It hadn't worked out like that. Certainly she was lucky in her teacher; remembering, and loathing, the harshness with which the monastic masters had beaten the arts of reading and writing into him, Brother Pinginn had eschewed the technical terminology of 'serifs', 'descenders', 'perpendicular ascenders' and the like, and evolved his own peculiarly juvenile, but effective, method. 'We won't bother about the formal script,' he'd said; 'presumably you're not going to write charters or royal letters. You just want legibility. I'm going to teach you a cursive style known throughout Christendom as "Bastard".'

And that, Finn decided, was a good name for it. She found transposing the oral word into the written – and in Latin, which she hadn't used for a long while – harder than she'd dreamed it would be. Furthermore, she resented in having as a fellow-pupil the former whore, Elfwida. Most of all, she resented Elfwida being a better pupil than she was.

Because it was the only place with a good light, the top floor of the tower where the two girls still had their bedroom, had been chosen as the schoolroom. On the first day Brother Pinginn and Finn had set up the tilted wooden board and slates under the north light, scraped their chalk into points, and sat down to begin the lesson.

Perse showed not the slightest interest, but lay looking at the ceiling. Elfwida, however, had been instantly curious. 'What you doing?' she asked sharply, 'I want to learn.'

'Well, you can't,' said Finn.

'Why not?' The question came from Elfwida and Pinginn simultaneously, and Finn, who was flouting all convention in learning herself, had no answer to it. The former English prostitute became the second pupil in the Swan school. She spoke fluent, though crude, Irish, but her knowledge of Latin was restricted to such dirty bits of the Bible as her clerical clients had liked to murmur in moments of arousal, so Pinginn taught her to write a form of Latinised Irish. Her progress was astonishing and soon he'd begun to employ his spare time in teaching her Latin itself. His only problem was in stopping her from working too hard.

'It's a wonderful thing,' he said joyfully, 'to fill that dear little bucket with the clear water of knowledge.'

'I'll give her dear little bucket,' grumbled Finn. There was something about Elfwida that repelled her.

But the possible disgrace of falling behind an English harlot pushed her into a fury of study. At nights she lit a candle in the dead middle room and forced her tired hands to practise her letters, and her tired eyes to study the primer Pinginn had written. Her literacy improved daily but her temper worsened.

'She loves you, Finn,' said Pinginn, unexpectedly as they went into the common parlour after one such session. 'That child's working like she is because she wants to do everything you do. She'd like to be a hag – she's already asked Bevo to teach her the Ploys when she's better. Poor little thing, she humbles me. You and I think we've known horror, but that girl has been into the Pit, and come out of it. Of course she loves you. You're the only true mother she's ever had.'

Finn's hand came out and hit Brother Pinginn's face so hard that his head rocked. 'I'm nobody's mother,' she said, 'Not hers. Not anybody's.'

As her net became more fine it seemed to become part of her own physical system, as if her veins and nerves were spread in extended branches over countries and seas, able to communicate itches, tickles, vibrations, aches back to her brain where they became translated into pictures. She saw the Celtic world restive and waiting to move at the extended ends of her arms when she gave the impulse.

She gained insight into the subtle, terrifyingly wonderful character of her enemy, Fitzempress, and knew that she was up against genius and strength that made her puny. Her hope lay in its instability; in the way it was overstretched, its greed and impatience.

But as time went on she came to recognise another character active within her web; a mind that concentrated on her sphere, working to counter all that she could bring about, probing the Celtic mists to find her, as she was reaching out of the mist to blind it. She could recognise the pattern of the agents this person used, all of them male and all of them paid informers; men who had position in the courts of Wales, Scotland and Brittany and who were prepared to betray their ancestral lords to the new, overwhelming power of the Angevin.

She knew that Rhys of Deheubarth had a nephew who hated him and gave information to this other spider. She knew of a blacksmith whose smithy stood on the pass between Gwynned and Chester who sent messages along this enemy web whenever Owen of Gwynned moved in the north. She knew that William the Lion was being made promises by this controller of agents if, when he inherited it, he would suppress Scotland into obedience to the Angevin Empire. She knew the promises would not be kept.

Gradually, she began to know her opponent, whoever he was. The way he used agents, how much he paid, what importance he attached to which area, gave him a personality. She 'felt' him through her web like a blind woman passing her hand over somebody's face; he was clever, with some understanding of Celtic thinking, and he had resources not open to her. But he was limited. He built his web by offering money and playing on envy. Her web was better because it had a common cause, a love of country and it was feminine and therefore unexpected.

She gave him a name – 'Duckweed'.

'We've got to get closer to William of Scotland,' she told Pinginn, 'and break the hold Duckweed's got over him. I'm going to send Tailltin to see what she can do there.'

'Why do you call whoever-it-is "Duckweed"?' asked Pinginn.

'I don't know.' Subconsciously she was intimidated by this controller of Fitzempress' Celtic spies; he was formidable and she needed to belittle and domesticate him in her own mind.

'He's at the centre of everything,' she complained, 'and I'm stuck here on a bank of the Liffey. If only Muirna would hurry up and make contacts at court. I don't even know who bloody Duckweed is. But when I do he'd better look out.'

She was sleeping badly, disturbed by the vibrations of her web. The sound of the confluence of the rivers beneath the tower remained bothersome. It would wake her up in the early hours to lie worrying over Aragon and Muirna, her web and petty details of the Swan's administration. The only cure was to creep up the stairs of the tower, through the top room to the roof and pace its four sides as the dawn came up.

At first it was just an exercise; the night breeze from the estuary acted like smelling salts and cleared the mind. For a long time, when the moon provided her with a view, she had perceived her surroundings merely as Not Lough Mask and ached for the summer scents of inland water. But then habit enforced familiarity, even affection. There was a lone seal which came up the Liffey estuary on the tide, twisting an apparently boneless body through the water after fish, occasionally turning over on its back to clap leisurely flippers.

She became accustomed to certain landmarks, counting on them; the tall, unnatural shape of the Thing-mound to the west and, beyond it, the Abbey of St. Mary's on Hogges Green, the castle and the walls of the city, the uncluttered Dublin mountains which partly scalloped the edges of her flat, river-infested world. She could see the shadows of deer across the river moving among the trees of the north bank. There was always something new on the Liffey, a boat moored in one of its channels waiting for the tide to take it into the wharfs, a *curragh* on some nefarious pre-dawn purpose.

It became a drug to see the first gleam come up over the seaward horizon of the bay and with it wild geese, honking their way inland. As the year wore on they were joined by thousands of knots which landed to ripple over the mud-banks like a grey carpet. Dunlin rushed over the estuary looking like wisps of smoke against the grey sky, skimming the water, sweeping upwards in bunches and then spilling out into a long, wavering line. As if they were a signal, a dog would bark somewhere in the city, a cock crowed, the geese in her own garden woke up, and the bells of the convents clanged out for prime. Just across the Stein, there was the sound of rushing water as Molling released his mill race, his paddle wheels turned and the deep echo of the mill machinery began its daily grinding.

Reassured that it was worth guarding, the watcher on the tower would go down to her inn to begin her day.

'I can hear her footsteps going round and round,' Elfwida reported to Brother Pinginn. 'They stop longest over there . . .' she pointed a skinny finger to the east, 'what's she looking for?'

'Invasion. She thinks the Normans will attack Ireland.'

'I could look out for it. I'd do that for her. Why don't she ask me? But it don't take that long to see the coast's clear. She's watching something.'

'She's worried about Muirna and Aragon.'

'Is there a man?'

Brother Pinginn sighed. 'Yes. On the opposite side.'

'She hit you, didn't she? I saw the mark. What did she hit you for? Do you hate her for it?'

'Release. No, I don't. She was put into my hand by God and I must look after her.'

'I'd look after her if she asked me to. She won't. She hates me. Why does she hate me? I wish I was a hag. I want to be a hag.'

Brother Pinginn dug his pupil in the ribs. 'So do I. But we're happy, aren't we? *Et ego . . .*'

Elfwida grinned back at him. '*Sciant qui sunt et qui futuri sunt quod ego in Arcadia vixi,*' she said fluently.

The Liffey rippled the months out to sea and lost them. Their passing was marked on the Swan Inn promontory by acquisitions and departures.

Finn now occupied the middle room alone. Even when the others were in residence they preferred to use the staff dormitory off the gallery in the inn. They found the tower creepy they said.

There was the day, just before the seas closed for the winter, when Aragon came home. Her ship limped up the main Liffey channel on the evening tide, so battered by a storm in the Bay of Biscay that Blat, who had gone up Lazy Hill to gather hazel nuts, didn't recognise it at first. Then the old ululating yell of triumph that had rung through the tower on Inis Cailleach sounded over the peaty-brown river, to be answered by another from the ship.

That night bales of silk, tuns of wine, and exotically-shaped bottles of scented unguents were passed up by the light of candles through the trap door in the tower's undercroft. Down in the parlours the guests grumbled at the slow service as Brother Pinginn, Gundred the serving maid, and Art sweated to keep them happy while the hags gathered in the tower room to hug Aragon, drink her health and gloat over her success. She had made contact with the rebels in Aquitaine and had brought back a full report. 'Fitzempress is in for trouble down there,' she said.

The next morning she took her ship upriver and unloaded what remained of her cargo onto Wood quay, paying the toll without complaint. The hags didn't want to make the royal officials in Dublin suspect that they were smuggling, and, anyway, the sale of even the legal cargo – mainly wine – enabled them to pay off most of their debt on the Swan, while the illegal profit outfitted Aragon for another voyage in the spring.

Aragon was home, and in the spring Bevo came back, also with news. The staff of the Swan gathered in the tower to hear it. On the social side Muirna was homesick but well, having been adopted by Eleanor with the sort of amused affection she reserved for monkeys, parrots, little black boys and other foreign exotica.

But as an agent, Muirna had already made a useful contact. Since the Queen was acting as Regent of England during her husband's absence, there was more coming and going between her personal court and the king's various administrative departments. 'Basically, Eleanor's just a figurehead and a signature,' said Bevo, 'the real power is in the hands of Fitzempress' chief justiciar, a man called Richard de Luci. Funny old man, looks like a turtle. Anyway, out of courtesy he keeps the Queen informed and there's a lot of to-ing and fro-ing with documents for her to sign. I think she'd like to play a bigger part in running the country, but they think she's only fit for all that courtly love and poetry and such.'

'Get on with it,' said Finn, shaking with impatience.

'Aren't I telling you? Anyway, there's this clerk who works for the Exchequer – that's the name given to the accounting department at court; it deals with every penny coming into Fitzempress' treasury and every penny going out. He's fallen in love with Muirna – honestly, they're a decadent lot in Eleanor's court, all drooping about with love, even the servants can hardly move for unrequited, hopeless passion for some lady or another.' Bevo's unromantic, stolid face showed digust.

'And this clerk's fallen for Muirna?'

'He certainly has. And Muirna eggs him on, and listens to his troubles – he's very unhappy about the situation between Fitzempress and Becket. He's a Becket-admirer, so there's no love lost for his king.

And one day he asked Muirna if she realised that Fitzempress had got her country in his pocket. He was showing off. And Muirna said what did he mean, and he said there was a document in the State archives which showed that Ireland belonged to the King of England. Muirna made him copy it out – he didn't want to, but she said he could prove his love for her if he did, all that nonsense. And, well, here it is.'

'It' was a torn, scraped membrane, obviously discarded for official purposes which Muirna's informant had used as, greatly daring, he had copied the document in Fitzempress' archives.

'Read it,' Finn told Brother Pinginn. Although her literacy was advancing, she was still slow making out words.

Pinginn skimmed through, reading it to himself, and went pale. 'This is awful.'

'Are you going to tell us or not?'

He looked up, all his usual artificiality gone. 'It's a privilege from the previous Pope. It gives Ireland to Fitzempress.'

There was silence in the room; downstairs they could hear shouts for ale – but nobody moved.

'It begins *Laudabiliter*. . . . Laudably and profitably does your magnificence contemplate . . .'

'Skip the courtesies,' said Finn, 'We'll read those later.'

'You have indicated to us, most well beloved son in Christ, that you wish to enter the island of Ireland, to make that people obedient to the laws, and to root out from there the weeds of vice . . .'

Finn got up. 'I was right. God help us all, I was right. Fitzempress can take us over any time he likes. With the Church's blessing.'

The magnitude of the business paralysed them. The massivity of church sanction gave weight, a duty, to Fitzempress' invasion if and when it took place that would make it impossible to dislodge. He would be not a conqueror but a saviour, snatching Ireland from the fire of barbarism.

'If ever he needs to save his soul,' said Pinginn quietly, 'Ireland will be his salvation.'

'Perhaps Fitzempress doesn't intend to invade,' said Tailltin in desperation. 'The document's old, after all.'

Finn turned on them. 'You haven't met him. I tell you he means to. If he hasn't invaded yet it's because he's got too much on his plate elsewhere. Well, Scotland and Wales and Brittany and me are going to heap more on it. If he thinks he's had trouble with the Celts so far, it's nothing to what he'll get now.' All compunction had gone. She would give the signal for war.

'We're with you,' said everybody.

Finn paced the room. 'I'll leave for England tomorrow,' she said.

*　　*　　*

241

It was late that night before they had finished laying plans. They were to disperse at once. Tailltin to Scotland, Bevo to Wales, Aragon back to Aquitaine and Finn herself to Brittany after she'd visited London.

As they prepared to go to bed, Finn called Bevo back into the room. 'Did you see him?'

'No. He was away on the king's business. Muirna says she isn't sure what his position is, but he's away a lot.' Bevo shuffled her big feet. 'He's married, Finn. Fitzempress awarded him an heiress for his services in Ireland. A Lady Isabel, daughter of a deceased Welsh marcher lord. She's got property in Cumberland, Kent and Wales. Her mother was Welsh. She was at court for a while when I was there.'

'And?'

'Bad cess to her. She's fat and middle-aged and dull, a typical Norman. The Pilgrim's welcome to her, for all her wealth.'

Finn smiled. 'You're a rotten spy, Bevo. I happen to know she's young, fair and pregnant. The Jews told me.'

Bevo reached out and eveloped her fellow-hag in her large arms. 'She's dull anyway. He's still welcome to her.'

It was cold in the tower that night. Eventually Finn got up and took her primer to read down by the still-glowing fire in the common parlour. The table had been cleared and wiped, but the sand on the floor was still scuffed from the guests' feet. The room smelled comfortably of peat, ale, herbs and long eaten dinner. Irritably she picked up an empty beaker that had fallen to the floor and been overlooked, then went to huddle by the grate. On the other side of it a long pair of legs shifted. 'God damn it,' swore Finn, 'what are you doing here?'

'Yust sitting.'

Lief had taken up residence at the Swan. One day he hadn't lived there and the next he did. Nobody had remarked on the change, so natural a progression did it seem. The man never seemed to initiate anything, yet gradually more and more responsibility accrued to him so that he had begun to attend staff conferences, without any permission being sought or given. Blat said he was a tower of strength and Finn had sniffed: 'Tower's right. We could squeeze two more customers into the space he takes up.' But she had shifted so much reliance onto the big Norwegian without realising it, getting him to represent her with agents and merchants who didn't want to be seen dealing with a woman, that she could no longer get rid of him.

She bent her eyes on her primer. 'I need you to take me to Bristol tomorrow.'

'Sure.'

'And then to Brittany.'

'Sure.'

She was becoming crosser. His presence always made her feel

242

physically little, like ivy against a tall tree. 'But if you've got business of your own, I can manage. Aragon can take me. We're not reliant on men here.'

'No.'

'They're not reliable animals.' She looked towards him, wondering why she was saying things she hadn't meant to say.

From the shadows his eyes were straight on her. 'You'd been my lady,' he said, 'I wouldn't have left you.'

He saw her go slack, all the courage she'd kept up for too many years gone out of her in a second. He got up and went over to her, put his hands under her armpits, lifting her like a doll to carry her up to the tower where for that one night the middle room was neither cold nor terrible.

She was furious the next morning, all her fight returned, ashamed of how vulnerable, how feminine, clinging, wet, responsive and generally stupid she'd been the night before. She felt, oddly, like an adulteress. 'It was an aberration,' she yelled at him, 'and don't you presume on it. It didn't mean anything. I was just . . . not myself. Do you hear me? You can go and never come back. Do you hear me?'

'Sure,' said Lief, 'We still catching the tide for England?'

'Yes.'

The Plantagenet court with its hundreds of clerks and courtiers moved around the palaces of its empire in turn, using up the food of each area, hunting through its coverts, transacting its business and then moving on, leaving behind it an army of indigenous servants to catch their breath, clean the rooms, empty the sewers and generally get ready for the next visitation. There was often little warning of the court's arrival and none at all of its departure. Frequently its impatient king arrived ahead of it, would stay in a fury of business for perhaps a month while the court caught up with him and then, one morning, all hell would break loose as he announced their departure for the next stop.

When Finn arrived in England it was to discover that the court, which had been at Winchester, was now at Westminster. Fitzempress, she was told, was away and the Queen was still acting as his regent in England. She knew she was taking a risk that Eleanor might recognise her, but the risk was small. The Queen had met Boniface, a very young nun, her hair scraped back and hidden under the Fontevriste wimple. She was unlikely to see Boniface in the older woman who had been through so much and who wore her hair round her face in the Irish style.

Lief had refused to stay behind in Bristol. She had commanded him to - his presence making her uncomfortable - but he had taken no

243

notice, so together they rode through the pleasant west country of England to Newbury where they embarked on a boat which landed them on the watersteps of Westminster Palace.

It was a bewildering place, one of the biggest royal residences Finn had ever seen, bigger than Chinon and not nearly so beautiful. The various kings who had occupied it since Saxon days had all added bits to it in the style of their particular age so that it ran for over a quarter of a mile along the north bank of the Thames like a ragged, architectural calendar. Its courtyards were crawling like wasps' nests with petitioners, hawkers, entertainers, and stallholders. The Great Hall itself which William Rufus had inconveniently built at a point where the river could flood it at exceptional tides was not now the feasting place of kings, as he had intended, but doubled as a permanent court of justice and a chancellory where litigants could purchase the king's writs, no longer having to chase all over Europe after the royal presence to acquire one. Fitzempress was centralising his new law.

Lief's height and Finn's Irish mode of dress attracted stares and questions from the men and women who milled around them, and giggles from small boys. Eventually Lief smacked one of the latter and paid him a half-penny to take them to the Queen's section of the palace.

Finn sighed with relief when they came to it; even in this hotchpotch of a place Eleanor had created beauty. At the west end of Westminster, beyond the great cathedral, as far as possible away from the encroachment of the city of London, she had built a smaller palace among gardens which ran into each other through archways in walls of rose-red brick. As they neared it bustle and traffic faded. At a lodge under a willow tree by a stream, they asked for Muirna, gave their names and waited, hearing the sound of a lute coming from a pleasuance further in.

Muirna cried with pleasure at the sight of them and flung her jewelled arms around Finn's neck. She had changed. To the court she was still very much an Irishwoman, exotic and foreign even among that cosmopolitan collection of peoples. 'Eleanor calls me "Lady Erin",' she told them. But to Finn it was apparent that she had absorbed the manners and sophistication of Eleanor's world, if not its values. She maintained an Irish mode of dress, though it was even richer than the one they had sent her off in, she spoke Norman French with a deliberate Irish lilt, but these things were her way of asserting her personality in a world crowded with personalities. Otherwise she walked with the slow sway of Eleanor, laughed and talked with affectation, batted her kohled eyelids at the male courtiers who pretended to swoon as she came among them, just as Boniface had seen Eleanor do.

She interpreted Finn's glances and became defiant. 'I'm one of her

244

regular ladies-in-waiting now,' she said, 'I'm fond of her. But I'm still a hag.'

Finn didn't want to waste time. When they'd exchanged greetings and news, she said, 'I want to meet the Exchequer clerk. I want a copy of Fitzempress' seal.'

Muirna's jaw dropped. 'And how about the moon while you're about it? He'll never do it.'

'He will. He's taken the first step in betrayal by showing you *Laudabiliter*. I'm going to force him to take the next.'

Among her web were double agents – the smith at the crossroads to Chester was one of them – and in turning them she had gained insight into Duckweed's methods; once a victim could be blackmailed or persuaded into treachery, however minor, he was his controller's agent for life.

'Are you sleeping with him?' she asked Muirna bluntly.

The Lady Erin smiled with pity at her naivety. 'It isn't how it works. Courtly love is for the unattainable; he just likes to moon over me.' She added, 'I may take a lover here, but when I do he's not going to be anyone as minor as a clerk.'

They walked through gardens where peacocks strolled among exquisitely-dressed courtiers, the men often more exquisite than the women and, with their short tunics, showing a great deal more of their person. Finn's eyes bulged at the bulges. Every so often they stopped while Muirna introduced Finn, 'May I present my friend, the Lady Hibernia?' As Bevo had reported, everybody seemed to be mooning over somebody else, the young men draping themselves at the feet of their ladies and either murmuring poetry to them or singing their beauty.

'Oh come on, Finn,' said Muirna as her friend's mouth pursed tighter and tighter. 'Confess that this is an advance on the way women are treated everywhere else, even Ireland. At least this give us status.'

Finn hadn't thought of it like that. It was true. Outside this daisy-chain garden women were discounted, mere receptacles for male seed, or work-slaves, or child-bearers, or heiresses to be bought and sold. Here, perhaps for the first time, Eleanor had insisted that womanhood be placed on a pedestal. But was it any more realistic? Weren't women still objects being hymned for the luxuriance of their hair, their white breasts, their delicate hands and not for who they were?

She felt a touch on her foot and looked down to find a young, male courtier fondling the end of her shoe. 'Give me the right to compose a sonnet to your wonderful eyes,' he moaned. She gave him a kick. 'Get off.'

Had she realised it, by the time they reached the centre of this romance, Eleanor herself, her face was expressing all the deprecation

245

it had shown years before when Boniface had first been introduced to the Queen of England.

'Madam, may I present my good friend, the Lady Hibernia,' said Muirna and Eleanor, extending a languid hand, found herself wondering where she had seen those dark-blue disapproving eyes before. 'How nice,' she said.

She too had changed. Her youth had gone in childbearing, though instead of losing her figure she was almost too thin. The contentment that Boniface had seen had given way to dissatisfaction; Eleanor was an intelligent, dynamic woman who was being eclipsed by her more dynamic husband, and forced into being merely a figurehead of a queen instead of the ruler she had hoped to be and was capable of being. Frustrated, she had made herself the centre of a world of culture, but it was still an artificial world.

There was a feast every night in Eleanor's palace; at least two hundred people, a mixture of officials, courtiers, visitors attended it if they wished. It welcomed too many foreigners, Christian and even Islamic, for Finn's presence to be questioned. In the crush she seated herself between a man and a young woman and wondered why Muirna, who had been pushed to the other side of the vast table, was making frantic faces at her.

The young lady at her right turned to her. 'Shall we exchange names? We haven't been introduced. I am Lady Isabel, wife to my lord of Llanthony.'

For a moment Finn stared straight ahead. Muirna spread out helpless hands and shrugged. Slowly Finn looked round at the woman her lover had married. 'I am Hibernia,' she said.

'Ah yes,' said Lady Isabel, 'You come from Ireland, I hear.' She shivered dramatically, 'all that ice and snow.'

'That's Iceland,' said Finn, and took a deep breath. 'They're easily confused.'

If the Pilgrim had informed his wife that he had ever been in Ireland, he hadn't told her anything about it, and that warmed her. More warming yet, as Isabel chattered on and on, was the revelation that he shared very little of his life with her. He had spent enough time in her presence to give her two sons – Finn heard a lot about the two sons – but most of the time he was away 'on the king's business. He's one of the king's marshals, you know.'

Finn studied the girl – she was still in her late teens – as she talked. She was extremely pretty, very blonde, well-born, and a complete bore. She kept the ball of conversation firmly in her court all through dinner, happy to enlarge on her estates and family as if Finn were familiar with them, never questioning Finn herself, content with her world of babies, stewards, servants, castles and a husband who rarely came back to interfere with any of them. The jealousy, which had shot through Finn like a poison, dissipated. She told herself she was almost sorry for the two of them, locked in a marriage which had so little partnership of minds. But she wasn't. She was hideously glad. She was exultant. She could have stood up on the table and shouted, 'He does not love her.'

She was ashamed at her joy. 'God damn the man, it shouldn't matter to me.' She consoled her conscience because Lady Isabel didn't mind it, had no idea that partnership of minds between man and woman was possible. And the Pilgrim had got what he wanted, presumably; from everything Isabel was saying his position in the king's administration was high.

'But you wouldn't think so sometimes,' chattered Isabel, 'for only two months back – we were up in Chester in our castle on the marches – he came home of a sudden and he was in rags, would you believe. Rags, as if he were impersonating a beggar.'

'Why?' asked Finn. What was a king's marshal doing dressed in rags in Chester, when the king and his army were in Aquitaine?

'I don't know,' said Isabel, 'He never tells me anything.'

The next morning Finn and Lief rode across the bridge over the river Tyburn and into the forest beyond it to keep the highly secret assignation that Muirna had arranged for them with Robert, the clerk from the Exchequer. Finn had refused to allow Muirna to accompany them. 'It isn't going to be a nice interview,' she said, 'and I want you to remain his object of affection. Better keep out of it.'

Robert was waiting for them in a glade. He was young, pimply and nervous. When he doffed his cap to Finn she noticed his tonsure, but apart from that sign of his clerkship, he had attempted on an obviously limited budget to dress like a young courtier. His short tunic appeared to have been made out of cheap, red cloth by his mother, and there were holes in his hose. He was disappointed at not seeing Muirna and became fretful, though he looked with alarm at Lief.

'I don't know you,' he said, 'I'm going back.' Lief stepped forward and Robert decided to stay where he was.

'Young man,' said Finn, taking a large purse from her sleeve, 'I'll get to the point. I have here some wax and I wish you to make an impression of both sides of the king's seal for me.'

It took time to sink in, then the clerk's jaw dropped. 'You're mad.'

'No,' said Finn, 'I'm rich. I'm offering you ten gold pieces,' – she showed them to him – 'one now and nine when you deliver the impressed wax back to me.'

Robert was pale, but his eyes were on the gold. 'It's death,' he said, 'I can't do it.'

'You're an Exchequer clerk,' said Finn, coldly, 'you use the seal one hundred times a day. Use it one hundred and one times today and bring it to me here this evening. If you don't, I shall let it be known that you have been copying the king's private records.'

Also death. Finn watched the boy sag at his bony knees and thought, 'What a wonderful thing it is to fight for your country and blackmail young English lads.' But she'd got him: she knew it and he knew it. The gold piece passed.

Finn's voice became harsher. 'And while you're about it, I want to see the account of expenditure incurred by the Lord of Llanthony. You need only show it to me, you can take it back with you tonight.'

Miserably the boy nodded. They could only hang him once.

It was a long, nervous day. If the boy was caught he would talk, and even though he didn't know who she was he would be able to point her out. Just in case, and to give herself the chance of escape, she borrowed Muirna's headdress which was of the latest fashion and had a strip of veil attached to one side which could be brought over and attached, to cover the lower part of the face, a compliment to Eleanor's crusading days. Muirna said it was a 'yashmak'.

She could take no interest in what was going on around her, the games, the entertainments, the continual and, eventually, irritating drone of the love songs. 'Extend your contacts,' she kept telling Muirna, 'we must know more of what's going on. Try and encourage Becket's rebellion.'

Muirna said: 'He doesn't need encouraging. He's turning half Christendom against the king.'

And then, in the late afternoon, a man came in through the gate and strode across the lawn to where Eleanor was picking cowslips, bowed to her and said, 'From Aquitaine my lord king sends greetings and his heart's love to his queen.'

Eleanor's voice saying, 'My Lord of Llanthony, how nice,' became the twitter of a far-away bird, the royal English garden became an island in an Irish lake. Finn, sitting on a stone bench, leaned against the yew hedge behind it until its spikes went into her skin and stayed still. Muirna who had been sitting beside her running her fingers over her harp, leaned over and tugged the yashmak across Finn's face. She got up, and crossed to the other side of the path. 'If he comes this way, I'll distract him.'

I don't know what to do, thought Finn, I just don't know what to do. She felt too weak to move and her soul bounced up and down between heaven and hell to find each unbearable.

She heard Eleanor say: 'And what a pity that your lady has gone falconing, towards Smithfield I believe. Is the king well?'

'I'll see her tonight,' said the lord of Llanthony perfuntorily, 'Yes, lady, he is well.'

There was some more conversation which Finn's ears buzzed too loud to hear. 'At least he's been in Aquitaine,' she thought, 'which is where a regular king's marshal should have been. He's going to come this way, he's going the other way, it doesn't matter in either case, oh bugger him.'

He was walking in her direction and she was on a bench. The years rolled away so that it was Boniface who sat there. She didn't look up, just heard his footsteps coming closer along the gravel. She would recognise him among millions, how could he fail to recognise her even though she was veiled?

He was level, and looking at her. Then she heard the sound of Muirna's harp ripple into sound. Playing the first tune she could think of to distract his attention, panicking. Muirna had picked on a song by Niall of the Poems. Would he recognise it? Would he recognise Muirna? No, he'd only seen her once, and that in the dark.

The tune hit her with memories, and it hit him. She felt him stop, knew that his guts were twisting, just as hers were.

After a long time, with both of them an armslength away from each other, she heard him say, 'Where did you learn that tune?'

Muirna said, 'It's Irish, my lord.'

'Well, stop bloody playing it.'

She watched him walk away.

That evening in a summer glade, a frightened young man gave two rounds of wax and a scroll into Finn's hands. All the way to the forest she had wished that she hadn't put the boy into extra danger by demanding the Pilgrim's accounts since it was no longer necessary; the dreadful suspicion that had flickered at the back of her mind as Isabel had talked, had been lulled. He'd been in Aquitaine with the king. He was the king's marshal and nothing more.

She had said goodbye to Muirna; she did not dare to stay any longer in case she encountered him again.

Hardly bothering, she ran her eye down the list the clerks in Fitzempress' careful Exchequer had written down in careful hand. Then she held the membrane tighter and read down it more carefully. 'To Huw of Buckley for services rendered. . . . xls.'

Huw of Buckley was the name of the smith on the road from Chester to Wales.

There were other names and other amounts. Further down she came across: 'To Alan of Galloway for services rendered. . . . 10 L.'

Alan of Galloway was the jealous nephew of William the Lion of Scotland.

The list swooped down onto the grass. She felt Lief's arm round her. 'You all right?'

She looked up at the Norwegian. 'He's Duckweed,' she said.

'Yust sit down a minute.'

'No,' she tore herself away. 'Don't you understand, the bastard's Duckweed.' Eleanor's garden had been an enchantment, just as it had on another occasion. She'd mooned about in it quite as sloppily as all the other poor fools. And all the time this man had been planning harm against nations that did not, and should not, belong to him. Had been planning harm to her.

'Give me that bloody list.' She ran her eyes down it, memorising each name as if she were cauterising them into her brain. Here was every agent he used; here was every agent she would put out of action.

When she'd finished, she thrust the membrane at Robert and slammed the gold pieces into his hand. 'Not one word of this.'

'Don't worry,' he said with feeling, and ran.

It was twilight as Lief and Finn made their way along the strand of the Thames to spend the night at the monastery of the Black Friars near Ludgate. Lief kept his hand on his sword hilt; the shadows that gathered in the bushes were watching out for unsuspecting travellers. He tried to urge Finn on quickly, before the City of London closed its gates for the night, but he couldn't get through to her. 'Oh God, oh God,' he heard her whisper. 'He's Duckweed.'

Chapter Ten

Within months of each other, the Celtic countries of Fitzempress' empire began to give him trouble.

William the Lion of Scotland moved south into the disputed borders of Scotland and England because he had reason to suspect that the King of England was about to bring an army against him. A woman traveller had turned up at his castle in Lothian saying that on the road from England she had come across a dead man, who had been robbed of all but a pouch containing a letter. Since the letter carried the seal of Henry Fitzempress, William read it – and swore terrible oaths. The letter was to the Earl of Chester and contained a plan to extend the frontier of England beyond the Tees and into his, William's, territory. Since the woman traveller was obviously ignorant of what was in the letter – since women could not read – William let her go.

Suddenly there was a conspiracy in the marches between the barons of Brittany and Maine to resist Fitzempress' lordship. Duke Conan, who ruled Brittany in the name of the King of England, was unable, or unwilling, to put the rebellion down.

In North Wales, Owain of Gwynnedd all at once moved an army east across the river Clywd and snatched land which belonged to the Norman Earl of Chester. He also wrote to King Louis of France, offering help against Fitzempress because, he said, he had learned that the English king had designs on Gwynnedd. A friendly monk had shown him correspondence bearing the seal of Fitzempress, which proved it.

In his castle at Chinon, where the Plantagenets had gathered for Christmas, Fitzempress went into a temper that seemed to the man standing by unnecessarily violent. He rolled on the ground, biting at the straw and swore on the various limbs and organs of God in a way which threatened to bring a thunderbolt through the roof. Eventually, spitting and shaking, he was persuaded to quieten down.

Even so, he raged. 'I'll have your balls off,' he said, 'John, I swear I'll have your sodding eyes out. You might as well be blind. Why wasn't I warned?'

'You were, my lord.' The Lord of Llanthony was pale, but firm.

'Ever since Woodstock, I've been begging you to ameliorate your policy to the Celtic nations.'

'Ameliorate?' The king made five syllables riccochet round the tower room. 'I'll ameliorate the bastards. I'll castrate the entire sodding race.' For once, he sat down and drummed his fists on the table. 'Why all of them? Why all at once?' He looked up towards Heaven. 'God, you sent me Becket, did you have to send me Celts as well?'

'My lord, you can have my resignation. I've failed you. But I'll tell you this much; there's a common factor behind these rebellions. Somebody is orchestrating them.'

'Who?'

'I don't know. But somebody, somewhere, has been forging documents purporting to come from you – and with your seal. If you were to keep me in your service, I should want permission to question your clerks.'

'You think it's a clerk who's stirring up the Celts?'

'No, my lord. But one of them has given an impression of the seal to the somebody who is. And I think that somebody's an Irishman.'

He outlined his reasons to the king. He had traced the people who had carried the inflammatory letters to Scotland and Gwynned. One of them was a woman, the other a monk. The monk was found to have taken ship at Milford Haven, the jumping-off point for Ireland from Wales. The woman had been described as having an Irish accent. 'And as far as Brittany is concerned, I believe Conan to have been bribed to go soft on the revolt there. He is under the thumb of a wise woman called Jehane. I've had her castle searched and in it I found some gold pieces minted in Ireland.'

Fitzempress had recovered his calm. 'I'll say this for you, John. You haven't been idle.'

'No, my lord.' God, he'd worked and if he could scent down this man who opposed him and his king, he'd work more. To find and scotch this elusive, hinted-at enemy who ran through his troubles like a vicious fleck of Irish green, had become his obsession.

Henry asked, 'What the hell would a sodding Irishman be doing in all this?'

'I don't know, my lord.'

'Better find him, John.'

'I will, my lord.'

'And kill him.'

'I will, my lord.'

The news of *Laudabiliter* had shaken even Ruairi O'Conor's complacency in the inviolability of Ireland, though it strengthened his faith in his watcher by the sea. As a result, Finn was given all the gold she

252

asked for to spend on her agents. With it she fuelled the rebellions which kept Fitzempress and his army rushing back and forth to quell yet another outbreak.

And with some of it she bought pigeons.

For several mornings while she was making her pre-dawn patrol of the tower roof, just as Molling began his mill, she had noticed a pigeon rise from behind his house, circle, and fly towards her over the Stein to disappear behind her own inn. At first she thought nothing of it. The Abbot of St. Patrick's had tried to forbid laymen keeping pigeons and doves since the birds' depredations of church cornfields cost bushels of lost wheat. But Dubliners were too independent and too fond of pigeon pie for the ordinance to be strictly enforced. Nearly everybody had a pigeon cote, the Swan included.

But on the fifth dawn that the pigeon took almost exactly the same course, Finn became curious and followed its route to find Art standing in the far gable door of the roof.

'What the hell are you doing?' She climbed up the ladder. Around the loft were wooden cages in which pigeons were murmuring throatily. One of them, the flier from the mill, was upside down between Art's hands as he untied a scrap of cloth from its leg.

'Become a bird fancier in your old age?' In the morning light she saw suddenly how old he had become. The fingers that fumbled with the knot of cloth were distorted with arthritis. It had never occurred to her that Art could age; he had seemed eternal. 'I'll have to get him a stable boy,' she thought. They had recently opened a stable for post-horses, a business which only just broke even, but attracted long-distance travellers.

Art was grumpy. 'Be minding your own business,' he said, 'this is between Gorm and me. If he's coming over for a drink at night he puts a cross on this ribbon, and if he's not he doesn't. A pigeon always flies back to the coop he comes from, if his mate is there and if he's fed.'

He scratched the pigeon's head with his crippled finger and put it into a cage with another. 'Could they fly from another country?' asked Finn, interested, 'Across the sea?'

Art shrugged. He didn't know. But on Aragon's next trip, which was to Brittany, partly to trade and partly to make trouble for Fitzempress, she took a crate of pigeons with her. Finn had forgotten the matter, being busy, when a month later Art came stumbling down the ladder from his loft with a scrap of cloth in his hand and shouting. 'Didn't I tell you? Ah me little darlin', all that way and he comes back to me.'

So Finn devised a code for her most important agents, like Muirna; she allotted each a colour. Since almost none of them could write they would communicate in symbols – a crown for king, a collar for a *brehon*, a castle for a Norman and so on – which in each case referred to

253

the people of the area, with crosses and other signs to mean various things according to their number. It was a crude method and Finn longed for universal literacy with ardour, but it would at least enable her to keep track of where various people were and, to a limited extent, what they were doing.

The next time Bevo travelled via Wales to see Muirna she took a pair of pigeons with her. When she came back, two months later, it was to inform Finn that the young clerk Robert had died under torture. He had confessed to making a wax impression of the seal 'for an unknown lady', but he had taken the secret of Muirna's involvement to the grave with him. Finn had grieved for him already – ahead of Bevo had arrived a pigeon carrying Muirna's sign on the leather round its leg on which had also been drawn a young man under the lash. Above him were four crosses, which Finn had designated as the symbol for death.

That night Elfwida was kept awake by footsteps which paced the tower roof until early morning.

On a day of late winter a pigeon flying from the north landed on the roof of the Swan and fluttered into its loft. Art brought Finn the pouch from its leg. 'Bilberry,' he said, 'that means Oriel.'

She smoothed out the soft vellum. The drawings on it were vertical. At the top was a triple crown. Below that were pincers clasping a round shape from which dripped red tears onto a single, patterned crown. 'The High King has blinded Eochy,' she said.

'Isn't he the bastard,' said Art, 'for didn't he guarantee Eochy's safety?'

'Yes.' There was more here than the usual savagery by which one king safeguarded his position from another. Eochy, king of Ulidia in the north, had rebelled against MacLochlainn of Ulster, Ireland's High King. After much skirmishing, in which he had come off worst, he had been induced to go under the roof of MacLochlainn to talk things over and make his peaceful submission. It hadn't been easy to persuade him – MacLochlainn was not a king to inspire trust – but both the Archbishop of Armagh and the King of Oriel had guaranteed his safety. Therefore, by blinding him, the High King had not only deprived Eochy of his eyeballs – and other bits as well – he had offered the grossest insult to the honour of Ireland's premier Archbishop and a royal ally on whom he depended.

Finn called the hags and Brother Pinginn to her room. 'I can't be sure,' she said, 'but I think this is it. If MacLochlainn's allies turn against him, Ruairi O'Conor can move at last.'

Two days later a man rode his horse into the Swan's livery stables and told Art to look after it well. 'He's come a long way,' he said. Art rubbed the gelding down, fed and watered it and went to find Finn. 'He's from Armagh,' he told her, 'the horse carries the cathedral brand. He'll have been delivering a message to Archbishop O'Toole.'

254

It didn't surprise Finn that the messenger had come out to the Swan after discharging his duty, rather than stay overnight in the city.

Laurence O'Toole had been elected to the Archbishopric of Dublin at the insistence of Dermot of Leinster, but it had been a popular choice – Dublin felt honoured by having such a saintly man as its primate.

After his inauguration, however, it became less sure. There was such a thing as too much saintliness. Laurence O'Toole had extended the austerity of his own life to curb the excesses of the monasteries and, by gaining influence over its king, of Dublin itself. Church sergeants patrolled the streets arresting drunks and unlicensed prostitutes. Visitors still fed well in the monastery guest houses, but they had to listen to uplifting readings from the Bible while they did it. Being outside the city limits, the Swan had escaped the general holiness which was pervading Dublin – and its custom had gone up accordingly. Finn stood in the doorway of the common parlour to get a look at the man.

Finn read the situation in the sailors' parlour as easily as she could now read the written word. The central fire was burning high, sending its smoke up straight to the roof and making the room and its crowd slightly over-hot, which was deliberate policy – the drinks bought by thirsty men more than paid for the fuel. The shepherd from St. Mary's was playing a reed pipe and one of the sailors off the Breton ship was dancing to it. Asgall's hog-keeper had brought a girl tonight who was not his wife and was kissing her. There were a couple of well-ordered games of chess going on in one corner and a rowdier dice game getting nasty in another. Ever since there'd been a stabbing over a wager, Finn had made Lief ensure that her order banning all weapons in the inn was strictly enforced. She looked towards the settle where Lief always sat and the Norwegian nodded; everything was under control.

Finn felt affection for him; she blamed herself for the weakness of the flesh which had led to their one intimacy; she didn't love the man, but he had relieved her of the burden by never referring to it and had gone on being his old, dependable self as if there had never been anything between them.

She turned her attention to the central table at which Perse was doling out tonight's speciality, pork and cabbage. Almost reluctantly, Brother Pinginn had pronounced the English girls finally well, and it had been accepted by everybody else as automatic that they should become part of the Swan, and by Finn because she needed more staff and reckoned they owed her a year's wages. She had dispossessed them of the tower's upper room, moving into it herself, and – because the staff dormitory was overcrowded – put them in the middle room. They didn't seem to mind its atmosphere. Perse was an asset, a slow but long-working carthorse, and popular in the sailors' parlour because even the stupidest customers could run intellectual rings round her.

255

Elfwida was a problem. She too was a good worker and now served permanently in the nobles' parlour because, to Finn's amazement, it transpired that the more upper-class the customers, the more they lusted after Elfwida whose skinny body and fast repartee made an apparently irresistible challenge to them. King Asgall himself had boomed at Finn: 'Teach the elf-maiden to dance and I'll give you twelve cows for her.' Knowing Brother Pinginn would object, Finn had turned the offer down with regret; she couldn't fault Elfwida's behaviour to the customers; the girl titillated yet kept the response at arm's length. It was off-duty that she threw tantrums and pestered as if she were testing everybody, particularly Finn, to see how far she could go. Like Brother Pinginn – the only person with whom she was calm – she flirted outrageously with Lief and, like Brother Pinginn, was ignored.

Perse ladled out a second platterful of pork and cabbage in front of the messenger from Armagh and he tucked into it with the concentration of a man who had ridden too fast for two days to stop and eat.

'Jesus,' said Finn, aloud, 'I wish I knew what he knows.'

Elfwida was at her elbow. 'I can find out, Finn. Finn, let me find out.'

'How?' Messengers were chosen for their ability to keep their sender's counsel.

For answer, the girl crossed to the back of the messenger's bench and put her arms round his neck. Through the noise of the parlour, it was impossible to hear what she said but it was provocative, and the messenger responded as if he'd been even longer without women than food. Finn wasn't surprised: the man was unattractive.

There were surprised looks at the entwined couple – the Swan had never provided girls: you had to bring your own. Brother Pinginn came up: 'What's Elf doing?'

'What does it look like? She's going to get information.'

'Stop her. Finn, stop her.' When Finn didn't move, Pinginn rushed forward, but Finn held him back. 'Leave her alone.' She dragged the little monk into the kitchen. 'Leave the girl alone. It's her decision.'

'It's not. It's yours. I'll never forgive you if that child goes into danger of her soul and it's your fault the poor little thing you're as bad as a pimp . . .'

Finn shook him. 'Stop being silly.' Perse came into the kitchen. 'Elf and that chap have gone to the stables. Persingly, I thought she'd stopped all that.'

'Finn,' begged Brother Pinginn, sobbing. 'I beg you.'

Finn took up a tray and headed for the nobles' parlour. 'Stop being silly.' It wasn't her doing. She hadn't asked the girl. They needed that information. If war had broken out in the north it was the beginning of the end for the north's ally, Dermot. Asgall could be persuaded to desert his overlord and fight for O'Conor, she was sure of it, but it would have to be done soon, before Dermot commandeered the Norsemen of Dublin to fight on his side.

Her customers were calling for their mead, but Finn didn't hear them. She stood still, gripping the tray. In all her watching and scheming against Fitzempress she had never forgotten that Dermot was the cancer within Ireland. Her planning, her sacrifice, all the work she had put in these last few years might bear fruit now. She might actually rid Ireland of Dermot. The weight of the rape that had oppressed her body and mind might at long last come off it. It might actually come off.

She woke up to find Ragnar shaking her arm. 'Thirst-quencher, we're waiting.' Finn slammed the mugs down on the table and looked at Ragnar without seeing him, 'And what's an English whore to all that?' she asked.

Late that night when the inn was quiet, Elfwida dragged herself up to Finn's room. ' "To my beloved brother in Christ, Archbishop O'Toole, from the primate of Armagh," ' she said carefully, ' "Know that for the crime of sacrilege and murder we have cut off MacLochlainn, High King of Ireland, from the body of Mother Church. Know also that Donnchad, king of Oriel, has foresworn his allegiance to the High King and that at our urging others are expected to follow his example and to declare war on the High King that he may be deposed for his sins." '

The news was of such magnitude that unconsciously Finn turned to go up the stairs to the roof where she did her best thinking. All kings everywhere held their throne with the blessing of God and His Church. If the Church removed that blessing they were no longer a proper king.

Excommunication was the axe being held over the head of Fitzempress by Becket at this moment. And in Ulster, another Archbishop had actually brought it down on the High King of Ireland. An excommunicated king lost the faith of his people and could not last long, especially if the Church was commanding his allies to desert him.

MacLochlainn was virtually finished, which left Dermot of Leinster isolated. She'd give the bastard isolation. She'd fix up a meeting between Dublin and Connaught, she'd bring the curse of Brigid to bear . . .

'Am I a hag now?' said a voice behind her.

She turned round. 'What?'

The girl Elfwida's face looked odd, as if its bones had slightly warped. 'You don't want to know, do you?' she said, and her voice was as unnatural as her face. 'But I want you to. That was the first fuck I ever got a thrill out of. Know why? Because he thought he was screwing me. But this time I was getting something out of it. For you. For the first time it was me doing the screwing. Does that make me a hag?'

Finn fought down her repulsion. 'I didn't ask you. But the

information is useful. Thank you. And go to bed. You must be tired.' She turned back to the steps and went up to the roof to plot in the good, clean air. Towards dawn her calculations were interrupted by a sound which reached her from the middle room, the whimpering of a girl returning to a recurrent nightmare. Finn covered her ears so that she could go on thinking.

Knowing that King Asgall would not take seriously any negotiations which had been set up by a woman, Finn used Lief as the go-between. Grudgingly she admitted to herself that the man was not only calm but intelligent, and literally had the stature that the two kings would respect, though why men had faith in someone just because he was taller than they were she couldn't understand.

Lief performed well, and it was some satisfaction to Finn that the meeting between the two sides took place in the tower of the Swan Inn. It was the natural venue; Asgall could visit it in the normal way without attracting the curiosity of Dermot's spies in the city, and O'Conor's negotiator Eoin, his *mór-maer* was met on the north bank, rowed across the river and smuggled into the tower via the trapdoor. This was, after all, part of Dermot's territory.

The talks between the two, with Lief as guarantor for both men's safety, took all night. At one point Lief, climbing up onto the roof for some air, discovered Finn listening at the top of the stairwell. 'There's yust one point they don't agree,' he said, 'Asgall wants 6000 cows for his homage to the O'Conor. Eoin offers 1500.'

Finn considered. Six thousand was a ridiculously large amount, but on the other hand fifteen hundred was ridiculously small. O'Conor, who had only one large trading port in his kingdom, Galway, had probably no idea of how important a city Dublin had become. 'It's worth 4000,' she said, 'but only on condition that Asgall persuades the Norsemen of Waterford to join him in the rebellion against Dermot.'

Lief nodded. 'That should do it,' he said and lumbered back to the council chamber. It did.

It seemed at very long last, but it was only early spring, on one of those mornings of pearly mistiness which indicate frost, that a rider appeared at the summit of a hill on the north bank of the Liffey. He was cloaked and, though without stirrups, the sun reflecting on his and his horse's head threw back a gold light. He was still and the city he looked at across the river was silent. There was a drum of hoofbeats and the hilltop around him sprouted hundreds of horsemen and banners, like sudden barley.

On the roof of the tower by the Stein stood a small group of people, gripping each other's hands. They had been waiting and working for this day. As the banner of Connaught unfurled on the north bank, another, smaller version, streamed across the roof of the Swan Inn from where ululating howls of triumph went vibrating across the Liffey.

The bells of Dublin woke up and began ringing. Its gates swung open and Ruairi O'Conor with his Connaught clans rode down to be received into it and be proclaimed king of its king and High King of Ireland, a post that MacLochlainn had relinquished when an Oriel spear pierced his lung during the recent battle at the Gap of the North in Armagh.

Two days later the O'Conor rode out of Dublin with his ranks swelled by its Norsemen – but not before he had gone to an inn on the Stein promontory and asked for a drink.

It was still in Irish Lent, which didn't exactly coincide with anywhere else's Lent, that Dermot of Leinster was defeated in the Blackstair Forest. His defeat was due as much to the defection of his friends as the victory of his enemies. Only the Hy Kinsella and a few others were with him at the end.

The clans of north Leinster like the O'Faolain who'd already been wavering in their allegiance to Dermot were finally convinced that they should desert him by a strange visitation from a woman bearing a striking resemblance to the ex-Comarba of Kildare, who told them to remember Kildare.

And what to do with him now they'd caught him? O'Rourke wanted him castrated and blinded but Ruairi O'Conor, benificent in his High Kingship, wouldn't allow it. They compromised on a punishment which, to Dermot, was nearly as terrible. They commanded him to go into exile and turned the exiling into a public event. They practically sold tickets.

The long ship carrying Dermot and the sixty or so companions who had chosen to go into exile with him came down the Slaney. Along the upper reaches of the river the banks were lined by his silent, disarmed Hy Kinsella. Whether he was defeated, whether God and St. Brigid were against him, Dermot had their blood as they had his. The hills above them echoed with shouts of encouragement to their lord from those who remained uncaptured as they retreated into the mountain forests.

But down the lower reaches, near the protection of Norse Wexford, other clans were delighted to watch him go. They spat at his ship as it passed and allowed their children to run along the banks throwing cow pats at it.

Two miles above Wexford, at Ferrycarrig, the river narrowed to squeeze between jutting cliffs. The right was impregnable from north and east and on its top some long-forgotten chief had built a *rath*. It was on the grandstand provided by its walls that the noble haters of Dermot Mac Murrough stood to witness his passing; kings, ex-hostages, former vassals, maimed chieftains – and the staff of the Swan Inn, Dublin.

As they waited there was an air of holiday. Ruairi O'Conor moved blithely among the crowd, pressing everyone to eat and drink the provisions his stewards had provided, making sure Dermot's victims were comfortable and describing the springtime scene to those whom Dermot had blinded. When he came to Finn he said, 'Isn't this the great day? And didn't I promise it to you?' He congratulated the hags on their part in the war – he had refused to let them fight in it, saying it was against his honour to use women warriors but, when they pointed out that as Connaughtwomen it was their war as much as his, he had allowed them to carry despatches through enemy lines for him. He had a special word for Brother Pinginn who had taken messages to the monasteries, and who had fallen in love with him.

Finn barely heard him. She was rigid with tension that something could still go wrong. Dermot had contaminated the air she breathed for so long it seemed impossible that it could be cleansed, that the easy river below her could debouch him out to sea as simply as it did all its other detritus. She barely noticed the one other person who was as intent on the river as she was. Tighernan O'Rourke had waited fourteen years for revenge on the man who had abducted his wife. If O'Rourke could have had his way, Dermot would have floated down the Slaney in pieces.

Finn's attention was caught for a second by the sound of Lief's deep voice behind her saying something about 'a mistake'.

'But why, Lief my little Viking primrose?' she heard Pinginn ask. 'This is the Christian way – exile rather than mutilation.'

'Maybe. But keep him here. Better Dermot in the tent pissing out, than outside the tent pissing in.'

As usual when the Norwegian spoke, Finn became furious. What did he know? Then somebody shouted, 'There he is!' and she forgot everything else.

The ship slid down the river in long pulls, its fifty oars making tiny scars in the water, like stitchmarks along an old wound. Dermot stood by the mast – they recognised his grey hair. Everything the wits among them had planned to shout at him died as inappropriate; he wouldn't have heard them. The man might be a weasel but he'd been a royal weasel, fighting until the last second. When they'd overrun his beloved stone castle at Ferns it had already been set alight by his own hand so that they should not have it. Even now he did not look around him like a man saying goodbye but stared ahead, ignoring the last chance to see his kingdom. And, after all, they were sending him into the outer darkness, to the rest of the world which orbited the sea around Ireland like the sun orbited the earth.

As the ship manoeuvred the bend in the river between the promontories one of the girls on board began to sing; unselfconsciously, beautifully, her voice said goodbye to Leinster on Dermot's behalf in some Hy Kinsella lament and for just one moment the men and women on the clifftop re-experienced the transfixing freshness of a child's countryside.

Finn walked along the edge to keep pace with the ship a hundred feet below; there were several girls aboard, all of them young. The one who was singing had long, dark hair, but as she felt the breeze from the estuary touch it for the first time she fell silent, smelling exile.

Tighernan O'Rourke and the landlady of the Swan Inn watched the ship until it was out of sight. Finn shook herself. 'What did you do with Dervorgilla?' she asked. The king of Breffni turned his one, hating eye on her. He was ugly, old and short and his temper was even shorter. 'Get out of my way,' he said.

Finn stretched and went to join Pinginn and the others. They saw that she looked younger than she had for years. Tailltin gave her a drink and toasted her. 'Can we all go home now?'

'You can,' said Finn, 'I've got one last call to make.'

Mór had grown tireder and fatter in the years of her Comarbship of Kildare. She was upset by the visitor who had been smuggled into her private apartments and now stood looking out of its window at the courtyard below. 'You cut down the pear tree,' said the visitor.

'It was diseased,' Mór told her. 'Why now? After all these years why do you want to know now?'

The woman at the window said, 'I had to clear Dermot away first.'

' "Vengeance is mine",' quoted Mór, 'The only thing worse than not getting what you want is getting it.'

The woman turned round and Mór saw that she too had grown tireder, but that she was still beautiful, the greying of her hair merely gave it a quality of dark mist. She said: 'It bloody nearly killed me to come here. Are you going to tell me or not?'

Mór sighed. 'It was a girl.'

A girl. 'What happened to her?'

'We gave her to Dermot.'

The Abbess fetched some wine and put it in Finn's hand. 'My dear child, what were we to do? He demanded her. If we needed an example of what came to those who opposed him, we had only to look around us. We were still rebuilding the town and burying those who took time to die from their injuries. There.' She wiped Finn's face with her trailing sleeve and went back to her chair. The bell was ringing for None and outside the quietness of the room the bustle of the abbey was moving into another rhythm. Mór ignored it. 'As a matter of fact, my dear, it was perhaps no terrible thing to do. Dermot has a fondness for children, especially girls and especially his own. And he felt responsible for this one.'

Finn went back to the window. 'Well he was, wasn't he?'

'Are you all right, my child?'

'Yes.'

'The king took Dervorgilla's little girl as well, naming her after her mother. The child, the one . . . you know,' she did not know whether or not to say "your child", '. . . he called Slaney, after his favourite river. They have both been brought up with his other daughters and I have taken care to reassure myself of their wellbeing and could find no fault with it; I myself taught them their catechism and the Bishop of Lismore himself confirmed them. If she could only quell a tendency to tomboyishness she would show fair to progress in the favour of God, his Holy Mother and St. Brigid.'

The Abbess had begun to speak with proprietorial fondness. She's forgotten I'm here, thought Finn.

'I would have received her into our convent here, but she was not willing, and I fear Dermot indulges her in everything. She preferred to be promised in marriage to one of the young princes Mac Brain who was brought up as a hostage of the court and whom she has therefore known since childhood.' The abbess sighed. 'The poor lamb. That's one wish which can't be granted to her now. Dermot was not that indulgent.'

'Why?' Then Finn remembered. 'The Mac Brains deserted to O'Conor. Was the boy still Dermot's hostage?'

'And paid for his clan's defection. Dermot had him blinded. Our monks have been looking after him and wish him to be a novitiate, though he rails against God. I understand Dermot's blinding also included having him, er, physically disqualified from marriage. It is a good thing the world is coming to an end, such times do we live in.'

'Does she know?'

'I imagine not, or she would not have agreed to go with Dermot.'

The patchwork of abbey sounds, a far-off *Jubilate*, a brush sweeping some corridor, the linnets in the courtyard, were remembered but alien.

'Would you wish to return to us, my daughter? I could get permission. Dervorgilla has been received into the nunnery at Clonmacnois these many years.'

Finn shook her head.

The Abbess said gently: 'She is a happy child, Boniface. Much like you in looks and colouring and God has blessed her with a most beautiful voice. You ought to hear her sing.'

Finn turned to her. 'That's a humorous God of yours,' she said, 'I just did.'

Chapter Eleven

The train of the exiled Leinster men and women crawled through the landscapes of Aquitaine for three months like a beetle. Names the Irish had difficulty pronouncing, Perigeux, Bordeaux, Toulouse, Saintonge, became goals, then shapes on a horizon; then buildings and streets which lost none of their strangeness when surrounding them. The scale of everything was oppressive, distances were too far, cathedrals and castles too big, mountains too high. They became unwell from unfamiliarity with smells and plants and music, their stomachs revolted by alien food. Three died on that journey, Nuala, Dermot's aunt, and two of the Hy Kinsella who had elected to go with him. All of them were elderly, but it wasn't age nor illness which killed them, it was disorientation.

They moved in and out of areas ruled by brigands but their party was too large to warrant attack and was anyway protected by its air of poverty and pilgrimage. What was strange to the people it passed by was that it didn't keep to the pilgrim routes nor ask for the local holy places. It enquired after one man and when they heard his name the inhabitants would shrug; he had been there last month, last week, yesterday, he would come back in two days, forty, next year. He was never there today. They passed through towns still shaking from his visit. At Castillon-sur-Agen they were told that he had reduced its castle, well fortified by nature and artifice, within a week to the wonder and terror of its Gascons, but that now he had gone elsewhere and a good thing too.

Their real enemy moved with them. Back home in Leinster, even on the hottest day, sun was a diffuse element, dappling on the ground of forests, splintering on streams, and generally flirting with the possibility of going away again. You ran out to enjoy it. But here it was permanent, an entrapment of heat like an endlessly large prison from which the only freedom was to enter the dim, unhygienic shelter of stone walls. At first Dermot's daughters, being young, had enjoyed the alien ferocity of colour, the enamelled blue sky on land burned ochre, clashing sandstone castles and red tiles. But a month of travelling in it after the elusive king their father was seeking, making detours to find water for thirsty horses, balked by unfamiliar language, developing rashes and saddle sores, unable to change their menstrual cloths often enough . . . 'Frankly,' drawled Aoife, 'it's beginning to pall. It's doing nothing for my complexion.'

'To hell with your complexion,' said Slaney, 'what about mine? Will Cennsellach Mac Brain still love me now I'm old and freckled?'

'You're not old enough to know what love means,' said Dervorgilla from the superiority of her sixteen years, but she said it kindly and once again alarmed her younger sister by leaning over to pat her hand. They usually communicated by banter and her sisters' sympathy indicated to Slaney that they knew something she didn't know about the boy she had grown up with. She'd begged them to tell her if they did, but they said they did not. She'd begged Dermot to tell her what had happened to Mac Brain, who'd been his hostage, but he'd said, 'Would I hurt anybody whose hurt would hurt you, pigling?' And she'd believed him, and loved him and been so sorry for him that she'd agreed to go with him into the outer darkness into which Connaught and Breffni and all the other treacherous bastards had driven him. 'It won't be for long,' he'd said.

Outer darkness had proved to be this blinding country which had changed Dermot. He had become silent and deaf, refusing rest, insisting on going on until it was too dark to see and they had to make camp on rock- or mosquito-infested riverbeds. It had got to the stage where his daughters and followers reckoned he had gone mad and that the compulsion to find Fitzempress, the Duke of this appalling eternity, was a disorder of his mind.

'I swear we passed that castle two weeks ago,' said Dervorgilla, squinting ahead at an elaborate fortification on the mountain ahead, 'except then it wasn't hanging clothes from its crenels. . . . Oh Mother of God, they're not clothes.'

What had looked like two flesh-coloured pillow slips writhed and kicked for a minute and then hung limp. The daughters of Dermot reached out to clasp each other's hands for comfort.

From the direction of the valley below the castle an approaching train of dust indicated a horse and rider travelling fast. 'It's Phelim.' The scout slid off his horse two yards from Dermot onto one knee – all Dermot's men and women maintained a meticulous standard of respect to him in his exile – 'Found him, my lord. He's sieging that castle and will be happy to receive you, he says, if you will forgive "lack of ceremony caused by the exigencies of warfare".'

'Let us come with you, Father,' said Slaney, 'those barbarians are hanging men from that castle wall like you would hang flags.' Dermot patted her head and didn't hear her, just as his ears had attended to nothing but the name of Fitzempress for three months. 'Tell them to make camp here,' he told Phelim, 'but first get them to unpack the best linen, my ermine cloak and the gold filet and jewels. I must look like a king.'

'I do hope you don't mind sitting under this awning while we talk,' said the King of England, 'only the rebels in that castle over there are hanging some of my subjects to try and frighten me off and I feel the least I can do for the poor bastards is to count them as they go. How many's that, Ursus?'

'Three, my lord.'

'You see,' said Henry, turning back to Dermot, 'until I married their Duchess these Aquitanians had no more idea of political entity than my arse. Less, actually. Any lord who owns a castle – like the fellow in Talmont over there – thinks he can do anything he likes. In fact, that fellow over there – he's a Gascon; have you met any Gascons? Don't bother – is even disputing that he's part of Aquitaine at all. So I sent my uncle-in-law, a man in whom my Duchess reposes somewhat misguided trust . . .' Fitzempress looked venomously towards a beautifully-accoutred but agonised knight who was watching the castle in the distance and biting his nails, '. . . to tell the sod that Aquitaine begins and ends where I say it does.'

'Three more,' said Ursus.

'And what does he do?' asked Fitzempress of Dermot, 'He sends his vanguard galloping into the castle bailey ahead of the main force and the portcullis bangs down and traps them in there. Oldest trick in the book. If I've told you once, Ralph . . . how many of your men do you reckon they've got?'

'Twenty-five, my lord,' said Ralph de Faye, 'My lord, couldn't we treat with . . .'

'No, we couldn't. I'm not having this anarchy spreading. You stand there and watch them hang. Teach you to be more careful next time. Now where was I?'

'Four more,' said Ursus.

'So I've got to reduce that sodding Gascon, and his castle in . . . how long did you say it would take to capture Talmont, Ralph?'

'Three months, my lord, it is strongly positioned and . . .'

'Three days. I haven't time to stand about.'

There was a moan from the knights standing around them; like straw scarecrows, men were being tossed over the crenels to jerk and kick and then slump at the end of ropes invisible in the heat haze which swam between the castle and its besiegers across the valley.

'Five in a row,' said Ursus. 'That makes eleven.'

One of Fitzempress' hands slammed into the palm of the other. 'Anyway, my lord, you will understand why I am forced to receive you

265

without the ceremony which is your due, and I beg that, as one king to another, you will overlook it. Now then, in what may I serve you? Will somebody get some wine for my lord of Leinster?'

There was a scamper for wine which was politely handed to Dermot by, had he known it, the Earl of Salisbury – a Fitzempress campaign usually moved too fast for its supply train to keep up and lords of the Angevin empire frequently found themselves acting as their own menials.

Dermot looked at his hand holding a chipped beaker of wine which had been poured from somebody's private flask and apparently previously boiled. The king he had come so far to see wore a leather jerkin which had seen better days and sat on a camp stool, having given Dermot the only decent chair in the place. Apologetically, Fitzempress got out a needle and thread to mend a tear in the finger of one of his gloves. 'I concentrate better if I'm busy. Do go on.'

Molloy, Dermot's cousin, muttered in Irish, 'This is against your honour, Mac Murrough. Where are the footbaths, and the trumpets, the oils of welcome? This is a kern, not a king. Let me teach him manners.'

But Dermot's madness made everything around him, the knights, the tapestried pavilion, the hanged men, the countryside through which he'd travelled, this low-class king, merely a background that moved past him while he himself stayed still. Part of him was in Ireland and the rest of him wriggled for the means to rejoin it like a worm cut in half. Carefully he got up and carefully he sank to one knee before the young king. He had learned the words he had to say by heart, he had repeated them to himself every day away from Leinster and, though he recited them in the Latin, he gave them the musical artificiality with which important speeches were made in High Irish back home, so that it seemed to his listeners as if he were singing.

He cried as he sang, and his hearers may have thought that he cried with self-pity at his wrongs, but Dermot's insanity at that moment was such that it gave him insight into the millenium of wrong he was bringing on Ireland. In full knowledge of what he was doing he wept for his country and sang his song just the same.

Inside the tent a hidden knight, perspiring with heat, put his ear closer to the calico.

'May God who dwells on High ward and save you, King Henry, and likewise give you heart and courage and inclination to avenge my shame and my misfortune that my own people have brought upon me. Hear, noble King Henry, whence I was born, of what country. Of Ireland I was born a lord. . . .'

It was ten minutes before he finished recounting his lineage and got to his own achievements. Some of the knights sniggered but a glance from Fitzempress' eye converted the sound into coughs.

'Six more,' said Ursus, 'Seventeen.'

'In the presence of the barons of your empire, good sire,' chanted Dermot, 'Your liegemen I shall become henceforth all the days of my life. On condition that you be my helper, so that I lose not everything, you shall I acknowledge as sire and lord.'

The song ended and the silence it left was filled with the stridulation of cicadas. Dermot got up and resumed his chair, staring at nothing. Molloy threw himself at his feet. 'What have you done, Mac Murrough, selling us to the foreigners?'

Fitzempress knotted the last stitch on his glove and bit through the thread. 'You honour me with your confidence, my lord,' he said. 'Obviously such a great matter cannot be decided without great thought. Allow my men to find you some fit place where you and your retinue – did I understand there are ladies in it? – can be comfortable while I take counsel with my barons.'

He stood up and bowed and gave orders in rapid Norman patois: 'See he gets the best we've got, and any bugger who insults him or even winks at his girls will suffer immediate loss of balls.'

When Dermot and a sobbing Molloy had been escorted off, Fitzempress went into the tent to his sweating knight. 'Lucky you were here, Spymaster. Did you or did you not hear that old man with the comic beard offer to sell me Ireland?'

'I did, my lord.'

The two men emerged from the sweltering tent into the sweltering evening air and strolled towards the one tree, a cedar, which had not been cut down to make siege engines and pit props.

Ursus came up to them. 'That's all of them now, my lord.' The sun setting behind them had turned the white stone of Talmont castle to blonde and was gilding the row of bundles which hung, untidily but still, below its battlements. 'That Gascon,' said Fitzempress, 'is a fool. He had twenty-five cards to play against me and he's just thrown them away. Tell the priests we'll attend a mass for their souls, but tell them to make it quick. We'll start the diversion at dark and the miners can go in.'

Ursus lumbered off at a run. 'Well,' said Fitzempress, 'you're my Ireland-watcher. Shall I buy?'

'You know my opinion, my lord,' said the Lord of Llanthony, 'Don't touch it with a bargepole. Dermot of Leinster . . .' he tried to keep his mind and voice balanced, '. . . is untrustworthy and no better than a criminal.'

'Haven't you traced that fleck of Irish green yet?' asked Fitzempress.

'Not yet. He's been lying quiet yet, as if he's got something else to do. And since your lordship managed to quell the great Celtic rebellion, perhaps we've sent him off with his tail between his legs.' He

267

took a deep breath. 'I've told you and told you, Ireland's unwinnable. The terrain is bloody awful – you're either up to your hocks in bog or you can't see for trees. It's all . . . misty. One clan might be your ally one day and the next it would be creeping up your rear with its knife in its teeth. It sort of runs between your fingers. Try to grab it and it slips away. Nobody will ever own it in the sense that we mean ownership.'

Fitzempress broke off a frond of cedar and smelled it. 'I wish I'd met her.'

'Who?'

'Your lady.' He patted his spymaster's shoulder. 'She got to you, didn't she? Every time someone mentions Ireland you fulminate against it, but you get that moony look in your eye. I can practically hear the mystic harp chords playing in the air. Was she anything like my Rosamund?'

'No,' said John, 'she was an unfeminine, ungrateful, treacherous bitch. Are we discussing Ireland or women?'

'It appears to be the same thing. So what do we do with Dermot's offer to make me his king?'

'Stuff it up his arse.' John was put out. How the hell did Henry know about the harp chords?

'Ah, the anal school of diplomacy. We could stuff Becket up there as well. He'd be in his true element. Is he still stirring up shit?'

'I've brought the agents' despatches, my lord. At Pentecost in Vezelay he spoke from the pulpit and excommunicated Richard de Luci and Jocelin de Balliol for drafting the Constitutions of Clarendon and swore that you too would suffer Anathema unless you speedily gave satisfaction for what he calls your injuries to the church.' John was a brave man, and now an important one, but he got ready to run. Fitzempress' temper was something outside him, an elemental force; it could enter into him and turn him uncontrollably destructive, like a typhoon. And Becket's was the spirit that called it up. The messenger who'd brought the news to the king that the archbishop had slipped abroad out of his clutches and joined up with Louis of France, had been tossed in the air like a wheatsheaf, breaking his arm, though Henry had apologised later by awarding him nice little serjeantship in Surrey.

Nothing happened and he relaxed. 'I heard,' said Fitzempress, shortly. 'And that's why we've got to help this mad Irishman of yours because if we don't he's going to go to somebody who will, like my royal overlord in France. A French Ireland – that's all I need.'

John shut his mouth. Fitzempress wanted information and not opinion; he merely asked for it to shape his own. Anyway, he thought to better purpose than anyone else in the world. John had no mean regard for his own brain, but in Fitzempress' presence he was humbled.

268

He looked through the striped shade of the tree at his sturdy, unglamorous king and loved him because John's affection followed John's ambition; he could not separate the two. It was why, in an unexcited way, he loved his wife Isabel that Fitzempress had given him and loved the lands and sons she had provided him with in her turn. He gave thanks at every mass for his escape from that liquidising passion which had once run through his bones in Ireland. He liked the duller colours, the even tenor of his deliverance and if, every so often, all sound became muted to a hum and he heard staves of music rising from a path, or saw a lakeland that sent him into a dream which lasted for hours . . . well, that was his cross to bear.

'So what I think we'll do, John,' Fitzempress was saying, 'is temporise. We'll not help old Dermot ourselves, but we'll give him permission to seek help among our subjects. And God help anybody who gives it to him.'

'Brilliant.'

'I know.' Fitzempress linked his hands over the branch above his head and swung on it. He got bouncy when he was clever. 'I want you to go back to England ahead of him, and go to Richard de Luci, bless his excommunicated heart. Tell him to look out a papal bull Adrian sent me once. Tell him to look for *Laudabiliter* and get copies made. Tell him I'll give him "L" if he doesn't find it.' Fitzempress collapsed at his own joke.

'What is it, my lord?'

'It's another bill of sale for Ireland. It shows I've been king of that bog hole all along. We might need it one day, you never know. And John, if Dermot does succeed in putting together an expeditionary force to win back his lands, I want you to be part of it. I must know what goes on over there. I can't have some sodding mercenary setting himself up as High King of Ireland.'

It was getting dark. Frogs down by the river were taking over chorus-work from the cicadas. Fitzempress said, 'It's got to be you, John. You're the only one I trust who's got any idea about the situation over there.'

'I know.'

'Get on with it then. And John.'

'Yes, my lord?'

'You're wrong about Dermot being the biggest bastard in the world.'

John nodded. 'I know, Henry,' he said. 'You are.'

In the last days of August, Dermot, former king of Leinster, was to be found sitting on the steps of a cross in the centre of Bristol's market place while above him a crier shouted an advertisement.

'Hear, all men who love adventure, honour, reward and feat of arms, hear what our king Henry hath promised this king from over the sea. Listen to his words. 'Henry, King of England, Duke of Normandy and Aquitaine, and Count of Anjou, to all his liegemen, English, Norman, Welsh and Scots, and to all nations subject to his sway, greetings. Know that we have received Dermot, Prince of Leinster, into our grace and favour; wherefore whosoever within the bounds of our territories shall be willing to give him aid, as our vassal and liegeman, in recovering his dominion, let him be assured of our favour and licence in that behalf.' Listen to King Henry's words and to what liberal promises of land and pay to all and sundry who may help him this prince offers. O come near, ye men of spirit, and enrol under this prince's banner.'

He was a good crier and he repeated the advertisement in English, Norman French and Welsh from the strike of Matins by the bell of St. Augustine's to the strike of Terce with half-an-hour's break for lunch. If he flagged, his employer nudged him into remembering how much he was being paid. The rest of the time Dermot just sat, facing westward, his hands knotted on the head of his staff, spattered by passing carts, sniffed by passing dogs.

Plenty of people came to listen and a few threw the odd cabbage stalk to show their independence and because they always threw things at the conspicuous. But it was boom-time in Bristol and such adventurers as there were had other things to do, or had long ago been scooped up by Henry II who treated his mercenaries to good pay and certain victory. Dermot got a few drunks, one madman who insisted on standing beside him holding a wooden sword at the salute, and several small boys. But he sat on, resisting attempts by his daughters and followers to pull him away.

The girls were no more eager to see him use foreigners to regain their country than Molloy was, but as the days of humiliation dragged on they began to pray for somebody, anybody, who would volunteer and end them. 'I'd fight for the poor old thing myself if it would do any good,' wailed Slaney.

'I confess I am disappointed,' said Robert Fitz Harding, their host, when they appealed to him, 'I had hoped the King would provide more co-operation to MacMurrough than he has; no doubt he is overstretched. He will have good reason, good reason.'

Fitz Harding was a dear old man, Bristol's most distinguished citizen, whose trading connections with Leinster went back a long way and who was anxious on that account to see Dermot reinstated. It was to his magnificent house in the city that Dermot had first gone to on being exiled and it was a letter from Fitz Harding which had procured his interview with Fitzempress. Henry of England owed a lot to the old merchant; when he was still a child in the midst of his mother's and uncle's civil war, Fitz Harding had given him shelter, money and ensured him the loyalty of Bristol. Fitz Harding had been repaid by the gift of Berkeley Castle and half of Gloucestershire for only one knight's fee. The girls were lodged in his home as if they'd been Norman princesses, with more luxury than they'd known in their lives.

They didn't like it. They didn't like being hemmed in by houses, they didn't like the restrictive clothes and shoes which were provided to bring them into the fashion, and they didn't like the male guests at Fitz Harding's vast dinner table who excluded them from all the interesting conversation, patronised them with elaborate chivalry when they did talk, yet tried to pinch their bottoms in the darkness of the corridors as if they were serving wenches. 'Sex mad, these Galls,' said Dervorgilla. Yet, perversely, they resented the chaperonage which Lady Fitz Harding insisted on giving them. 'But my dear young ladies, you can't walk down the streets unattended. Look at the undesirables you've attracted already.'

It was true. The girls felt peculiarly watched. One morning when they'd been showing helpless solidarity to their father during his market square calvary, a Jewish woman in bright colours had said to them, 'So you're the Leinster ladies. And which one of you darlings is Slaney?' It had given them all, particularly Slaney, a nasty turn. It was dangerous to be named by evil spirits, and if anybody looked like an evil spirit, that woman did. On the other hand, good spirits were also on guard over them for when a horse, maddened by flies, broke round the corner of Frome Street, its cart toppling in its traces, a huge blond man had stepped out of a doorway and calmly gathered Dervorgilla and Slaney, who were in its path, out of the way. When they thanked him, he looked at Slaney and said a strange thing. 'Yust like your mother,' he said, and went away.

They discussed the incident over and over. Everybody knew who Dervorgilla's mother had been, the naughty thing, and Aoife's, who was his latest wife, but there was a mystery about Slaney's – probably some war prize who had gone back to her clan. Dermot acknowledged any child whose mother said it was his, but he insisted on having it brought to his court for rearing. Who had actually borne her had never bothered Slaney; she'd had all the mothering she needed – and sometimes more – from her eldest, and legitimate sister, Urlacam. Now she found herself unsettled.

'I want to leave this creepy city,' said Aoife, 'Good or bad, these spirits are foreign. I want to go home.' They ached for Ireland. That night they knelt before Fitz Harding in a rehearsed plea. 'Good seigneur, in your puissance find aid for our father.' To help his thoughts and because he liked her voice, Slaney sang to him the song

271

with which she had said goodbye to Leinster, and the only one who didn't cry at the homesickness in it was Dermot.

As the song came to a close and a green countryside faded out, leaving them in a carved, gilded room, Fitz Harding frowned. 'I suppose there's Strongbow,' he said.

Dermot talked and Strongbow listened, biting his nails. Every so often he interrupted. 'But did the king mean that?' Or 'Are you sure that was what he said?' He got Fitz Harding's scribe to come and read the letter from Fitzempress to him as if he didn't trust what Dermot said it said.

Hidden in the gallery of Fitz Harding's hall, their ears pressed to the balustrading, the sisters listened. Dervorgilla whispered: 'Now how can a man with a nickname like Strongbow be so wet?'

It didn't fit him. The girls knew it wasn't his, anyway; his father, Gilbert de Clare, had won it fighting for Fitzempress' grandfather, Henry I, as well as the earldom of Pembroke. Richard had attached it to his own middle-aged, balding person after his father died, to give himself grandeur. He needed grandeur. For Richard de Clare was not the second earl of Pembroke as he should have been. He'd made one, colossal mistake – he'd been sure that Stephen would win the Stephen/Matilda war. He'd been so sure that a woman couldn't win or rule England that he'd been one of the few marcher barons to persist in Stephen's support all through. In one sense he'd been right; Empress Matilda didn't win the war: her son did. When the battle dust cleared, Richard de Clare found himself without an earldom, with a king who didn't love him, and in terror of another mistake.

'Isn't he the indecisive,' said Aoife, as her father persuaded, coaxed, cajoled and Strongbow wavered back and forth.

Heavy steps pounded up the stairs to the gallery and Lady Fitz Harding tracked her charges down. 'Girls, girls,' she said, shocked at their eavesdropping. So un-Norman. The daughters of Dermot stood up shamefacedly, showing themselves, and the men in the hall below looked up.

'There, there,' cried Dermot in his madness, reaching out an arm like an actor. 'There is your prize if you throw in with me. My eldest daughter, my fair daughter, heiress to all my lands. You shall have her and all my inheritance after me if you throw in with me, if your throw in with me, my lord.'

'Which one?' said Strongbow, while his brain made calculations.

'That was very naughty of you, Father,' said Aoife, later. 'I'm not your eldest daughter and how can the poor man inherit anything through marriage to me, or any woman? It was false pretences.'

The girls were in the large bed of their own private bedroom in Fitz Harding's wonderful house, the linen sheets drawn up to their chins and their heads, one fair, one red, one black, sticking over the top. Dermot sat down the end of it, looking more normal than he had in days. 'How is he to know that? Women can inherit land here, in abroad. Men marry them for it. It's the law.'

'They can do what they like,' said Dervorgilla, 'it's not the law back home, thanks be to God.'

'And I wouldn't marry a balding old vacillator like him if it was,' said Aoife, sternly.

Dermot leaned over and tugged her long, fair plait. It was lovely to see the father they knew come back to them. 'You look like a row of toffee apples, the three of you,' he said. 'So Aoife won't help her poor old father trap this innocent Norman into helping him win back Leinster? Not one teeny little worm of a lie to drag the poor fish to Ireland so that we can throw him back later, unmarried? Even though God overlooks fibs when they're made to barbarians? You wouldn't do that for an old man who loves you?'

Aoife smiled her beautiful smile. 'You know I will,' she said.

Dermot had to pile offer on ludicrous offer before the pact was agreed; his daughter, riches, Ireland on a plate decorated with parsley. At last Strongbow said carefully, 'Very well, my lord. From henceforth your honour is mine and together we shall fight to defend it.'

They embraced. Then Strongbow said, 'But, of course, I shall have to ask the king's permission first.'

When the girls heard, Slaney said, 'That'll take forever.' But Dermot was buoyed up by hope. 'We're going into Wales in the meantime. Strongbow says there are landless men there who will join us. He'll come over later with the main army.'

'When all the fighting's done, I suppose,' said Aoife. 'Mother of God, that's a fine betrothed you've landed me with. I'd not marry him if I was sainted for it.'

'You won't have to,' said Dermot, 'When they've done their work, we'll get rid of these foreigners.'

'Will it be easy to do that, Father?' Slaney was doubtful.

'Sure it will, sure it will,' promised Dermot. 'And when he finds out he can't inherit as much as a stone from the marriage, Strongbow won't want it anyway. Who'd want to marry an ugly old lump like any of you?' The girls threw themselves on him and scuffled him to the ground in delight. Their father was back in his old self, the man who could make everything all right and trick the sun into thinking it was night-time.

*   *   *

Standing on the healthy side of the bars of the deepest dungeon in Wales, Dermot called out, 'Is there a Robert FitzStephen among you?' Shapes stirred and scrabbled in the darkness his eyes couldn't penetrate and he covered his nose against the smell of urine and faeces.

'I'll tell the butler to fetch him,' said a voice. 'Who shall I say it is?'

'Dermot, king of Leinster. With his release.'

'Now you're talking.' A tall scarecrow emerged into the light of Dermot's flare, brushing down his rags as if he'd been taking his ease on a haystack. The gaoler unlocked the gate and the scarecrow nipped through, just avoiding the rush of other prisoners to get out. 'Bye, lads,' sang FitzStephen, helping the gaoler club them back, 'Don't let's be dog-in-the-manger about this.' The screaming and babble drowned any further conversation and, after mouthing and bowing to each other for a moment, Dermot led FitzStephen up the staircase which circled the hole in the mountain until it reached the floor of the tower of Aberteivi castle.

'My lord . . .' began Dermot but FitzStephen raised a long, filthy hand and stopped him. 'Just a minute, my lord.' He crossed to a niche in the wall in which stood a crucifix and knelt before it, shaking, sobbing prayers of gratitude. 'My lord . . .' began Dermot when he'd finished, but again FitzStephen stopped him. 'Would you mind if we went outside? I've rather gone off walls.'

They went through the bailey where guards allowed them out of the gates to the grass slope with its view of mountains and river. It was an overcast day, but FitzStephen squinted against the light. 'Now, my lord, who did you say you were? The Archangel Gabriel?' he said.

'I am Dermot, king of Leinster.'

FitzStephen nodded kindly. 'I've heard of it. Did Fitzempress send you?'

'In a way.' Dermot explained his mission. FitzStephen listened carefully and was then silent for a while. 'So Fitzempress didn't send you to get me out?'

'No,' said Dermot, 'I heard of your predicament through my lord Strongbow, and since your . . . host . . . Prince Rhys has shown me kindness and hospitality, I bargained with him for your release. He is prepared to let you go if you leave Wales and don't come back.'

'Three years,' said FitzStephen, gently, 'I've been in his fucking prison for three years because I tried to hold these bits of rock for England and failed. Our glorious king Henry doesn't believe in failure. Prepared to let me rot, was he? He should try fighting these fucking Welshmen and then he'd see.'

'I thought you were half-Welsh yourself.' FitzStephen was tall like a Norman, his carefully lcaonic speech was Norman, but the emotion which had shaken it just then, like his sallow skin and curly, black hair, was British.

'Unavoidable accident,' he said, 'Mother was an accident waiting to happen to practically every Norman who set foot on her bloody mountains. A Welsh counter-attack all by herself, was Nesta. Well, my lord Leinster, your intervention was timely and your invitation timelier still. It appears I'm no longer welcome in my mother's country and Fitzempress' silence indicates I'm not welcome in my father's any more either.'

'You can have Wexford and two *cantreds* of land,' said Dermot, generously. Wexford and its environs belonged to the Irish-Norse who'd jeered him out of Leinster.

'Done,' said FitzStephen, 'and thank you. It'll take until next spring to gather a good force together, but not longer. Thanks to my mother, I've got more half-brothers, uncles, nephews, what-nots – especially what-nots – all hungry for land, than you could shake a stick at. And talking of hunger, my lord, you haven't got on your person something really valuable, have you? Like a piece of cheese?'

'And may I present somebody or other, another nephew. He begs to be allowed to show you ladies how he hunts larks with a sparrowhawk, a custom I believe is unknown to you in Ireland.'

The daughters of Dermot bowed and whoever it was leered at them, thick fleecy curls hiding the eyes. 'Sparrow hawk or not, I'm not moving a step with it until I hear it speak,' muttered Dervorgilla. In the past weeks they had made dizzying forays to Welsh mountaintop to enlist pack after pack of FitzStephen's cousins, halfbrothers, half-nephews, full brothers, full nephews, legitimate, bastards, tall and blond, short and blond, tall and dark, short and dark, all of them called Fitz something or something Gerald but all of them with the rapacious mouth they had inherited from their common denominator, the ubiquitous and fecund Nesta. Whatever education they had picked up in their windblown, straw-littered keeps had not, except in a very few cases, included the social graces. Some grunted lustfully at the girls and grinned at them with lupine teeth. Others just grunted and turned away to a more interesting occupation which usually involved killing something. FitzStephen tried to invest each with some charm as he presented him, but privately the girls categorised all of them into 'wolves' or 'pigs'. This one was a pig. Although the girls still stood he sat down, spat onto the head of the sparrowhawk on his wrist and rubbed the saliva into its feathers.

'He's shy,' said FitzStephen, shooing some hens off a bench so that Dermot and his party could be seated, 'And over in the corner, my lord Leinster, is my most distinguished cousin. May I present archdeacon

275

Gerald de Barry?' A young man with ginger eyebrows put his forefinger in the book he was reading and looked up. 'Giraldus Cambriensis, *if* you please,' he said. 'Let us by all means use the civilised tongue.'

'This is our royal visitor from Ireland, the king of Leinster, Giraldus,' said FitzStephen gently, 'and the princesses.'

Giraldus got up, his finger ostentatiously marking his place, ignoring the girls. 'Do you intend, sir, to root out the weeds of vice in your barbarian country, to establish in it the holy Roman Church and the jurisdiction of blessed Peter?'

His daughters' heads turned to Dermot and saw that for the first time in this whole humiliation, their father showed displeasure. 'I intend to win it back,' he said, softly, 'and to remind the world that there would most likely be no Church of Peter had not the saints and scholars of my country kept it alive during the Dark Ages.'

'Good for you,' whispered Slaney.

'Well answered, my lord,' – nothing could dint the patronage of Giraldus' self-satisfaction – 'and the noble valour of the FitzGeralds will be the sword of Christ in that land of darkness. For while I myself tread the harder, lonelier path of learning, we are all descended from the heroes of Troy and the celebrated prophecy of Merlin Silvester will clearly be fulfilled by my cousin, FitzStephen here, that a knight sprung of two different races will be the first to break through the defences of Ireland by force of arms. But I would remind you all that it is better for any prince to be loved by his subjects than to be feared. For it follows that whatever is loved with human love is also feared . . .'

The girls' eyes were watering with boredom halfway through and, since he'd shown them no courtesy, they showed him none either and went outside to look out across the sea at the ill-defined smudges like clouds which were the hills of Ireland.

' "If I had seven tongues in seven heads I could not sing all the beauty of Leinster",' said Slaney softly. 'Oh Mary, Mother of God, when can we leave these terrible people and go home?'

Above them, where sheep the size of cats with long coats cropped the thin grass, somebody else had left the keep and was also looking at the smudges on the horizon. The knight sprung from two races was finishing Merlin Silvester's prophecy. ' "Break through Ireland's defences by force of arms," ' said FitzStephen, ' "and conquer it for himself." Why not? Why not?'

One by one the Breton, Welsh and Scottish rebellions failed against the overpowering efficiency of Fitzempress' army. But Aquitaine had exploded again, and so it was there that Finn spent most of her resources.

Her staff saw that she had lost the energy which had once fuelled her

276

spying activity. With the going of Dermot she had achieved one of her goals, but it had brought its own loss. Also it had brought its own dangers. She concentrated on what Dermot was doing, worrying about his search for allies, however ineffectual it was proving to be. She watched through her web for the threatened invasion by Fitzempress with the old intensity, but her hope now lay in the trouble that Becket was creating for his king, in Aquitaine. Not in herself.

Time had leached out of Finn the disgust at giving birth to a baby that had been forced into her. She had gone to Kildare to find out what had happened to it from a terrible, compulsive curiosity. When the child took shape, the distant shape of the girl in the boat, there came the realisation that she had not just been the receptacle for a man's semen but that, in receiving it, her body had been activated into the function for which it had been built and that her blood, not just the man's, had gone into the baby. The child looked like her. She had exiled her own daughter.

Finn's mind teetered on an edge, then looked back. In that moment of choice the option of breakdown was foregone. She couldn't afford its luxury. She couldn't abandon her child for a second time.

The whole world changed. Instead of being flat, as she knew it was, it rounded into a sphere in which there were no ends or beginnings or disconnections, but only a cycle to which war, ambition and nations were irrelevancies; time-fillers pursued by men to disguise uncreativity. With the agony of her own irrelevant years came a dreadful and overwhelming compassion for all parted things, a crying baby, every lost duckling, Mary at the foot of the cross, and, more importantly, for herself. She could have wailed at wasted time but she let even herself off that hook in her new pity. It was as if only now she had become a mother and while her love was centred on a girl seen just once, the edges of its vortex gave a kinder understanding of everyone else.

She saw more clearly than ever the lopsidedness of the Word of Man. 'How could they leave out Motherhood in the Bible?' she asked Brother Pinginn, 'when it's the most important thing in the world?'

He was her only comfort in his understanding. 'I don't think they left it out,' he said, 'they just downgraded it.'

She remembered the Thing on the Wall at Kildare, and the weighty, breasted idol in Scathagh's gallery. 'It was too much for them, wasn't it? Scathagh referred to God as She.'

'From what you tell me, Scathagh made the same mistake as men, only the other way round. I've been thinking lately that if we're made in the image of God, all of us, then he must be both male and female. God the Father, God the Mother and God the Son. And Jesus was the combination of the best of both.'

She looked at the little monk and tears plopped down her cheeks. 'I do love you, Pinginn.'

'I love you too. It's nice, isn't it?'

'Will you make me some vellum?'

They had to wait until one of the inn's cows aborted her calf and then, crying for the mooing mother and the little dead thing, Pinginn scraped, soaked and rubbed its skin and stretched it on hoop-frames to dry. The ink he made from oak galls, copperas and gum, and the quill from a crow, which enabled smaller writing than did a goose quill. He went to a whitesmith and at his own expense had two lead inkwells made, one for Finn, one for Elfwida.

While he was doing it, Finn set her spies not only to watch Dermot, but to guard her daughter. She felt gratitude as the reports came in of an apparently happy, well-rounded girl who had affection for the man she believed to be her father. If it turned out that the child's happiness would depend on her keeping that affection, then Finn was amazed to find that in her new-found motherhood she was prepared to opt for that.

But it gave her a satisfaction in serving her daughter, to go back to Kildare and offer a home to Censellach Mac Brain, the boy whom Slaney had loved, and whom Dermot had blinded and castrated. Mór arranged for the interview to take place in her room. He was very young, but his milky white eyes gave him an ageless look, like a statue. The brassard he wore on his left arm – a snake biting its own tail – showed the excellence for which the Mac Brain goldsmiths were renowned.

'Why?' he asked, when she made her offer.

'I'm told you don't take to monastery life.' There was no point in telling him their connection. 'If you're not going to go back to your clan, you could help me watch Ireland.'

'Who is this silly bitch?' he asked of the monk who'd guided him into the room. 'Is she blind as well?'

The monk, who was new, mouthed apologetically at the well-dressed lady, 'I'm afraid he's got very bitter.'

She wasn't surprised. The boy was fifteen years old and the coffin lid had already closed for him. She said, 'You won't need eyes for the sort of watching I do. Dermot Mac Murrough is trying to gather a force of mercenaries together so that he can win back Leinster. Some of us are trying to put a spoke in his wheel.'

She looked at the monk, but he didn't seem to be paying attention. Nobody in Ireland seemed to be paying attention. When she'd given Ruairi O'Conor her agents' reports of what Dermot was up to in Bristol and Wales he'd been undisturbed. 'My dear cousin, Ireland is uniting at last. What can a few mercenaries do against the size of army

I can bring into the field?' While it was true that the clans of Ireland were, in an exhausted kind of way, showing signs of accepting the rule of Connaught and O'Conor as their High King, she knew that they had never faced mailed knights and had no idea of their effectiveness – she said so. 'Call no new thing fair,' Ruairi had said, as he so often did of things outside his experience. To her chagrin he was using the fine herd of cavalry horses that Iogenán had bred out of her Fitzempress' mare as hunters.

But as least she had the blind Censellach's attention now. 'Mac Murrough? You're opposing the Mac Murrough?' His thin, adolescent fingers reached out and were crawling over her face. 'Will we hurt him?'

'We'll stop him.'

'I'll come.'

In her eagerness to serve her daughter by taking the boy into her care, Finn had discounted the difficulty. The few unsighted people she had met in her life had been blind from birth and had trained themselves in various skills as harpers, story-tellers and such. The hereditary *brehon* of the O'Faolain clan had been blind, carrying the massive weight of Irish law in his memory. Familiarity of place had enabled them to move around fairly freely with the aid of a stick or a slave. It hadn't occurred to her that the newly-blinded Censellach would be virtually helpless, nor that his scarred mind would refuse to help itself. It wasn't that the Swan staff didn't do their best – Blat cooked special little delicacies for him, Art took him out riding on a leading rein and tried to get him interested in pigeon-rearing, Lief carved him a stick and Brother Pinginn went into contortions of sympathy, devoting much of his time to reading and talking to the boy. Finn gave him his own chair in the nobles' bar and, to her relief, found that the jarls were so moved by what had happened to him – not so much the blinding as the castration, which was their nightmare – that they tried to include him in their talk. But when, inevitably, they got onto subjects like hunting which had been his joy, he spat at them and ran across the room, nearly blundering into the fire. 'Don't those pigs have any feelings?' he screamed at Finn, 'why do they have to remind me?'

He had been a good-looking, charming, careless, extrovert young man who had not been fed on enough intellectual protein to sustain him now that his sexual and active life was over. Pinginn watched in agony as the boy dug himself into a time trench, refusing to look back and rejecting any advance to the future. Finn longed to hear anecdotes about Slaney but he had wiped out his past for his self-protection and she learned nothing. He spurned the help of Art, and when Tailltin suggested that he might like to take charge of feeding the poultry, he turned on her furiously. 'I am high-born, not a hen-keeper.' Pinginn offered him the consolation of religion, but he said, 'Don't talk to me about God. How could He let this happen to me?' He took the stick Lief gave him and gradually learned to tap his way round the inn and its environs, screaming with frustration whenever a guest left a stool out of place and he fell over it. Since he couldn't abide the company of his peers, Finn put his chair in the commoners' bar, telling him that by listening to the sailors' talk for information he could be useful to Ireland. He sneered – he had no conception of Ireland as an entity, like so many of the clan aristocrats – but the only alternative was to sit brooding in the tower, so he did it. But even as a spy Censellach was limited because the one subject which interested him was Dermot. 'Why didn't you tell me what the Manx sailor was saying, about FitzStephen trying to recruit men from the King of Man?' Finn asked him crossly, one night, 'Even Perse realised that was important.'

He sulked. 'I was listening to the trader who said Dermot had gone back to Bristol.'

'But we know that.'

'Well, if you know that why don't we send someone over to kill him?'

She was silent. She'd dreamed of it. A few years ago, when it was impossible, she had spent happy hours plunging hypothetical knives into the Mac Murrough neck; now that it was a feasible proposition she no longer had the necessary hatred.

'I could do it, Finn.' The boy's hands crawled over her face again. 'One of his daughters used to love me, she probably still does. I could trick her into getting me close to him and I could do it.'

'No.'

During the daytime while the staff were busy preparing for the guests, Censellach took to wandering outside the inn, stick-tapping excursions along the quay and over the bridge to the mill, but most frequently up Lazy Hill behind the Swan where he was often to be seen in conversation – at a safe distance – with the lepers. 'What on earth can he find to talk about with them?' she asked Pinginn, who had followed him at first to see he didn't fall. The lepers were still her *bêtes noirs* and, though they had learned to keep their distance, she suspected them every time a clutch of eggs or a hen went missing.

'Hatred for the unafflicted,' said Pinginn sadly. 'I'm afraid for that young man, Finn. And of him.'

She didn't have time to pursue it. She and Tailltin and Pinginn were preparing for a mission. Thanks to the information that Dermot was sounding out the Isle of Man for mercenaries, she had been able to thwart him by getting Asgall, his fellow Norseman, to warn the Manx king that it would be regarded as an unfriendly act if any of his people joined forces with the exile. It would be less easy to stop the

280

recruitment of Welsh and Scots mercenaries, but they were going to try.

That spring the most innocent of parties, two nuns and a priest – a very small priest – journeyed through Scotland, by chance following in the wake of some knights who were trying to recruit men for an expedition into Ireland. They were like an eraser, for wherever they passed the enthusiasm for the expedition among those who had promised to join it in two months' time was obliterated. The knights had offered good pay – sixpence a day for axemen, a shilling for mounted men with armour – and rewards of land. The nuns and the priest said with compelling earnestness that the expedition was doomed because St. Brigid, of whom even non-Irish Celts were in awe, had cursed Dermot Mac Murrough whose expedition it was with a deep, long curse. Her disfavour had already exiled him; if he returned to his native land to face it again the fate of Gehenna awaited him and all his soldiers with him.

Some were prepared to take the chance, but the superstitious majority were not.

Elated by their success, Finn, Tailltin and Pinginn took their message of doom into the enemy's territory, into Wales, to counteract recruitment under the noses of the recruiters, the sons of Nesta themselves, which was how they got caught.

Chapter Twelve

'Well, well, my lord,' said FitzStephen, welcoming his visitor to Strongbow's castle at Chepstow, 'who'd have thought it?'

'Not me,' said the Lord of Llanthony, dismounting, 'but these are chancy times. And Fitzempress is a chancy king.'

'He's let you keep your lands?'

'So far, but you know what he is. I could be deprived of them any minute. He won't have me in his sight just now, so I thought . . .'

A groom led the horses away. Stiff-legged, John followed his host across the bailey and up the steps to the hall. FitzStephen ushered him in and gave him wine: 'So you thought you'd better acquire more, just in case.'

'I regard this expedition to Ireland as a crusade,' said John with what he considered just the right touch of hypocrisy. 'To bring the enlightenment of the True Church into Celtic darkness.'

'Don't we all. And in what did you offend our noble king?'

'Well, I happen to think he's going too far in his animosity towards Becket. He'll bring the country under interdict if he's not careful. Like a fool, I said so.'

'And the sky fell in? Dear me, I thought you were so close to Fitzempress.' FitzStephen's foxy eyes flickered at his guest.

'So did I. I reckoned myself the best of his marshals.' John stamped the mud off his boots and alarmed the falcon sitting on its be-dropped perch. 'How's the recruitment going?'

'Not well. We'll be glad of any men you can bring. Jesus, I'll swear someone's deliberately blocking our attempts. Is Fitzempress playing one of his games?' Again his eyes went sideways.

John said with perfect truth, 'He's got too many troubles everywhere else just now.'

FitzStephen nodded. 'Well, Strongbow's gone off to lick the king's arse and make sure he's not offending him. The damned Jews are being backward about advancing the money. You'd have thought on a venture like this . . . and that Manx idiot refuses to let any of his people join us and the Scots have proved broken reeds. I thought there'd be some Welsh surplus, and I was sure we'd get a lot from the

Flemings who've settled here, but there's this odd reluctance. There's a rumour going round among wives and mothers that Dermot's been cursed by some Irish saint and that if we join him we'll never have sons, or be struck down by disease or something.'

John became alert. The green fleck again. 'I bloody know somebody's blocking you. I've had an idea for some time that someone over in Ireland is causing trouble all over Europe, and when I get my hands on them . . .'

FitzStephen was pleased. 'Now I'm glad you said that, because we've had a bit of luck. One of the FitzGeralds was in Caerleon three days ago when he heard that a woman had been spreading the curse-rumour in the market place the day before and, not being the fool he looks, he chased along the road she was supposed to have taken and rounded up every suspicious looking woman he met. I told his rider to bring them here for questioning . . . ah ha.'

Down in the bailey there was a sound of horse-shoes on cobbles, shouts and muffled screaming. The two men moved to the doorway and looked down on some large, sheep-skinned riders who were escorting a train of pack mules, each one with a skirted figure tied across its saddle. Feminine legs kicked at one end of the bundles and from the other, under the sacks over their heads, issued feminine curses.

'Bit wholesale, wasn't he?' shouted John to FitzStephen who shrugged.

'That's the FitzGeralds for you.' Over the noise he told the man in charge. 'Take them to the keep.'

He and John went back into the hall to finish their wine and conversation. 'It's a strange place, Ireland,' said John, 'and while I discount all this business of curses and ill-wishing, it might be that we should delay any move . . .'

It's got to be now,' said FitzStephen sharply. 'Dermot Mac Murrough's information is that the O'Conor is making a success of the High Kingship. We've got to get over there before the clans cohere for the first time in their history.'

'My lord.' A man had appeared at the door. 'My lord, one of the women is asking for the Lord of Llanthony.'

A cold trickle went down the backs of the men in the hall. 'How did she know he was here, for God's sake?'

'She heard his voice, my lord. She says she knows him.'

'Who is she?'

'She's a nun, my lord. But she said . . .' the man was ill-at-ease, 'she said to ask him, did he remember Bertha the Bosomy?'

She had been taken to the keep's top room, so that he could speak to her alone, and flung into a corner. The fight she'd put up before she was captured had forfeited her captors' respect for the nun's habit. Her veil was off and hanging around her neck. She had a black eye and a bruise on her jaw. She looked a mess.

He had the beginnings of a paunch and the years had taken away most of the amusement from his face. He stood in the doorway for a long time before he spoke. 'Just tell me why.'

'Why what?'

'Why Glendalough?'

Mother of God, after all these years it still ate away at him, and how familiarly beautiful he still was, how beautifully familiar, he was a shock near her in a doorway and just the same; it was Christmas and Easter and every saints' day and spring. She shouldn't have asked for him; but she'd known she was in danger of her life. Anyway, she couldn't bear to have him just pass by again.

She said, 'I couldn't leave Ireland. But it nearly killed me to do it.'

He softened. So she'd gone back to the convent; there'd not been another man. All the resentment and the nights swearing vengeance if he saw her again melted into not mattering now that he'd found her. The damn harp staves were at it, louder than ever.

He shut the door behind him and the minutes switched into Lough Mask time. 'It bloody nearly killed me. They kept putting me in herbal baths.'

She grinned and winced. 'Very good for you.' There was an iron cup with water on a shelf. He took off his surcoat and dipped the sleeve of his fine lawn shirt into the water and squatted down over her.

'Don't you come near me,' she said. She had begun to breathe fast, ridiculous.

'Wouldn't want to, a bruiser like you.' He wiped her face gently. She could smell his skin. 'Loon, you were the only thing that was good for me.'

The scents of lakeland, juicy and full, were in the room. The floorboards were the grasses of Swan Island. 'God almighty, you never used to wear all these buttons.'

When he eventually got back to the bailey, he found FitzStephen still talking with the woolly FitzGerald. He went over to them: 'As I thought, my lords, nothing more sinister there than a nun on her way to Much Wenlock Priory. I used to know her a long time ago. I'll escort her so that I can explain to her superior why she was waylaid in this fashion. There shouldn't be any trouble.'

FitzStephen glanced up at the keep. 'That's what she told you, did she?'

'Certainly.' He was still light-headed. 'Of course, she's furious but . . .'

'She didn't explain where she learned to use sling-shot and fight like a gutter-rat, by any chance?'

The FitzGerald grunted. 'She killed one of my lads outright and bloody near crippled two more. She fought so the two people with her got away.'

'Ah well . . .'

'And she didn't happen to explain what she was doing with this in her saddle-bag, did she?'

FitzStephen held out 'this' on his open palm. It was a double-sided seal. John took it. The obverse portrayed a king enthroned with orb and sceptre. The reverse showed him mounted, his hand thrown back and clutching a sword. It was the seal of Henry II. Somebody had carved a pretty fair, but imperfect copy from a matrix. 'It's a forgery.'

'No doubt. But one like this was good enough to make Owain of Gwynedd rebel – and take all the mercenaries in north Wales with him. She's a spy.'

He kept turning it over and over, not seeing it. All these past months, years, he'd been trying to fit a figure and face to the personality of the somebody in Ireland who'd been causing problems for him and his king, the personality he'd come to think of as 'the green fleck'. They had eluded him, so that he'd been able to envisage only a black, person-shaped hole. Slowly, in his mind's eye, he slid a body he knew into the gap and saw it nestle home. It was her. Now it had struck him it was obvious; she was about the only person in Ireland with enough cosmo-politan knowledge – and the audacity – to do it. She'd used women, the hags probably. That's what had fooled him, he'd been thinking in the masculine when all along the feminine had kept cropping up. The O'Cornor wouldn't have had the brains. It was her. She might be working for the O'Conor, but it was her.

Because of her, the best king in the world had been troubled nearly to madness. Because of her, lesser men had risen against their ordained overlord. Because of her, some of his own best agents had disappeared. Rebellion, war, murder had taken place – because of her. Judas priest, because of her he had been within an inch of losing his position.

And the smell of her hair was still in his nostrils and his body was still warm from hers.

'I'll have her guts,' he said, quietly. 'Stay here.'

The door rocketed open as Finn was adjusting her respectability and veil. Her lover stood again in the doorway, not so beautiful.

'It was you,' he said. He had the Fitzempress seal in his hand.

She was shaken by the viciousness of him. 'I don't know what you mean.'

'Then allow me to tell you.' The compartment in his brain that he had kept secret from her in Lough Mask was in charge, making his voice steady, showing the calculation that reduced his emotion, his love, and now his dreadful rage to subsidiaries. It had made him Fitzempress' spymaster and it put her in mortal danger. She didn't know this man, except as a long-range enemy. She had made love to somebody else. This man she couldn't reach.

'It all fits. There've been Irishwomen in it all through. It was you and the hags. The letter in Scotland. The woman who gave Irish gold to Jehane in Brittany . . .'

'I don't know what you're talking about.'

'The mysterious woman who bribed the Exchequer clerk.' His rage burst through the control for a moment and he slammed his fist against the wall. 'I should have known.'

'I don't know what you're talking about.'

He paid no attention. He was a good, intuitive spymaster. He knew. She could protest until she was black in the face; he still knew.

'You've fooled me all along, you bitch. You got me to trust you. I trusted you in Ireland and you drugged me into Glendalough. Were you working for O'Conor then? Were you working for him at Lough Mask, you treacherous bitch?'

She didn't care then whether she gave herself away, or gave Ireland away; she'd give the whole world away to vent at long last the pain and resentment she'd carried since Lough Mask. 'Trust? And who are you to talk about trust, you bastard. I trusted you. I loved you. It wasn't until the end of Lough Mask that I found out you were Fitzempress' spy. You gave yourself away.'

'Keep your bloody voice down.' Without looking behind him, he slammed the door shut, nearly taking off the ear of the man who had crept up the stairs behind him and was listening from outside.

FitzStephen walked back down the stairs, rubbing the side of his head reflectively.

Behind him the two spymasters fought face to face the battle they had waged over the Irish Sea, both too furious and too hurt to notice that it had more to do with personal betrayal than the war of countries.

'That was why I drugged you into Glendalough. And you were lucky: I should have killed you. Treachery. How can it be treachery? You want to conquer Ireland, you and your filthy king. But it's mine, and I fought for it clean.'

'Why killed my agents, you murderous bitch?'

'Who tortured that little clerk, you stinking butcher?'

'So you admit it was you?'

'Yes. And I'd do it again.' She leaned her head back against the wall, voided of all emotion; the only beautiful thing she'd ever had was Lough Mask, and she'd lost it. Now she would probably lose her life as well. Let him hang her; she'd given him a run for his money. She'd go with the whole truth between them at least. She opened her eyes. 'And do you know the worst? I went on loving you. Right up to when I found out from the clerk that you were the one I'd been fighting all along. I didn't know until then that you were Duckweed.'

'Who?'

'Duckweed. It's what I called you.'

He blinked. 'Bit bloody undignified.'

God damn him, he'd always been able to make her laugh; even here, even now. 'Oh bugger you,' she said hopelessly.

For both of them the anger in the room had diffused into something she was too tired to analyse. Acceptance? But the echoes were still there and she heard the words: Love. Trust. Betrayal. Relationship words. Marriage words. They might be espoused to different sides, he had gone through a wedding ceremony with somebody else, but God, who always got the last laugh, had inextricably and eternally mated them to each other.

She knew he'd had the same revelation because he sneered at it: 'Our first quarrel.'

She could have wept for him, for both of them. 'I'm sorry.'

'So you bloody ought to be. Why couldn't you have been an ordinary woman?'

'You wouldn't have loved me.'

'No.'

He walked to the window. 'Well, this is a fine bloody mess.'

'What are you going to do?'

'I ought to hang you.' He saw her with a rope round her damned neck. Mentally he locked her up in prison with rats and, for a second, enjoyed the vision and then didn't. They'd question her. He remembered the men he'd had questioned and what they'd looked like when the inquisitors he'd employed had done with them. They hadn't intended the Exchequer clerk to die, but his heart had given out under the torture. She'd always had lovely skin, even the freckles.

Tonelessly he asked, 'If I got you away, would you promise not to work against Fitzempress again?' and heard her say, 'No' because she wouldn't lie to him any more.

'Sod you.'

Movement down in the bailey caught his eye. Men were unsaddling horses. FitzStephen and the FitzGerald were talking hard, glancing up at the window. They wouldn't wait much longer. In a minute they'd act, shut the gates, send guards up. They wouldn't have any mercy on her and he didn't blame them. But she wasn't their woman. She was his, God damn her to hell. He wished he wasn't going to do what he knew he was going to do. He wished he could reflect and put her in the balance against his country and everything that was really important. But he didn't have time.

'Come here.' He put his arm round her shoulders and pointed. 'See that horse there? Still saddled? We're going to walk down the stairs in a moment and across, as near as we can get to it. When I tell you, you bloody run. Get on it and go like hell. Can you still ride?'

'Pilgrim, they'll kill you.' Would she have let him go if the situation was reversed? Yes, she would. He was right, it was a bloody mess.

'No they won't. They think I'm on their side.'

'Aren't you?'

'Mind your own business, woman. Can you still ride?'

'I could still beat you.'

'I beat you. Can you make it?'

'If I get to the Severn. They're waiting for me there in a boat.'

'For Christ's sake, move.' As they went down the steps he said: 'One thing. Did we have a child?'

'What?'

'I used to wonder. I'm a very potent man. Did we have a child?'

Oh God, I love you, she thought, and that cosy wife of yours has given you sons, and I have a daughter whom I love and love is indivisible and I must give you something and we may both die in the next few minutes.

'A girl. I called her Slaney.'

'Bloody awful name. A daughter.'

'Yes.'

They were out in the air now, going down the outside steps to the bailey, and heads had turned to look at them. His hand was holding her arm as if he were a gaoler but they were moving diagonally, away from the men towards the still-unsaddled horse. 'Go.'

She broke away from him, and despite her skirts did a steed leap Art would have been proud of, and was galloping out of the gates and down the steep track to the Wye. Behind her the Lord of Llanthony turned to face FitzStephen. 'Damn the woman,' he said, 'she was too quick for me.'

'Shoot,' screamed FitzStephen to the guards on the gate. 'Shoot her.'

What saved her was that it was Strongbow's castle and FitzStephen only the temporary castellan. Strongbow's men were unused to taking orders from him, especially when they involved bringing down a nun. They havered until it was too late to hit anything. By the time they'd re-saddled the remaining horses, it was also too late to catch up with a woman who could ride like the bloody wind.

*　　*　　*

The Swan drew her in lovingly. The staff treated her as if they knew she'd left most of herself in Wales. But they couldn't protect her from the latest news. Eventually they took her up to the tower room to tell her.

'Dermot's back.'

'Mother of God.'

'He landed in August near Wexford,' said Bevo, 'He had a tiny force with him, some Welsh and Flemings. Our system worked well – we got a pigeon almost at once, and Art went to tell the O'Conor. He moved fairly quickly, for him, and marched with Tighernan O'Rourke against them and fought them at Cill Osnadh. Twenty-five of Dermot's force were killed and the rest sent back where they'd come from.'

Finn saw something in Bevo's face. 'And?'

'I don't know how to tell you this, Finn. Against O'Rourke's advice, our High King O'Conor refused to re-exile Dermot. Seemed to be sorry for him. He took two of Dermot's sons hostage and made him pay one hundred ounces of gold to O'Rourke for having abducted Dervorgilla all those years ago. But he allowed him to stay as lord of the Hy Kinsella as long as Dermot recognised him as High King and foreswore his claim on the rest of Leinster, which remains under Donough MacGiolla Phadraig.'

There was silence in the tower. Then Tailltin said, 'Why didn't Ruairi give him the High Kingship while he was about it?'

Finn thought, 'We're fighting for his life, and he's treating it like some gentleman's game.' The she thought of her daughter.

Censellach Mac Brain spoke from his corner: 'We can kill him now.'

'Where's Slaney?' asked Finn.

'Don't look like that. She's all right. Dermot left the girls with Fitz Harding in Bristol. They'll be safe with Fitz Harding.'

Finn began to shake. They gave her wine and comfort. MacGiolla Phadraig was Dermot's great enemy, they said; he'd never let him get the rest of Leinster. At least the O'Conor had done something. It would be all right. Finn fought for control and tried to believe them, but she couldn't stop shaking.

It was a winter of storms and high, treacherous seas which formed a wall between Ireland and the world. Finn spent it in love and terror. She sent extra pay to her agents in Wexford and Ferns to redouble their watching. She would have gone herself to see Dermot's every move, but, having nearly lost her in Wales, the Swan staff persuaded her it was too dangerous. Besides, Dermot was doing nothing.

She had changed. She was kinder to all of them, and especially Lief to whom, when he'd brought her, Pinginn and Tailltin back from

Wales, she had said, 'I'm sorry.' He shrugged: 'The best man won, he better be.'

'I don't know best any more. I'm just sorry.'

She began writing. At nights after the inn had gone to bed she sat in her top room with a candle near her board, first putting the shapes on a slate with chalk and then, when she'd got them right, scratching them onto Pinginn's vellum with the crow quill. 'Know all who live now and who will be,' she wrote, 'that I am Finola of the clan of Partraige, once Sister Boniface of Fontevrault, once Abbess of Kildare whom Dermot of Leinster had raped for the evil of his self-gain.' It was dreadfully difficult. She ran after words like a dog trying to enfold errant sheep. Brother Pinginn offered to do the writing for her, but she thanked him and refused. It would be a form of forgery. This was her resurrection from the oblivion of male history into which the chroniclers of the monasteries had consigned her. But it was to be more than that. This was to be the Word of Woman.

Once, when she heard whimpering from the room below, she got up and went down to stand beside Elfwida's bed, hesitating, then she knelt on the floor and took the girl's unconscious, twitching hand in her own and put it against her neck. 'Comfort my daughter wherever she is, dear God,' she prayed, 'Comfort this daughter and all daughters. Comfort the Pilgrim and all pilgrims.'

The daughters of Dermot Mac Murrough were polite to Bristol society all that winter, wearing the foreign clothes they had been given, eating sparingly of the massive meat dishes which the foreigners loved, and ravishing the too-few vegetables, worrying about their complexion in public and their father and the messages he sent them when they were alone. 'What does he mean by he's all right but we're to stay here?' said Aoife. 'If he's all right, then we can go back. We ought to be near him. We could stay in the Hy Kinsella mountains.'

'Och, Och, I can't stand this place much longer,' sobbed Dervorgilla, punching her pillow in place of the latest insulting, Norman lordling.

It was Slaney who said, 'How much money have we got?'

They watched the Bristol weather above the rooftops that enclosed them and, on the first clear, early spring day when the swans were flying they followed them, dodging their chaperone and making their way down to the harbour to look for a friendly, Irish boat, and took passage in it. As they passed Lundy Island where conscientious monks kept a beacon alight to warn shipping of its dangerous brown cliffs, the master of their ship pointed out the little sea-parrots which inhabited the ledges, but the girls' eyes were on the swans, going home.

*   *   *

291

In the bleak, beautiful, red-rocked harbour of Milford Haven three ships were at anchor, rocking chaotically as nervous horses were pulled and pushed aboard them. The cursing that laid their ears back were in strata of tones, screech of Welsh, full, rich Devonian, hoarse Flemish, thin Norman and, deep under, the grunts of the sons of Nesta. With horses and provisions, a longboat could take one hundred and twenty men. In fact, only about ninety men filed up each gangplank. They were under strength. FitzStephen's eyes flickered back and forth. 'How many do you reckon have come?' he asked his cousin, more for comfort than counsel because few of Nesta's sons could count. The FitzGerald took a stab at it: 'Three hundred,' and stumped off to kick his men into embarking faster.

'Innumerate bastard.' FitzStephen looked at the Lord of Llanthony, who had come to wave them goodbye. 'I'd prefer it if you came with us now.'

'I've got to gather my own men. I'll join you within the month.' He'd been in danger ever since he'd let Loon go; they hadn't liked it, but they hadn't been able to prove anything, except negligence. He'd put himself in even greater danger by trying to delay their departure; they were suspicious that he wasn't going with them. But he had to get word to Fitzempress that this unauthorised invasion was under way. He would join them later. 'Keep an eye on them,' Fitzempress had said. And, like the good spymaster he was, he would keep an eye on them. And while he was about it, he'd look for his woman.

Now that he'd admitted to himself that she was vital to him, he couldn't return to the distance he'd kept between them. He'd gone back to see his wife once since then, and had found her so tedious, poor thing, that he'd had to cut short his visit. The bloody Irishwoman was everywhere, in his bed, in his office, roaming his estates, confusing the job he had to do.

Up at the pier Giraldus Cambriensis was holding his arms out to the tiny fleet, howling prayers of victory and the prophecies of Merlin.

Beside him, he heard FitzStephen muttering, 'Can I rely on Merlin? Should I wait for Strongbow?' And he envied him for his ambition. There was a man who wasn't encumbered by a woman. Straight and simple, this man was out to get himself an empire. But he'd stop him. The only one who was going to include Ireland in his empire was Fitzempress. Loon or no Loon, Fitzempress should have Ireland if he wanted it, not this rabble. And if he did and when he did, well, then the Loon would have to stop fighting for it. She'd be beaten and they could be together.

Suddenly FitzStephen vomited into the sand. John could almost have pitied him. The risk he was taking was colossal. When the attack was over he crooked his helmet in his elbow and sank onto one knee.

'Dear God of hosts, Jesus and Mary the Virgin, St. David and St. Ann, take us into your hand this day and prosper this venture for the sake of your Holy Church – and me.' He got up. 'You'll join us?'

'I'll join you.'

FitzStephen raised his voice: 'Let's go.'

John watched the ships move easily down the haven and stood, even when they were out of his sight and encountering the currents of the sea which surge with energy between the islands of Skokholm and Skomer where they would bob like corks.

'Madmen,' he shouted after them, and then rode to tell Fitzempress that, whether he wished it or not, the invasion of Ireland had begun.

They were on horses larger than any ever seen in Ireland, the spring sun glinted on mail and pointed iron helmets with nasals which, to those who knew no armour, made them uniformly sinister. Back in Europe, where the pot helm, closer-linked mail and wider shields had come in, they would have seemed old-fashioned and rather comic. In Ireland, the shepherds who looked round at the sound of their hoof-beats saw a machine, a multi-headed juggernaut, and they fell on their faces in terror. They were so outside the experience of one old hermit whose beehive they passed, that when he looked straight at them his brain rejected them as impossible and he didn't see them at all.

Their own terror made them brutal; this island had floated in its uncharted sea on the edge of knowledge for aeons, misty with harp-music, sacred wells, strange saints and senseless language. The people were unrelated to them, another species. There was no Arthurian legend here like that which formed the basis of their knighthood, neither Joseph of Aramithea nor the disciples nor any saint they knew of had planted familiar, revered feet on these hills to make a path for a Christianity they recognised.

So, like dogs piddling scent to mark a territory for their own, they were impelled to superimpose their own reek on this alien place by sword and semen.

It was the spring equinox and the daughters of Dermot were back where they belonged. With other girls of the Hy Kinsella, they went to the lonely countryside of the southern Wicklow hills to express joy at their youth and homecoming, and to dance the Mayday in through a ritual which connected them to dancing ancestresses in a cowslip chain of vitality.

Sun welcomed them, Irish grass laved their bare feet as they circled in the ancient rhythm to the point where its mystery lifted them two inches in the air and they skimmed like the Children of Lîr at take-off – until Dervorgilla saw the mailed horsemen above them on the hill.

The horsemen saw a bunch of peasant girls playing silly buggers. Asking for it.

'Who were they?' whispered Dermot.

'Foreigners. I don't know.' Aoife's voice was toneless between puffed lips.

'They kept their hats on,' said Dervorgilla. The iron of the nasals had torn their faces as the penises had torn their vaginas. Her nose was broken and still bleeding and she rocked forward, giggling out of control. Slaney regarded the enraged, shouting Hy Kinsella men around her out of uninterested eyes. A flap along her cheekbones hung open.

Dermot wept. 'They're spoiled. My little flowers, all spoiled. They smell of men.'

Murchadh brought the two army doctors into the tent. 'Lucky that Morrow saw them. Their clothes were blowing around the hill; he thought they were sheep.' He watched the doctors begin work, then raised Dermot and took him outside. 'Will we go to Wexford and burn the foreigners alive, brother, and let the wind blow their filthy cinders back to Wales.' It wasn't a question.

Dermot wiped his eyes. 'No. We must feast our guests. What are you thinking of, Murchadh? Feast them. We'll give them the meat they tainted.' He smiled at his brother. 'They'll marry their own poison. Where is the woman that teaches other women to kill?'

It was only then that Murchadh saw how deeply the disease had eaten into his brother's brain. 'Will you destory everything, Mac Murrough?'

Dermot patted him, amazed he had to ask. 'Destruction's all there is.'

'I can't tell you how sorry I am, my lord,' said FitzStephen with complete honesty. 'My fault, really. We were short of supplies, you see, and I'd sent this lot out foraging. But they had strict instructions . . . I had no idea.'

'What did you do with them as a matter of interest?' asked Dermot. He was taking it very well.

'Hanged them,' said FitzStephen. 'Flogged them and strung 'em up immediately. They suffered before they died, I can tell you.' He'd certainly had them whipped *and* rubbed salt in the lashes to remind them to keep their hands to themselves, but hanging was out of the question: he was short of men as it was. He approached his next question with delicacy. 'The ladies concerned, were they, well, anything special?'

'Peasant women, just peasant women,' said Dermot. 'Mind you . . .'

'Oh, indeed,' said FitzStephen, 'One will be happy to pay their eric or whatever recompense you give over here. I mean, it's not pleasant whoever it is. But there you are, Flemings will be Flemings. Well, my lord, it is good of you to show such Christian forebearance. Not a good beginning, but we'll go on to a better. With your men and mine our army must be, oh, nine hundred strong. Shall we proceed to get Leinster back for you?'

'Yes,' said Dermot. 'And when we have, you shall marry my eldest daughter and be my beloved heir. All you brave, strong knights must marry my daughters. I want you to have your reward.'

If the Normans had been less greedy, or more imaginative, they would have been frightened to death of the odds against them. The High King whose country they had invaded could whistle up an army five times their strength by merely pursing his lips. Their enemy was on familiar ground which enabled it to disappear into the vast forests, cross the deadly bogs as if they were streets, blend into the camouflage of the mountains – and pop up again, refreshed, to attack from some completely different quarter.

To some extent the Normans were prepared for that; most of them had fought in Wales and had experience of ambush in difficult terrain. They had an advantage in being armoured. In a cavalry charge they could chop and axe their opponents from a greater height and, therefore, with greater force than a rider without stirrups. Their Welsh archers had a new and terrible weapon, the longbow, which released iron-tipped arrows at such speed that the sound of the air they displaced as they flew ripped the courage out of an opponent even before they stuck through him – and a longbow arrow could pierce a thick oak door.

But Ireland was the enticement to landless men that a bitch on heat is to roving dogs; they were out of control with the excitement of her, and what would have been a defeat had one Irish clan inflicted such damage on another, to the invaders was a temporary set-back in which to pant while they worked out some other form of assault.

When, outnumbered by three to one, they sieged Wexford, the defenders chucked bits of their city down on the Normans' heads. Robert de Barry, brother to Giraldus Cambriensis, was struck on his helmet by a great stone and fell down into the moat. But his companions dragged him out and he threw himself at the walls again with the rest of them. The Norse of Wexford were worn out by besiegers who were either bravely insane or insanely brave but either way couldn't be stopped. Their arms were tired with throwing things at them and, anyway, there was nothing left to throw. They sent their bishops out to sue for peace and submitted to Dermot Mac Murrough.

So Wexford fell. The annalist of Innisfallen, sitting in his monastery scriptorum, with the rest of Ireland as remote to him as if it were mythical Cathay, recorded, 'This year was a bad one for hazel-nuts.'

295

He dipped his quill into the inkwell and added, 'Also did Dermot Mac Murrough bring a fleet of foreigners to the shore of Erin.'

The High King, Ruairi O'Conor, had no time either to pay attention to what was happening in the south-east. He ignored the warnings that came from his watcher by the sea. He was having trouble subduing the clans of Thomond who were pursuing a vendetta against him.

Three weeks later Dermot and his army crossed the Blackstairs mountains and invade Ossory which was the kingdom of Donal MacGiolla Phadraig, who had been given Leinster when Dermot was exiled. MacGiolla Phadraig held Dermot's eldest son, Eanna, as hostage against just such an attack. Now he blinded him.

Ireland was lost during that long-running battle, though nobody realised it. MacGiolla Phadraig did all he could. He made the most of his thick forests, ambushed the invaders, skirmished, killed their stragglers, fell back into the bogs and emerged – to find Dermot and his Normans waiting for him. He was forced into a pitched battle which lasted for three days and he lost it. Outnumbered several times over, the Normans had encountered the best that an Irish force on its own territory could do, and the best had not proved good enough.

Two hundred Ossorian heads were cut off after the final battle. The Normans watched as Dermot roamed among them, talking to himself and turning them over one by one.

'What's he looking for?' asked Maurice de Prendergast to his friend, the Lord of Llanthony. He was a Flemish captain, and not usually a squeamish man.

'The face of the executioner who blinded his son.'

'I tell you, John, there are times I think even Ireland is no reward for being an ally to such a man. I don't trust him.' Straws in the wind, a glint in the Mac Murrough eye, made him suspect that Dermot did not intend to reward his allies once they'd won back his throne for him, but that he would turn and send them back where they came from – with or without their heads.

Beside him the Lord of Llanthony sucked in his breath: 'If I had my way, I'd kill him.' But Fitzempress had sent him on a watching brief. Keep Dermot safe, Fitzempress had said, we may need him. But when we've finished needing him . . . John dwelled on what he would then do to the King of Leinster.

They heard a squeal of delight. Dermot was holding one of the heads up by its ears like a two-handled chalice. Slowly he brought it down to his own face as if to drink from it, and tore off its lips with his teeth.

The loss of Maurice de Prendergast and the two hundred mercenaries who went with him back to Wales, consigning Ireland and its mad kings to the devil, was made up by the enlargement of Dermot's army as he overran more and more territory and forcibly enlisted the men of his old kingdom.

It was left to his brother to attend to the details, such as supplying the army, dispensing justice, raising taxes – and now making the arrangements for a group of girls who, in Murchadh's view, were more trouble than they were worth. Left to himself, Murchadh would have married them off quickly. The fact that they had been raped was not an obstacle – the Irish didn't set much store by female virginity, except nuns'. That foreigners had raped them, and thereby shamed the clan, was much more serious. It had to be kept secret or Dermot's honour would be in the sewer. Nobody, and especially the foreigners themselves, must ever know of it. Dermot's plan to have them turned into warrior-women and then married off to the foreigners' leaders to carry out his revenge on them was, to the unsubtle Murchadh, another example of his brother's over-deviousness. Nevertheless, Dermot had ordered it to be done and all his life Murchadh had done what Dermot wanted. Not for him the game of blinding and assassination which other clan chieftains played to ensure kingship for themselves. During Dermot's exile he had been given the kingship of the Hy Kinsella in the share-out of Leinster ordained by the O'Conor, and on Dermot's return he had handed it back as easily as if Dermot were reclaiming an old coat he'd left behind. As far as Murchadh was concerned, his brother was the true king and that was that.

The problem was that Dermot had not said exactly where, to whom and with what assurances for their security the girls were to be sent; once he'd given the order he had refused to see his daughters again; he had lost his enjoyment of them. Doggedly, Murchadh sent an ambassador to the only warrior-woman he knew of, the one in the Western Isles of Scotland, the ancient home of warrior-women where Cuchulainn had learned his legendary skills. On receiving assurance that she was apolitical and would return the girls, suitably militant, back to the Hy Kinsella in a year and a day, he sent off the girls themselves and went back to his other, overwhelming duties.

Murchadh was not to know that Scathagh would decide to, reconvene her Academy on its old site at Lough Mask in the territory of the greatest enemy of her candidates' father and king. Nor that she was short of instructresses for so many candidates and would, therefore, send to Dublin for help from some old pupils.

Patriotism, politics, spying went for nothing when Finn heard what had happened to Slaney and the others. She'd have sold Ireland, she'd have watched the Pilgrim die and most certainly she would have died herself, if she could have saved her child from this. As she rode to Lough Mask, her own rape dwindled into an incident. What the hell had she made the fuss about? The suffering was transmuted away from herself and became a vehicle to experience the suffering of someone-else. 'I'll do anything,' she promised the God who had whipped her back in her impotence to bleat with the rest of the flock, 'only let her be all right.' She was not capable of much coherent thought on that ride, but among the panic and grief grew a suspicion, later a conviction, that if God was capable of feeling the supreme suffering of his human beings, then he had not stayed in Heaven and watched while his Son was on the cross, neither was he on the cross himself, but he was where the greatest agony was, with Mary, screaming and scrabbling with her fingernails at the wood of the cross's foot. Mary was God.

Lough Mask was always silent in high summer, with the mother birds sheltering their broods in the reeds and grasses. Its water reflected an amethyst sunset and the tower of Inis Cailleach was casting a shadow blacker than the tower itself, whose stone was pink in the dying light. From Scathagh's gallery it was a shock to see so many girls trooping quietly in to the main beehive of the courtyard; at least three were dark.

'Which one is Slaney? I'm taking her home with me.'

'Why?'

'She's my daughter.'

'Still, why?'

Finn looked at the bulk beside her. 'I can't let her go through it. All the hardship, the wolf-hunt. . . . It's too dangerous.'

'You managed it.'

'Niav didn't.'

'My child.' Scathagh had not aged and her voice was still lovely. 'My child, you cannot deprive her of the chance to find what you found. Nor have I the right to let her throw it away. She took the Academy oath with the rest. If you love her, you will help her and not keep her crippled as she is.'

'Is she crippled?'

'She has an advantage you didn't have. She isn't pregnant, though two of the girls are. She was one of a group and they will help each other more than anything you can do. At the moment they are hungry and they will go on being hungry until they can forget their present misery and do something about it. You remember.'

She remembered. Dagda brought them up steaming bowls of stew, carefully wafting them past the doorway of the beehive which answered with the smell of plain fish. As they ate, Finn put her problem to Scathagh. 'So do I tell her I'm her mother?'

Scathagh munched greedily as she considered. 'You don't owe Dermot Mac Murrough any favours, that's for sure. On the other hand the child thinks he's wonderful – they all do. Whatever else he does, Dermot inspires love from his kin.'

'Not his wives.'

'Probably not. But the girl has lost so many illusions from the rape, that I think the loss of one more at this stage would be harmful. Leave it until she can cope with it.'

The next evening Scathagh, Dagda and Finn ate with the candidates in the beehive, helping themselves to their own rich dishes, apparently ignoring the fare apportioned to the girls, and with Finn trying not to watch every move her daughter made. The scar along the girl's cheekbone gave what had once had been a chubby, innocent face a piratical look which might be intriguing if ever humour came back to it and drove away the bewilderment of perpetually-relived horror. Nevertheless, Finn saw that Scathagh was right and that while mass rape brought its own particular abasement, its victims would be more quickly formed into a team than she and the hags had been. Already they had got to the sullen stage. Next evening one of the girls – actually, Aoife – said angrily, 'When are we going to be treated properly and have decent food?'

Finn leaned back in her chair and watched. Scathagh said, lifting a choice morsel to her mouth, 'You want some nice venison like mine?'

'Yes.'

'Then kill it.'

The different perspective as she helped to teach the girls how to handle a *curragh*, watched them fetch peat, then began the training sessions with sling and javelin on the far side of the lough, made Finn realise how unselfish Dagda had been in allowing the girls to ally themselves against her for their own good. It was a lonely business to be outside the team spirit as, very gradually, the girls became all-for-one and one-for-all hags who resented, and often said so, the women who drove them so hard. But Finn drove as hard as any.

'You devil,' Slaney screamed at her one day, bleeding from a cut knee after an unsuccessful steed leap, 'I can't do it. I'll never do it.'

'Then fail,' Finn said indifferently. She was beginning to know her daughter. Slaney mouthed some highly promising swear words and tried again. She had inherited no natural expertise with horses; Dervorgilla, Caitlin and several of the other girls mastered the jump before she did, but she had endurance and was beginning to get a sense of her own worth which Finn, at last, was prepared to make her suffer to achieve. She had missed out on the stage when she could have kissed a little girl's knee better; all she could opt for now was to make the little girl into a better woman.

What qualities Slaney had inherited from her she didn't know, but the girl was fearless, vain, and honest to the point of being able to laugh at herself. Finn became fond of all the girls, especially Aoife who was at once kind and deservedly their acknowledged leader, but Slaney she began to admire as well as love. Her daughter's humour reminded her time and again of the Pilgrim and increasingly she became his child as well as her own. That personality couldn't have been formed in the terror of Kildare, it belonged to Swan Island.

It occurred to her that none of the young hags had the resources which, as Connaughtwomen, her class year had known among the Partraige. The Partraige life went on around the shore just the same as it always had, more or less ignoring the activities on Inis Cailleach.

So when the girls had stopped resenting their training and were beginning to see the point of it, Finn chose one night to say to Slaney: 'If ever you want some privacy, you're welcome to use my island. It's the one over there. I stay there sometimes.'

'I've watched you sail over to it. Are you really a Partraige woman?'

'Yes. Why?'

'I don't know. Scathagh has the eternal wisdoms, if you know what I mean, but you've got all the other sort. What did you do with your life after you were qualified?' The girls used 'qualification' as an ironic euphemism for rape. Finn had obeyed the Academy rule and given them a censored account of how she had become a previous candidate.

'I opened an inn in Dublin with some other hags.'

'Didn't you want to marry?'

'Do you?'

'I did. I was going to marry Censellach Mac Brain – he was a hostage at our court for years, but Father regarded him more as a foster-son. He's gone back to his clan now and, I don't know, do you think he'll still want me? Since my qualification, I mean?'

Tell her, Finn commanded herself. Tell her what Dermot did to the boy. Wean her away from the bastard she thinks is her father. She longed to let the girl know she was her mother. But it was too soon; the child still had periods of depression and Finn wasn't going to make them worse. She said merely, 'It's best not to set your hopes too high.' She watched her daughter's eyes go dull.

Sometimes it was the three daughters of Dermot who came and joined her on Swan Island in the evenings, but more often it was Slaney on her own. It was a shock to find that the girl admired her as sophisticated and mysterious and wanted to talk. She, who had never been chatty, found herself engaged in woman-to-woman conversations which were at once delightful and exhausting. 'Talk more,' Slaney would say, 'You don't tell me things.'

'What do you want me to tell you?'

300

'You know, things. Have you ever been in love? Did any man love you after your qualification? Like that.'

'You're man mad. Well . . .' Because it was so pleasant to do, she told Slaney about the Pilgrim, and deluded herself that secretly it was a 'how-your-father-and-I-met' story that an ordinary mother might tell. Slaney loved it. 'Why didn't you go back to England with him?'

'Reasons. I didn't want to leave Ireland.'

'Tell me how you ployed him again.'

'I won't. It's your turn to provide the entertainment, then it's time you were going back.'

Always before she sent her home, she got Slaney to sing. The girl's voice was extraordinary, mature, strong, yet catching a remembrance of being very young. Hearing it echo across the water was heart-rending – and it wasn't only Finn's heart it rended.

Watching the girl as she sang outlined against the late sun, Finn saw her conjure a memory into form; a horse with a man bending low against its neck swimming across the lake towards her island out of the past. Time circled and then jinked; this one came out of the present. The horse was smaller, a pony, and the man was taller, younger and darker. His eyes were on Slaney, not her. A birthmark covered his left hand. The pony scrabbled up onto the tiny beach and its rider dismounted and led it up to the fire they had lit on this warm night to provide light and keep the mosquitos away. 'There should be a law against a song that drags men across lakes,' he said. 'I think I'll make one.'

Slaney looked back at Finn, glowing and amused. 'Shall I give him Scathagh's Number One?'

'It's not obligatory. Try "Hello". I'll go and get him a drink.'

She stayed in her hut a long while, giving them time to talk and herself some room for recovery. For one moment she'd thought God had suspended the laws and given her back an option on happiness. This time she wouldn't have turned it down. But it wasn't a God for second chances. She was being greatly obliged in seeing it perhaps offered to her daughter. Well, well. He'd be about Slaney's age. What had she done with the years? The last time she'd seen that birthmark it had been on a baby's fist. She'd heard he'd been officially acknowledged as a prince of Connaught by the O'Conor, now that the jealous queen was dead. He'd be home on a visit to his mother, Cuimne.

There were raised voices outside. Slaney stamped into the hut, grabbed the beaker of mead from Finn's hand and stamped out. Finn went out just in time to see her throw it after the retreating Cathal. Together they watched him and the horse swim back into the dusk. 'And don't come back,' shouted Slaney.

'What happened?'

'He's a stinking Connaughter. He asked where I came from. When I said I was a Leinsterwoman he said he was sorry for me. Me. Because an evil man was my king. Stinking Connaughter.'

Finn grabbed her daughter by her shoulders and shook her. 'Don't you dare, don't you dare. You're breaking Ireland into pieces between you.' She took a deep breath and dropped her arms. The girl's fury directed on her; she had, after all, been brought up a princess of Leinster – then it changed.

'And I thought it was just a cup,' she said.

What a nice child you are, thought Finn. More adult than I'll ever be, and the Pilgrim's your true father, whoever sired you.

'What do you mean, breaking Ireland?'

They sat down. 'There isn't any time left for clan war. The world's moved on. If we don't start thinking of ourselves as Irish, rather than Connaught or Leinster or Breffni or whatever, we'll soon be something else entirely, or not anything. England has its eye on us. I know, I've been watching it watching us. Dermot Mac Murrough has brought the Normans in and unless we combine against them they'll never go away.'

Slaney said loftily, 'Father is only regaining what is his by right.'

'Just think about it. What they did to you and the others, they'll do to Ireland. I'm sorry. I'm so sorry.'

The girl's scarred face had gone into a spasm of pain. Finn put her arm around Slaney's shoulders and rubbed her cheek against her hair. 'I know. But we survive.'

They sat together for a long time. Eventually Finn said, 'If they'd just stop. All of them. Even Ireland and England aren't important. Men and women together, equal and loving, that's all that matters.'

In the winter, just as the new hags were beginning to investigate wolf traps, Art arrived. He looked older than ever and the journey had taken so much out of him that Finn put him to bed in her hut. She'd been doing it up so that it would be habitable all the year round. 'Is everything all right?'

He nodded, gasping.

'You silly old fool,' she said, 'why didn't they send somebody else? Who's looking after the pigeons?'

'Thanks I get,' wheezed Art. 'See you're all right. Away long time. That Belaset harpy. In Dublin. Wants . . . see you.'

'She can wait.' Whatever was happening it wasn't more important than Slaney going out to get her wolf. Even now she wasn't sure she could let the girl do it alone. She hadn't been alone when she'd got hers.

She sat by Art's bed all night, giving him sips of balm and honey to ease his cough, wrapping hot bricks in sheep's wool to keed his feet warm. When she helped him out of bed to use the pot, he wanted her out of the room. 'Oh, for God's sake, don't be so bloody prim.' But he began to cry, so she went. At a point before dawn he broke into a sweat and then slept. She knelt and thanked God for the life of her oldest friend, settled herself back in the chair, covered herself in furs, and slept well.

'Art,' she said, when he was better. 'I'm worried about the horse-breeding situation here. Iogenàn's letting the strain go. I want you to stay here for a bit and see to it. And keep an eye on Slaney – you know why, but don't tell her.'

Art cast a ghastly eye on her. 'Are you trying to keep me safe, woman?'

'And Blat will come back to keep house for you.'

'You're trying to keep her safe. You know something. I don't trust the look of you.'

She shrugged. She didn't voice it because she didn't dare admit to herself, that Ireland was seeing the beginning of its end. 'Whatever happens I'm going to need a secure base here. Nobody's going to be safe, but they'll be a long time getting as far as this. I might need to come back in a hurry.'

'Shan't.'

She took his hand. 'You looked after me. Look after my daughter.'

She'd defeated him. 'Bloody women,' he said.

On the night of the wolf hunt, it was bitterly cold, but clear and dry. Somewhere up in the Partraige mountains a grand-daughter of Blat's bitch was tied up in a hut, full of night-time promise. From Inis Cailleach a *curragh* set for the western shore and landed fur-wrapped figures who fanned out into different directions. Agonising, Finn was on the point of following Slaney when she spotted another, smaller *curragh* making for the same shore. The hands that rowed it had been left ungloved in his haste, but one of them was dark.

'Ah well,' she said, and consigned her daughter to the care of Cathal of the Wine Red Hand. He seemed a nice boy.

The next day, while a load of girls with wolf-tails pinned to their hair roistered in the tower of Inis Cailleach, Finn left Lough Mask for the last time.

The madder Dermot Mac Murrough became, the more beautifully he played his game. Like a chess master he moved each piece, bishop, castle, knight, queen and pawn with remorseless clarity of purpose, knowing he would win. And he did. The flaw in his strategy was that in his madness he had played the wrong opponent.

John of Llanthony sent a message to his king by one of the agents

303

he'd brought with him. 'My lord, every week more men come to join FitzStephen, and yet Dermot of Leinster still believes they are playing his game and that when he has won it he can return them whence they came, but he cannot.'

It was still the middle of the game, when he'd overrun most of Leinster, that Ruairi O'Conor decided Dermot had gone far enough and again brought the army of Ireland to meet the swelling mixture of a force that was Dermot's. There was no question of a pitched battle; the O'Conor's men outnumbered Dermot's and FitzStephen's rag-bag to an extent that merely by advancing – longbows, armour, stirrups notwithstanding – they could have crushed it to death. Smiling to himself, Dermot made a tactical retreat to the fastness of Mount Leinster and produced his bishop. Actually, it was an archbishop, Laurence O'Toole, that good, sainted, peace-loving, silly man.

'Let us avoid blood, O'Conor, in the name of Christ,' pleaded Laurence O'Toole to the High King. 'Mac Murrough has won no more than was his orginally. Forgive his sins, recognise him as King of Leinster and he will abide by all your terms.'

'He must acknowledge me as High King of Ireland,' said the O'Conor of Connaught.

O'Toole rode up to the barricades of Mount Leinster. 'Will you acknowledge the O'Conor as High King of Ireland if he lets you keep Leinster?'

'I will and gladly,' shouted Dermot.

'He swears he will,' reported back O'Toole.

'Will he send away all the foreigners he has brought into Ireland?'

Back trooped the archbishop to Mount Leinster. 'Will you send back all Galls from the land of the Gael?'

'I will and gladly.'

'Then come down to make oath on your assurances, and give the kiss of peace to your rightful overlord.'

Dermot went down. He swore on bibles and the bones of saints that he would not look beyond Leinster ever again, that he acknowledged the O'Conor as High King, and that he would send all the foreigners he had invited into the country back to where they had come from. Then he went back to Ferns and ordered his scribe to write a letter to Strongbow urging him to hurry up and come, so that between them they could win Ireland for themselves.

Down in Wexford FitzStephen, far from going home, cut down an entire area of woodland and built a strong tower on the very vantage point of Ferrycarrig from which the nobles of Ireland had watched Dermot go into exile four years before. It was the first Norman castle in Ireland.

* * *

304

In Dublin Asgall confessed his uneasiness to the landlady of the Swan. Did these proceedings mean that the High King had abandoned Dublin, the city which had supported him? And even if he hadn't, would he protect it if Dermot moved against it? He certainly hadn't protected anywhere else in Leinster – Dermot was building a small pyramid out of the eyes and testicles of the men who had deserted him four years previously.

'I don't know,' Finn told him, miserably, 'I don't know the O'Conor any more. He won't listen to me. All we can do is take precautions.'

Acting on that advice, Asgall made sure that the walls of Dublin were fortified as never before and contingents of archers practised at the Hogges Green butts.

The Lady Belaset hurried to the Swan Inn as soon as she heard of Finn's return home. 'You take my advice, you'll pack your traps and all these funny people of yours and come to Bristol,' she said, 'I'm getting mine out. I don't like the breeze that's blowing.'

'Vives is going?' Finn felt a pang of loss; the Jew had seemed a rock. Although she had paid off her mortgage years ago, they kept up their weekly meetings. He had given her a vat of kosher wine so that he could drink with her.

'Vives, Rabbi, the whole ball of wax,' said Belaset, and Finn saw that under the belligerent make-up, the Jewess's face was shrivelled with concern. 'Not for always maybe, but definitely for now. You know why?' Finn shook her head. 'Because it's got big and getting bigger. Raymond le Gros and another army of half-breeds has landed to join his uncle FitzStephen down in Wexford. And Strongbow's finally made up that mind of his and he'll be coming over with two thousand men any day.'

'Two thousand? Are you sure?' Her spies had given her no such information.

'Who'd you think lent him the money?'

'Bela!' She couldn't believe it; the Jews, especially this raddled old woman, had seemed her allies.

'Sure, Bela, Bela. Finn, you listen. If it hadn't been me gave him the money he'd have gone to some other Jews, the damned Ashkenazim maybe, and why should they have all the profit? Besides, this way I keep tabs on what's happening so I can I tell you. And I'm telling you get out. Sure as God made little apples, them Normans is going to take Ireland over. One time I thought that High King Ruairi of yours would stop 'em, but if he ain't stopped 'em so far he never will. They're going to rape and pillage this little country, and then they're going to ask God to forgive 'em for it. And you know that Normans do to get God's approval?'

Finn shook her head. She couldn't bring herself to speak to the woman.

'They build churches and they kill Jews. So I'm taking mine out. And they ain't going to like you much neither.'

'They haven't won yet,' said Finn, coldly.

'They're going to.'

They parted without warmth, something for which Finn was sorry when she had time to reflect. Like all Jews, Belaset was a permanent exile; she did not truly belong even to the part of Spain where she had been born, so why should she feel any patriotism for Ireland? Besides, she had done what she could in warning Finn of Strongbow's invasion.

Almost hopelessly, Finn sent on the news to the O'Conor; but the panic she had seen in Belaset's eyes infected her. If he hadn't stopped Dermot's and the Norman's advance yet, would he ever?

She began to make arrangements to get her staff to safety before the worst came to the worst, and, because she was in a panic, she did it badly.

'I've decided that the time's come to start thinking about a strategic withdrawal,' she announced at the next staff conference, 'Perhaps we'll open a new Swan Inn over in Connaught somewhere. On the coast, near a pilgrim route. Dublin will be the next place the Normans and Dermot make for, and Dermot's not going to treat it kindly for having fought against him. So I'm going to divide up the profits so far between us all. Tailltin, Bevo, Blat, Lief and Brother Pinginn can go ahead and make their base at Lough Mask for the time being. Aragon goes on her next trading trip soon and when she comes back she can make harbour in Galway.'

She looked at them sharply. Everybody was staring into space. 'Well?'

'And what are you going to be doing all this time?' asked Tailltin.

'I shall run the inn with Perse and the Elf and the servants until I hear from Muirna.' They hadn't heard from Muirna for some weeks and were worried about her. 'Then I'll come and join you.' She didn't add that she was also waiting for news of the Pilgrim; she had the feeling that he was in Ireland or in trouble, or both. She'd tried contacting her agents down in the south-east, but they had disappeared; dead, perhaps.

'Well, Lief and I aren't going without you, are we Lief?' said Pinginn, waggling his shoulders.

'No.'

Eventually she had to tackle them individually. 'I beg you,' she said to Tailltin, 'I must have somebody I can trust keeping an eye on Slaney,' and because her anxiety was touching, Talltin agreed to go 'for the time being'.

306

Blat also agreed when Finn begged her to go and look after Art. 'To be honest with you, Finn,' she said, 'I've been dying to set me eyes on Connaught before I die. Not that I wouldn't stay if I was of use, but I'm getting old so I'll go and keep house for that ugly little man of yours, though how the Swan'll get on without me marrow pudding is more than I can answer for.'

Bevo's big-boned face went puce as she refused to join the exodus to Lough Mask. 'Actually, Finn, I'm getting married.'

It was so unexpected that Finn's astonishment was almost insulting until she recovered herself. Why shouldn't the hags find love? 'I'm happy for you,' she said, 'who's the lucky man?'

Bevo blushed some more. 'Ragnar.'

'Ragnar?' On the few occasions that Finn had seen him since her return from Connaught, the jarl had been better behaved than formerly, but he was so fixed in Finn's mind as a drunken nuisance that she couldn't have been more surprised if Bevo had said she were marrying Dermot.

'He's calmed down a lot lately,' said Bevo fondly, 'and, well, with me chucking him out so many times it's formed a bond between us. My share of the profit will be my dower. I won't be his first wife, of course, but he's fond of me and he's got a nice little property up Swords way.'

'I wish he'd got a nice little property out of Ireland altogether,' said Finn.

'Is it going to be as bad as all that?'

'Yes.' Finn kissed her friend. 'I'm so pleased. Be happy. Have lots of babies.'

It was a fruitless business trying to persuade Brother Pinginn and Lief to leave her, but she did get Lief to agree to accompany Tailltin to Lough Mask and bring back an assurance that all was well there. Besides, the country was dangerous to travel through with more and more Norman bands roving deeper and deeper into it.

The only people for whom Finn had not thought to make arrangements were Perse and Elfwida because she honestly did not know what arrangement they wanted. As it turned out, Perse had made her own.

'I'm getting married and all,' she said.

Finn was beyond surprise by now. Obviously a lot had been going on while she'd been away. 'Who to?'

'Miller Molling.' Perse smirked while everybody congratulated her; from her point of view it was a marvellous match. But Finn reckoned that the miller, who was a widower, wasn't doing too badly either; Perse was one of the world's workers and Molling was getting a first-class cook, laundress, seamstress, and general dogsbody as well as a bed-fellow considerably younger than himself. When he came over a couple of days later and asked Finn formally for Perse's hand she ensured that some of Perse's share of the profits were safeguarded for Perse's own use, and not his.

'And what about me?' shouted Elfwida jealously, as the plans for Perse's wedding went ahead. 'What are you going to do with me?'

'What do you want me to do?' asked Finn, 'you've got money of your own now. You can go to Lough Mask with the others, if you like, or you can go back to England.'

'I want you to care what happens to me,' screamed Elfwida, and Finn shouted back, 'I do care. I just don't know what you want.'

It was true that she did care about the girl, but never so much as when the Elf was out of her sight or asleep. In the girl's presence, she always felt that more was being asked of her than she could give.

'I'll stay here then,' grumbled Elfwida, and Finn took the easy way out by agreeing, telling herself that she was bound to get warning of the Norman approach when it came, and that they could both escape then in plenty of time.

Molling's and Perse's wedding was celebrated sedately at the Swan. Perse took her pitifully few belongings over to the mill, and as a quid pro quo, Gorm brought his pitifully few belongings over to the inn to take Art's place in the pigeon loft.

Two days later, and much less sedately, Ragnar's and Bevo's wedding wrecked two shutters, four settles, most of the crockery and a frying pan in a party that ended with Ragnar and Bevo together throwing most of Dublin's nobility into the Stein. In a dawn made hazy by hangover, the Swan staff cheered and threw wheat as Bevo, clinging onto Ragnar's ample waist, rode off on Finn's wedding present to them, a descendant of Fitzempress' mare and the only horse for miles around strong enough to bear the weight of them both.

There was no hangover to mist the distress the next day when Blat, Tailltin and Lief rode off to Lough Mask.

Finn and Brother Pinginn stood on the tower roof for a long time after they had disappeared into the trees of the north bank. 'I can't bear it we're not a company any more and I'll miss them so much and I hate it when you cry,' sobbed Pinginn. Finn snivelled as she shook him. 'Stop being silly.' She tore her eyes away and looked around at the orchard, speckled with the geese that had been Blat's genius suggestion, but now was so lonely. She spotted a figure up on Lazy Hill talking, as usual, with the lepers. 'What are we going to do about Censellach?' She had suggested to the boy that he go to Lough Mask and told him all about the Academy. She didn't see why Scathagh shouldn't take him in and train him; God knew he was damaged enough. She described it, told him where it was, and then made the mistake of telling him that Slaney was already there.

He screamed. 'I won't have her see me!' So that idea had been abandoned.

Pinginn cheered up at the thought of responsibility. 'I'll look after him, the poor dear,' he said, 'and he's getting ever so sweet. You know that lovely arm bracelet of his? Well he gave it to the worst of the lepers – you know, the suppurating one. Wasn't that a lovely Christian thing to do?'

But, as it turned out, Cennsellach was another one who made his own arrangements. That night a party of pilgrims on their way to Lough Derg and Croagh Patrick stopped for a drink at the inn, and the next morning Finn discovered that Censellach had gone with them, without saying goodbye.

Miller Molling agreed to allow Perse to become temporary cook-in-charge at the Swan on the understanding that he ate two free meals a day at the Swan and had his washing done by the inn's skivvies. Finn accepted gratefully, partly because Perse was a good cook and partly because she had hardly any money left to hire extra staff with. Besides, the custom at the Swan had diminished to the point where her staff, small as it now was, could cope sufficiently.

News that Strongbow was about to invade with a strong force had gone round like wildfire, and rumour had it that he would land at Dublin. Besides, the advance of Dermot and his Normans and the weakness of the High King in not stopping it had persuaded many Dublin citizens who had homes elsewhere that elsewhere was a good place to be just now. The thought of what Dermot might do to a city that had allied itself with his enemy caused a steady daily exodus of carts from Dublin's gates, while fewer and fewer entered them. Trading ships still came up the Liffey but these were mostly from the furthest foreign parts which had not yet been apprised of Ireland's invasion by the Normans; Welsh, Bristolian, Scottish and Manx merchants were more careful and decided not to risk valuable cargoes being seized as booty. They began sending their ships round to Galway instead, on the premise that hazard of the seas were still safer than a possible surprise attack by mercenaries who, as everyone knew, werre little better than pirates.

One of the few from Bristol that ventured up to Dublin brought a message from Muirna. Most of it was an account of the latest atrocity in the war of denunciation between Henry II and his Archbishop of Canterbury. Finn was glad to see that England and the Continent were still in turmoil over the Becket business – it would keep Fitzempress busy. He was still the greatest threat to her country; given time Ireland might absorb the freebooting invaders, however much it suffered in the process, as it had absorbed the Vikings, after all. But Fitzempress with his codes and constitution and common law could, and would, alter it forever.

'. . . this threat to our Mother Church. Moreover, my lady and yours wishes me to inform you that she is well and happy and has come under the kind patronage of the Bishop of Salisbury in whose palaces she now makes her home when she is not in attendance on the queen. She further wishes me to write that the aforementioned queen has had the scales ripped from her eyes with regard to the king's liaison with the adulteress, Rosamund Clifford, and is likely to vent her fury on the aforementioned king should he return to England, as is the nature of a woman scorned . . .' (Jesus, Fitzempress *would* be busy.) '. . . She has news of the pilgrim of whom you enquired and sends word that he is in Erin and that he may be in jeopardy with these adventurers to the end of the world, since it is common talk among us here that he is a king's man and that his interest is with the king and not the aforesaid adventurers for which shame should attend him since it will not profit any man that he should throw in his lot with the Devil . . .' The letter went back to villifying England's king and ended on the same note.

Her sleeve was tugged by the sailor who'd brought the letter. 'The lady said I'd get a free meal and a bed.'

'So you shall. Did she look well? Did she say anything else?'

The sailor pulled his earring as an aid to memory. 'Something about Wales. She said the news from Wales, that's it, the news from Wales was Waterford. Make any sense to you?'

'I'm afraid it does.' She was ashamed of her relief that it was to be Waterford and not Dublin which was to receive Strongbow's onslaught. She'd send word to the High King to warn him to get his army into position . . . why the hell did she still put faith in the O'Conor doing anything to protect his High Kingdom? Because he was all there was.

So Muirna had become the mistress of a bishop? Well, if it suited her . . . He'd better be kind to her. Suddenly she was enraged at the hyprocisy of a Church that condemned the Irish for immorality in allowing their churchmen to marry when practically every high prelate in Europe was known to have a beautiful 'housekeeper' keeping his bed warm.

Underneath everything was a nagging anxiety for the Pilgrim. She must warn him. But where was he? Her spywork system was breaking down as travel became increasingly difficult and more and more of her agents in areas which had fallen under Norman control were, ominously, no longer reporting. Supposing that by warning the Irish side of Strongbow's impending invasion she was putting the Pilgrim in danger? On the other hand he was in danger already. And so was

Ireland. She glared at the sailor: 'Have you ever thought how lucky you were not to be born a woman?'

'No,' he said, 'What about that meal?'

As if it could not digest so many, the sea spewed a thousand moving iron fragments onto the beach of Dun Domhnaill. They formed themselves into patterns which flowed towards Waterford, four miles away, like massed black insets all crawling in the same direction. At their head was that most dangerous of all creatures, a man who is determined not to show weakness. Strongbow was going to live up to the name won by his father. He would be forceful, terrifying, he would make an example of the first to oppose him so that nobody would oppose him again.

Waterford's leader, the lord Sitric, had news of the Norman's coming. What had happened to his fellow Norsemen at Wexford, where they had given in to Dermot and FitzStephen, and been dispossessed for their trouble, had reawakened the old Viking spirit in him and his people. They resolved to fight. As the Normans breached their city wall and poured through the gap, that's what they did.

As was usual in such cases the churchmen intervened and asked for a truce. When Strongbow refused to accede to one, they were at a loss and so was Waterford. This wasn't what the Irish were used to; one clan always stopped short of annihilating another when it asked for terms. It was at once the strength of their civilisation and its weakness in that it preserved the clans to fight another day. But that day total warfare came to Ireland. Sitric was beheaded in his own hall. Waterford, its men and many of its women and children died to provide a lesson to the rest of Ireland.

With the smoke of his example still staining the sky behind him, Strongbow marched away – heading for Dublin.

Chapter Thirteen

Slaney missed the woman Finn; their brief relationship had seemed significant in a way she had been unable to define. In the woman's absence she visited Swan Island frequently and pestered the funny old man Art with questions he rarely answered. They got on, despite his insistence on playing gooseberry when Cathal happened by, as if he were some hideous, self-appointed, chaperoning guardian angel. On this evening he'd nodded off to sleep as he frequently did, and she was still sitting on the island's beach, watching the sun down, when a voice called her name.

'Yes?' She was unnerved; the boat was between her and the sunset and the two figures in it were mere two-dimensional shapes against the strong light.

'Slaney.'

'Yes?' She stood up. She couldn't see which of the shapes was calling her, but she knew the voice. 'Is it you, Censellach?' The girl had loved him; the woman she now was wished him well.

'Your father wants you, Slaney. He's asking where his daughters have gone.'

'Is he all right?'

'He needs you.'

'Are you all right? Why don't you come here? What's happened to you?'

Lough Mask was always eerie but she had never known it threaten her as it did this evening with its water like oiled silk and the voice echoing over it, the same but different. Unless it was her that was different.

'Slaney,' called the voice again, 'Give your father a present I have for him. Will you do that for me, for the old days?'

The boat came nearer but she still couldn't see him properly; although he looked in her direction she had the feeling he wasn't seeing her either. Closer, his voice whispered across the reeds. 'It's my present to him, Slaney, gold, the finest. Give it to him as if it came from you. Let him wear it and be admired and then, one day, I'll tell him it was my gift. It will help him look more kindly on me.'

So complicated, so un-Censellach-like. 'Why don't you give it yourself? Censellach, come and talk to me.'

'Let him think it's your gift. Please, Slaney. For the old days.'

She would do anything to compensate him for not loving him any more. 'All right.'

The man at the boat's oars stood up and threw a heavily-wrapped parcel across the reed bed.

'And Slaney. Don't touch it. Give it to him in its wrapping. There's a *geasa* on it that no woman must hold it.'

'Censellach, this is so silly.'

'Swear.'

'I swear. Don't go. Where are you going?'

Her eyes watered so that the figures in the boat had rays about them. It had begun to drift away from her. She had a precise vision of him as he had once been; he was hunting, yelling with joy at the speed of his horse, ahead of everybody else and everything beautiful waiting to happen to him. Conviction came over her; Censellach was dead. His shape and voice had been impelled from the underworld to obey some frantic wish of his soul which she, too, must obey.

A skein of geese passed overhead crying like musical squeaking doors. Art was still asleep. Sobbing, Slaney picked up the parcel and put it in her *curragh*. She must go back to the hags and tell her sisters that a ghost, which could not lie, said their father needed them. They had to go back.

When the party from Dublin, which had been badly delayed on the road, arrived at Lough Mask it was to find that the daughters of Dermot had said their goodbyes and gone without anybody being able to stop them.

Although they each carried a dagger and sword beneath their cloaks, the girls were cautious on their journey home; they would never be incautious again. They rode from convent to convent, getting an escort from each one to take them on to the next.

As they rode through Leinster the landscape reflected back their own loss of innocence; whole woodlands through which they had once hunted and knew like the back of their hand had disappeared, taking with them light and shadow and in their place were naked acres of stumps. The trees had gone for assault machines, scaling ladders, battering rams and other requisites of war, or they had been transformed into scaffolding and cranes on which men worked around the untidy, skeletal props of other trees, incorporating them into the erections which would be castles dominating a ruined countryside. Time and again the girls had to make wide diversions to avoid them, warned by the chop of axe into wood, a sound more common than birdsong.

It was as if a giant breed of termites had been introduced into the country and was gnawing Ireland into the shape of its own environment.

'But why doesn't Father stop them,' Dervorgilla kept saying, 'why doesn't he stop them? He must stop them.'

It still didn't occur to her that he couldn't, but Slaney heard Finn's voice in her head. 'They won't go away again.'

At Ferns there was the same febrile activity. The castle Dermot had burned down to stop anyone else having it, was being rebuilt bigger and more Norman. There were only men about and these were too busy to give the girls much greeting. So was their father. 'Good, you're back,' he said, 'Did you learn to kill?' In a way it was a relief; they had been afraid of what he would say if he discovered they'd been sojourning all this time in Connaught, but it was odd that he kept his eyes away from them.

He didn't look the same at all; his arms were bare like a young warrior, though the exposed upper flesh on them was old and sagging. He wore the crown of Leinster and was decorated with torques and bracelets and brooches as if he were grabbing at the authority given by royal jewellery. On the wall behind him a suit of mail was on a hanger topped by a helmet like those worn by the rapists. Eyeless, it stared in their direction.

'What's happening, Father?'

'We're off to Dublin. Strongbow's coming.'

'Do you need him now? You've got Leinster back.'

'Leinster. I'll have more than Leinster.' He calmed down and became dismissive. 'I'm not discussing it with you. Get ready to ride.'

Except for the time in Aquitaine when they had been looking for Fitzempress, he had always been solicitous for them; now he didn't enquire whether they were tired or not. The love for the person he had once been turned to pity for this abstracted, pathetic old man and Slaney knelt before him. 'Accept this, Father, before we go.'

She held out the mysterious parcel, waiting to give some explanation, but Dermot took it impatiently, tore it open and just slid the beautiful snake bracelet it contained up his arm to join the horde of gold already on it. He frowned. 'It scratches. Go and get ready.'

They were heavily guarded by Hy Kinsella on the journey to keep them safe from the Norman troops who marched with them, though there was a moment when Slaney felt oppressed even by these men she'd known since childhood. She felt Aoife looking at her and saw the same panic in her sister. 'You don't think . . .?' 'He wouldn't.' They smiled reassurance at each other.

'Anyway,' said Slaney, 'We're not the women he sent away; we're hags.'

315

But only three hags. And there wasn't another woman in the column, unless you counted the camp-followers who dragged along in the rear. Aoife kept coughing, as she always did when she was nervous. 'Any trouble and I'll give them Scathagh's Number Three,' she said.

When Dermot's army joined Strongbow's and turned towards Dublin, it took with it Dermot's daughters and one prisoner who, although he was a Norman, was kept in chains.

The chances that the Normans could conquer all Ireland and set up their own kingdom over it were becoming better and better, though none of them mentioned it to Dermot. But as their expectations rose, so did their fear that Fitzempress would come over and stop them before they were ready. 'And that, my dear old soul,' explained FitzStephen as his men bound the arms of the Lord of Llanthony behind his back, 'is why we can't allow you to send him any messages.'

'What the hell do you mean? I'm not Fitzempress' man. We quarrelled.'

FitzStephen smiled at the struggling figure. 'Oh, yes you are, oh no you didn't. You're his spy and always have been. A little bird told me . . . well, she told you actually, but I was listening behind the door. That was before you let her go.'

'Fuck you.'

'Naughty,' said FitzStephen and put a gag in the spymaster's mouth. 'I'm going to hand you over to Strongbow with your full history. He won't find it amusing, but then, he's got no sense of humour. He may keep you alive because he's also a timid bugger and won't want to offend Fitzempress even more by killing his favourite marshal. And he may have a use for you. On the other hand he may not.'

The inertia of indecision had settled over a Dublin divided between belief that because nothing dreadful had happened so far, it never would – the 'Ruairi-O'Conor-will-save-us' school – and the conviction that something was going to happen but it wouldn't be as dreadful as all that – the 'God-will-save-us' school.

Asgall came more than once to the Swan during those days of waiting so that he could drink and worry and beg for reassurance in the privacy of Finn's tower room, freed of the necessity to display confidence and courage before his court.

'Have you heard anything?' he'd ask. Ever since his secret negotiations in that very room with the O'Conor's agent he had regarded Finn as his pipeline to underground information.

'Only that the High King is camped with most of Ireland at Clondalkin, ready to intercept Strongbow,' Finn told him, 'but you know that.' There had been no news from Lough Mask and she was worried.

'Why isn't he here?' moaned Asgall, 'Strongbow doesn't have to come via Clondalkin. Dermot can lead him through Wicklow like silver-finned salmon leap a fall. Yet my assistance-pleas bring no High King to my aid.'

Finn poured him more wine. He was right. The O'Conor had entrenched himself across the major roads leading to Dublin and was apparently ignoring the fact that Dermot knew the backways to it like his own hand. She'd begged him to ring the city, but he'd said it was cleverer to catch the Normans at Clondalkin. She lost all faith in him; she suspected his obtuseness was a subconscious fear of a confrontation he might lose.

'If they come I shall go to my brother-king of Orkney for reinforcements,' said Asgall. 'Our combined Viking blood shall smite the upstart Norman.'

Finn raised her eyes. So far Viking blood had combined to smite bugger-all, but the idea comforted Asgall in his terror that Waterford could be re-enacted at Dublin. He drained his cup and then stood up to fling it away. 'And where is Dervorgilla now? Has the harlot hanged herself in shame at bringing this disaster on our shores?'

'Dervorgilla?' Finn tried to understand him. 'You mean O'Rourke of Breffni's Dervorgilla?'

'Who else is so blameworthy?' roared Asgall and ticked off his reasoning on his stout, chewed fingers. 'Did the bitch not betray her husband with Dermot of Leinster? Therefore did not her husband in his righteous desire for revenge force Dermot into exile? And was it not that which sent Dermot into the arms of the Normans? Her name shall be written with dishonour in the annals of Ireland.'

'That was eighteen years ago,' Finn shouted back at him. 'How could you possibly . . .?'

'Time does not rob an act of its infamy.'

'Oh,' said Finn, 'Oh . . . go away, you stupid oaf.'

It was not the courtesy which the landlady of the Swan usually accorded her guests, but Finn had completely lost her temper and Asgall was so put out by it that he weaved down the stairs and left, making a rift between him and his favourite inn.

Finn slammed the door behind him and paced her room. The idiot, the great, swag-bellied, jelly-hearted, pose-striking, booze-brained . . . male. Realisation made her go cold.

That's what they would say. In this room she had heard the verdict of male history. With their ambition and conniving and the blood of their filthy wars still on their hands, they would look around for a scapegoat so that they did not have to blame themselves and find their

317

oldest, deepest fear. Not Dermot, not O'Rourke, not O'Conor, not the Normans, all these had only been misguided in the way of man. They would blame a woman, a romantic, gentle, silly woman.

'I'll give them scapegoat,' said Finn and fetched the Word of Woman from Vives' box. She would write it as it was, now, quickly, so that the truth could exist somewhere. Where was the harlot now? Finn knew where she was. The Abbess of Kildare had told her, and on her way back from Lough Mask this last time she had called in at the monastery of Clonmacnois sprawling its great size along the flat, wide, banks of the Shannon. She had skirted the long wall to the causeway where waders bobbed their beaks into the mud, and climbed up the rise between trees to the tiny church and its outbuildings that were out of the monastery's sight and there, in the habit of a nun, she had found Dervorgilla and told her that her daughter was alive and well.

Dervorgilla smiled. 'She was my sin, you know. They took her away from me. I do penance for her every day. Do you think God hears the prayers of a wicked woman?'

'Yes.'

'O'Rourke let me build this church so that God would not think so ill of me. He's been very kind. I was allowed to help the mason with the design. Do you like it?'

'Very much.' Miniature, beautiful, its perfectly-proportioned doorway and roof were a feminine placation of a disapproving god. The nuns who looked after Dervorgilla stood at a distance, watching like wardresses.

'I hope they let me stay here.' Dervorgilla's little face under its veil had not aged but its vagueness had become impenetrable, like a mist between her and a harsh world. From behind it her pansy eyes stared at Finn. 'I know you, don't I? We met somewhere.'

'Once. A long time ago. I did you a great wrong and I beg your forgiveness.'

Dervorgilla nodded. The nuns were signalling her to come away; she had talked long enough. 'Everything was a long time ago,' she said.

'Men begin to say, now that affliction has come upon them,' wrote Finn in her tower room, 'that Dervorgilla of Breffni by her adultery with Dermot of Leinster brought down God's wrath upon Ireland, but this is the alteration of reason by which men excuse their own actions, for Dervorgilla was a victim . . .'

She wrote for a long time, experiencing her usual difficulty, until exhaustion forced her to break off. She sprinkled sand over her manuscript, cleaned her quill as Brother Pinginn had taught her, blew the sand off the words, rolled up the vellum and put it back in Vives' box. Having begged God to safeguard all who were precious to her and made special mention of a nun of Clonmacnois, she blew out her candle and went to bed.

Crouched in the centre room of the tower at the foot of the stairs leading to the upper story, Elfwida saw the light go out. As she always did, she waited until Finn's breathing became regular, then she climbed up the stairs and crossed on bare feet to Vives' box, opened it and took out the vellum. Back in her own room she lit her candles from the brazier and set it by the board which Pinginn had made for her, wriggled her hand down inside her dress and took out a membrane which she had scraped and prepared by herself.

Putting Finn's manuscript by the side of hers she began to copy it.

Because Finn didn't know what to do, she did very little. She wanted to be at Lough Mask but was afraid that if she set off she would miss the arrival of Lief and Tailltin; besides, she would be out of the way if any news came in of the Pilgrim's whereabouts. She made some preparation for an emergency, provisioning the tower with food and arms and keeping a *curragh* moored in the secret cave beneath the tower. Thinking of every possible scenario, she and Pinginn dragged the Jews' vat of still-untouched kosher wine over the trapdoor so that intruders into the tower wouldn't see that there was an exit and intruders from below couldn't use it as an entrance. She got Gorm to make slots and a bar on the inside of the tower door leading to the inn – its only other entrance.

One of the many burdens on her during those waiting days was the Word of Woman. Apart from the fact that it gave away who she was and what she had done, that it should exist, a tiny, whispering descant to the deafening roar of men, became daily more important. She started carrying it in her sleeve by day and tucked it under her pillow at night. 'If anything ever happens to me,' she told Brother Pinginn and Elfwida, 'try and get the manuscript to safety.'

'What do you want done with it?' asked Pinginn.

Elfwida asked, 'Why, what's in it?'

That night she was back in Lough Mask but a fog was over the lake and the dead were moving in it, laughing at her. Niav; her mother; Scathagh; were laughing at her inability to move. 'Wake up,' they jeered at her, 'wake up.'

She woke up. It was Elfwida. 'The geese are cackling.' She could hear them.

It could be a fox, or a dog, or one of the lepers after her chickens again. 'You and Pinginn and Gorm get down to the boat,' she said, dragging on her boots and putting a dagger down the sheath she'd sewn into the right one. The rest of the staff had taken to going back into the safety of the city at nights. But Elfwida was looking out of the north window. 'There's movement on the other bank.' Finn pushed her out of the way. There was a weak moon but enough to show her, who knew every tree on the bank, that there were shapes where no shapes should be.

They might still get out to sea, but she didn't know what lay behind the hill on the south bank. It could be O'Conor's army come to defend Dublin properly at last. She dressed the rest of herself. 'Well, stay here. Fetch the others and lock yourselves in and don't answer until I tell you.'

'Oh, yes,' said Elfwida, following her down the steps into the dark inn. Pinginn and Gorm were already there. 'The geese are upset.'

She gave up trying to keep them safe and led them out onto the quay and round to the orchard by the inn's gable end. To have gone out by the kitchen door would have silhouetted them against the banked-up fire. Scathagh-craft. You'll need it. The milch cows were moving restlessly in the byre.

Lazy Hill and the leper hospital were outlined against a dark-grey sky by the beginning of dawn. The hill had sprung crocuses overnight, hundreds of them, colourless steel crocuses which rose up in accelerated growth to become helmets with bodies underneath, advancing down the slope.

'Back.' They ran for the kitchen door but more shapes stood in their way and then surrounded them so that the four of them became the sepals in a flower of swords.

Chapter Fourteen

If she hadn't been sure the Normans were going to do it for her anyway, Finn would have cut her own throat. She deserved to die for her criminality in allowing Elfwida and Brother Pinginn to fall into their hands. While the Normans searched the inn and she stood under guard in her own kitchen with her arms round the girl and the priest, she was terrified only for them.

'Don't be frightened God is with us I'm not frightened' babbled Pinginn. Finn hugged him closer. 'Stop being silly.' These metalled men would kill him for being silly. They would rape Elfwida. She'd kill them first; she still had the dagger in her boot. If they got a chance to reach the tower they could still get away, if the vat hadn't been moved to expose the trapdoor. Oh Jesus, the Word of Woman was underneath her pillow.

Disinterested eyes watched them from the shadows of the guards' helmets.

A bigger, rounder metal figure came through the door from the common parlour. 'Nice inn, this,' it said in Norman French. 'Too many arms in the tower, though. What have we got here, Jacques?'

'The staff, I reckon,' said one of the helmets, 'and a priest.'

'Get the interpreter.' The big figure put up its hands, took off its helmet and became a fat-faced young man whose fair, curly hair stuck to his scalp in sweaty leaves. He ran his fingers through it. 'Anything to eat?' One of the soldiers took down a ham and began carving it with his dagger, another brought the bread jar and a cheese. 'Give me a plate and then fill yourselves.'

The were disciplined, thought Finn; they hadn't touched the food until the fat man told them, though now they fell on it like starving dogs. The fat man turned up his nose at the offer of ale. 'There's a vat of goodish wine in the tower cellar. Bring a couple of jugs.' The prisoners stood very still.

The interpreter who came in looked like an ex-sailor and certainly wasn't Irish, though he spoke it adequately, if without refinements. 'Yes, my lord Raymond?'

So this would be Earl Raymond – they all called themselves

'Earl' – the nephew of FitzStephen, another Geraldine, and known to his contemporaries as 'Le Gros'. He'd come over in the second wave of invaders.

'Tell these people they're lucky. They've been occupied by the kindest man in Christendom if he's obeyed. Tell them he's a demon from hell if he isn't.'

While the man translated, Finn thought, 'You're all bastards, whoever you are.' Raymond had been one of the attackers at Waterford. Now he distorted his fat face as he jumped about, scratching his armpits, to show how terrible he could be. Under their helmets a couple of his men smiled.

'Right. Ask them where the owner of the inn is.' He turned to his men. 'Nice inn. I'll take this land, I think. Might build a castle here. Good position up on the hill.'

Brother Pinginn answered in Irish. 'We don't know.' He sounded dull-witted.

'They probably don't,' Raymond said, 'I expect he got out days ago, Irish scum. Ask them who is it in this place who can scribe. We found two writing boards upstairs and a manuscript under a pillow. Wouldn't think it, would you?'

There was a silence. 'I can,' said Pinginn.

'Irish? Norman? Latin?'

'Irish and Latin.'

'Good enough. You can scribe for me. Never thought to bring a bloody secretary and I don't trust Strongbow's. Or Dermot's. Ask them what a nun's habit is doing here? Found it in the cellar.'

Pinginn was at a loss and so was Finn, but the interpreter saved them. 'The innkeeper's probably got a relative who's a nun. Terrible, isn't it, a nun in an inn, but that's the way these Irish carry on.'

Raymond jutted his jowls at Elfwida and Finn. 'Can't you two talk?'

'That's Irishwomen all over,' the interpreter said, 'Faces intelligent and minds as thick as pigshit. Good workers, though.'

'Tell them they're now working for me,' said Raymond. 'Tell them if they look after me and my soldiers properly, they won't be harmed. And I mean that, Jacques. If one bugger so much as looks up their skirts I'll have him flogged. They can make do with the camp followers and any willing girls in the city when we get there. You hear me? If we're going to live here I don't want to keep looking over my shoulder for a dagger in the back.'

'Yes, my lord.'

There was a disturbance in the nobles' parlour and more soldiers brought in Perse and Molling. The miller looked appalled, Perse looked just the same.

'Says he owns the mill over the creek, sir. We got them crossing the bridge – I think they'd heard the troops and were coming to the tower for safety.'

Raymond smiled. 'Wrong on both counts. Tell him it's my mill now. He just runs it.'

Perse saw that the inn had visitors and reacted accordingly. 'I got nice soup ready,' she said, 'I'll heat it up. Persingly, I think hot soup's always better when it's heated up.'

As they watched her stoke up the fire and hang a cauldron over it, the interpreter translated. Raymond looked at Pinginn. 'What does she do here? Apart from push back the frontiers of thought for the rest of us?'

'She's the cook.'

'I like her. Right. I now annexe this inn in the name of God, Earl Richard of Striguil also known as Strongbow, the king of Leinster and me. I'll want hot meals and palliasses for fifty. The women can sleep, when they do sleep, down in the tower cellar. Locked in. Safer. My quarters are at the top. You, sir priest, can start taking dictation. Jump to it, the lot of you.'

It was a long day. Elfwida, Perse, Finn and Gorm worked like slaves, preparing food, cooking, serving, filling mattresses. Each one could have escaped twenty times over, but alone. Only one of them at a time was ever allowed into the tower by the sentry at the door. Most of the soldiers spoke Welsh, a few Flemish, even fewer Norman. There was no doubting the efficiency of Le Gros for whom his men – even if they called him 'Fatty' among themselves – had respect and liking. The soldiers guarding the hill and the river were relieved regularly for food and sleep. Captain Jacques had relayed the order that the women were to be treated with propriety and it was obeyed; anyway, most of the men were too tired to be anything but surly. Finn gathered the forced march through Hy Kinsella country had been hard going. Bitterly she admired the achievement in encircling Dublin while the Irish army which was supposed to protect it was still unaware the city was besieged.

In the early afternoon a look-out shouted, 'Lord de Cogan crossing the bridge.'

Raymond Le Gros met his fellow-commander in the inn's doorway. 'Nice place,' said de Cogan.

'Keep your eyes off, Miles. I liberated it. Everybody in position?'

'Yes. The river's the problem, trying to stop the bastards getting word to O'Conor. Dermot's parleying across the walls with Asgall, demanding hostages, but the Vikings can't make up their minds who to give as hostage.'

'God, Miles, we can't wait for this crapping about. We need to be in that bloody city before O'Conor moves.'

'That's what I say . . .' Their voices moved out of Finn's range as they climbed up to the tower. Later they sent for food and wine, but Le Gros ordered Perse to fetch it. He'd taken to her.

Most of the men drank ale, for which Finn thanked God; nevertheless, Le Gros' consumption would finish the kosher wine quickly at this rate, in which case somebody might move the barrel. She told Perse to serve the Aquitanian Aragon had brought on the last trip, and hoped to God the Normans would be kept too busy with their own concerns to wonder why such heavy goods should be transported to such an inconvenient place as a tower cellar, and whether they had got there by some other route than through the inn.

She must get Pinginn and Elfwida away. She wasn't worried about Perse, who could obviously look after herself, or Gorm who had a universal camouflage in being the sort of silent, capable, elderly, jack-of-all-trades to be found in inns all over the world. Already he could move about without the continual watch kept on the rest of them. Jacques had got him mending broken harness.

It was still only mid-afternoon – she cast an amazed look at the sun, wondering whether it had stopped – when Pinginn was allowed out of the tower to the garden privies.

She managed to look as if she were gathering herbs and move into Pinginn's path. As he passed her, he said in Irish, 'They're going to storm the city tonight,' before his guard pushed him on.

'Can we warn them?' asked Elfwida when the two of them could exchange a few words in the kitchen.

Finn shook her head. 'We must get away.' If Dublin wasn't prepared for a surprise attack by now, nothing she could do would help.

'It's a shame,' said Perse, 'but never mind, the wedding'll cheer things up.'

'What wedding?'

'Lord Strongbow's. I heard two of the Welshmen talking, but I didn't let on I understood because they're southerners and persingly I don't like southerners.'

'But how did you understand?' She stood there, bovine and confiding, her fingers making knuckle-shapes in dough.

'Well, it isn't what we spoke up in the north exactly, but near.'

'Perse,' said Finn, smiling for the first time that day, 'you're Welsh.' She'd never thought of Perse as having nationality; she had seemed to belong to some unique breed of her own, descendant of a long line of Perses.

'Was,' said Perse.

'Who's the swine marrying, anyway?'

'One of Dermot's daughters.'

* * *

324

Their dependable, lovely, refined, intelligent Aoife was trying to crawl under the canvas of the pavilion. When the Hy Kinsella lifted her back she ran around it, snatching at hangings, throwing over stools, battering her father, howling.

Dermot pushed her off and sat down in his camp chair, rearranging his cloak. 'This is unseemly. I told you, it doesn't matter.'

'It matters to me,' shrieked Aoife.

There has been a mistake, thought Slaney. God has put us into hell while we're still alive. That is not Aoife. That is not Father. This not me. All this is outside what I am capable of believing.

'You were never free to marry whom you liked,' said Dermot.

'Irish, Irish.' The pavilion smelled of bruised grass. Aoife was on her hands and knees, clawing at it, hitting her head on it. 'Not a thing from another world entering me. You said it was just a ruse. You said it was a ru-u-u-use.' Her body went limp as the word throbbed out of it.

'It's still a ruse,' said Dermot. He was puzzled at her reaction. 'This way he'll win the High Kingship for me. He'll think he'll inherit it after me, not knowing he can't. You can kill him then if you like. When he sleeps or something. Or I'll send him back to England. But you must understand, Aoife, that Tara is attainable now, so close. I can feel the wind on its hilltop.'

There were spots round his mouth and he scratched himself continually. He is dead, thought Slaney, and the body still twitches to drag itself up a grass-covered mound where ancient kings stood once for a ritual. You're a corpse. Die now, decently, before you do this thing to Aoife.

'You must see,' said Dermot, 'It doesn't matter who enters you. You've been defiled already. Again won't matter. Take them away and prepare them.'

As the Hy Kinsella closed in, Slaney said, 'If I can, Father, I will kill you.'

Dermot focussed on her. 'I forget who your father was, but I know he raped your mother.' He frowned and put a flaking hand to his head. 'I can't remember why.'

Scraps of food were chucked down into the undercroft after them. 'Tell them not to touch that bloody wine,' they heard Le Gros say, and the trapdoor which sealed off the undercroft from the upper floors slammed down. Bolts rusty from disuse scraped home, boots thudded overhead and they were in a darkness so complete it muffled the eyes. There was silence, apart from Molling's whimpering. The man had completely gone to pieces.

'Gorm, Pinginn, get that vat rolled away. Elf, help me find the chest.' They stumbled and tripped in their disorientation but eventually Finn's hands were on the nun's habit. In the maelstrom of horror into which she was going it would be little enough protection, but it was all she had. 'I'm sorry,' she kept saying as she dressed. 'I'm so sorry. But I've got to get to her if I can. To help her, at least to be there. If it is her.'

'Whoever it is, the poor thing,' said Pinginn.

It would be terrible going upriver when their only safety lay the other way, but the boat was small and couldn't take all of them; she would have had to make choices whatever she did. She felt Elfwida's hands buttoning up the back of the habit and turned round to clasp them. 'I'll be back. I promise, I promise. Say it.'

'You'll be back,' said Elfwida tonelessly.

'What'll we do if the Normans find you gone?' shrieked Molling. Perse said, 'It's not very nice, all this.' Oddly, she was a comfort.

The trapdoor was raised to let in the smell of river and an impression of light rather than light itself. 'What time would it be?' 'About prime.' Everything was quiet outside apart from the hiss of rain. She stumbled over to the opening, sat down, felt about for the thwart with her feet and dropped down. The *curragh* rocked as she was pushed aside by Pinginn dropping down beside her. 'You can't come,' she said, clutching at him.

'Did God put you into my hand or not?'

She was so afraid that she didn't protest any more.

'What'll we do if the Normans come back and find you gone?' shouted Molling again, but his voice resounded in an empty cave.

A bad August was turning into a worse September and the moon was obscured by cloud but there was a glow from the fires along the north shore which would illuminate them. They hauled the *curragh* round the rock face by pulling on their hands against its surface, with the river trying to pull them in the other direction, as if it knew something. Sculling across the mouth of the Stein and into the view of anyone on top of the tower or along the quay was an exposure so blatant it seemed obscene, but they had to break cover at some point. The sculls creaked in their wooden rowlocks and Pinginn, always a clumsy oarsman, missed his stroke and hit the water like a child batting a stick against it. If there was anyone on the tower, he was blind and deaf.

'We could land and make it on foot,' he whispered hopefully. She considered. Out here they were a target and the impulse to get among trees was strong, but in the darkness of the shore they could blunder into a group of soldiers before they knew it whereas in a boat, if the first arrows missed, they could lie down and let it take them back to where they'd come from. 'Not yet.' She watched the north shore bonfires as they rowed but saw no movement, one or two were being damped down by the rain, which was increasing. Presumably the troops which had lit them had been pulled in for the coming attack on the city. Nothing was happening yet. Behind them as they rowed Dublin looked as it had done on the thousands of nights she had watched it, a faint patina coming from the braziers and flares in its streets, tiny arches of light which were the illuminated upper windows of its castle where men were talking, worried but not worried enough, still relying on the old Irish custom of last-minute negotiation to save them, unaware that everything Irish was about to be swept away and that negotiation was gone for ever.

The satin sheen from mudflats on their right told her that further inland stood the Thingmount, another vantage point from which arrows could fly at them; she had no plan, there couldn't be one; she was just moving upstream to save her daughter, a clumsy salmon likely to be speared at any moment but unable to disobey the summons of its body.

The sculls creaked and water splashed off the blades in the same sound she had listened to a hundred times as she had pulled over the gentle surface of Lough Mask. Out there were men wanting to kill other men and harm women who had legs, arms, breasts, a head, like their own women at home. Tonight there would be children experiencing a fear that would darken the rest of their lives, if they lived them at all. *God, stop it and send us all home.*

From the far side of the city there came a single battle-cry, the voice self-conscious as it broke the peace of the night, its false note followed by a roaring drum of sound sweeping on and on round the ouside of the city, engulfing it, bouncing back off its walls in a wave that ran down the river like a bore, so violent it seemed to rock them. 'Oh, Jesus.' If they went on it would consume them as well as Dublin.

They pulled for the shore, hid the boat under a clump of alders and climbed up through mud until they found a path. They were stupefied into carelessness by the assault of noise but there could be no danger in the no-man's land of Hogges Green now; every invader in Ireland had to be contributing his throat in that immense shout, magnetised towards the city by its promise of power, booty and killing. Their own heads were turned to it and when they came to an avenue of beeches by a wall they stopped and positioned themselves to look in its direction as if they were the audience to some riveting entertainment.

The lights of the stage wavered as torches were set to buildings and then went up so that it was flared, showing ridiculously miniaturised shapes fighting along the top of the walls, a theatrical effect, a puppet show. The roar of shouting became ragged, augmented by screams, steel hitting steel, and the whoosh of fire. The rain became insistent and beech leaves turned down into small chutes which soaked them, but they didn't notice and it wasn't enough to put out the flames which bounced up and down in cascades where one house went up more quickly than its neighbour. They watched all night. The slope of the city to the river gradually skidded the action of the fighting down the walls to the right of their stage's wings, so that all they could see was unchecked burning. They tried not to imagine what was happening as the people and army of Dublin were jammed down into the roads leading to the river, but the squealing from that direction was like a slaughterhouse and went on and on until that Finn found herself saying, 'Stop it, stop it,' not to the butchery, but to the noise of butchery.

She heard Brother Pinginn calling on his God and wondered why.

It was still raining when dawn came up and showed that Dublin had assumed different shapes, walls messily incomplete, spars where there had been comfortable clusters of thatch; the smoke over it was general instead of rising up from particular, domesticated fires. The stretch of land between it and where they stood, wet to the skin, was empty of living things except for birds which were going about their brisk morning flights and landings as if the world were still the same.

'Where are we?'

'It's St. Mary's Abbey. If we go towards the city from here they might think we're coming from it.' There was no question either of their minds that the Normans had won Dublin; the absence of people proved it. All the vultures had gathered in that one spot to gorge on whatever was in there. Pinginn said, 'After all, there'll be a need for priests. They'll let us in.'

Almost aimless with shock they began wandering out from the shelter of the trees and then dodged back as they saw a horseman coming towards them at full speed from the direction of the city. He dismounted at the convent gates and rang the bell with energy, but they didn't open; the nuns of St. Mary's had also had a grandstand seat to the destruction of their city. The horseman persisted after a long while they heard a squint-door being unlatched in the gate. They couldn't hear the conversation that went on through it, though the horseman's tone was peremptory. Apparently reluctantly, the gates opened and a nun, the superior by her dress, came out, her head up. She and the horseman spoke together without warmth for a moment or two, then she turned to beckon to her sisters who emerged, more hesitantly, in ones or twos.

Finn, who'd been watching through branches, let them spring back and closed her eyes. As the Mother Superior had turned she had seen her face. She knew it. She'd seen it before. She associated it with dread, but why? She'd seen it a long time ago in connection with something terrible. Terrible. A cold, flat voice in her memory said, 'I don't know what he will do to you, but it will be terrible. He is a terrible man.'

The horseman remounted and turned his horse in the direction he had come, leading the twenty or so nuns at walking pace towards the city.

'Come on.' She and Pinginn sprinted over the grass, their wet skirts flapping against their ankles, and joined the procession. The nuns were being taken into the city and whatever it was for, even if it was to be killed, it was a passport through the gates. A few of the nuns looked up as Finn pushed her way towards the Mother Superior but they were too afraid to question anything; their mouths moved in ritual, issuing a whisper of prayers, while their fingers flickered frantically over the knots of their rosaries.

The Mother Superior wasn't praying. She walked stiffly with her eyes straight ahead and her face blank. Finn nudged her and said quietly: 'Do you know me?'

The nun turned her head and focussed with an effort. The last time they had met it was Finn who had been the Mother Superior. 'Yes.' Whatever peace she had found in her sanctuary all these years it had not revived emotion in her, or perhaps the summons to Dublin had taken it away. She was as bloodless as on the night when she had warned the abbess of Kildare that Dermot was on his way.

'What's happening?'

The woman who had once been Dermot's wife glanced at the horseman riding ahead and said, 'My sisters and I have been invited to a wedding. We are to lend respectability to the marriage between Strongbow and Aoife of Leinster.'

Aoife. It was Aoife who was to be sacrificed to a conqueror forty years older than herself. Finn shut her eyes in relief that it was not to be her daughter, then opened them wide as she remembered: Aoife was the daughter of the woman walking beside her. 'I'm sorry.' It seemed inadequate, but she didn't know what else to say.

The Mother Superior shrugged. 'I gave up my right to her by leaving, but Dermot had taken her away from me before that. He can share nothing. He would be delighted to know that he was inflicting this extra cruelty in making me attend the ceremony.'

'Doesn't he know then?'

'No.'

Finn's brain made more links. After all, one of the most powerful churchmen in the land, Laurence O'Toole, was this woman's brother.

329

He would have protected her. 'Suppose Dermot recognises you?'

'I hope he does.' The former queen of Leinster's smile was not religious. 'I should like him to know before he kills me that I aided his enemies. I gave all his jewels to Asgall to buy arms for use against him.'

So the two of us have been working to bring Dermot down, thought Finn, and for all the good it's done we could have stayed at home and played with dolls. Such is the might of men and the powerlessness of women.

They were approaching the Dames Gate bridge. The horseman looked round to make sure his flock was keeping together. He hadn't counted them at ay stage, and the fact that there was a monk among them caused him no surprise, so usual was it for nuns to be accompanied by a confessor.

'I'm going to try and get my daughter away from that madman,' said Finn, 'I'll take yours with me if I can.'

Again the Mother Superior shrugged; her face showed not only hopelessness but an acceptance of hopelessness that was almost satisfaction.

To judge from the crowd of nuns and monks around Dames Gate waiting to go in to the city, Strongbow had commanded every religious within heralding distance of Dublin to attend his wedding, hoping perhaps that the odour of so much sanctity would make it smell sweeter. The gates were open, but whatever was holding them up had sent most of the habited figures to their knees.

As the nuns from St. Mary's approached they saw the obstruction. Fifteen foot high in the gateway was a pile of bodies. A burial detail consisting of the non-combatants of Strongbow's army – men and women – was working to clear a path through them by clambering up the shelves of trunks, legs, arms and heads and rolling the upper corpses down to loaders below who swung them into waiting carts. The nuns, Finn and Brother Pinginn knelt and prayed. Most the dead were men, but a few were women, and both sexes had already been stripped of cloaks, weapons and jewellery.

One of the burial detail – a female camp follower – high up on the pile had her boot firmly planted on a corpse's cheek. She bent down to retrieve something that had been hidden under one of the bodies and called to her mates further down. 'Oh look,' she said, 'In't it sad?' She lifted the corpse of a baby from its mother's dead grasp. The other women of the detail went 'Ah.' Some crooned, 'Poor little thing.' Others, 'What a shame.' The baby was laid carefully in the cart and a sentimental moment spent on arranging its shawl until the horseman in charge of the St. Mary's nuns sharply told the detail to hurry up.

Eventually a path was cleared and the monks and nuns were

urshered between walls of dead whose rigored arms stuck out to brush their skirts as if in supplication. One of the nuns stopped as she saw a pallid face she recognised, a father, a brother, but another sister clasped her round her shoulders and hurried her on. Nuns or not, they were Irish and must not display pain before the enemy.

The cramped, carved wooden frontages of the streets Finn had come to know well had disappeared so that there was an uninterrupted view over the entire eastern side of the city up to the castle and down to the river wall. In their place were wide rows of ashes and fallen timbers patterned into charcoal by the fire, sending up steam in the rain. The shrivelled, featureless shape of a Norseman stood against the stone portal of a doorway with his sword still stuck to the bones of his hand where the melting flesh had glued it.

The cathedral, when they reached it, was untouched except for its great doors which had been rammed and hung splintered on their hinges. More carts were being filled from another pile of corpses; this one consisting of the women, children and old men who had sought sanctuary in the great church. Whether or not the Norman leaders had tried to prevent the massacre when their men had broken in, they hadn't been able to. On the hideous roundabout of the ages it had come to the descendants of Vikings to be hewed to bits at an altar by berserkers.

A mass for the dead was being conducted on one side of the cathedral steps where a large congregation from the religious houses of the city was kneeling in the rain. Perhaps it was the rain which was damping down hysteria, or perhaps the release of brutality which had ejaculated over Dublin the night before had brought its own peace, but there was a sense of calm, almost purposefulness, over everyone – even the nuns and monks, even the few survivors who ambled the streets like sleepwalkers – which seemed as nightmarish to Finn as anything she had ever known. The ordinary priest who was taking the mass – there was no sign of Dublin's Archbishop or bishop – wandered from psalm to psalm, sometimes penitent, sometimes pleading for help, but never angry. 'My soul is among lions,' he said, quietly, 'and I lie even among them that are set on fire. Deliver me from the workers of iniquity and save me from bloody men. O God thou hast cast us off, thou hast scattered us, thou hast been displeased; O turn thyself to us again.' He paused. 'Be still, and know that I am God.'

Behind him, brawny camp women were washing down the flags of the cathedral interior and jovially chatting together in Welsh as they brushed out water which was pink with diluted blood.

There was a squeak from Brother Pinginn kneeling beside Finn and she felt him nudge her. She looked up and followed his eyes which

331

were trained on a helmeted Norman soldier who had his arm round a raddled camp follower and appeared to be looking intently in her direction. She found she had been crying, wiped her tears off with the back of her hand, and looked again. The Norman was very tall and the camp follower seemed familiar. 'Deliver my soul from the sword,' said the priest, 'my darling from the power of the dog.' Finn sobbed. The floozie was her friend Tailltin and the soldier was Lief.

She and Pinginn got up and walked with their heads bowed round the steps and into what had been Fishanger Lane beside the cathedral, where a row of once-respectable stone houses still stood, windowless, doorless, ransacked but otherwise intact. An arm drew her into a doorway and for a long time Lief held her close, then he passed her onto the embrace of Tailltin and hugged Pinginn, who was still squeaking with joy.

Finn wanted to say that she had never seen anything so beautiful in the whole world as the two of them, but none of them could speak. Ridiculously, they stood in the filthy doorway and patted each other's faces.

A file of soldiers marched down the lane outside and the four of them backed into an inside room. Suddenly Finn was cross with relief. 'You buggers,' she said, 'Where have you been?'

'We yoined Strongbow's army,' said Lief.

When he and Tailltin had arrived at Lough Mask and found that Slaney, Aoife and Dervorgilla had already left for a destination unknown, they had decided not to inform Finn until they had news of the girls' whereabouts.

'You had worries enough,' said Tailltin. They'd rested for a day, packed themselves food for another long journey, and set out on fresh horses to pick up the trail. It had been easy going until they reached Leinster where, although by that time they'd guessed Dermot's daughters were heading for Ferns, the country had been so criss-crossed by Dermot's patrols and pickets that they had to keep hiding or wasting time in wide diversions. 'The trouble with him is,' said Tailltin, jerking her thumb towards the Norwegian, 'he looks like a Norseman, and after Waterford stray Norsemen were being killed on sight.'

Eventually Lief had decided to make for Wexford, a town he knew from his trading days, where there were still sufficient Norse-Irish left alive for him to pass unremarked, and which was close enough to both Ferns and Waterford to find out what was happening. 'He's not the fool he looks,' said Tailltin fondly – Finn had already seen that the two of them had become close. For their purposes Wexford had turned out to be perfect. Mercenaries were still arriving from across the Irish Sea and, a few days after their arrival, Strongbow and his army had passed nearby on their way to join up with Dermot, his army, and his daughters, at Ferns. 'So we joined too,' said Tailltin. 'it's a real dog's breakfast; old hands, new hands, recent arrivals, all nationalities, as well as individual mercenary bands. Nobody knows who anybody else is and nobody questions much. There's even some Irish-Norse turncoats and levies, so Lief didn't look out of place. I made out I was his wife and mucked in with the rest of the camp followers, but I could have joined on my own and nobody'd have thought anything of it. There's a terrible woman; Alice of Abergavenny; her man was killed at Waterford and in revenge she's supposed to have chopped off seventy Waterford heads – she's still with the army, drawing a soldier's pay. Another hag didn't make any difference.'

Along with the rest they had made the terrible march through the Wicklow mountains to Dublin. Tailltin closed her eyes remembering it. 'I wouldn't like to do that again,' she said. 'We tried to get near to the girls but Dermot had them under guard. You know the bastard's marrying Aoife to Strongbow? Well, we were with Miles de Cogan's lot by then and we had to take up a position to the west of the city. We'd hoped to sneak away and get to you, but De Cogan was making sure nobody gave away the surprise attack and kept the camp surrounded by his men. And, well, that's it.'

It wasn't it. She hadn't mentioned the attack on Dublin, which indicated that Lief had been forced to keep his cover by taking part in it. Finn decided she didn't want to know. The loyalty and courage these two had displayed was something she could never repay.

'And Slaney?'

'Lief's done a reconnaissance,' said Tailltin.

'Not good, but maybe,' said Lief. He squatted down and drew a shape in the dust of the floor with his finger. 'If Dermot won't bring her and the other girl to the cathedral for the wedding, then we go to his house and steal them, maybe. Yust now it's surrounded by guards in case somebody try to assassinate him.' He spat. 'But if he bring them, he put them there,' he jabbed at the transept in a rough drawing of the cathedral, 'in the Lady Chapel with the other women.'

'Yes?' For the first time in her life Finn blessed the separation of male and female congregation in church.

'Ja. Little door in the back of the chapel. Here.' He jabbed a point which meant the door was in the north wall and opened out into St John's Lane.

'It's full of inns, that lane.'

Lief shook his head. 'Not now. Mostly rubble. We get horses maybe, many as we can. Arms too. We wait for you there. You get the girls out some time in the ceremony.'

'And Aoife?'

Lief shook his head. Nobody could help Aoife.

333

'We'd better get back to the steps,' said Tailltin, 'in case it begins. Better not go out all together.' Lief went first. Then Pinginn. Tailltin put her hand on Finn's arm. 'I didn't just pretend to be his wife, Finn. I was.'

'I know.'

'You don't mind?'

'How could I? I'm glad.' In all this annihilation it was beautiful, even if it made her own loneliness even more dreary by the loss of them both. 'Tailltin, you listen to me. If we get the girls out and we make it, try and get them to Lough Mask. But if there's choices at any point, yours is Lief. The two of you have got to get away and have babies. Promise me you won't ever come back.'

Tailltin's mouth was moving. 'But you're coming?'

'If I can. But I swore to Elfwida I'd go back for her. I'm not risking heroics from the rest of you, you've got to promise now.'

'I don't want to leave you, Finn.'

'Well, you're bloody going to.'

Tailltin sighed. 'Then I might as well tell you. I wasn't going to for fear you'd stay, but if you're staying anyway . . . The Pilgrim's here.'

'Here?'

'He's a prisoner. I saw him on the march and he had fetters on. One of Strongbow's followers said he was a spy for Fitzempress, and that if they didn't keep him locked up he'd get word to England that Strongbow was setting up a rival kingdom here in Ireland.'

'They'll kill him.'

'Well, they haven't yet.'

I can't worry about him, Finn thought. Slaney comes first. I'll give him spies. And, God, I love him. 'Is Strongbow setting up a rival kingdom?' she said.

'He means to be High King. Marrying Aoife is symbolic, his claim to Ireland.'

'Jesus help her.'

The crowd of nuns and monks were allowed into the cathedral at mid-day. Its floors were still damp but splashes of blood on its pillars had been overlooked. As they waited, anger began to replace shock and one or two of the abbots started out again with the intention of protesting to Strongbow, but guards on the doors turned them back. While they weren't looking, Finn went into the Lady Chapel and tried the tiny door in the north wall. It was unlocked.

Some of the camp followers showed charity by bringing soup in pails and passing cups around, but most of the sisters and brothers refused to touch it. Finn and Pinginn accepted gratefully, not knowing when they'd have nourishment again.

334

They heard later that while they waited Asgall was on trial in his own hall.

Strongbow sat in the great, carved chair that had once belonged to the man who, with his arms and legs in chains, had been kicked to the ground before him. Close by stood the executioner with a raised axe.

'Do you ransom your life, Norseman,' asked Strongbow, 'or do I take your head?'

A true Viking at the last, Asgall, son of Thorkil and king of Dublin, looked up. 'We were few this time, Norman. You had better take my head, for if you do not I shall come after you with greater numbers.'

Strongbow nodded to the executioner and there was a swish as the axe came down. 'Asgall MacThorkil died,' wrote the chroniclers afterwards, 'not for his armed defiance but for his impudent words.'

Through the high slit windows of the cathedral the dull light of the rainy day outside turned duller as the afternoon progressed, making a muted tapestry out of the brightly-dressed Norman leaders who had begun to come in; they had already learned to appreciate the beauty of dyed Irish wool and linen, as well as the huge gold Celtic brooches, enough to filch them off the shoulders of dead Irish nobility. They milled around, talking, planning, calling each other 'my lord' of this or that Leinster cantred, discussing the advisability of their own marriages to Irish heiresses.

More and more of them arrived, to be joined by flustered Irish bishops whom Strongbow had summoned to his wedding. He was packing the cathedral with as many dignitaries as possible so that nobody could say he had been married to this heiress improperly.

The monastic community looked at the Normans and the bishops with contempt. Even if the bride was willing, and it was known that she was not, didn't the fool Strongbow know that a woman could bring him nothing?

Brother Pinginn, who had been praying next to Finn, sudddenly said, 'Now there's a thing.'

'What?' Finn was irritable with nerves. She and the nuns were still herded with the monks. If, against custom, they were kept together during the ceremony, and out of the Lady Chapel, there would be no escape for anybody.

'I've had a revelation.' The little man tugged at her sleeve in excitement. 'A real one. God has just showed me that women will win after all.'

She buried her head in her hands.

'They will, Finn. It's just a matter of taking the long view, God's view. All these men, they'll marry and Irishwomen will bring up their children and Ireland, female Ireland, will absorb them. Gradually they'll speak Irish, or their children will, and think Irish and copy Irish customs and it'll be lovely because after a time, quite a long time, you won't be able to tell the difference. That's how women win. That's how God wins.'

'For Christ's sake, shut up,' snapped Finn. They were among the last words she spoke to him and she regretted them for the rest of her life. She sat up. 'Hell, if they separate the men and the women, you'll be trapped in here. Get into the Lady Chapel quick, and get out.'

There was such a crowd by now that, small as he was, Pinginn was able to scurry into the chapel unnoticed. He disappeared into the shadows.

From somewhere Strongbow had found trumpeters. Not very good trumpeters, more used to sounding a battle charge than a fanfare, but they produced a discord which turned all heads towards the great, shattered doors. Strongbow entered, flanked by Le Gros and De Cogan, both of them taller than he was which may have been why he still had his helmet on. It gave him a warrior status which was lost when he took it off and revealed his bald head. His eyes went round the congregation, counting.

Murchadh came in behind him, disliking the whole business but, as ever, making sure it was properly conducted. He clucked when he saw that men and women were mingled together and hissed instructions to some Hy Kinsella. To her relief, Finn and the nuns were directed to the Lady Chapel. They were joined by some of Dermot's female relatives. Finn placed herself near the rail at the front, next to the Mother Superior of St. Mary's. 'God help me. If I ever disbelieved, forgive me and help me now.'

The chatter in the cathedral rose to fever pitch. Choir monks, adjusting their surplices, dithered at the altar steps. Were they supposed to sing and, if so, what? There was a shriek from the chancel and a dead body flopped forward onto a choir stall from under the curtain which had hidden it. The sacristan who had dislodged it by opening a cupboard flapped his hands in horror and indecision. Murchadh clucked again and, striding the chancel steps, picked the corpse up, put it in the sacristan's cupboard and shut the door.

Again the trumpets set everybody's teeth on edge, but now quiet damped down the echoing tumult of the cathedral as outside the rain was putting out the Dublin fire. Dermot stood in the entrance.

A church, candles, armed men, the circumstances in which she had last seen his face were around her now. Bracing herself to look at it, Finn had gripped the chapel rail. Slowly she let it go. She had been expecting to remember terror but there was nothing in the figure whose legs were jerking it towards the nave to bounce it back at her; the metamorphosis, her own and his, was too great. The Abbess of Kildare had died long ago and so had the man who'd had her raped.

This wasn't him. This was a corpse as dead as the poor thing in the chancel cupboard even if this one was walking; its eyes as lifeless and its face more advanced in putrefaction. Automatically people drew back as it passed them.

Finn felt no pity; if she had contributed anything at all to the destruction of that creature there she was glad, but there was no point left in hating a man who was being so obliging as to be consumed by his own evil. It was just a disaster for the girl who walked beside him that it wasn't happening quicker.

Somebody had dressed Aoife in white and gold. Somebody had piled her fair hair into a convoluted shape on her head and somebody had stuck flowers into her hand, but they had done so without any co-operation from Aoife. Unresisting, she was permitting this thing to happen to her because she couldn't do anything else, but she had withdrawn so far into herself that in her way she, too, looked dead, as if the rest of her life were a waiting period until, in the same dress and with the same flowers, they put her in her coffin.

For that moment Finn forgot why she was there, not even seeing her daughter and Dervorgilla as they walked behind the girl being buried alive. She looked around, amazed, at the people who were going along with this travesty by adding their own pretence to it. 'Help her,' she said, 'Help her.' But just as she had onced asked for help in a church and received none, there was none for this girl now. Beside her, the Mother Superior of St. Mary's might have turned into rock.

At least Strongbow wasn't pretending. He waited in the centre of the nave for Aoife's approach with less emotion than a housewife calculating the contents of her larder. Up in the choir the monks began a hymn. Aoife suddenly turned round and looked at her sisters, but a guard of the Hy Kinsella moved round them. Imprisoning them in a lobster-pot of their own bodies they walked the two girls towards the Lady Chapel and, pushing them into the crowd of women, took up position in front of them.

Strongbow put out his arm to beckon Aoife forward and Dermot put a hand on Aoife's arm to urge her towards him. It was the colour of fungus against the white cloth. Aoife kept staring after her sisters though the Hy Kinsella blocked them from her view. Finn put up her hand. Aoife's eyes shifted towards the movement, and recognition came into her face. Finn's hand made the sign of the cross, then she gave the signal which Scathagh had taught them to use when the hags needed a diversion.

Beauty returned to Aoife for a moment as she smiled at Finn. Then she threw back her head and screamed.

The choir stopped, its singers' mouth still open in chant. The congregation, which had turned its head to watch Aoife come up the aisle, stayed in that position. Strongbow's hand remained outstretched. It was as if a disastrous drop in temperature had frozen everybody into ice figures, except Aoife who kept on screaming. Even Finn couldn't move for a second, then she pushed her way to Slaney and Dervorgilla. 'It's time to go.'

They didn't hear her, they could only hear Aoife. Finn took her daughter by her shoulders and shook her. Nobody noticed; she could have gone out into the nave and danced and nobody would have noticed. 'You've got to come with me. Listen to her. Listen to what she's saying.

Aoife's screams were formulating words. 'Go.I.Don't.Need. You.Go.'

Slaney sobbed. She took Dervorgilla's hand and Finn took hold of hers and together they pushed their way through to the back of the Lady Chapel. Nuns stood on tiptoe as they got in the way of their view, so that they could see what was happening in the nave. Aoife was still screaming but as her sisters disappeared through the door in the wall, she turned the scream into an ululation of triumph.

Outside there was rain and grass, a wall and Brother Pinginn. They hauled each other up, hardly aware they were doing it. Aoife's voice clanged through their heads. Vaguely Finn noticed it was still light; she'd hoped it was night by now. They'd stand a better chance.

Lief had found only four horses. In the hope that she'd look the part of a military escort Tailltin had put on a leather hauberk and wore a helmet, but her slightness compared with Lief robbed them both of conviction; one too small, the other too big. Finn and Slaney got up on the bigger of the two spare horses and Pinginn, oohing with nerves, was pushed into the saddle of the other. Dervorgilla steed-leapt up behind him and held on.

'Trot,' commanded Lief. 'Not walk, not canter, trot. More official.'

The lane was cobbled and the shod hooves stuck like hammers. Some soldiers who were lounging on the cathedral wall jumped down in front of them. 'Give us one of the girls, mate. You got two spares.' They were drunk. One of them put his hand on his hip and minced. 'I'll have the fairy.' They made a grab at Finn's bridle, but she put her horse at them and knocked them out of the way so that they rolled on the cobbles, shouting abuse. As they trotted away Finn glanced at the grey bulk of the cathedral. How long had they got before somebody, Dermot, Murchadh, noticed the girls were gone?

Lief paused at the end of the lane; left, Fishamble Street went past the fish market and down to the wharves, right, it followed the wall of the cathedral. They went left and turned into the market heading for Dames Gate. They had to slow to a walk because of the rubble which

littered nearly every yard of ground. 'There'll be a curfew,' called Tailltin. They would lock the gates.

They passed more soldiers staggering from looted liquor. In the aftermath of capturing the city, they were free to take what they could; conquerors' perks. Some of them had boxes under their arms with furs and dresses thrown across their shoulders. Dazed from killing and rape, they didn't question the odd cavalcade that passed them, though frequently they stopped it, offering comradely wine to Lief and Tailltin, grabbing the girls' skirts. It was getting darker by the minute. 'They'll lock the gates, they'll lock the gates,' Finn whispered to herself.

In the absence of orders, the army was disorderly; so it was the cavalcade's back luck to come across one of the few men in Dublin who had been given a command and insisted on carrying it out. He was the soldier in charge of the Dames Gate guard. 'Can't come through,' he said.

'Open up, mate,' said Lief. 'Got to escort these people to Mary's Abbey. Orders of Earl Raymond.'

The sergeant picked his teeth. 'Gate's closed. Orders of Earl Miles.' He looked closer. 'Who are they, anyway?'

Lief wheeled his horse left and trotted off into the maze of devastation downhill, heading for the river. The others followed. Behind them the soldier called out the guard.

Following the city wall, making detours past collapsed buildings, they were heading north and west when all the time the only safety lay east. They'll close the gates. They'll be after us by now.

They had got so used to having smoke in their nostrils that the smell of the river was like the scent of home, but it came from over the wall. St. Tulloch's Lane was on their left; any moment they'd be at Fish Slip, the southern exit to the wharves. There were flares ahead of them and shapes moving.

The steep slope of Fish Slip had been lined with drinking taverns. Most of them had survived the fire and now they had attracted large numbers of Strongbow's common soldiery. It had never been a salubrious area; tonight it was a scene from hell. At least three landlords were hanging by the neck from their own eaves like pub signs; swinging and dripping in the rain. The others were sensibly dispensing free drink as fast as they could hand it over to the crowd of soldiers, camp followers and city prostitutes who crammed the bars, sat in the windows and overflowed into the road to watch carts carrying corpses go by down to the river. The Dublin dead were being thrown into the Liffey.

Survivors ran alongside the carts searching for their relatives while watching Normans shouted joking encouragement. Every so often one of the soldiers would see a woman he fancied and rushed into the road to take her, struggling and shrieking, into an alley. A very young girl was being raped in front of one of the inns while a queue of men stood by waiting their turn.

Lief slowed to a walk, keeping his horse's head well up, smiling, returning the jovial obscenities of the crowd as, slowly, the cavalcade threaded its way down the slip. They were halfway down, three quarters. They had an unobstructed view through an archway to the river. The open gate to the quay was blocked with carts. Beyond it each pony was being taken out of its shafts and the contents of its cart tipped over the edge of the wharf. More soldiers, more torches lighting green-white corpses as they splashed into the water and bobbed.

Lief's teeth showed under his helmet. 'Get the bloody carts out the way,' he shouted amiably to the soldier in charge. He'd misjudged it. Slowly the man waved one of the carts through, leaving a small gap, but he stood in it, looking up at Lief. He had a sword in his hand and he was fed up. 'Think I like this?'

Lief put his hands up, conciliating. 'Sorry, mate.' But the soldier still blocked the way: 'Well I don't.' He was drunk, but not enough. 'I don't like you, come to that.' He peered. 'You look like one of those fucking Vikings from Waterford. Didn't like them either.'

From up the hill behind them the great bell of the cathedral began to clang. Around them men laughed. 'That's old Strongbow getting his end away.' But the soldier in the gap said, 'It's not. It's the alarm. Got to shut the gates on the alarm. Orders.' He turned to his detail. 'Shut the gates.'

Lief's mailed boot landed under the man's chin and broke his neck. 'Get through.' They put their horses at the gap and were through. Behind them somebody shouted, 'Bastards. Mount up. Get them.'

The wharf was crowded with carts, men and equipment. They turned right and galloped through, kicking at baskets, heads, everything in their way. Finn knew they wouldn't make it. She got the dagger from her boot and slashed at a face. Slaney kicked out at another. They were at the end of the wharf, it was clearer here, but darker. They had to follow the narrow ledge of a walkway right round, back the way they had come on the other side of the wall to Dames Bridge. There was a howl of recognition from the guards at Dames Gate, hooves clattering, orders to stop. A sentry on the bridge leapt into the water to get out of their way as they charged across it.

The blessed open space of Hogges Green was around them, but there were horses pounding behind. Finn tightened her grip on Slaney's waist and looked back, there were a dozen torches at least flickering as they were galloped through the rain.

'Where's the boat?'

'Opposite the convent.'

She wouldn't know the tree she'd tied it to; in this murk all trees looked alike. The rain had turned the ground to marsh and their horses were slowing in the mud. Christ, Christ, where was the river? The tide was leaving it. It was in channels with wide stretches of slit between. They couldn't make it.

She saw Lief wheel between branches, dismount and fumble at a painter she had tied to a trunk in another life. There was a vast expanse of mud between them and flowing water. It gleamed in the wet. They couldn't make it. They threw themselves off the horses and dragged at the boat, silt sucking their feet down into itself so that each step was a jerk of the knee and they moved like sleepy puppets. There'd been nightmares when she ran and ran on the spot like this as horror advanced at her back. Slaney slipped. Finn hauled her up. The boat was heavy but it glissaded over the silt as they pulled. Tailltin had an arrow sticking out of her leather arm and there was a spear rattling between the thwarts of the *curragh*.

She heard somebody, Pinginn, say crossly: 'Oh, this is hopeless. I love you, Finn,' and he'd gone. She had no breath to call him back. She would kill him when she got hold of him. They were splashing through water, they were up to their waists and the boat was floating. She pushed Slaney so hard that the girl went headlong into the *curragh*. Tailltin was in, and Dervorgilla. She was in and they were low in the water. Lief? She saw him swimming beside her, one hand pushing the boat. 'Row.'

Somebody else rowed. She looked back and saw Pinginn, a small crab, wading towards the torches where men stood still, not pursuing, not now if the boat got away as long as they had somebody to kill. She heard his voice, artificial, pretending to be brave. 'Now don't be naughty, boys,' before they closed in and held the torches high so that they could see what they were doing. 'Where are you?' she was shouting, 'Where's God?' She heard Lief say something important but it didn't register then. The scene on the mudflats got smaller and smaller as they pulled away from it. It had activity and from it came the scream of a hare being torn to bits. It followed them out onto the peace of the Liffey where dead bodies floated quietly alongside them.

'I am very tired,' said Finn to herself. 'Very tired.' There were things to be done and the shape of the Thingmount was travelling by her in the darkness. Ahead the tower of her inn stuck up against the clouds like an admonition. 'Well,' said Finn. She took a deep breath. Slaney and Dervorgilla were doing the rowing. She leaned out towards Tailltin's helmet and tapped it. 'You promised now,' she said and saw Tailltin's hands grip hard onto Lief's wrist. Finn cupped her own hands round Slaney's face. 'That's my girl,' she said, gently, 'I must go home,' and slithered overboard.

She heard Lief splashing and crying, and Tailltin shouting at him. Don't let him come after me; he can get into the boat now. The current took her away from them towards the Stein where it would push her out into the river again and then back, with luck, into the undercroft cave, but it didn't matter if it did or it didn't. Her habit weighed her down and it wasn't nearly as nice swimming here as in Lough Mask with Pilgrim, too many difficulties. Somebody tapped her on the shoulder and the corpse of a young man bumped against her. She pushed it away though she was quite polite about it. 'I'm afraid I can't stop.'

Elfwida and Perse waiting by the trapdoor saw another body float into the cave – there had been several – but this one talked gently to itself as it sank and rolled in the last stages of drowning. They hauled it in.

Chapter Fifteen

Alarmed by the glow of fire in the distance, and much too late, Ruairi O'Conor moved his ponderous army to Dublin. Even then he ringed it at a distance out of range of the enemy's longbows for which the Irish had learned respect. They'd also learned not to face a Norman cavalry carge so they kept clear of the flat land around the city, like Hogges and Stephen's Green in the east, and the Poddle marsh and the Horse-market to the south and west. Nevertheless with the numbers at his disposal O'Conor was able to make his siege tight enough to stop any living thing bigger than a squirrel crossing its lines. That night he sent his herald to arrange a meeting.

Since he didn't trust Dermot and Dermot didn't trust anybody, the two sides met at the top of Lazy Hill, near the leper house, from which both contingents could see the other's forces and, in case of treachery, retire easily back to their own.

Glimmering with jewellery and fine linen, the Irish outshone the Normans in their war-stained mail, although even they did not lower the tone as much as the lepers who had refused evacuation, knowing that they were sacrosanct, and leaned out of their windows jeering with even-handed animosity at both sides.

At first the O'Conor directed his remarks to Dermot. He still thought of Strongbow and the other Normans as transient mercenaries.

'Contrary to the terms of our treaty,' he said, 'you have invited a host of foreigners into this island. So long as you confined your operations within your ancient kingdom of Leinster we bore it patiently, but now you have passed the limits assigned and insolently crossed even your hereditary boundaries. Either you restrain yourself and your foreign troops, or I shall certainly send to you the decapitated head of your own son.'

An interpreter murmured a translation to the Normans. It all seemd very procedural, nothing to do with life and death. A soft, damp breeze moved the bannerets as courteously as the words had been uttered. Those standing beside Dermot shifted upwind; he was beginning to smell awful.

'These are my ancestral lands.' Dermot's voice was cracked and seemed to be laughing. The arm he swept around at the river, the forests, at Ireland, shook like his nodding head. There was a gold bracelet on it in the shape of a snake. 'I am the rightful *Ard-Ri* of this land. I am High King.'

Ruairi raised his eyebrows. Then he gestured to the herald in turn who gestured down to the Irish tents. Out of them were pushed two young men with their arms tied behind them. 'Do you recognise them, Mac Murrough? Your son? Your grandson?' Ruairi asked the question because there was doubt whether Dermot did; he peered down the hill briefly and then looked beyond it.

'They are my hostages, Mac Murrough,' insisted Ruairi O'Conor, 'You gave them. You broke our treaty and it is my right to kill them.'

'How beautiful Tara is,' said Dermot.

Helplessly, the O'Conor said, 'He thinks he really is High King.'

'He isn't.' Strongbow stepped forward. 'But I am. I inherit Ireland through his daughter whom I have married.'

The O'Conor was amused. 'You own nothing of Ireland, not even the bits of coast you presently occupy. Dermot should have told you, there is no inheritance through the female line in Irish law.'

'There is no Irish law,' said Strongbow.

Perhaps at that point full realisation came to Ruairi O'Conor, perhaps not, but from then on he addressed himself to the Norman.

Raymond Le Gros stopped listening; it didn't matter what was said anyway; he and the others would possess Ireland sooner or later. He liked Ireland. He liked the way the Irish dressed and the way they spoke and the ridiculous way they thought, their funny music, even the bloody weather. He didn't mind killing them, but he liked a rest between doing it. The two hostages down there were about his own age: they probably wanted to live as much as he did; if it was up to him, he'd let them. He switched his attention back. The O'Conor tribesman was getting ruffled. He was saying, 'Why should I talk terms? A nestling has more ground for negotiation than you, who are outnumbered twenty to one. If you won't go, I shall starve you out.'

'You can try,' said Strongbow.

Ruairi O'Conor was a kind man, but he was a traditionalist.

Later that night two heavy leather-wrapped balls were thrown across No Man's Land to Le Gros' men who were holding the lines along Lazy Hill. 'What the hell are they playing at?' said Captain Jacques, picking them up. 'Oh, Christ.' He took the heads of Dermot's son and grandson down to his commander at the inn.

The sight of them made Raymond cross. 'Bloody unnecessary,' he said. 'What's the point of revenge on a man who doesn't count any more? Barbaric bloody carry-on.'

344

He was already in a temper from having found, on retrieving his staff from the undercroft, that one of them was missing. 'And it was the scribe, the only bloody useful one among 'em,' he complained to Captain Jacques.

'Where'd he go?'

'God knows. I slapped the rest about a bit, especially the miller, but they wouldn't say. There was a bloody chute into the river down there all the time, hidden under the wine. He got out that way, little bastard, hope he drowned. The rest were too scared to follow him. Anyway, the older woman's ill. Get her over to the mill. I'm not having the bloody plague in my inn.'

'She'll get away.'

Raymond looked at his second-in-command and asked God to give him patience. 'Where's she going to go? Across the lines? If O'Conor's got any sense, which I doubt, he'll shoot anything that tries to get through his lines. Friend or foe. To encourage the others. He's going to starve us, you stupid sod. He'll want every mouth to stay inside the perimeter and eat up our food. That's what he'll do if he knows anything about war. That's what I'd do. That's what Fitzempress did at Verneuil.' He stopped short. It had been a nasty moment on that hilltop when Strongbow had revealed his hand. It didn't matter about the Irish, but if Fitzempress ever learned that one of his earls was making himself king of a neighbouring country . . .

Raymond Le Gros crossed himself. The only comfort was that nobody was going to be able to get out of Dublin and tell him.

Brother Pinginn and Aoife held each other's hands and danced, laughing and balancing stars on their noses. Finn was so pleased to see them happy she tried to clap her hands, but the music wasn't worthy of the brave and beautiful dance; the harp played the wrong notes while the drum kept to a different time. She complained to the band. 'Get Niall of the Poems,' she said, 'He'll play the right tune. He comes from Lough Mask.'

'Who's Niall of the Poems?' asked somebody.

'She's raving, poor lamb,' said somebody else.

Finn began the effort of explaining and then gave up as the drum beat her back into unconsciousness. It was still hammering away when she woke up again but this time it turned into the grinding stones of Molling's mill. The beams over her head were vibrating with the working of the huge mechanism above, and there was a white, floury spider's web spun into a corner while pervading everything was the not-unpleasant smell of oats. Finn's eyes rested on the web because they were too tired to move anywhere else. Brother Pinginn was dead, Aoife buried alive. Slaney, Lief, Tailltin, Dervorgilla . . .? Her lips tried to move. 'Slaney.'

Blat's face, or was it Perse's, came between her and the web. 'You're ever so much better.' Some broth was spooned into her mouth. Pinginn was dead. The joyful dance had been a fiction; odd that her mind couldn't be rid of the happiness it gave her. Anyway, there was nothing she could do any more. She went back to sleep.

Elfwida took up quarters at the mill to help Perse run it, to nurse Finn and because the inn had been invaded by women whom Raymond Le Gros's men had brought with them to Ireland or picked up since.

'Where's Molling?' Finn asked when she was able to sit up and take notice. Perse's plain face became plainer as tears ran down her cheeks. 'He was a good husband,' she said, 'He's up there.'

'Where?' Perse was pointing up Lazy Hill which was just visible through the mill window. It looked as it had always looked, its long slope up to the leper hospital an elegant sweep against the late autumn sky. 'There.' There was a lump on the skyline like a low bush.

'They won't fetch him in, poor thing,' said Perse wiping her eyes. 'Persingly, I think the dead ought to be buried, especially if they were good husbands.'

Finn looked at Elfwida for elucidation. 'He ran,' said Elfwida, grimacing. Unnerved, and certain that the Normans would kill him, Molling had made a break for the Irish lines, but as he'd pelted, shouting, over the hill horizon a slingshot at his head, from the very force he was trying to reach, had killed him – at least, he had fallen and not moved since; a decomposing monument to the fact that Ruairi O'Conor was at last learning the rules of total warfare. Even by night it was too dangerous to bring the body in because marauding Irish kept making incursions through the lines.

Finn looked at Perse as she stood at the window grieving for a man who had been prepared to desert her, and saw what, if she hadn't been so preoccupied, she should have seen some months before. 'Oh Perse, you're pregnant.'

Perse cheered up. 'Good, isn't it?' Suddenly the need to protect the body which was incubating new life in all this horror overwhelmed Finn. She could have killed Molling, she could have killed the men who killed him, and the men who, by their invasion, had disrupted the life in which he had been confident. 'You shouldn't be hauling those sacks about.'

Perse shrugged. 'Got to. Anyway, there won't be anything left to mill soon.' Large as the besieging ring round Dublin was, it had been placed so all open ground was within range of Irish fire. Most of the herds of cattle, sheep and pigs which had roamed Hogges Green were still on it, lying on their sides, killed by spears or slingshot from the north shore and the southern lines. Sorties by Norman soldiers, even those wearing mail, to bring in the carcases for food, had proved disastrous and left more than a few of them dead among the dead animals. Being under the shelter of the hill, the Swan still retained some of its livestock, 'but they're being eaten like there's no tomorrow,' said Elfwida, 'those camp women have got no idea about rationing. And they've stolen everything in the mill except the unground corn. I don't know what we're going to eat.'

Supply ships from Wexford had tried to row up the Liffey by night, but had encountered a boom of boats, each one containing armed men, stretching across it and had been sunk. Crossly, Finn said, 'A fine time for the O'Conor to become efficient.'

It was as if her pneumonia had provided a defensive embankment between what had happened in Dublin and this bit of the present. Her very weakness had robbed her of the ability to experience the grief that waited on the far side of it in ambush. She kept her mind away from it, from what might have happened to Slaney and the others, and concentrated on Now, narrowing her responsibility to what she could cope with. If it hadn't been for Perse's baby she might have clambered back over the embankment; as it was the greatest emotion she felt was irritation at the mess they were all in.

Her legs ached when she did it but that night, daring Irishmen and Normans alike, she walked from the mill, over the Stein bridge and into her inn. It was very cold and everything was still.

The Swan was a mess. There were no women about – Le Gros had sent them back into the city by night so that they could eat up Strongbow's provisions, not his – but during their occupancy they certainly hadn't killed themselves with housework. There were also fewer soldiers in it, since a heavy guard was needed along the line of Lazy Hill, but those that lay around asleep had been drinking; there was a pool of vomit on the floor. It was a wonder the place hadn't burned down, each man seemed to have built his own fire on the floor on which to cook his own individual meal. There was still plenty of peat stacked at the back door, but they had smashed up most of her benches and one of her tables – her lovely oak, nobles' table – for firewood. Dirty pots were piled high in the sink of the kitchen which looked as if it had been sprayed with grease. There were no hams hanging from the beams, though the bunches of herbs were still there, and the flour bins were empty. No geese, no hens made any sound in the orchard. There was one milch cow left in the byre but the pigsty was unoccupied.

Finn forgot the pain in her legs. She stalked through her inn and up into the tower. Le Gros was sitting gloomily by a brazier which was burning the remains of one of her writing boards, nursing a cup of wine.

'What have you done with my bloody inn?' Finn shouted at him.

He jumped. 'This is my command post, madam, kindly leave it.' The wine had befuddled him; for a moment he didn't recognise her.

'I'll give you command post,' yelled Finn; fury had made her careless, 'You'll be in command of sod all if you go on like this. You won't have anything to eat; what's worse my women won't have anything to eat and one of them's having a baby and that's a bloody sight more important than your bloody war. Now get up off your fat arse and let's get things organised.'

It came to le Gros that he was being berated in Norman French and, moreover, by a personage, woman or not, who knew her own mind. It gave her the advantage. She had caught him during one of the few periods of his life when he was at a loss. Raymond Le Gros was good at war and good at leisure, but he had never until now had to live through a period which was neither. Sieges imposed great anxiety and great boredom on the besieged, a combination which sent some men mad and others into melancholy. In Le Gros' case it had induced a physical and mental lethargy made deeper by the knowledge that his mercenaries were drifting into indiscipline and that he ought at least to be doing something about the food situation, but wasn't sure what. He was no housekeeper; he wasn't a fool either.

'What do you suggest?' he asked.

The former kitcheness told him. At length. She took him down to the undercroft and counted what was left of the provisions she had laid in before the occupation. The kosher wine barrel was empty and had been pushed aside from the trapdoor. The Aquitanian vat was still a quarter full. 'And you make sure it stays there. For medicinal purposes,' Finn snapped.

Le Gros followed her into the inn where she pointed out each atrocity while he listened. She reminded him of the Norman nurse, a woman of spirit, who had brought something like order into the draughty, lax, Welsh castles where he and his Geraldine cousins had careered through their childhood. His men woke up to find their commander being commanded by an angry Irish skivvy, but Le Gros was unperturbed. 'Hear that?' he said to them, 'One communal meal a day from now on. There'll be a guard on all stores and this lady will be in charge of issuing and cooking them. Hear that, Jacques?'

'And a guard at the mill,' snapped Finn, 'I'm not having them take that flour when they feel like it.'

'And a guard at the mill, Jacques,' said Le Gros.

'Nobody slaughters that cow out there, either,' said Finn.

Le Gros sighed. 'For the moment nobody slaughters the cow. The lady Perse is having a baby and apparently that is more important than our war.'

'We'll move back into the inn here,' said Finn, 'but I'm not having that baby born among a lot of soldiers. We'll sleep in the middle tower room.'

Captain Jacques said: 'There's the trapdoor to the river, my lord. Supposing they get out?'

'Where to?' Finn stamped her foot. 'There's no boat. And from here on in at least one man will be sitting over the trap door day and night catching fish. Fish is about all we'll have to eat.'

'Fish and pigeons,' nodded Le Gros.

'And no more . . .' Finn stopped. 'What pigeons?'

'The occasional pigeon drops in to the loft up there,' said Le Gros, 'Only the other day . . .'

'Did it have something tied to its leg?'

'Did it, Jacques?'

'I think it did, my lord.'

She made them search for it and searched herself, kicking recumbent men out of her way, ruffling through the dirty sawdust of the floor. Eventually, one of the soldiers remembered he'd picked up a bit of leather and kept it, never knowing when he'd need a patch for his jerkin. 'This it?'

She tried to snatch it, but Le Gros got there first; he wasn't as intimidated as all that. Smoothed out, there was nothing of strategic importance on the leather, just a picture somebody had scrawled on it. 'Not very good,' he said, 'Four birds, swans from the look of 'em, landing on a lake.' He looked up. 'Mean anything?' Good God, he thought, she's beautiful.

The relief of knowing that Lief, Tailltin, Dervorgilla and Slaney had reached Lough Mask made Finn better; not well – she needed good food and rest for that – but better. She transferred herself, Perse and the Elf to the inn and began reorganising the situation there with an irritable efficiency that wrong-footed the soldiers into obeying her. It was illogical, she knew it was illogical, to be assisting men she had spent her strength opposing, who had destroyed her city and massacred its inhabitants. But her own side was effectually just as much the enemy now as the Normans, and she was rapidly narrowing down her loyalties to individuals. She had done what she could for Ireland; if she could create a niche in which a baby could be safely born then she had achieved something which dwarfed everything else, even saving the Pilgrim. Through Perse, God was giving her a second baby: she wasn't going to fail this one.

Oddly enough, her confederates in the enterprise were the Norman mercenary soldiers themselves. Perse was their favourite anyway and the sight of her growing waistline as she waddled through the inn domesticated it for them. She reminded them of home. They all ate their meal a day together in the commons parlour, even Le Gros – the men on duty had to do with oatcake – and little as it was, several of them slipped food off their own platters onto Perse's. 'Get it down you, Perse, you're eating for two.' Dai from Caerleon and Raoul, a Fleming from Ghent, made a cradle for when the baby was born out of slats from the empty pigeon loft. Robert the Breton ran a book on whether it would be a boy or a girl and the colour of its hair. The Scotsman Macwilliam got a punch in the mouth from Captain Jacques for his bad joke in suggesting that when the baby was born they should eat it.

Gradually the became comrades in adversity, even Finn, whom the men had disliked as 'too stuck up' at first, even Elfwida, who'd been a sex object – they were all becoming too weary to bother about sex. Finn relaxed. At the moment they were just hungry; if the sieges went on they would be starving and unpredictable, it would be as well that by then they were all bonded in camaraderie.

Oddest of all was the growing liking between Le Gros and herself. Raymond had been cheered by the way she'd taken at least one problem off his shoulders, and called her 'Quartermaster', but he still had plenty of others and in the evenings he'd join her by the fire in the kitchen – she wouldn't allow one anywhere else but the Common Parlour in order to save fuel – to discuss them. The fact that she was no threat, being a woman, yet obviously of his own class, while remote from Norman politics, encouraged his confidences, especially as she was in no position to repeat them.

'I ought to be in the city,' he'd grumble, 'in the Castle with Strongbow. They'll all be plotting and scheming, putting in their bids for lands, and I'll be left out.'

'De Cogan's in an outpost as well,' she pointed out, 'and you can't get any lands, any of you. You're bottled up.'

'Temporarily, temporarily. It's just a matter of waiting until the Irish slacken their guard; they will eventually, you know.'

She was silent. She was afraid they would. The Irish weren't used to long campaigns, especially sieges.

'Who are you, Finn?' he asked one night, 'You're not Irish.'

'I am. But I was brought up at Fontevrault.'

'A nun? What made you leave it? Man trouble?'

She found herself smiling. That just about summed it up. She steered him away to a subject which interested him more, his career: 'Who are you going to marry?'

He stretched. 'I'd thought of one of Dermot's daughters, which would have given me an Irish connection and therefore more land. He was offering them round like playing cards at one time. However, they've disappeared. At the moment I've got my eye on Strongbow's sister, but that's the trouble with being stuck out here – Miles de Cogan might get her.'

'Is she worth getting?'

'Good Lord, woman. With Strongbow owning Ireland? I'll say she will be.'

'He doesn't own it yet.'

'He will. That's if Fitzempress doesn't interfere.'

His fear of Fitzempress, which he made no attempt to hide, cropped up constantly in his conversation. As far as Raymond Le Gros was concerned Ireland was a piece of cake to be carved up between its invaders if, if, if, they could only do it and become established before Fitzempress tried to take it away from them. She saw an opening: 'I heard Strongbow's got one of Fitzempress' spies locked up in Dublin Castle.'

Le Gros turned on her. 'How the hell do you know that?'

'Gossip.'

'You worry me sometimes, Finn. As a matter of fact it's true, the poor bastard. My Lord Llanthony, brilliant chap, knew him in Aquitaine. Strongbow's taking a risk keeping him a prisoner – Fitzempress wouldn't like it if he knew. But if he lets John go, John'll bring Fitzempress whistling over here so fast our feet will be dangling from the gallows before we know they've left the ground. Dear God, I wouldn't like to be a prisoner in Dublin just now; we think we're on short commons here, but it must be hell in the city. Still, I don't suppose Strongbow'll let him die. Might need him as a bargaining counter if the worst comes to the worst.'

In a succession of bad winters, the one of 1170-71 was the worst the eastern half of Ireland had ever known; refugees from the war zones who imposed themselves on relatives in the safety of the mountains were welcomed under the sacred laws of Irish hospitality, but providing food for two families instead of one meant a shortage for both which the weak, very young and very old did not survive. There was no snow at first, just a griping cold that manufactured complicated and beautiful crystals on the outlines of every blade of grass, every twig. Travellers unwary enough, or desperate enough, to venture any distance in it were frozen in mid-stride so that they were later found lying with a knee raised in frantic effort to elude the elemental robber which had taken their life. Small rivers froze.

The Irish besiegers of Dublin piled more skins over their cosy tents, built fires big enough to roast an ox and roasted oxen on them, flapping at the turning carcases with their cloaks so that the smell of cooking wafted towards the silent, starving city. The winter was their ally, a force even greater than their own thousands; nothing could withstand

351

it and them. They relaxed in the security of their confederation, and went hunting while they waited for the gates of Dublin to open and the Normans to come out, suing for peace.

And the gates did open. Twice. But the thin heralds who crossed the lines to speak to the O'Conor under flags of truce were not offering surrender, merely asking for safe conduct for two Irishmen who had business elsewhere. And O'Conor acceded to their requests.

The first figure to emerge was that of Dublin's Archbishop, Laurence O'Toole, on his way to Armagh where an assembly of Ireland's greatest bishops and clergy was waiting for him. It had finally impinged on the Irish Church's consciousness that the battle in the south-east was not just another, personal feud between the High King and a recalcitrant subject, but an invasion that could change the face of Ireland. The bishops were going to discuss it.

The second time the gates of Dublin opened, a small bunch of horsemen came out escorting a cart. Some sheepskins had been cobbled together to roof the man who was lying inside but it was open back and front and somewhat dirty. Behind it rode the superior of St. Mary's Abbey of Hogges Green. Occasionally she leaned forward to hiss sentences at the figure tucked up in the straw on the cart's floor.

Magnanimous as ever, the High King of Ireland rode around the siege lines to greet the cart at Rathfarnham. He was shocked. 'Jesus God, Abbess,' he said, 'Let the man die in peace.' After all was said and done, it was the greatness of Leinster lying on that straw.

She smiled up at him with a pleasure which made the crystalline day warm by contrast. 'Make way, O'Conor,' she said, 'Make way for Dermot on his road to hell.' She whispered again to the body in the cart and Ruairi saw it try to raise its black, gangrenous hands to its ears to shut out the things she was saying. He stood back and stared after the cart as it bumped and swayed over the iron-hard ruts of the road to Ferns.

Back in Dublin, Strongbow hadn't even bothered to watch it go.

Later an Irish chronicler recorded with satisfaction of May, 1171: 'Dermot Mac Murrough, king of Leinster, who had spread terror throughout Ireland, after putting the English in possession of the country, committing excessive evils against the Irish people and churches, died this year of an intolerable and uncommon disease. He became putrid while living, by the miracles of God. He died at Ferns without making a will, without penance, without the Eucharist and without Extreme Unction, as his evil deeds deserved.'

It's doubtful if the loving monks of Ferns refused absolution to their king. But nobody else cared whether they did or not; Dermot of Leinster had become irrelevant.

*　　*　　*

A long way away, at Bures in Normandy, it was snowing and bells rang out over muffled rooftops. In the castle where he was about to celebrate Christmas, another king received yet another despatch telling him of the latest piece of arrogance perpetrated by his archbishop who had now returned to his See in England by an agreement between them, which he had broken. The king fell down as he read it, and rolled around on the floor, biting the rushes, and he shrieked out words that out-rang the bells of the churches, that reverberated through the castle, through his future and for centuries after his death. They formed a question. 'Will nobody rid me of this turbulent priest?'

Four of his knights, who had their own grievances against Thomas Becket, slipped quietly away and rode for England to answer it.

Raymond Le Gros and his unofficial quartermaster stood together in the white, brittle orchard of the Swan inn and looked at the cow standing in the byre.

'She's got to go, Finn.'

'I know.'

'I'm sorry.'

'I know.'

Le Gros tightened his belt; it kept slipping. 'I mean, she'll die soon anyway with nothing to feed her on . . .'

'*I know*.' Finn fought down the exasperation which came easily. Perhaps, she thought, it's because there's no fat to absorb them that extreme emotions erupt and then die away like this. Within the space of an hour she could experience anger, deep grief, even spurious exhilaration. The next stage would be inertia and that would be the finish. She patted the cow's bony rump. 'You did us proud,' she told it.

Le Gros said, 'She can have a couple more days to fatten up on the last of the hay, then she must go.'

They turned away and walked slowly – they could do nothing very fast – towards the turnip pile, counting the twenty roots on it in case by some miracle they might have multiplied in the night.

'My guns keep bleeding.'

'So do mine.'

The Norman put his arm round her and dragged her out of the way as the branch of an apple tree, petrified by the cold, cracked off from the trunk and fell down, splintering as it hit the ground. The tiny sounding of a bell in the city had sent out a vibration which had been too much for it. They listened to its separate, slow rings, as if whoever pulled the bell rope was very tired.

'Good God,' said Raymond Le Gros, 'It's Christmas. May our sins be forgiven for the blood of the Saviour born to us this day.'

'Merry Christmas, Raymond.'

'Merry Christmas, Finn.' He still had his arm round her.

On the bitter air, wafting from over the hill, came the beautiful, warm smell of roasting oxen. Le Gros looked down at his quarter-master. 'You're bloody torturers, you Irish.'

He let her go and tightened his belt another notch. 'Well, better go and cheer the boys on the hill. Tell them Christmas will be late, but there'll be a Christmas feast. Will you get Gorm to see to the slaughter-ing?'

'I will.'

His breath steamed down at her. 'It won't be long now, Finn. The siege is getting slacker every day. I had no trouble getting to and from De Cogan's outpost yesterday. Well, a stone and an arrow or two, but they missed. Once we've got some meat in our bellies we can attack.'

She was irritated again. 'What do you want me to do? Wish you luck?'

But as he climbed the hill to his look-out posts, he heard her shout, 'Take care.'

Take care, take care, thought Finn. What a ridiculous thing to say to an enemy. That young fat man, who was fat no longer, puffing up the hill today could tomorrow be puffing down the other side of it in a charge at her people; he could kill her friends – there might be Partraige in that section, Nessa, Niall, Iogenán. But the thin fat young man wasn't the enemy any longer either. He was an uneducated, ambitious man, who was enduring hardship without complaint and with humour, who put himself on the same pitiful rations as his men, who tolerated her bossiness, who was allowing Perse's baby to grow into what looked like monstrous proportions in Perse's belly.

The ironies involved in living were nearly as wearing as the walk across the orchard; she had to lean against the kitchen door jamb to let the spots clear from her eyes. Elfwida was in the kitchen, with Perse.

'You're too thin,' Finn told her, still irritable. Like everybody else, Elf was giving Perse some of her ration.

'Look who's talking.'

'It's Christmas Day. Happy Christmas. Raymond's having the cow slaughtered soon.'

'Yum, yum,' said Perse. Unworried, she ate everything they gave her. She was like an enormous cuckoo being fed by exhuasted blue tits.

'Finn, it's Jacques,' said Elfwida, 'He wants me to marry him when this is all over.'

'When what's all over?' She recovered herself, she had been expecting it. 'I'm glad for you both.'

'It's not fraternising with the enemy is it, Finn? He's got a wife in

Normandy, but he likes Ireland, he wants to stay.' The girl always wanted reassurance.

'Become enamoured of Irish cuisine?' She leaned over and rubbed Elfwida's thin knees. 'There isn't any enemy, just organisations. Be happy. You deserve it.' She got up. 'I must go and speak to Gorm.'

'Ow,' said Perse, 'Got a pain in my tum. Ow.' She breathed in. 'It's gone now. Think it was indigestion?'

It was an unexpectedly terrible labour; somehow they'd all expected it to be as easy as a sow farrowing. It was dreadful to see Perse, who had ambled with such amiable indifference through the vicissitudes of her life, sharpened by the pain. Between the contractions and the untempered screams, she kneaded Finn's hand. 'I'm not going to die, am I?'

'You dare.'

But after twenty-four hours of agony for all of them, it was obvious that she was getting weaker. Finn put on her cloak while Elfwida, very pale, took her place at the bedside.

Le Gros was at the door. 'Where are you going?'

'I've got to get to the convent. There might be somebody there who can help her.'

'You're not. It's snowing and you'd be a target.'

She pushed him with all her strength. 'Get out of my way. I don't know what to do, I don't know what to do. They'll die, the two of them.'

For the first time to his knowledge she was showing vulnerability. He held her close and shouted down the steps over her head. 'Anybody know anything about babies?'

One of the men shouted back. 'Dai might. See what you can do, Dai.'

Dai was small, middled-aged, agricultural, competent, comforting. 'Know more about cows, really. Put your hand in and turn; I suppose it's the same isn't it?'

She studied his hands. 'Not until you've washed it isn't.' She was better with something to do and she scrubbed his hands until they were raw, then turned back the covers to expose the massive mound of white, contracting flesh. He spat on his palms. 'Right now. Hang on, girl.'

Finn and Elf held Perse's arms as she screamed. Dai's head nestled against her thigh and he looked towards them with unseeing eyes. 'Feels like a breach to me.'

The candles round the bed flickered in the draught that came down the steps from the upper room where snow was blowing in through the eastern light. I know I have worried you too much, prayed Finn, but I never will again. Intervene just this once. It is the season for it. Let just one lovely thing happen on this special night.

'Turn, you little bugger now,' said Dai.

'It's all right, Perse.' Turn, you little bugger. Please God, just one lovely thing.

'Now then,' said Dai.

He had a small triangle of a nose which was firm to the touch of her lips. She carried him out onto the steps of the parlour. 'Perse's compliments to you all and she's going to call him Raymond or Dai, probably both. And oh, boys, Merry Christmas.' She sat down and wept into the baby's shawl while they crowded round her and sent word to the guards up on the hill.

She was too exhausted to sleep and she clambered up the far staircase to the pigeon loft where Gorm lived to tell him the news. Then she sat down beside him, her knees up to her chin, and looked out at the snow, hypnotically white and whirling against the dark grey of the sky. 'Poor Molling,' she said. It was a time to be alone, and up here was as alone as you could be; Gorm never talked.

He spoke now: 'Pigeon.' He showed it to her. It had come in that morning. He'd already wrung its neck and begun to pluck it. 'For Perse.' In his other hand was the membrane it had carried in its leather pouch, black with writing. 'Muirna.'

With the bad light and her eyesight failing from starvation, it took a long time to decipher the cramped, angry scrawl of Muirna's scribe and then she sat and looked out of the gable at the sky for even longer. When the hand of God opened, it opened with a vengeance. Have mercy on us all. But it could save the Pilgrim.

'Gorm, go and slaughter that cow.' She tucked the membrane in her sleeve, and went downstairs, the pigeon dangling from her hand.

Like herself, the men were too hungry and too exhausted to sleep. Their eyes went to the pigeon. 'Feast tomorrow,' she told them, 'We're slaughtering the cow.'

It was today they needed food. Their eyes were deep-sunk and there were starvation sores round their mouths. Dai said, 'Just what a nursing mother needs, pigeon pie.' The others nodded.

They had sacked and raped Dublin. There might be men in this room who had torn Pinginn to bits. If she hadn't been so bloody tired, she would railed against the torture of human complications; as it was, she was crying again.

She and Elfwida fed the Magi in the common parlour; beef a bit tough, but who cared, dumplings a bit suety – she'd never been a hand at dumplings – but they said they were wonderful, turnips a bit

356

stringy, but who cared, who cared. They heaped their own plates and hers. 'Who's a clever little quartermaster, then?'

Raymond said, 'Medicinal purposes?'

'Definitely.'

Toasting Dai-Raymond, Perse, all mothers, God, the mother of God, herself, the Normans, the Irish, Elfwida and Jacques, bless them and send them happiness, Wales, Flanders, change the guard and more food, more toasts, Dai-Raymond suckling at Perse's gorged breast, all gods, God of all mothers.

She poked a finger into Le Gros' arm. 'I've got to talk to you. Alone.'

'Definitely.'

They climbed up the tower room while the Magi cheered them like a honeymoon couple.

'I love you, Finn.'

'No you don't. We've got to talk.'

He was fairly drunk; she'd never been drunk, she wasn't drunk now though she was having a hell of a lot of trouble lighting the brazier. But if she waited until they were both sober, she wouldn't know how to attempt the difficulty of putting it to him.

'You're beautiful.'

'I'm old. Listen to me.'

She cracked the ice on his wash basin, laved her face and made him do the same.

'You're still beautiful.'

She shook him. 'Becket's murdered.'

That sobered him. It was sobering the whole world. She helped him get his chair nearer the fire. 'Read this.'

He looked at the membrane. 'I can't read.'

'I forgot. "This infamous day was our lord Archbishop of Canterbury murdered on the steps of his own cathedral. Woe to the . . ." ' She couldn't see. 'It was four knights of Fitzempress' entourage. They hacked the top of his head off and stirred his brains onto the floor. They say Fitzempress ordered it, whether he did or not . . .' The king of sixteen years ago had run his hands down his wife's pregnant stomach, like Perse's. He was capable of anything, that joyful, cunning young man, but too cunning to bring Christendom down on his own head. He couldn't have really wanted it, but they'd crucify him just the same.

'Where did you get this?'

'A friend of mine in England sent it by pigeon. She's my spy. I am a spy master . . . mistress, for Ireland. I can read, I can do anything, except protect my country from you.'

She wasn't beautiful to him now. She saw his small blue eyes go blank and she wondered why it was that devious men were clever but

357

devious women were unnatural. 'Why tell me, you bitch?'

To reassure him, she went down on her knees.

'My lord, because there's no point in concealment any more. Ireland, *my* Ireland is doomed. This affects you and me, both in different ways; we can help each other. My friend, my spy, says all hell's broken loose. The Church may excommunicate Fitzempress and put an interdict on his realm.' There would be no dead buried, no marriages, children going to hell through lack of baptism, the dying fearing hell through lack of last rites, no God from the Tweed to the Pyrenees. As if a Church could remove God. But it could if people believed it could, and they did.

He needed time to encompass it all so she went downstairs for another jug of wine and two cups. It was going to be a tricky night. When she got back he was looking out at the snow and didn't turn round. 'So you've been a traitor all this time.'

Dear Lord, they always got deflected by side issues; they never kept their mind on the point. 'No,' she said patiently, 'I'm Irish. I've been a patriot, but I'm trying to give it up. Do you want some more wine?'

'Not from you.'

'Oh for God's sake . . .' Keep calm; you'll only get what you want by using every wit you've got. 'My lord, if I'm your enemy I'm a singularly unsuccessful one. Physically, I'm in no position to betray you and, anyway, I wouldn't want to now. I admire you and I'm grateful for your kindness to me and mine.'

That was better, more feminine. And it was true. He turned round and let her pour him wine.

'You see, I'm in a position to know what will happen. I promise you, I know.'

'What?'

'Fitzempress will buy the Church off. He'll do penance and he'll give the Church the one thing it hasn't got. He'll give it Ireland.'

He was sober now, by God, and he sat down while she told him who she was, what Fitzempress had said to her, how importantly the Cardinal had regarded the acquisition of Ireland for the Church, *Laudabiliter*, what had happened. She didn't care how exposed she was any more: she could save the Pilgrim – though him she didn't mention.

'Fitzempress knows the Church wants Ireland brought into its fold and he's kept it, you see. Stuffed it up his sleeve for later when he'd need it. Well, he needs it now.'

She could see she was persuading him of the likelihood which to her was a certainty. Like another Norman had done once, he reassessed her because of her connection with great people and great events; he might not like her as much, but he respected her more. She would never understand men.

Apparently it went both ways: 'You never cease to amaze me, Finn.'

'My lord, he is going to invade this island one way or another. You know better than I do what that will mean to you and Strongbow and the others when he does.' They would be pygmies overwhelmed by a massive eruption. He'd grind them until they disappeared from history with no prowess nor achievement for their sons to boast of, no riches with which to build churches to buy off the God they had sinned against while amassing those riches in the first place. If they were allowed to live, it would be as no better than peasants. Worse, they would be humiliated for having chosen wrong.

She went to the window to give him some privacy while he absorbed it all. The snow was settling on the sill in a long, perfect cushion and formed a speckled blind between her and the view.

'So?' he said after a long time, and she turned round to find an older man facing her – and reality – in the place of the young magician who had sat there before and who, by waving his sword, had thought he could make the world do what he wanted.

She took a drink herself. Now then. Better kneel at his feet again. 'It's not too late to placate him, my lord, if you are in Ireland on his behalf, not anyone else's, not your own. You can still be the great earl you should be, but Fitzempress will be your king and not Strongbow.'

He chewed his lip. 'Bloody difficult.'

'Not if you get the . . . the man who's in prison in Dublin castle on your side. You said he was Fitzempress' man and that the king would be angry if anything happened to him. Make him your ally. Get him released so that he goes back to Fitzempress and puts your case.'

'Strongbow won't let him go.'

That was the difficulty. In fact, Strongbow was even more vulnerable to Henry II's wrath than Raymond, having set himself up as a rival king. He might see the wisdom of crawling to Fitzempress and begging his forgiveness, but then again, he might not.

'But it's a thought,' said Raymond. He'd got some confidence back, 'Give me some more of that bloody wine.'

She wanted to go down to the middle room and go to bed and leave him to work on it, but he wouldn't let her. 'Oh no you don't. There's a lot I want to know yet.'

They went over the same ground, then he asked question after question, who she was again, what she'd done in Ireland, why she'd worked against Dermot, why she'd set up the inn, what she'd done there, why she'd done it.

When they ran out of wine, he fetched more. 'There's not much left, but, by God, if ever there were medicinal purposes they're with us this night.'

They went over it all again. And then she went into error. He asked if she knew the Fitzempress spy and she said, 'Yes,' and because she was tired and not completely sober and she'd been so lonely for the Pilgrim for so long and so frightened for him, she said it with love and didn't expect him to notice.

His eyes flicked down at her. 'Was he the man trouble?'

'We've been on different sides.'

'Was he the man trouble?'

'Part of it.'

'Does he love you or hate you?'

'He doesn't even know where I am, for God's sake. I'm going to bed.'

He grabbed her shoulders. 'He loves you, doesn't he? I remember FitzStephen telling me about it. There was this nun and John let her escape. That was you.'

'Young man,' she said, 'you are getting away from the point. This is not a romance and love has nothing to do with it.'

'It explains why you want him freed. It's not for the sake of my skin, is it?'

'I told you, we can help each other.'

He poured himself some more wine. 'Happy Christmas, Irish. Perhaps we can.'

The Normans counter-attacked the Irish in a snow storm. Miles de Cogan and Raymond Le Gros each headed a detachment with Strongbow bringing up the rear, as usual. They led their scarecrow horses over the Liffey Bridge without anyone seeing or hearing them, scarcely able to see or hear themselves, so thick was the snow.

Knowing that nobody but the mad would venture out on a day like this, let alone fight in it, the main Irish army had retired deep into the woods of Finglas to continue celebrating the birth of its Lord. They were singing round their fires; Ruairi O'Conor had ordered a sweat house to be built and was actually having a bath in it.

The while element around them solidified into white shapes. White-crusted horses reared above them. They were killed by snowmen like the ones they had built in play as children so that afterwards their dead faces were found to have frozen into a rictus of horrified recognition. Like enormous metal flakes the enemy kept falling on them, as relentless as the snow and more fatal. Within fifteen minutes, the huge Irish army was either killed or running away from a force one sixth of its size. Ruairi O'Conor just made it, only just by escaping naked.

He took what was left of his people back to Connaught. He could have borne being defeated, what he couldn't bear was the embarrassment.

On plundering the Irish camp, the Normans found it to contain enough corn, meal and pork for a whole year. Raymond Le Gros took his share back to his inn so that he could feed up his victorious men, his servents and his woman.

As they brought him into it, the Lord of Llanthony blinked at the light in the Dublin Castle tower room; actually, it was dim because the sky outside was still grey and there was only one candle, but it seemed strong to him. He squinted around him. 'Hello, Miles, Hello, Le Gros.'

'Hello, old chap. No hard feelings.'

'I'll tell you in a minute.' They'd set out a tureen of stew for him, as big as a cartwheel and he fell on it, but after a few minutes' eating he began to retch. 'Eyes bigger than my belly.' Le Gros poured him wine; in case he was cold they'd brought him an ermine cloak and put it round his shoulders with the care of a mother. 'Like a wash, old man?' They took him into the ante room where a bath had been prepared. There were clean clothes and there was a barber to shave him. He took his time and made them scrub his back. Let the bastards sweat.

'Strongbow well, I hope?'

'Fine, fine,' De Cogan assured him. 'Gone down south to secure the Leinster bridgehead.'

'Oh, good.'

They took him back to the stew and he did better this time, then he went to the window and looked out of it for a bit, examined his nails, found them unsatisfactory, pulled a Viking chair with horns on it close to the fire and toasted his feet. The news that Becket was dead had been like the snow, it had permeated everything, his cell included. Well, Becket had it coming, had wanted it. No tears for the blessed martyr Becket. But he'd cried for Fitzempress.

These two lads were about as subtle as horseshit and he was way ahead of them; what puzzled him was how they'd had the brains to work out the prognosis. They couldn't know about *Laudabiliter*. They were the sort who'd think that because Fitzempress was down, he was also out. Strongbow didn't think at all. The way they'd work it out, left to themselves, they could become kings of Ireland while Fitzempress' back was bowed under the clerical lash. Somebody had done their thinking for them.

'Well?' he said.

'It's like this, old chap . . .'

He eyed them while they went through their rehearsed routine. It was all a mistake . . . hadn't meant to upset him . . . doing it for King Henry . . . glory Fitzempress's, the country Fitzempress's . . . King had given them permission, after all . . . itching to do the king homage for it . . . welcome the king to Ireland to lay it at his feet . . . if he,

John, would just put their case for them . . . grateful forever and show it in material fashion . . . always liked him, comrades-in-arms in Aquitaine, did he remember . . . jolly old times.

De Cogan was sweating with the effort of verbal crawling, but Le Gros, thinner now, but not as fucking thin as he was himself, had something at the back of his eyes.

'Is Strongbow in on all this?' he asked them abruptly.

They wavered. He saw them weighing it up. Abandon Strongbow? Better not; if one went down, they'd all go.

'The Earl is as eager to recognise Fitzempress king of Ireland as we are ourselves.'

'How do you I won't sell you out once you let me go?' Actually, Fitzempress would probably have to confirm them in their lands – he wouldn't want to fight them and the Irish – but they'd be bigger fools than even he thought they were to let him sail to England on the pious hope that he'd recommend it.

'As we are Norman knights, we accept your word as a Norman knight that you will speak well on our behalf to the king,' said Le Gros, 'And we've got your surety.'

You've no surety of mine, you bloody Welsh half-breed. 'What surety?'

'My quartermaster.'

'I don't know any quartermasters.' They'd gone bloody mad. Too much Irish air. Who the hell were they opening the door to?

'This one's rather special,' said Le Gros, smiling.

And Loon walked in.

He was weaker than he thought. It had got very dark. Time must have passed while he'd looked at her. Too skinny as always, skinnier than ever, hair getting grey in it, nothing to write home about, eyes . . . oh, fuck it . . . nobody else had eyes like that.

He said, 'Can I speak to her alone?'

'I'm afraid not.' Le Gros was more triumphant than ever.

He said in Irish, 'Are you all right?'

She used the same tongue: 'Say anything, but get out as fast as you can.'

'I'll take you with me.'

'They won't let you. Just go.'

'We'd prefer it if you spoke in French,' said De Cogan. 'We are prepared to accept this surety . . .'

'Hostage.'

'. . . surety, for your favourable representation to the king on our behalf.'

'I told you my quartermaster was special,' said Le Gros.

The bastard was proprietorial toward her. He'd probably even had her. And she'd bargained with that skinny body of hers for his safety. She'd got nothing else to bargain with. Why couldn't she leave him alone? Why had she entered his sodding life at all? He was jealous of the conferences she must have had with them. He was jealous that she was saving him, not him saving her. Jesus Christ, what a mess.

'I see.' It was an effort to stand up. 'When's the next boat?'

He saw her take it all in; she'd always been too clever by half, the whore. It was her who'd done these bastards' thinking for them. As he passed her in the doorway, he said, 'Bit young for you, isn't he?'

She'd always had spirit as well. 'Get out of here,' she said, 'And don't come back.'

He went, and he didn't mean to come back.

Henry II showed his genius on many occasions – in warfare and even more in peace, in the institution of a Common Law and the jury system – but he never displayed it better than by coming to Ireland as its saviour.

He was at the lowest ebb of his career with his enemies calling for his blood and his allies wavering. The Church everywhere condemned him as a murderer. But by scolding and apparently punishing the Norman adventurers who were making their life hell, he made the Irish forget all that. He made them grateful. In effect, he said to them, 'Look on me as an instrument of cohesion. Recognise me, an outsider, as your High King – it's just a title – and your clans will not feel that one has triumphed over another. I suppose we'll have to confirm this upstart Strongbow and the others in some of their lands to keep them quiet, won't we, but they'll be answerable to me and, by God's eyes, I'll keep them in check, and preserve your ancient liberties.'

Behind him, just in case, he'd brought the biggest Norman army yet seen, but it was unnecessary. He had *Laudabiliter* in his hand, and the backing of the incumbent Pope. The reforming bishops of Ireland, who wanted to see their church abandon its peculiar individuality and come under the Church of Rome, were behind him and recommending him to their people.

To the men of Meath and Leinster and Ulster, and all the other clans outside Connaught, Ruairi O'Conor had been a foreigner, just as MacLochlainn had been a foreigner to all the clans outside Ulster. So here was just another foreigner passionate for the title of High King which didn't mean that much anyway.

Sick of war, the Irish lined his route from Wexford to Dublin and cheered him, thinking his titular reign would be just a passing phase like all the others.

*   *   *

363

'God is at once male and female and more than both,' wrote Finn, 'a Being of limitless power that has chosen to be represented in vulnerability. For, as men were the only ones to write the words of the Bible, they were unable to see the femininity of God but recognised only the masculinity.'

That was telling them.

'Yet, in that Jesus came to us not in strength but in the weakness of a poor human baby, not to experience the power of the world but its pain, he was partaking of the common lot of its women. Nor can I find any condemnation of women in his teaching such as are heaped on our heads by the bishops. Indeed, he understood the body of a woman so well as to cure it of the bloody flux. In that he loved and forgave prostitutes and adulteresses and rejoiced at marriages as at Cana, and frequented the company of women, he reflected the womanly nature of God as much as the manly. Therefore the saints who have regarded Eve and her daughters as evil, like St. Kevin, who cast women from him, have done violence to God who is both their father and their mother.'

She stopped. She'd filled up the skinside of the membrane and would have to go over on the other because this was the last of the membranes Pinginn had prepared for her and she doubted her ability to make more, even if she had any skins, which she didn't, and the energy, of which she had less.

She felt she ought to have been harder on St. Kevin but the torpor of one who has experienced too much in too short a span had left her unable to feel indignation about anything. Even her pleasure was in small, ordinary things, this lovely spring day, the baby, discovering the right words for her manuscript.

Leaving the ink to dry in the sun, she went over to watch Dai-Raymond sleeping in his cradle and gloat over the weight he'd put on and the curl of his hands and his little nose, she loved his nose. 'Time waster,' she said to him. Still, for the first time in her life she had time to waste. She looked down over the parapet of the tower at the Liffey which today had the colour of clear ale. Out towards the bay a school of dolphins leapt in and out of the water, a spectacle that stayed on the mind in curves. More time wasters.

She'd nearly finished the Word of Woman – just the matter of Pinginn to deal with. She wasn't completely satisfied with it, but it spoke up for herself, for Dervorgilla, for all voiceless women, for the female-ness of God. It had become the most important thing in her life, next to Dai-Raymond.

The inn had been put off limits for the Dublin garrison. Raymond's men, her Magi, were encamped on the north shore ready for what was being called 'a peace-keeping mission' into Meath. Shipping was beginning once again to come up the Liffey, but most of it was military and went straight to the city wharves. At least it was bringing grain and some of it was being milled by Perse and her new husband, Dai, over at poor Molling's mill. Poor Molling, buried at last.

Few locals had survived the invasion and the siege. With so little left to steal at the inn, even the damned lepers were leaving her alone.

She strolled over to the west parapet to look towards the fantastic structure that now stood between her and the city below the Thingmount. Since the castle was still under repair, the Irish had built Fitzempress a mansion of wattles to stay in during his visit and its woven walls had a white sheen under the thatch, like the stalks of a mushroom cluster. He'd charmed them by saying it was the most comfortable and beautiful of his palaces. They'd never seen Chinon.

Tiny figures swarmed around it, in and out of its doors, getting everything ready for when the clans arrived to do homage to Fitzempress for their lands.

One of the biggest misunderstandings in Irish history, thought Finn. To them land is a share of a river, a forest and plain for their herds to run in, an immortal paradise. To Fitzempress, it's property. They think he'll let them have their quick sweeping of the stream without having to pay him for it, and that he will disappear into the past with other kings. He knows Ireland belongs to the English empire for ever.

If she'd had any tears left, she would have wept for the lovely thing that was passing.

One of the figures detached itself from the rest and rode towards the Stein bridge. She went over to the inn side of the parapet and called down to Gorm who was hanging out washing in the orchard: 'Le Gros is coming. Take Dai-Raymond back.' It was time for the baby's feed. She could only have him for about three hours at a time, but even that much was a help to Perse while she was busy at the mill. She took the cradle downstairs and handed it over. She didn't give it to Elfwida because Elfwida was jealous of the child, now that she'd lost Jacques. One of the few Normans to have been killed during the assault on the Irish camp at Finglas had been Raymond's second-in-command. An Irish axe had severed his leg and he'd bled to death in the snow.

She returned to her manuscript. 'Not in the victory of one idea or one army over another is God to be found,' she said, 'but only in love. We are interconnected in that love and must recognise in each other the brightly-burning flame of God. When Brother Pinginn, whom men reviled as effeminate, gave his life for his friends, he was the incarnation of God.'

That was the important thing Lief had said that night as she'd pleaded to know where God was. He'd been holding onto the boat, looking back to the little bundle at the feet of men who were piercing it

365

with spears, and he'd said, 'I think that's Him.'

She was lonely for Lief, for all of them. She felt too ill to make the journey to Lough Mask, even if the Normans allowed her to leave. But she'd sent them word that she had survived and had heard back that they were well. She'd asked Le Gros to try and find out what had happened to Bevo, but apart from discovering that Ragnar's farm out in Swords had been destroyed, he could get no news of her. No more pigeons came from Muirna in England and none of the Normans knew, or cared, about some damned bishop's mistress. Every time she looked out at the Liffey she hoped to see Aragon's ship but so far none had come sailing up it with a black-haired woman captain ululating from its deck.

She heard Le Gros shouting for her and went down to greet her landlord. They sat down in the empty nobles' parlour, facing each other over a small oak table that Gorm had made out of the wreckage from the old one.

He was still proprietorial towards her and refused to allow any other troops to come to the Swan. He kept it just for himself and a few friends. It was somewhere he could relax and get away from his new wife, who was, he said, as old as Finn and not nearly so interesting to talk to.

He was going to pull The Swan down, anyway, and build a castle here if Fitzempress would let him. She didn't hate him for it; he had helped Dai-Raymond to be born and he had kept his word and saved the Pilgrim. She had this feeling that the world was coming to an end and there wasn't time any more to demarcate people into friend or enemy. Too little time to waste in hatred. Dear, dear, how mild she had become; must be middle-age.

'How's Basilia?'

He grunted. 'Good Norman stock, Basilia. But she's settling down. Do you know that Maurice Fitzgerald said the other day?'

'What?'

'He said that we, the Normans over here, that already we're Irish to the English and English to the Irish.'

'Did he?' Perhaps Pinginn was right; in time they would be absorbed.

'Dermot's dead.'

'Is he?' She rolled the information round her brain; once it would have chewed on the information, tasted it, regurgitated it, but now it hadn't any savour.

'Yes, and Aoife's pregnant.' He sighed. 'I wonder if Basilia's too old for children. It's funny, but not one of us except Strongbow has made a woman pregnant since we've been over here. Are we cursed do you think?' His fat face was anxious.

366

'Probably.'

'And we move out to Meath tomorrow and God knows when I'll be back. The king's dispersing us, the cunning sod. Gave us hell in front of the Irish, but he knows he can't do without us, and winked at us behind their backs. Put on a hell of a performance with FitzStephen because he was the first to invade – had him paraded in front of everybody in chains. But he's letting him keep his lands. Jesus, he's cunning. The Irish are eating out of his hand. Oh, and Llanthony's due to arrive in Dublin soon; the king's called him back to advise him on Irish affairs.' He grinned at her. 'He thinks you slept with me so that I'd let him go.'

'I know he does.'

Le Gros patted her. 'And I might have done if you'd been younger, and I hadn't liked you instead.' He heaved himself up. 'I'd better go. You'll be here when I get back? No escaping to Connaught?'

'No.' Anyway, she couldn't bear to leave Dai-Raymond.

'I suppose you've been at that damned scribbling again,' Le Gros said. He was mystified that she could do it. 'I can't think what you fill the pages with.'

'Heresy.'

'Well you be careful.' He finished his mug of ale. 'I mean it, Finn. The reformers are rampant out there now they've got the upper hand. Did you know the priest who was in charge of St. Patrick's Well?'

'No.' She vaguely remembered a jolly little man who'd stood outside the church of the well, shouting the blessing of St. Patrick on passers-by.

'He's been forced to throw his wife and children out of his house. No more married priests. The poor woman's begging on the streets now. And all the prostitutes have had their heads shaved. Bloody hypocrisy. I know for a fact that the first thing some of those bishops who came over with Fitzempress did when they arrived was take an Irish woman. But you can't turn a corner in Dublin without some damned preacher denouncing the evil practices of Irish marriages, and baptisms, church rites and tithe-paying – they've got to pay more now, of course. Everything's got to be according to the Church of Rome. I said to Fitzempress, "Henry," I said, "You'll be turning this country the same as the rest of priest-ridden Europe if you're not careful. Lose all its individuality." '

He was showing off to get her approval and she gave it to him. She really was fond of him. 'Spoken like a true Irishman. What did he say?'

'Well, he doesn't like it any more than I do. Rather fancied the idea of easy divorce, if you ask me – did I tell you that Eleanor's supposed to have poisoned the Fair Rosamund? But he said to me, "Raymond, old chap, what can I do? The sodding bishops are on my back. It's Ireland or me." '

'Are you sure you won't have more ale?' There was no point in blaming him for the coming of the new era; Ireland had refused to enter the modern age and so the modern age had come to Ireland.

'No. But incidentally, was this inn ever called The Amazon?'

'Yes. Why?'

'There was one of those bloody preachers standing at Dames Gate ranting to a crowd of monks that the Amazon Inn on the Stein was a den of iniquity run by women in trousers who killed men and took their spirit to foreign countries, or some such rubbish. That it wasn't their inn in any case, they had used Jews and other devils to get it away from its rightful owner. What's an Amazon anyway? I picked the little bastard up and chucked him over the bridge. "That's my Inn," I told him, "there's none of your bloody Amazons there, just a friend of mine, and you leave it and her alone," I told him, "or I'll come back and the place'll have a new name, The Ranter's Balls, and yours will be the inn sign." That's what I told him.' He reached out and caught her hands. 'There shouldn't be any trouble. But there's a boat down in the cave harbour below the tower. Just in case.'

He joined his men across the river and they moved out at dawn. Finn and Elfwida stood on the tower roof to wave goodbye. The early light was enough to distinguish their shapes as they moved into their column – there were no trees on the north shore any more, just stumps and watchtowers. The men's voices came across the water with an echo: 'Bye, Finn.' 'Bye, Elf.' 'Goodbye, quartermaster.' 'Who's a good little quartermaster then?'

'Take care,' she called. Take care of yourselves. Take care of Ireland.

The Normans moved out of her sight into the great uterus they believed they were conquering, and Finn was left to the greater enemy.

Dublin had become hysterical. Reaction and the fear of damnation had set in on conquered and conquerors alike; the conquered knowing that they had sinned or God would not have punished them like He had, the conquerors conscious of the sins they had committed during the conquest and afraid of God's retribution, and both, therefore, in a, terror which made them as wax in the hands of men who could point the way to salvation.

Preachers ordained and self-appointed, reformers, fundamentalists, madmen, had appeared like magic to stand on the battered streets of the city and howl damnation on such Irish as refused to take their particular recipe for its avoidance. Some were Irish themselves, having waited all their lives for this opportunity to bring their erring country into the fold, but many had travelled from overseas. A Praemonetratensian from Normandy shrieked, 'Kill the Jews and be saved,' at the Lord of Llanthony as he made his way past him to Dames Gate.

Further on a canon from Durham was telling a collection of traders, 'Your filthy marriage customs have condemned you at last. Repent for marrying within the forbidden degrees. Repent for your divorces. Repent and be saved.' Norman soldiers were being urged by Irish monks to pull down what few secular inns were left in Castle Street so that they would not be led into temptation by drink and the women who inhabited them. Prostitutes were having their heads shaved by nuns. Those with the authority to sell indulgences were doing a brisk trade.

As he crossed Hogges Green to the Thingmount, the Lord of Llanthony was surprised at his own resentment at this outburst of right-eousness. He had disapproved of Ireland's laxity in his time; now he felt protective towards it against these outsiders and clerics. He pushed angrily through the petitioners who crowded round the doors of the amazing woven palace the Irish had built for his king and was imme-diately ushered into its hall by the chamberlain.

Fitzempress was alone unless one counted four scribes who sat at their boards around the room, writing like maniacs as the king strode from one desk to another dictating paragraphs of four different despatches in succession. It was a nice hall, light, airy, with a view over the Stein and the smell of peeled twigs which took him back to his childhood.

'My lord.'

'Ah, John. How goes it in the city?'

'I haven't had much time to find out, but, since you ask, things are getting out of hand. It's the bloody canon courts. They're trying to dis-mantle in an hour a way of life that's lasted for a thousand years. The church courts are condemning everything that moves as long as it's Irish. Men and women who thought they were respectably married are being told they've lived in concubinage all this time and their children are illegitimate, which is a term they don't understand. It's chaos.'

'Hmmm.' Fitzempress picked up one of the scribes and hung him by his hood on a peg on the wall and stood back to see how he looked. He decided against it, unhooked him and put him back on his stool. 'A Holy Roman Ireland's what the church wanted, and a Holy Roman Ireland's what it's getting.'

'Well, but can't Archbishop O'Toole do something about it? He'd check the worst excesses.'

'Certainly not. How dare you?' He went to the window, 'They're blaming the sinful people of Ireland, nothing to do with the holy reforming bishops. No skin off my nose; the blacker its bishops paint the Irish people, the better I look for bringing them onto the true path. Look at that view, John. There's stags out there just begging me to come and hunt them. I like this country, makes me feel young again. And I'm putting you in charge of it when I go away.'

It took a moment to sink in. The Lord of Llanthony went on to his knees. 'My lord.'

Fitzempress looked round at him and grinned. 'Well, I wasn't going to let Strongbow govern it for me, the usurping sod. He'll have to stick with what he's got. Besides, your cover's blown as a spy-master *and* I trust you *and* it's not going to be a picnic. It was either you or Hugh de Lacy and you know more about the Irish than he does. Heard any good harp staves lately?'

John shook his head. 'Somebody cut the harp strings.'

Fitzempress winced at a pain of his own. The Fair Rosamund was dead; there were those who said Eleanor had poisoned her. 'Somebody always does. Be like me: give women up. They're either stabbing you in the back or they're dying on you. What the hell's going on?'

There was a disturbance at the door where a group of men were demanding entrance of the chamberlain, who was refusing it. 'It's the Archdeacons and some persons, my lord.'

'He's attending the Synod at Cashel. He just called in on his way from Armagh to give me the findings of the Council of bishops at Armagh. The Council has finally pronounced on the invasion or, as it put it, "the coming of the foreigners to the shores of Erin". Do you know what those holy men have blamed it on?'

'Tell me.' Fitzempress was shedding some of the age which had come upon him on hearing of Becket's murder. Ireland was a holiday for him, an opportunity to do what he loved best; increase his empire, manipulate men, and go hunting. He genuinely liked the Irish, he said they relaxed him, that the life was civilised.

But sooner or later, thought John, you're going to have to go back and face the Papal Legates and get whipped by the monks of Canterbury and all the other horrors they've got in store for your penance. Still, you've got Ireland to offer them as a sop.

'They've said it was the curse of God brought upon the Irish for their persistence in buying slaves from England.'

John had thought nothing about the Irish could ever surprise him again, but it could. 'They didn't.'

'They did. I think it's rather sweet. Doesn't blame the Normans at all.'

'What about the curse of God on England for selling its people as slaves in the first place?'

'Ah well,' Fitzempress said, 'I rather think that's the hole in their logic. But they're not a logical people, that's what I like about them.'

'But that means all those archbishops and what-nots are blaming themselves.'

Fitzempress sighed. 'Let them in.' The Archdeacon of Llandaff, who was actually an Englishman, and a zealot, had come over to Dublin some weeks before to make sure that the Irish Church was purging itself of the iniquities into which it had fallen, and had discovered in the Archdeacon of Dublin a soulmate who had long been pestering Laurence O'Toole to institute branding as a punishment for everything from divorce to simony, and had made a serious effort at getting him excommunicated when he refused. The two of them had yoked themselves together in what they called 'The Crusade of Reform' and which Fitzempress, to whom they were constantly complaining, called 'a pain in the arse'.

With them came an assortment of monks, one of them frothing at the mouth, a depressed-looking soldier, and a girl.

'My dear Archdeacons,' said Fitzempress, 'how good of you to disturb me.'

'Becket-killer,' shouted the frothing monk, 'Assassin.'

Fitzempress smiled politely at the Archdeacon. 'Excuse me.' He strode over to the monk, picked him up by the belt and handed him to the chamberlain. 'The Liffey,' he said shortly, and turned back, brushing his hands. 'Yes, reverend gentlemen?'

Neither the Archdeacon of Llandaff, who was thin, nor the Archdeacon of Dublin, who wasn't, lacked courage. 'Henry Plantagenet,' shouted Llandaff, waving his fist, 'as you were an instrument of the Devil, now be an instrument of Almighty God and send your army against the fortress of evil in which is harboured a daughter of demons, a fornicator, whom this virtuous monk here has discovered to be a heretic of such filth as no country save Islam has produced before and of whom . . .'

Fitzempress turned to the virtuous monk, a skeletal man whose shaking hands held a scroll and on whose dark-flushed face broken veins indicated a past of heavy drinking. 'You tell it,' he said, kindly. 'What's your name?'

'Madoc,' said Madoc.

'Well, Brother Madoc? And leave out the hellfire, there's a good chap.'

'My lord,' said Madoc, and put his hands, which had begun to shake uncontrollably, under his scapular. 'I have long had reason to suspect that the inn over there . . .' he jerked his head towards the Stein, '. . . was the haunt of a she-devil, a witch. She gained ownership of it by nefarious methods to which this soldier here, a brave member of your own army, Harold of Bristol, can attest since it had previously been his.'

'We'll take his testimony as read,' said Fitzempress. He crossed to one of the scribe's desk, took up a fat candle that was ringed with the hours and lit it from the brazier. 'And?'

'The inn was of ill-repute even in the days of King Asgall,' said Madoc, 'but since the king frequented it because he was attracted by the Amazons who ran it – they danced for him, my lord, in trousers – nothing was done.'

'Let not that omission stain your soul, Fitzempress,' shouted Dublin.

'And?' said Fitzempress. He looked over towards John and mouthed: 'Dancing girls,' but John didn't see it.

'And since the coming of your countrymen, the whore has been under the protection of one of your generals, Raymond Le Gros . . .'

'The dirty dog,' said the king, 'Old Fatty, eh John? Well, he's gone and she's unprotected. So?'

'My lord, I have been keeping watch on the place and this morning, I, and some others, apprehended one of the witch's familiars, this famale here, and searched her, and on her person we found an infamous document.'

Elfwida was pushed forward into the centre of the room. Her dress was torn and her fair hair hung over her eyes. Fitzempress smoothed it back. 'I thought you men of God weren't allowed to shed blood.' Elfwida's nose was bleeding.

'We tripped her, my lord, as she tried to get away and she fell. The blood is involuntary.'

'That makes it all right then.'

'My lord,' Madoc's voice which had been sing-song became suddenly vibrant and confidential. 'We made her talk. This manuscript was written by the witch, her mistress . . .'

Llandaff jumped forward, 'What further proof do you need of satanic origin, Plantagenet? A woman who can write.'

'So can my wife.'

John thought: He's showing off, playing games with them. He thinks they're comical. He'll still be amused and aloof when they destroy this woman, whoever she is. Dear God, don't let it be her.

Fitzempress was saying . . . 'So read the manuscript.'

Dublin raised its dimpled hand. 'Not so, my lord. Let not the ears of good men be infected by its filth. I have had merely a minute in which to peruse the document, but enough to see that it must be read only by those who are proof against its ungodliness. It must be sent at once to Cashel for the Archbishops to see and condemn, as this woman must be condemned.'

Fitzempress picked up a stool and put it near the window in the sun, then led Madoc to it. 'Read it.'

Madoc unrolled the scroll with hands that were no longer shaking. 'Know all who live now and who will be that I am Finola of the clan of Partraige, once Sister Boniface of Fontevrault, once Abbess of Kildare whom Dermot had raped . . .'

John, Lord of Llanthony went white.

Elfwida began to sob.

'. . . So I did learn at a lakeside that a man's and woman's body can meet in joy when they meet freely and that God must have intended this to be so,' she had written. There was an intake of breath from the Archdeacons and the monks. 'And that nothing is more important than love, because it comes from God who is our father and our mother . . .'

At last the Archdeacon of Dublin's voice stopped and allowed the sound of larks rising and falling on Hogges Green to enter the hall, like bubbles breaking. He had snatched the manuscript from Madoc when the man had faltered over the account of the nancy monk's death. Now Brother Madoc sat still, looking out at the Liffey.

'So that's what happened to her. I often wondered,' Fitzempress said quietly.

Llandaff's voice intruded like cymbals. 'We have already sent word to the Archbishop of Cashel that he may expect the manuscript, my lord. He will be wanting to hear that the woman has been captured and silenced.' He added a threat: 'I hope it will not be necessary to appeal to the Pope on this matter.'

John said, 'What are you going to do with her?'

'Send soldiers with us to the inn; you have heard she is a warrior, while we are men of peace.'

'What are you going to do with her?'

'It is not your concern. There are places.'

Fitzempress turned to the Lord of Llanthony. 'There's nothing I can do, John. I daren't cross the Church again. And anyway, this manuscript tries to alter the cosmos; we can't have that.'

'No.'

'Just take a detachment to keep order. They needn't do the dirty work.'

'Yes.'

'I can't do anything about it, John. Male or female, God's not with me any more. Becket saw to that.'

In the to-ing and fro-ing outside the doors, where more monks were

373

waiting to join the hunt, John managed to grab hold of the girl's arm. 'I'll delay them. Go and warn her.'

The only other person who saw her slip away was Brother Madoc. He clung onto John, crying. 'I didn't know,' he was saying, 'I didn't know.'

'Didn't know what, you bastard?' John shook him off and called out the guard.

The first thing Finn did was thank God that Dai-Raymond happened to be over at the mill. Then she told Elfwida to lock herself inside the tower, and ran to find Gorm. The pigeon loft was empty and she wasted vital minutes calling for him through the inn and outside until she discovered him sitting beatifically on the nobles' privy. 'A fine time to get caught with your trousers down,' she told him, and helped him pull them up. As she hustled him towards the Stein she said, 'Remember, you work at the mill. You've never worked anywhere else.' She couldn't bear it if anything happened to him because of her.

She watched his bandy legs stump over the bridge to where, in the far distance, a black mass was concentrating and moving towards her.

'Food,' she said and pelted along the quay and into the inn. With the sun coming in through the open shutters in long beams it looked as it had looked on countless mornings waiting for trade, shadowed, clean and expectant. In the process of going through the nobles' door to the kitchen and out through the commoners' she acquired a loaf of bread and some cheese. A new shadow was in the entrance. A monk had run ahead of the others to gain the glory of her capture. He bowed back and fore in an effort to catch his breath as he came at her so that it seemed she was being advanced on by a huge, hopping crow. She felt terror, but she had been activated at long last. She dropped the bread and cheese, went to meet him and gave him Scathagh's Ploy Number One. The old skill was still there even if the strength wasn't. The monk dropped, gargling. She picked up the food and yelled to the Elf to open the tower door. Then they were both inside and getting the bar into its slots with shaking hands.

'There, there.' She held the sobbing Elf close. 'There, there.'

'I didn't mean to, Finn.'

'Of course, you didn't.' She crooned baby talk to the girl as she led her to the basin and washed the blood off her top lip. 'But how did you get the manuscript? It was under my pillow this morning when you left.'

'Still is. That was my copy.' Elfwida collapsed on her again. 'I copied it every night when you were asleep. Sort of, to give me power over you. I betrayed you. Oh God, what have I done?'

'There, there, my treasure. Nothing.' The fault was hers; she'd never loved the girl enough. Well, she loved her now. Ferociously. She'd never been allowed to show her love to Slaney, but Elfwida was her daughter now. 'Stay there.' She scrambled up the steps to the top room and grabbed her manuscript and a satchel. 'Can you find Lough Mask?' she called as she came down again.

Elfwida wiped her eyes. 'Should do. You've talked about the place enough, you and the others.'

Why didn't I take her there? raged Finn at herself. Why didn't I pay her more attention? The sin is in overlooking people. She stuffed manuscript, bread, cheese and a couple of pinginns – all the money she had – into it.

'But I'm not leaving you,' said the Elf.

'You bloody are. Look at me.' She put her hands round the girl's face. 'Am I or am I not a happy woman at this moment?'

Elfwida stared at her. 'Yes. Yes, Finn, you are.'

'Very, very happy.' She jerked her head at the door. 'They've made me happy, bless them. They're scared. They've read the manuscript and they're scared out of their wits. They know mine's the truth. They know they can't own God for themselves. If they'd torn up the manuscript with a light laugh, it'd be different, but that's not a light laugh out there.'

It was more like the sounds the pack had made over the body of Pinginn. The door was shaking as they hit it.

'You take the Word of Woman, Elf, and add your word and then other women can add theirs and one day there'll be another voice in the world. Can you do it?'

Elfwida nodded and kissed her. 'Right.'

'Good. Get down to the boat and get ready. The tricky bit will be the north shore if you make it. Run like you've never run before, Elf. God bless you, I love you so much. Start rowing like hell when you hear me do this.'

At the other side of the door the black mass stopped for a moment at the dreadful sound which did not release them to attack again until it had throbbed away to nothing.

John and his men drove such monks as had run ahead out of the inn and back over the bridge to the Dublin side of the Stein, chucking a few into the water for good measure. It wasn't until he'd got them under control that he had time to look back – and saw the inn on fire. 'Suffer not a witch to live,' one of the monks was howling, 'Burn her.' They all took up the chant. 'Burn her. Burn her.' A stone cracked into the mouth of one of them with a force that broke his teeth. She was up on the roof and they could see her waving her sling at them.

'Water chain,' said John. But it wasn't any good; the inn's timbers and thatch were blackening already in flames that were almost invisible in the sun. There was the deep, satisfied roar of fire going up.

He ran to the far end of the quay so that the tower roof was in his view and saw her sling another stone, then throw a spear. Either the air between them was moving in the heated air from the inn or she was dancing. She let out the ululating yell he'd heard on a winter's night a long time ago, piercing the monks' chants with that most unnatural of songs, the vocal triumph of a woman.

But these weren't poor, simple wolves. He glanced at their upturned faces, primroses following the sun. These had God and Fitzempress' army on their side.

God was where the poor were, she'd written, suffering with them, crucified again: He was Mary watching the crucifixion. Bloody rubbish she talked. God wanted him to be Governor of Ireland. Then why the hell was every beautiful thing he'd ever known inextricably entangled with that stupid bitch up there? Why was he free to stand here remembering it, when he could be dead from starvation in Strongbow's prison? The stupid, loving bitch.

The monks were running towards the end of the Stein. He followed them on the inn side of the river so that he could see what they saw – a boat with a girl rowing it gliding out from behind the promontory, heading for the opposite bank of the Liffey. So that's what she was doing. Letting this one get away. It occurred to him that he hadn't asked the girl in Fitzempress' hall what her name was. She wasn't going to make it; there were some cockle-gatherers' *curraghs* beached on the silt. Some of the monks threw themselves at one of them, dragging it towards the water. A nice shot put a spear splintering through its side and immediately they ran for another and begin dragging that. She must be running out of spears.

He saw the monk Madoc, away from the rest, on his knees, praying. Behind him the front of the inn collapsed in on itself. One of the guards on the quay had a bow and quiver. He grabbed them off the man. God forgives everything except lack of love, she'd written. He hoped she was right. She'd better be right.

The staircase to the tower door had gone, and so had the tower door which was a hole with a flicker of flames round it. In the old days he'd have leaped that high, but now he had to burn his hands on a charred beam which was still strong enough to take his weight and clamber up it. Bloody rheumatics. You'd have thought God, male or female, would have made an exception in his case.

The staircase in the tower was beginning to burn, but he made it up to the roof just in time. There she was, and she *was* dancing, blast her. Shouting, throwing, having a high old time. 'This is bloody ridiculous,' he shouted at her over the roar.

She looked round and saw him. 'I can manage, Pilgrim,' she said, as if he'd offered to help with the shopping. 'Go down.' She had an arrow sticking out of her upper arm – his men had begun to shoot back at her because she was shooting at them as well as the monks. You couldn't blame them, a madwoman like this one. She wouldn't feel any pain yet. But soon.

He jumped away as the steps crackled and collapsed and a fireball shot out of the stairwell. He went to her side at the parapet and began shooting down at the crowd by the boats. 'What I came to ask,' he shouted, 'is that girl Slaney?'

'What?'

'My daughter. I don't want to think I've come up here for nothing. Is that Slaney?'

She looked towards the river and then turned to smile at him. 'She's our daughter.'

'That's all right then.' Come to think of it, the girl had fair hair; she'd taken after him. She was getting near the north bank. He wished he'd known her; he'd have liked a daughter. 'I suppose she's heading for Lough Mask?'

'Will she make it?'

The monks had launched one of the *curraghs*, but the girl had landed on the other side and was already running between the tree stumps towards the forest in the distance. He aimed an arrow at the monks' boat but they were getting beyond range and he missed. 'She might.' If she could run fast, if they didn't send cavalry after her, or dogs, if she avoided the countless dangers on her way.

The Loon shouted, 'Isn't it a lovely day, Pilgrim?' and coughed as the shaft of a longbow took her in her left side.

He'd no arrows left. Down there one of the best Welsh marksmen in Fitzempress' army was fitting another shaft into his bow. John picked his woman up and swung her round so that he could kiss her and receive the arrow into his own back.

What disturbed the Archdeacons of Dublin and Llandaff, as they searched through what was left of the tower the next morning, was to discover among the wreckage not one, but two, contorted pieces of lead which had been streaked with black. From their knowlege of monastery fires, they identified them as melted inkwells and were forced to draw the conclusion that there had been not one, but two, writers at the Swan Inn. Had the place been a factory of women scribes? A satanic spring of female heresy welling up from Hell? Was there a copy of the dreadful manuscript?

They gave orders that the two skeletons they also found in the wreckage be hacked apart; they had been welded together when the lead of the tower roof had turned into molten liquid. The male skeleton was put into a coffin and shipped back to England for burial in the state accorded Norman barons, however mad. They discussed for some time what should be done with the female skeleton. As a heretic she deserved to go into unconsecrated ground, but since she had also once been an Abbess of Kildare they decided in their charity to adjudge her mad as well, and put her wrapped in sackcloth in an unmarked grave in the lepers' churchyard on Lazy Hill.

In the room overlooking the plain of Cashel, the Archbishop pondered the information he had received, and stood up to find that it was evening and that his bones had gone stiff from sitting in one position for so long.

'The girl's heading for Lough Mask then,' he said. 'I'll send riders to the Archbiship of Tuam to intercept her. If she once gets among those islands we'll have trouble finding her. They're a funny people, the Partraige. I don't trust them. In fact I don't trust Connaught at all – no idea of reform. It may be well that the Normans conquer Connaught as well.'

He glanced sharply at the monk: 'You've been doing research on the dead woman.'

'Yes, my lord.'

'Not from sympathy, I hope?'

'No, my lord,' said Madoc.

But the Archbishop didn't trust him; the dead woman's life had impinged too much on the monk's, or his had impinged too much on hers. He might be penitent now, in fact he looked as if he were suffering, but his part in all this had not been creditable. He would have to be incarcerated somewhere far away to reflect on his sins and to keep his mouth shut. Now that he knew it all, the Archbishop was more frightened than ever that the story would get out. And the evil manuscript was here with him, in this room. They'd call it the Cashel heresy. He would show it to Laurence O'Toole and then have it burned. Heaven forfend that the escaping girl should have a copy. God as a woman, indeed. The obscenity of the idea panicked him again, and he lumbered across the room to the door to order the pursuit into Connaught.

As he opened it, he heard the loud cadences of Gerald of Wales' voice greeting a newcomer, and the gentle Irish voice of Laurence O'Toole making a reply. Thank God, he was back.

'I should think it shame, my lord Archbishop,' Gerald of Wales was saying, 'that in a country like this, which professes itself Christian, there have been no holy Christian martyrs.'

The Archbishop of Cashel tutted with irritation. 'I expect there'll be plenty now the Normans have arrived,' he muttered, and went down the stairs.

Brother Madoc remained looking out at the darkening plain of Cashel, his mind's eye seeing a tower on fire. 'There has been one,' he said to the empty room, 'only it was for a different Christianity. And it was a woman.'

Did she have a copy of the manuscript, that girl who was out there somewhere, struggling westward through the darkness? They'd catch her for sure; the odds against her were too great.

Suddenly he leaned out of the window.

'Run,' he called into the night, 'Run.'